The H...

H

Nick Kelly

About the author

Having been a volunteer teacher with VSO in Aswan, Egypt, and with a basic knowledge of Arabic, Nick went to the relatively unknown desert sheikhdom of Qatar in 1977, where he first worked as an English teacher before he was asked to read the English news bulletin on Qatar Television. Over time, he developed a fondness for the friendly Qataris and their uncomplicated desert land.

Working for the Ministry of Information, he produced and presented programmes on Qatar and the Gulf while living in the country until 2000, when he decided to return to Britain. Since then he has been a newsreader on the BBC World Service.

The House of Fortune is his first novel. He is currently working on a sequel, which covers the period from 1972 to the present day. It is due to be published in 2022. Nick now lives in Whitstable, where he enjoys walking along the Kent coast.

For Michael

Author's note

The house on which the story is based can, happily, still be found in the centre of what remains of the old part of Doha. When I lived and worked there it was known as 'the wind tower house' and was used as an ethnographical museum.

While I've tried to keep historical facts as accurate as possible, *The House of Fortune* is a work of fiction, taking place over the first seventy years of the twentieth century. My intention was to capture the hardship of the pearl-diving days and the colonial period leading up to the discovery of oil, through the prism of a fictional Qatari family.

I have included some famous names of the day. Of course, the exchanges between the characters may never have taken place. This is fiction, not fact.

I would like to thank all my Qatari friends who inspired me to write the book. It is all too easy to make judgements about a people who now have massive wealth, but I made many genuine and kind-hearted friendships in my twenty-three years in the country.

I am grateful to all those who helped me during the seven years it took to complete the book. John Lockerbie's excellent website, catnaps.org, was an invaluable source of material for the geographical and architectural descriptions of Doha's landscape and buildings. Jill Crystal's *Oil and Politics in the Gulf* was very useful. Thank you to everyone I met and interviewed over the years, many of whom have found their way into *The House of Fortune*.

Jane Hammett worked hard as editor. Occasionally I may have not taken her advice, in which case I am responsible for any remaining errors. Thank you to Peter Smith, Helen O'Neill and Fiona MacDonald for reading the initial draft and to Elizabeth Shedden, Tim Nightingale and Christine Lillington, who also gave me their views and constructive comments. Matthew Smith has been key in the overall production of the work. Sara Burgess and John Richards, with their tireless enthusiasm, gave me the impetus to get the book finished. My sincere thanks to them and to all those who have given me support over the years.

Cast of Characters

AL BAHR FAMILY

Lubna Al Bahr – a teenage girl living in a village on the north-east coast of Qatar

Nasser and Miriam Al Bahr – her parents, commonly known as Abu Salem and Um Salem

Salem Al Bahr – their son

Maysoon Al Bahr – Miriam's sister, living in Al Khor

Faleh bin Suleiman Al Bahr – Maysoon's husband, a wealthy trader living in Al Khor

Khaled Al Bahr – their son

Jamal – the captain, or *nokhdar*, of the pearling ship, *Firial*

Adel – a pearl-diver

Yousef – a pearl-diver

Ibrahim – a pearl-diver

Bilal – a pearl-diver

IN KUWAIT

Harold Dickson – British Colonial Administrator

Violet Dickson – his wife

Frank Holmes, or Abu Naft ('the father of oil') – an oil prospector

IN CAIRO

Sir Miles Lampson – British Ambassador in Egypt

Lady Lampson – his wife

IN QATAR

Um Jabor – servant to Khaled

Abu Jabor – her husband

Jabor – their son

Amina – their daughter

Lulua – Amina's daughter

Desmond Whitehouse – manager of the Eastern Bank

Maureen Whitehouse – his wife

Edward (Eddie) Parker – bank assistant

BRITISH INFLUENCE IN THE MIDDLE EAST 1930s

TURKEY

SYRIA

LEBANON

PALESTINE

IRAQ

PERSIA

TRAN SJORDAN

KUWAIT

BAHRAIN

QATAR

TRUCIAL STATES

EGYPT

OMAN MUSCAT

SAUDI ARABIA

SUDAN

YEMEN

ADEN PROTECTORATE

ERITREA

ETHIOPIA

SOMALIA

QATAR PENINSULA 1930s

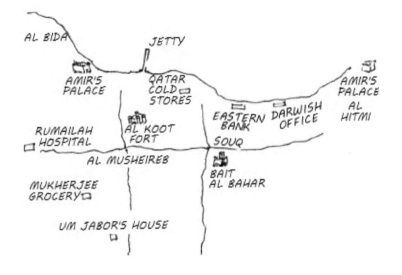

DOHA 1950s

ARABIAN GULF

AL BIDA

JETTY

AMIR'S PALACE

QATAR COLD STORES

RUMAILAH HOSPITAL

AL KOOT FORT

EASTERN BANK

DARWISH OFFICE

AMIR'S PALACE AL HITMI

AL MUSHEIREB

SOUQ

BAIT AL BAHAR

MUKHERJEE GROCERY

UM JABOR'S HOUSE

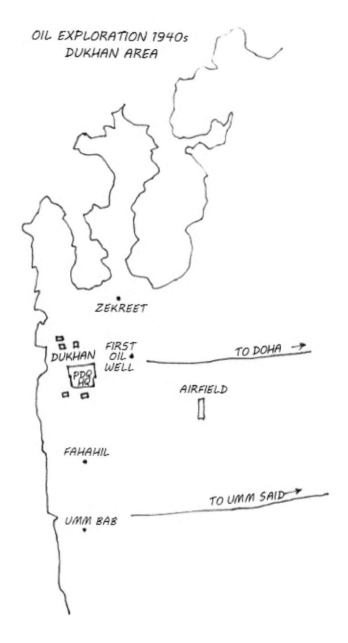

OIL EXPLORATION 1940s
DUKHAN AREA

ZEKREET

DUKHAN

FIRST
OIL
WELL

PDO
HQ

TO DOHA

AIRFIELD

FAHAHIL

TO UMM SAID

UMM BAB

PART 1

1

At sea, off the north-east coast of Qatar, 1928

The large black fly explored its latest landing place: a fine nose, long and noble. It crept boldly along towards the nostrils and down to the luxuriant moustache and sensuous lips, then upwards to the cheekbone. The fly searched for nutrition through the young man's beard. It inched its way along his eyelid, but all it found was the odd patch of crusty sea salt. Then he slapped at the fly. A signal to move on. On the man's skull, beads of sweat provided water for the fly, which buzzed down to the man's chest, bare and smooth. As the fly ambled along, over a taut, tanned abdomen, across the faded cotton of a well-worn pair of drawers, the diver's long limbs came to life. The fly left, unfulfilled. The diver's brief respite was over, and the luxury of dreams would have to wait until tonight.

'Ya Adel, ya kaslaan,' the captain shouted to the youngest member of his crew. *Adel, you lazy thing.*

The fly, after a hefty thwack from Adel, headed for calmer territory, a dead grouper floating a few metres away. The flat silence of the day, sometime after two o'clock, with 45° heat and 90% humidity, came to a halt with the harsh cries of the *nokhdar*; the strict, no-nonsense Captain Jamal.

Al Mafjar, 1928

The village of Al Mafjar is sixty kilometres to the north of Qatar, at the tip of the peninsula that juts out into the Arabian Gulf. Some would call it the Persian Gulf – those from Persia, but also the colonialist Ottomans whose empire stretched from Constantinople to the far reaches of Felix Arabia. The nearest town and port, Al Ruwais, is at the top of Qatar, from where ferries leave for Manama, the capital of Bahrain. The waters between the two contain tiny islands – or *fisht* – hardly more than spits of land. Here the water is shallow, perfect for the old *dhows* that travel between islands, plying their trade and carrying passengers.

Lubna Al Bahr hummed as she washed the pots and pans in the sea. She loved the early morning peace, with the waves gently bathing her feet. She could have brought the water to the house, but here on the beach, she used the sand to scour away the remnants of breakfast. It only took moments to pop down to the shore. Aged seventeen, she was unlike the other girls in the village, who liked to gossip and giggle their way through adolescence, vying for position in the hope of finding a suitor of whom their parents approved. As she toiled, her mind wandered. What would life have in store for her? Her mother and father were strict, and had taught her to be honest, dutiful and obedient. They had also encouraged her to think for herself, so she would be independent, whatever the future may bring.

'Ya Lubna. Where have you been, my lovely daughter?'

It was Lubna's father, calling from the old walled village.

'Here I am, dear Father. I thought I would come here to wash the dishes. You know I love it here by the water's edge.'

'I know. I know. But your mother wants you. Your aunt is coming to see us, and we need to make coffee and you know – '

'Yes, Father. I know. It's OK. I've nearly finished. I was just thinking.'

Nasser was known to everyone in the village as Abu Salem – the father of his son Salem. He took Lubna's arm as they made their way up the white coral beach towards the tufts of long grass that gave way to the little footpath into Al Mafjar itself.

It was quiet. An ordinary day.

'I'm getting old, Lubna. I wish your mother had had you sooner.'

'Don't be silly, Father. You're still young. Your grip is still strong, anyway.'

They laughed as Nasser released his hold on Lubna's arm when they were safely back up the slope. Although he was getting unsteady on his feet, he had the habit of grasping his children's arms when he was about to say something important.

'Sit down, Father, and rest a little before we go back.'

'Your mother's waiting.'

'A few minutes won't hurt.' Lubna found her father's favourite spot in the village. It was an old bench in the square where his friends gathered in the evening to mull over the day's events and the bigger problems they knew were going on in the outside world. It was mid-morning, but the single date palm that graced the centre of Al Mafjar still provided shade. Nasser heaved a sigh as he sat down heavily, patting the bench beside him.

'Tell me one of your stories, Father. You know I love those. When you won the battle against the Ottomans.'

'Oh, not again, Lubna.'

'Please, Father. Please.'

'Well. It was 1893, if my memory serves me correctly. I was quite young, but they put me in charge of a group of men. Sheikh Jassim asked for me personally. It was a great honour, as you can imagine,' Nasser began.

'Tell me again why there was a battle, Father,' Lubna said, feeling a sense of pride at the thought of her father fighting for her country.

'You know that Qatar is a small country. It only has about thirty thousand people, and there were even fewer back in the 1880s and 1890s. Qatar was ruled by the Ottomans. It was part of a swathe of land occupied by them, stretching from Iraq to the north to Oman in the south. Even when I was in my twenties I remember the mighty Medhat Pasha, who was the governor of Al Ihsaa, coming here with his army. Sheikh Jassim, then deputy to the Emir Sheikh Mohammed, agreed to this because they made him Governor of Qatar in exchange for having a fort at Al Bidda.'

Lubna looked puzzled. 'So, what was wrong with that?' she asked, leaving the bench and sitting on the ground and looking up into her father's eyes.

'That was fine, but when Sheikh Jassim became Emir in 1878 the Ottomans wanted to have more power – probably because Qatar was getting friendlier with Britain. In fact, Medhat Pasha wrote to Sheikh Jassim asking for more Ottoman soldiers to be stationed at Al Bidda. When Sheikh Jassim refused, Pasha ordered the Emir to resign. Sheikh Jassim agreed, but said he wanted his brother Ahmed to take over. A clever move, because he knew the Ottomans would never agree to that. They didn't and, outraged by the Qataris' resistance to the mighty Ottomans, Medhat Pasha demanded that the sheikh surrender. He was on board a ship off the Qatar coast at the time.

'Sheikh Jassim felt that something dreadful was about to happen. He sent his brother Ahmed along with fifteen elders to negotiate on his behalf, in the hope that a settlement could be reached. Sadly, no settlement came about. Pasha told Sheikh Ahmed that, until his brother resigned, he and the elders would be held captive on board the Ottoman vessel.

'The Emir had had enough of being ruled by foreigners and wanted to establish Qatar as an independent country. But he knew that if anything happened to his brother and the elders, it could cause even more trouble.'

'It must have been difficult for Sheikh Jassim. What did he do?'

'He decided that war was the only answer. Although two or three thousand Ottoman soldiers were already offshore, as well as those already stationed at Al Bidda fort, he knew the Qataris would never want to be dominated by the Ottomans again. He gathered together all the men of fighting age – young men from the desert regions, as the tribes had agreed to forget their differences for once, and men from the coast, like myself, who would normally have no interest in quarrelling with anyone.'

'Why were you asked to take part, Father?' Lubna asked.

'One day, one of the Al Attiyah came to the house. We hadn't seen anyone from that tribe in the village before. He was anxious and in a great hurry. He didn't even accept our hospitality, saying there was no time to lose. Behind him was a group of men from the village, and more from Al Ruwais and Al Fuwairat. He pleaded with them to fight the Ottomans. He said that all Qataris must come and fight for our country.

'So, I went. That was it. Thank goodness I could ride, at least. They gave me a horse and an old rifle. The horse was fine. The gun was something else. I didn't know what to do with it. One of the men from Ruwais had been a hunter so he gave me a quick lesson in how to load it and pull the trigger.'

Lubna drew closer to her father, gazing with pride into her father's sparkling eyes, seeing the long-ago warrior there. 'So how did you fight the enemy?' she asked.

Nasser heaved a great sigh, weighed down with his memories of that day.

'It was a huge undertaking. Sheikh Jassim had told all the elders who hadn't been taken hostage to gather as many men as possible. As I said, our group from the north rode down the coast past Ras Laffan, where some of the Kuwari joined us, then to Al Khor. Most of the men there were either away for the season at the pearl beds or fishing. We did manage to get a few, though, mostly youngsters who were at home with their mothers. Some were only fourteen or fifteen years old. There weren't enough horses, so we got some of the Bedu further inland to come with us. They wondered what was going on but when we explained we were fighting the Ottomans, they mounted those camels as fast as lightning!'

His mind vivid with the memories of battle, Nasser gathered his *thobe* around him as he recounted the day. 'Sheikh Jassim was there, fine and strong on his stallion at the head of the small army. He had a few of his personal retinue with him but the rest were all ordinary folk like me. "We are assembled today," he cried, "to wage war against these occupiers, who have had their day in this fine and noble land. We will not allow them to conquer us, for we are a free and proud people. Let us show them to whom this beloved land belongs." And then he gave the order: "Charge!"

'It was strange, Lubna, my love. I was afraid of the Ottoman soldiers – they had proper weapons like cannons and we had hardly anything – but we felt an inner strength. I looked around at my fellow Qataris. Although I didn't know any of them well, I felt we were all brothers fighting for our homeland. *Burq*, my horse, was frightened and wanted to bolt, but with a bit of encouragement he faced the front. We all shouted *"Yallah!"* and charged towards the Al Wajbah fort.

'We could see the Ottoman soldiers in front of us. They surrounded the fort. There were several blasts of cannon fire in front of me. As we rode on, men were falling from their horses, their swords tumbling to the ground, clanking as they hit the desert. Some of the men at the back managed to grab a sword, if they weren't armed, and others like myself rode ahead, not knowing if we would live or die.

'As we approached the fort we could see the fear in the faces of the young Ottoman army. Although there were more of them and they were better armed, we were determined. We galloped on, the noise of our horses' hooves deafening. I could hear the cries of the men as the guns, swords and cannon dealt their lethal blows. I was about to charge a group of Turks brandishing pistols when I felt myself falling. My dear old horse had been hit in the leg and had fallen. I was thrown off. I managed to get back near *Burq* for protection from the men behind me and the Ottoman army, which was in front of us. There before me was the infantryman responsible for maiming *Burq*. I took my rifle and aimed at the young soldier. As I did so, he got up and ran towards me. I don't know what happened but, instead of shooting the Turk racing towards me, I shot dear old *Burq* in the head. His death was quick.

'I heard the pistol fire straight away and for a moment thought that I would die too, but it wasn't me who had been struck. I saw a young boy from Al Khor lying in front of me.

The Turk faced me. My head was filled with rage. There was no time to reload my rifle so, summoning up all my strength, I grabbed the Turk's arm, forcing him to let go of the pistol. I was about to strangle him, but I couldn't bring myself to do it. There was panic and fear in his eyes as I wrestled him to the ground. He muttered something in Turkish and I could see he thought he was about to die.'

Lubna, her legs crossed, shuffled even closer towards Abu Salem as the memories become more vivid. She stared into his eyes, but they were focused somewhere beyond her right shoulder, the vision in his mind as clear as if it were happening here and now.

'Somehow I managed to control my anger. He was just carrying out his duty as a recruit under army orders. I dragged him to his feet and marched him to a group of others who had been taken captive. We led them towards Doha, trying not to lose sight of our main objective: to restore power to Sheikh Jassim. As we grew closer to the outskirts of the settlement I noticed another group of battle-scarred victims of the cavalry and infantry charge. At Wadi al Shaqab fort, which until now had been the Ottomans' base, men were surrendering to the Qataris. The gamble had paid off and we were on our way to taking back our country. Sheikh Jassim got word from the Ottoman flotilla offshore that an exchange of prisoners could take place. We had won the battle of Al Wajbah, and so began a time of peace for the people of Qatar under a much-loved Emir. What did I do? I was exhausted. The Emir ordered sheep to be slaughtered for a feast, but I was too tired to enjoy it. I had some dates and a little camel's milk then slept so soundly that nobody could wake me.

'After a night at the Mushairab fort I made my way back to Al Mafjar. Two days later I was back home being greeted by your mother. I had never been so happy.'

Tears rolled down Lubna's cheeks as she hugged her father. She could find no words to convey her feeling of pride at what her father had done, so she led him from the village square along the alleyway home.

'One moment, Lubna dear.' Nasser stopped in the alleyway and turned towards his daughter. 'You know, that night when I came home, I vowed to your mother that I would always be by her side and I would make her happy. We had to wait a long time for you and your brother, Salem, to come along, but we love you both so much.' The emotion was too much for him, and all he could do was hold Lubna in a fond embrace.

'Where have you been?' Lubna's mother, Miriam, cried out with a hint of annoyance. 'Your aunt is here. We have something to tell you.'

Adel stirred, summoned by the *nokhdar* to dive yet again. He had already been down fifty times, and it wasn't yet noon. Even at the age of twenty-one, fit and strong, he felt the strain of so many dives, and he still had the afternoon to go, until the sun went down. He had already been at sea for two and a half months. All they had to eat was fish, rice and dates. He longed to bathe in fresh water – the only fresh water they had on board was for drinking, and was never to be used to wash, so Adel had a permanent salty crust over his body and in his hair.

'Ya Adel. Come here now,' the *nokhdar* commanded. 'You'll have to go down. I know there are good pearls in this place and you have a fine pair of lungs. Let's go. *Yallah!*'

Although it was a large vessel with more than fifty crew, Adel had been singled out as the star diver. He was tall and handsome, yes, but more than that, he had confidence in his abilities – and his crewmates admired him. That's why he was permitted to take a nap in the shade of a furled sail and come along a little late for the afternoon diving.

The vessel was called *Firial* – a girl's name. Faleh bin Suleiman, the boat's owner, was a trader in the Gulf with a fleet of ten pearling *dhows* as well as a fishing fleet based at Al Khor. He commanded an empire of men and vessels that was the envy of Dubai, Bahrain and the Trucial states. He was a wily merchant with one goal: to make as much money as he could. He cared for *Firial* and the other boats in his vast fleet, but he didn't care what happened to the men who worked for him.

Adel was tall and broad-chested. His chest matched the smile he wore even on the worst days at sea. He was fortunate to have been blessed with a happy disposition and did not worry much, except about his family back home.

'Go on, Adel. Go and get that big one. Get the *dana*.' It was Yousef, the joker of the crew, who was probably the least able diver. He was slight, and usually stayed on deck as quartermaster and head singer. Other men, squatting on the deck repairing the divers' baskets, called out in unison. '*Yallah*, Adel. Allah maa'ak.' *May God be with you.*

In times of danger it helped to call upon the Almighty – in submission to His will, yes, but also for safe delivery back to the ship, and back home. The long trips, the heat, the hardship, the thirst, the waiting and longing could drive a man insane.

Wearing only a loincloth, Adel took one of the mended string bags from Yousef, hung it around his neck, then took a rope with a lead weight attached to it. He climbed onto the side of the vessel, put a wooden clip on his nose, took a deep breath and slid off the boat, disappearing beneath the azure waters of the Gulf. He had a maximum of two minutes to get to the sea bed, which was about 60 metres down, pick the choicest-looking oysters, put them in his bag and resurface. Once he had gone beyond the two minutes and had suffered hallucinations afterwards. The *nokhdar* had shown no sympathy, just anger that he had been out of action for the rest of the day.

At least the sea was cool. As he swam down, he enjoyed the wonders of the marine life that enveloped him. Even though he had grown accustomed to being underwater, he was still in awe of the natural beauty that lay all around him: first, the pale turquoise waters near the surface through which the sun glinted, and one or two large *hamour* glided lazily around. No doubt the crew would be after those for supper later, as they were an easy catch. Halfway down he could see sea plants swaying in the current, and then the coral came into view, some bright and white, their tree-like branches creating little forests in the darkening water. Among the sea plants were brain corals. Adel wondered how they came to be there. Why did they look like a brain? What did it all mean? It was an extraordinary place to be. It felt like home. After all, he and they were all living things.

He had a minute to go. At the bottom, he concentrated. No time for dreaming now. His eyes were used to the darkness. He investigated any light shapes he saw among the coral – and there they were. A cluster of grey oyster shells, clamped to the rocks, but it just took a quick flick of his wrist to prise them away and into the basket. Please let there be a pearl inside, he thought. Let it be a *dana*. That would be unbelievable. He knew – like every other man in his crew – there were only likely to be three oysters with a pearl for every five thousand they collected. Adel had collected about two dozen. His lungs were reaching their limit. He tugged on the rope. Up he went, slowly and carefully to avoid the bends.

He didn't want any more hallucinations – or brain damage, which one of his uncles had suffered while diving.

'*Ya* Lubna. Wein itch, ya binti?' *Where are you, my daughter?* Miriam called out again and again, walking up and down outside the house and looking along the alley that led to the sea.

'Ya Abu Salem,' she cried. Where had her husband got to? Had there been an accident? Was there a problem with the fishing boats? Was one of the family in trouble? These thoughts were constantly on her mind, as the matriarch of a family of whom she was justifiably proud. Her sister, Maysoon, had come to visit, and she had something important to say. The two ladies had taken coffee and chatted about their families, the comings and goings in Al Mafjar and the recent hot weather. Maysoon had travelled up from Al Khor specially to see Miriam and Nasser.

'I can't wait much longer,' Maysoon said, a harsh tone in her voice. She was Miriam's older sister – and had never forgotten it. 'I don't want to be late back. It'll take two hours at least with that stupid mule outside.'

She was talking about a real mule, but she could have used the term as a euphemism for her son Khaled, who had accompanied his mother and was loafing around outside the house, kicking stones in the dust. He had a neglected look about him, with a dirty, creased *thoub* and his *agal* at a rakish angle, barely holding his faded, ragged *qutra* in place on his long, greasy hair. Unlike most young men in Al Khor, who worked hard either pearling or fishing, Khaled didn't work. His father was well connected, and Khaled was able to come and go as he pleased, idling his days away. His parents were respected members of the community, although some of the elders frowned at the ways in which the family conducted itself.

'Ah, there you are.' Miriam sighed with relief as her husband and daughter entered the old house, arm in arm. 'Where on earth have you been? I've been waiting for you.'

'Sorry, my dear,' Nasser replied. 'I was talking about the old days. I don't know where the time went.'

'Don't know where the time went? What kind of answer is that? And you, Lubna. There's work to be done here. Where are those dishes? Are they clean? We need them for lunch.'

Lubna's face reddened as she realised she had forgotten all about the dishes. She'd left them at the shoreline. 'I'm sorry, Mother. I'll go and fetch the dishes and work hard when I get back.'

'That's all right, my dear. I'm just relieved you're all right. You never know what might happen with this weather, the tides– '

Nasser put his arm around his wife. Trying to calm her, he asked her to sit down in the *majlis*, where it was cool and quiet. Then Miriam realised her sister was sitting there.

'Oh dear. What am I like? Maysoon, Maysoon, I forgot about you. I'm so sorry. Lubna, Maysoon is here. All the way from Al Khor. I'm such a terrible host. I'm so sorry, Maysoon.'

Maysoon, bored and fed up with waiting alone in the majlis, looked up and started to get up from her cross-legged position on the floor.

'Don't get up, Maysoon. Stay, stay,' Nasser begged his sister-in-law. 'Lubna, bring tea. Let's all sit down.'

'Thank you, Nasser. That's good of you,' Maysoon said. 'At least you are polite to me.' She stared angrily at her younger sister. 'I've come all the way from Al Khor, you know. I had such a long, dusty journey.' She sighed.

'Maysoon, you are very welcome, and thank you for making the effort to come here. It is indeed a pleasure,' Nasser said, feeling he had laid on the compliments perhaps a little too much. 'To what do we owe such a rare visit?' Nasser knew that she was not just making a social call.

Immediately she said, 'I've come about your daughter. Lubna. I want her to marry my son Khaled. He's outside.'

As Adel rose slowly to the surface, he concentrated on staying alive. The last breath he had taken had been more than two and a half minutes earlier. It seemed like an eternity. Adel was an experienced diver, used to conserving every tiny bit of breath in his strong lungs, but he had been brought up to question things, and he did this now in the precious seconds between life and near death. One second too long and he would perish; a couple of seconds too fast and he would be brain-damaged. He was only too aware of this and had seen some of his fellow divers reduced to pathetic creatures after diving accidents.

The distance from the sea bed to the surface was hardly two hundred metres, the waters of the Gulf shallow even at this distance offshore. But having gathered as many oysters as he could manage he found it a luxury to enjoy the beauty that surrounded him. How wonderful nature is, he thought, his eyes feasting on the dancing sea plants. Wouldn't it be lovely to live down here, he thought, far from life's daily troubles? I wonder what will become of me. Will I be a pearl-diver for much longer? Will I find happiness?

An angel fish passed him, gloriously parading in orange and purple. A shoal of *saafi*, the best fish a Qatari could eat, zigzagged towards him, suddenly diverting when they realised they were about to head for his legs, which were now propelling him to the surface. Adel smiled as he spotted a lazy *hamour*, too slow to catch up with the speedy *saafi*. What a silly old fish you are, he thought. How easy it would be to catch you for dinner later, but he was content to let it go on its way, undisturbed. As Adel sped ever upwards, he realised anew how much he loved the world beneath the waves. It seemed to him a perfect universe where the water held treasures of pink coral, black spiky sea urchins, sea anemones of all shades and hues, straight-backed seahorses, bright red starfish, and fish of every shape and size. He felt honoured to be among these creatures he had come to know as friends.

One last kick, a sharp tug on the rope by the diver on deck, and Adel broke through the surface. The blazing afternoon sun brought him back from his reverie. He had made it back just in time. Gasping for breath, he lay back, his heart pounding, on the flat sea.

'Where on earth have you been, Adel? We almost gave up. The rope was too slack. Don't do that again, please. You were down almost three minutes.'

'Oh, that's good,' Adel said casually, catching his breath enjoying the business of breathing normally again. 'I got a big pile, as you can see.' Adel handed the basket, crammed full of large slate-grey oysters, to Bilal. 'I saw an angel fish and some beautiful coral too.'

'Angel fish? Coral? He's only interested in finding pearls.' Bilal glanced around at Captain Jamal, who was waiting impatiently on his throne-like seat towards the stern of *Firial*.

Adel was pleased that his best friend on *Firial*, Bilal, had been holding his lifeline. He knew him well and trusted the kind, gentle giant of a man. Big-boned and heavier than most divers, he was the colour of burned charcoal, the son of slaves brought from Zanzibar. For him life was a precious gift and he felt a kinship with Adel, who was his junior by ten years.

'Empty the baskets in ten minutes,' the fearsome Captain Jamal barked, ordering the crew to assemble with their day's catch spread out on the deck. Although the captain sat sedately with both eyes fixed on the goings-on on board, his mind was elsewhere. He knew, unless he brought back a few decent pearls of quality and size, he would be reprimanded by the merchants in Al Khor and Doha. He was getting older and feared his days as a nokhdar were numbered. He had done well over the years and had used his scheming ways to do a few side deals that would make him a bit more money at the end of the season. His masters were only too aware of the shady trade in which they were involved. No one could guarantee a regular income in this uncertain world.

Captain Jamal knew that the Great War had caused havoc throughout the Middle East and the Ottomans were determined to hold on to any last vestiges of power they had. Lawrence of Arabia had fought against them, blowing up the Hejaz railway from Amman to Medina, and the end of the war signalled an end to Ottoman rule. Qatar had become a British protectorate in 1916. Sheikh Abdullah bin Jassem had agreed not to enter into any relations with any other power without the prior consent of the British government. Percy Cox, the political resident who signed the treaty on behalf of his government, guaranteed the protection of Qatar 'from all aggression by sea'.

Like most of his fellow *nokhdars*, Captain Jamal was lugubrious, preferring to remain aloof and alone. He didn't mix with the younger crew members, merely giving orders, concentrating on the mercenary matter of delivering pearls in exchange for money. That was his sole task. In Captain Jamal's world there was no love. No love for his job. No love for the sea. No love for nature and not much love for his family either.

Looking worried, the captain shifted his weight from one leg to another as the crew brought their day's collection before him, crouching down and laying them out carefully on the deck like an offering before a god. Adel and Bilal had done well, bearing several baskets. The rest of the crew gathered around, some looking wearier than others, afraid of the consequences should Captain Jamal notice their efforts hadn't been enough.

'Open the oysters,' came the command.

Half a dozen men armed with short, sharp knives began to shell the enormous heap of oysters in front of them. They were exhausted by the strain of numerous dives that day, and had eaten only a few dates, but they dealt stoically with the job at hand. To help them along the way, they sang. Captain Jamal was not fond of this custom, but he knew it meant the crew were more productive, so he did not forbid it.

Bilal was a natural diver, story-teller and entertainer, and now he could play his favourite role: lead singer. Loudly enough to blast the sails from their masts, he chanted, 'Wish us luck in all we do, bring us fortune wherever we go.' The men sang back to him, echoing Bilal's verse as they picked oysters from the pile and prised each open.

'Bring us joy in all we do. Give us strength to face the day,' Bilal continued, smiling at his fellow crew, bidding them to join in.

Captain Jamal was the only one not singing. His presence somehow polluted the atmosphere. Since the men sat in a horseshoe shape in front of him, he was able to carry out a continuous crew-wide inspection, to ensure nobody stole a pearl.

By the time they had sung ten verses of their favourite pearl-diving chant, the men had opened about a thousand oysters. There was not a single pearl to show for their labours. The men were used to this. As they sang, some thought of their families back home, while others were more concerned with money. This had been a particularly bad year and one or two men had been forced to take advance payment from *Firial*'s owner.

During a break in the singing Adel managed to whisper to his friend, 'You should have been a singer, not a diver.'

'There's no money in that either,' Bilal replied, quick as a flash. 'At least here we have good friends and that lovely man over there.' He glanced at the captain. 'Who wants to sing at weddings? All those wealthy merchants showing off? Not me.'

'You're right, Bilal,' Adel whispered. 'What would we do without you?'

'Who's talking? Adel and Bilal. No fish for you.'

Captain Jamal did not let a single word pass unnoticed. The men ploughed on, waiting and hoping for at least one precious pearl. Nothing yet. It was approaching sunset, and the beauty of the scene around the ship belied the harsh conditions on board. Again Adel, confined to silence, dreamed about what life might have in store for him. Bilal was his best friend, that was certain, but sometimes Adel felt he wanted someone with whom he could share his life, someone to care for and to care for him and love him. Life is so precious, he mused. I must not waste a single second. I'm such a lucky man.

'Here, I got something.'

It was Ibrahim, one of the youngest divers. He had only been diving for two seasons. The men stopped chipping away at their shells while their master bade the youth to come forward. The men hoped that at last an oyster had borne a bright shiny pearl. Ibrahim felt proud as he showed the oyster to Captain Jamal.

'It's a pearl, all right. But it's useless. Maybe worth a few *baisa*. Can't you see, stupid boy? It's a blister pearl, still attached to the shell. Back you go.'

Ibrahim returned to his place among the men, getting encouraging nods from his mates. And so it went on. More singing, more searching, more hoping. It was well after sunset by the time the men had finished opening all the shells and Captain Jamal had declared the day's work done. More than five hundred oysters had been opened. Not one had contained a single whole pearl.

Wearily, the men cleared up the empty shells before them, downhearted at the outcome but glad at least that work had ended for the day and they had some free time. The Captain looked more miserable than ever. The future was bleak. He didn't want to think about the news he had heard last time he had been in Doha. The news that somewhere further east, clever people had made a farm where oysters produced pearls with no need for diving. He banished the thought as he ate his fish alone.

Adel and Bilal ate their rice, enjoyed joking with their shipmates, and slept under the stars.

Nasser looked at his sister-in-law, astonishment written clearly on his face. Nothing had prepared him for this. Miriam seemed less surprised.

'Well, what do you say?' Maysoon asked. It was as if she was making an offer that would benefit Lubna's parents to the detriment of her own family. 'Khaled is a worthy boy and your daughter appears to be suitable and hard-working.'

Miriam remained quiet, knowing she couldn't speak her mind with her elder sister sitting before her. Nasser gazed at his wife. Had she known about this before? Nasser was only too aware of the conspiracies that took place while the men were away from home. Young Khaled wasn't the kind of man he'd had in mind to marry his beloved daughter. There was a lengthy silence. At last Lubna arrived with a tray of tea and set it on the floor. It fell to her father to break the silence.

'Ah. There's a good girl. I need a cup of tea. It's been a long morning. Lubna made me tell all sorts of stories about the old days.' He tried to take their minds off the subject, but it didn't work.

'I haven't got much time. I have to be back by the end of the day. It's no good sitting around here chatting. Well, have you made a decision?'

Lubna looked puzzled, feeling the tension in the air. Her eyes met her mother's but after a moment Miriam had to look down. Lubna looked at her father. What were they talking about?

He turned to Maysoon. 'It is right and proper. Let the marriage take place.'

Lubna paled and felt as though she was about to faint. Unable to speak, she sat, her head in her hands, stunned.

'Mabrook.' *Congratulations* was all Miriam could say. 'Mabrook, ya Lubna. You will be married soon to Khaled, your cousin.'

Lubna was unable to react. She had been raised to be quiet and dutiful and now, as in the past, she was respectful of her parents' decision, trusting them to do what was best for her. However, her eyes searched for answers. Her mother still looked away.

'Well, Nasser, I'm glad that's sorted out. I'll be on my way.'

With that, Maysoon left the majlis with a brief glance at her future daughter-in-law, weighing up the slight figure before her with an air of superiority. Outside Maysoon found Khaled hanging around. She whispered to him, 'It's all done', and they departed for Al Khor.

Inside, the house was quiet.

'Father, can I talk to you?' Lubna asked quietly. 'I know you have done what you think is right for me, but I want to know more about this boy from Al Khor.'

'I have to agree with your mother, dear Lubna. She knows what's best for you. He is from a good family and he will be able to support you, so you have a comfortable future. That's important for your mother and me.'

'But who is he? What is he like?'

'He is the son of Faleh bin Suleiman, the owner of *Firial*, one of the finest vessels in the Qatari pearling fleet. You will be looked after, my love. I have to think of your future.'

'How can you be sure he is the right one for me, Father?'

'How can anyone be sure, sweet Lubna? Khaled has been a disappointment in the past, but I am sure he will adapt to his new responsibilities and grow to be a fine husband and father. It's surprising how men change once they are married and have a purpose in life.'

'But I want to love my husband like Mother loves you. I want to be happy, like you were when you came home from battle.'

'Yes. We were lucky, Lubna. On the day I came home, I promised to honour and obey your mother until the day I died. That's why I have to agree with her now. I hope you understand.'

'Yes, Father,' Lubna whispered. 'I understand.'

Firial was drifting lazily, her sails folded. It was still high summer, and there was not a breath of wind. They had been at sea for nearly three months. Tempers had begun to fray. Captain Jamal was even more morose with the crew, imposing harsh punishments on those who stepped out of line. Now was the time when insurrections grew, even mutinies. In all his days at sea the wily captain had only once had to deal with an uncooperative group of men. They were quickly dealt with, using rope and lead weights, and were never seen again.

'Not long till we go home.' Bilal beamed.

'Yes. It will be good to see the family. Mother, Father, friends too. I wonder how they all are. I don't suppose a lot has happened while we've been away. We'll have good food and fresh water. Oh, what luxury.'

They laughed.

'I wonder how much we'll get paid. That miserable old miser won't give us much, I'm sure. The catch has been bad anyway. The worst ever, I think,' Bilal said.

'We'll get what we get. At least we're still alive. Be thankful for that,' Adel mused philosophically.

Captain Jamal looked inside the wooden chest he had guarded the whole voyage. It was empty apart from a bundle of red cloth in the corner. He opened the cloth slowly and saw a cluster of pearls of various shapes and sizes, most no bigger than a pea. He began to count. There were no more than fifty. Fifty pearls in ninety days. The catch had never been so bad. He gave the order to sail for home.

2

Kuwait, 1928

Further up the Gulf in Kuwait, Violet Dickson was taking an afternoon nap. It tended to be more humid than elsewhere in the Gulf but at least they had the sea breeze. Her husband Harold was the newly appointed political agent, and they were looking forward to a new life in a different country. The couple had travelled together widely in the Gulf and had lived in India for a time too. Here they had chosen a magnificent house, the former home of a Kuwaiti merchant, right on the shore. A fine example of Gulf architecture, it had thirty rooms on two floors, where the Dicksons could entertain and live a comfortable life. Violet was used to the diplomatic life: hosting dinner parties and exchanging visits with local dignitaries was familiar to her.

'Darling? Are you there?'

It was Harold, calling from his study at the far end of the house.

'Of course, I'm here. Where do you think I am? In a tent in Al Bushire?'

They loved a laugh or two. Now they had their two children, Saud and Zahra, they were as happy as any young couple could be. Violet propped herself up on her day bed.

'I'm coming. Just a minute. Muzzafar, *hatni bared*,' she said to the house servant. She had asked for a cold drink.

When she had a refreshing drink in hand, she made her way along to the business end of the house, for it served as the political agency as well as their home.

'Now what is it this time, Harold dear? Don't tell me you're working on another book!'

'No such luck. Far more important than that. I've had a wire from HQ in Bombay. Frank Holmes is coming to town.'

'You mean the geologist we met in Bahrain? The New Zealander?'

'Yes. He reckons there's oil in these parts, just like in America. He's coming in from Basra this evening. You'd better get your glad rags on, old girl.'

'Muzzafar,' Violet called out. 'Another one for dinner, please.'

She ran along to their bedroom to make sure Saud and Zahra were all right. They were being attended to by the maid. 'Run along, you two little pickles. Fonseca be a dear and take them down to the beach for a walk, while I get ready. We have a visitor coming all the way from New Zealand, my darlings. How about that?'

The children looked puzzled, then ran to the large globe Harold kept in the playroom in the hope that his offspring would grow up with a lust for adventure like their parents.

Violet went up to the veranda, where she could look out to sea. Sometimes she slept up here when it was hot, enjoying the beauty of the stars. She waved to the group on the beach. Fonseca and the children had been joined by the neighbours' children – the girls in brightly coloured clothes, barefoot and with jet-black hair, the boys bare-chested in sarongs, also barefoot. They were playing with a piece of driftwood, happy and smiling in the late afternoon sun.

How lucky I am, she thought.

By the time she'd had a bath in rather rusty water, put on a fairly new long dress she'd bought in Bombay and fixed Harold's bowtie, it was time for the archaeologist's arrival.

'You'll do,' Violet said teasingly as she looked Harold up and down.

'You don't look so bad yourself, Mrs D,' Harold replied. 'I wonder when he'll be here. Bit of a journey from Basra, although they should have laid on a decent car and driver for him.'

It was only 130 kilometres from the Iraqi city of Basra to Kuwait, but the desert track was unreliable, and cars were liable to break down or get stuck.

Suddenly there was a loud honking. The latest in luxury automobiles drew up in front of the house in a swirl of sand.

'Well, hello Harold. The boss let me have his Rolls-Royce. Not bad, eh?'

The man from New Zealand certainly knew how to make an entrance.

'Violet. How good to see you; it's a long time since Bahrain. As you can see, I'm still sniffing around. I hope I'm not an imposition.'

'Not at all, Frank. It's a real pleasure. Come in. Come in.'

Violet guided the driver to the side door while Harold escorted his guest into the main part of the house, bags and archaeological paraphernalia in tow.

'I don't have black tie, I'm afraid, old boy. It'll have to be my best suit. I'll change and be down in a minute.'

'Don't worry about that, Frank. We shall wait for all your latest stories. I'll get you a large whisky and soda.'

'Why do we do all this dressing up, Harold dear?' Violet asked her husband as they made their way along the photograph-lined passage to the large room they used for entertaining guests.

'Got to keep up the traditions, old girl. Can't let the side down. Standards, dear, standards,' Harold replied, moving towards the mantelpiece, in front of which lay a tiger skin. He had shot the tiger on a hunting trip in Bengal.

The drawing room, although spacious, had a cosy feel about it due to the comfortable couches and wing armchairs they had shipped from the UK to India, to Bahrain and now to Kuwait. The style of the house was a mixture of Surrey country house and Oriental bazaar: there were marquetry side tables from the souq in Damascus, reading lamps from a bazaar in Istanbul and russet rugs acquired in Isfahan. More black and white photographs adorned the faded cream stucco walls: tribal sheikhs, grand viziers and wealthy colonial families in the so-called Happy Valley of Kenya.

'What a life we've had,' Harold declared, surveying the memorabilia around him. Each ornament had a tale to tell. 'But give me the desert any day. That's where my heart lies.'

'I know, Harold dear. I know. But times are changing. That awful war – and who knows what the Germans may be up to again? We won't be here for ever.' Violet sounded self-assured.

'Ah, Frank. There you are. Here's your drink,' Harold said, offering his guest a tumbler of single malt with a splash of soda. 'Your good health,' he went on, raising his gin and tonic. 'Good to have you back in Kuwait. We're lucky to have you – you're always on the move.'

'You're a fine one to talk, Dickson. You always seem to be out with the Bedouin, inaccessible in some tent on the Saudi border.'

'Violet and I enjoy nothing better than a night under the stars being entertained by our hospitable Bedouin friends, don't we, darling?'

'Absolutely. We've made so many good friends here and further afield – friends for life, I'm sure.'

'But things are changing, as you know,' Frank interjected. 'Don't fool yourselves that this way of life will continue for long. Those friends of yours will be extremely wealthy once we've got the black gold out from underneath them. I wonder if they'll still be living in tents then.'

'Maybe not, but we must try to preserve the traditional ways,' Harold said. 'It's up to us not to be greedy. We must not use the Gulf countries to suit our own ends. It will end in the people of the desert being deeply affected.'

'It's going to happen whether we like it or not,' Frank said with confidence.

Trying to lighten the conversation, Violet proposed a toast to the people of the desert. They clinked glasses.

'The people of the desert,' Harold repeated, holding his glass high.

'Let's go in to dinner,' Violet suggested to the two men, having spotted Muzzafar hovering near the door. 'I can't promise a banquet, but we do our best, don't we, Muzzafar?'

The old servant nodded and made his way back to the kitchen to bring up three bowls of cock-a-leekie soup. Muzzafar was oblivious to the incongruity of serving a hearty soup in the height of summer, having prepared the trusted starter countless times over the years.

'Ah, good old cock-a-leekie,' Harold said, sitting at the head of the mahogany table. 'It looks marvellous, Muzzafar. Stick the fan on, there's a good fellow.'

The Dicksons' house was one of few with newly installed ceiling fans. Kuwaiti families who could afford it had been reluctant to adapt their homes by adding fans, and the ladies had visited Violet on the pretext of tea and a chat only to stare in wonder at the new-fangled machines that whirred around noisily.

'So, what have you been up to, ya Abu Naft? Prospecting as usual?' Harold enquired, slurping his soup. Frank Holmes had been nicknamed 'Abu Naft' or 'Father of Oil' as his reputation for discovering oil in the Middle East grew.

'Well, as you know, I've been sniffing around in eastern Saudi Arabia, Bahrain and Qatar for some time with reasonable success, except for Qatar.'

'Why's that? Surely the Qataris want to find oil if there's any there,' Violet said

'Sheikh Abdullah is all for it. Goodness knows, when I saw him last time he was most hospitable.'

'Only because you gave him that marvellous motor car,' Harold reminded his guest.

'Well, that helped, I suppose!' Frank said, and they broke into laughter. 'It wasn't the Qataris. It was the British Colonial Office, for heaven's sake. Can you believe it?'

'I'm afraid I can,' Harold said. 'That sounds typical of my lot.'

'Blow me down if that confounded fellow from Anglo-Persian hasn't gone down there and scuppered all my plans,' Frank said.

'Ah. George Martin Lees. Yes. He is a fine geologist, though. He was here too.'

'Was he indeed? The scallywag. I thought I was Abu Naft, not him.'

Violet thought a change of mood was called for, and summoned Muzzafar for the main course. It was likely to be roast mutton, as this was Muzzafar's main standby should guests turn up unexpectedly. He had good contacts with the cold store in town and could easily obtain a leg or shoulder with a few hours' notice. Sure enough, there it was on a silver platter, looking rather dry and overdone. The ever-optimistic Harold declared it a marvellous-looking piece of meat.

'Very lucky for us to have meat. Well done, Muzzafar,' he said.

'It does look rather well done too,' Violet said as though this was an old joke between them.

Some grey vegetables were placed near Frank, and some watery gravy.

'Have we got any mint sauce left, Muzzafar?' Harold asked as if they were dining in the English countryside.

'I think it's had its day, my dear,' Violet said.

'There you are, sir,' Muzzafar said as he came back from the kitchen. 'I kept it in the larder in a jam jar.'

'Perfectly fine. Marvellous,' Harold said, sharpening the carving knife. 'So, any news of that queer fish, Lawrence?'

'Captain Lawrence?' Lawrence of Arabia, as he's known now? Well, he's changed his name to T.E. Shaw and lives modestly in a little cottage in Dorset. What a funny business all that was.'

'Funny, maybe,' Violet said, 'but he certainly got Britain back in the Middle East and got those damned Turks out of the way.'

'Gertrude always thought he was a spy,' Harold said, handing a plate to his wife.

'Gertrude Bell should have known. She knew everything about Arabia. When she finally ended up in Baghdad as Oriental Secretary, she told me Lawrence had had secret meetings with Amir Faisal before he became King of Iraq – and Syria, of course,' Harold said. 'But I'm not so sure. If he was a spy, how come Churchill asked him to join the Paris Peace Conference in 1919?'

'Oh, I don't know. It was so sad the way Gertrude died. All alone in Baghdad. Too many sleeping pills, they said. It must have been an accident, surely. I know she was upset about her brother Hugo's death, and of course she was in love with Doughty. But you would have thought, after all those years of exploration and discovery, she would have been happy in retirement. Buried in Baghdad with no husband and children, and not even sixty.'

'I know. It was sad. But King Faisal watched the funeral procession, and all those people. It was incredible.' Harold chewed on a piece of meat. 'The king thought the world of her. Now Lawrence and Bell – what an odd couple. Both the same height. Five foot five. Did you know that?'

'Harold, you are a mine of information,' Violet said, laughing.

'She wouldn't have had much luck marrying T.E., that's for sure,' Frank said.

'Now, now,' Violet interjected. 'Some things need never be said. Thought, perhaps, but not said. How about dessert?'

The plates weren't entirely clean when Muzzafar came in to clear the things away.

'You mentioned Churchill,' Frank said. 'Haven't heard much from him since he made a mess of things as Chancellor.'

'I met him at the Paris Peace Conference when I was a junior in the diplomatic service,' Harold said. 'He was better at dealing with wars, I think. They say he's writing a history of England now he's out of favour. Baldwin out, Ramsay McDonald in. Who knows what may happen?'

'Churchill never liked the Middle East much anyway, and he certainly didn't want to have anything to do with India. Wait until Mr Gandhi gets his way,' Violet said, directing Muzzafar to place a pink blancmange in the centre of the table. 'Now that does look nice, Muzzafar. Well done. I see the new refrigerator has come in handy.'

'Yes, ma'am,' Muzzafar said dutifully. 'It's raspberry flavour, ma'am.'

'The world is certainly going through a lot of change,' Violet said, passing a pudding bowl to Frank. 'President Hoover will have to do something about the economic situation pretty soon.'

'It's not his fault, Violet. People were spending too much. Too much wealth and opulence,' Harold chipped in. 'Everyone overdid it after the Great War and now they're paying the price. Times are going to be hard, that's for sure.'

Frank was more positive. 'All the more reason to get some oil out of these vast deserts around here, then. America may be in trouble but it's a long way away, and the Empire is still in good shape.'

'Not so sure about that, Frank.' The usually optimistic political agent was unusually down to earth. 'It's all changing. The Egyptians have independence. Balfour is carving up the rest of the Middle East. The Indians are getting restless, thanks to Mr Gandhi, and don't even mention Africa. We'd better make the most of it because we won't be here for ever. Cigar?'

Violet left the two men to talk. She thought the evening had gone rather well and went along to thank Muzzafar. We have been lucky, she thought, having such a happy life. I'm so grateful to the Arabs for giving me the guidance towards a wholesome and peaceful existence. I wonder what will happen to them all.

As the two men enjoyed their cigars and whisky, the discussion came around again to Frank's favourite subject – oil. Violet joined them, carrying a tray of tiny coffee cups and a silver pot of coffee.

'I wonder if you could do me a favour, old chap,' Frank said.

'Ah. I wondered if you had an ulterior motive. Although it's good to see you, of course,' he said.

'The thing is, I'm concerned about Qatar. I'm sure there's oil down there, but the Colonial Office has refused permission for me to carry out more work. Would appreciate it if you can help out. You're the only one who can.'

Harold thought for a while, then said, 'Very well. I'll see what I can do tomorrow. Violet, how about a trip to Doha?'

Lubna walked along the beach in Al Mafjar. It was the place she loved the most, and where she went when she wanted to think. She'd found a sense of freedom there all through her happy childhood. It had been rocked by this shock. Her father had agreed. There was no question of trying to change his mind. Of all the men who could have been chosen for her, it had to be that good-for-nothing lazybones.

Why, Father? Why? was all she could ask herself. She kept recalling the long conversation they had had earlier in the day, sitting contentedly under the tree in the quiet village square. She had always been happy carrying out her daily chores, at ease with whatever life may have in store for her. She had not thought about marriage. She presumed that one day she would get married, but to whom mattered not a jot. She sank down onto a piece of driftwood as harsh reality began to sink in. Khaled? The lazy boy she had seen occasionally on childhood visits to Al Khor? Surely not. He doesn't know anything. He doesn't work or do anything, she thought. She wanted to cry, but she couldn't. So, this was her destiny? She had been so happy in Al Mafjar. Suddenly she realised that life would never be the same again. She stood up, took a deep breath, squared her shoulders and walked back to the house, ready to deal with the situation.

When Lubna arrived back at the old mud-brick house Nasser had rented since returning from battle all those years ago, there was a commotion going on. From the alley, she heard men's voices, raised with emotion – perhaps anger.

Then she realised that her younger brother was home. No doubt he had heard the news.

'Salam aleikum,' Lubna said softly, but clearly, to her family.

'Aleikum salam,' came the reply. After a moment's silence Salem began to mutter, his downcast look betraying a feeling of disapproval at his future brother-in-law. He rose to embrace his sister.

'Oh goodness me. You are so kind, dear Salem.' Lubna smiled. 'How nice of you to congratulate me in this way.'

'I don't know why Father– '

But she wouldn't let him finish.

'Yes, I am soon to be married. It will be such a happy time. Thank you, my dear, for all your kindness to me. You have always been dear to me, and now I give thanks for your support during this next stage in my life.'

Salem was speechless. He smiled awkwardly, bidding his sister good health and happiness. He left as soon as possible – no doubt to carry on his conversation outside with his friends. Lubna was left alone with her parents. They were silent, barely able to look at their daughter.

'My dear mother and father. You know I love you both,' she said, squeezing herself between the two.

Miriam began to cry. 'We've always wanted the best for you, sweet child,' she said as tears trickled down her lined face. 'We didn't know what to do, your father and I.'

'I understand, Mother. It's quite all right. I shall be happy, I am sure, whatever happens,' Lubna said, hugging her parents. 'You're all that matters to me.'

'You see,' Miriam said, 'we are so poor. Your father can't work anymore, and we only have the little money from your brothers and the help we get from your uncle. We felt we– '

'It's fine, Mama,' Lubna said quickly before she heard any more, knowing but not wanting to hear what she was about to say. 'I understand. Don't worry. You want me to have a good future, which is what all parents want for their children. I couldn't ask for more.'

'You see what a wonderful daughter we have, my dear?' Nasser said to his wife as Lubna got up, ran outside and called her brothers. 'Hey, you two, I'm starving. Let's have dinner together.'

Salem looked surprised at this sudden change of mood and came back indoors.

'Mama let's cook and give these hungry men something to fill their tummies. We can all sit down together as one happy family.' Lubna led her mother to the kitchen, leaving the men of the house to gaze at each other in awe at her generosity of spirit.

'What will we make, Mama? *Fassolia?* Beans with *bagdounis*, parsley, some *adiz*, lentils with the chicken broth we have left over and maybe a little rice. It's a feast!' They laughed as they prepared what would be a humble supper to most, but to them would be a memorable feast.

Harold and Violet Dickson loved nothing more than spending time in the desert, as far away from the trappings of modern life as possible. In 1928, life was certainly not luxurious for expatriates. Harold was in touch with the Colonial Office every day and burdened by the daily grind of diplomatic correspondence as well the constant round of courtesy calls – 'being on parade,' as he called it.

Violet had jumped at the opportunity to visit another desert country. In order to carry out the mission Frank had requested, the couple had called on the assistance of the ruler of Kuwait, Sheikh Ahmed Al Jaber Al Sabah. He was fond of the eccentric Harold. The sheikh admired the British for their sense of justice and love of all things traditional. Harold was told by the Amir that he could visit the sheikh's palace any time, day or night, if he needed anything, so one evening, after the obligatory coffee and dates, the political agent mentioned that he wanted to travel down the Gulf, exploring some of the areas towards the lesser-known sheikhdoms of Felix Arabia.

'You British are great explorers, Colonel Dickson, and I am not surprised you and your wife want to go for another adventure.' The Emir was gracious, although concerned for the couple's safety. 'I will give you my best desert guide, camels, and two or three servants to help ease the burdens of travel. Your caravan should be adequate. I would have to go with a lot more, but that's another story. I haven't travelled far since I had to go and see that old rogue Abu Saud in Riyadh. He still wants our land. All this talk of black gold. I wonder where it will lead. I suppose I'll have to go and be nice to King Faisal in Baghdad too, one of these days, in case he wants to invade too. These are difficult times, Colonel Dickson. Difficult times.'

'Your Highness is perfectly correct. We have many problems to face in times of international crisis. The economic situation in America must be a cause of great concern too. Be assured that His Majesty's government will do everything it can to protect your country from harm.' Harold gave his best diplomatic speech to the frail-looking Emir.

'Thank you. May I call you Harold?'

'It would be a great honour, Your Highness. Thank you so much for making our journey to Qatar possible.'

'Give Abdullah bin Jassim my best wishes. I must invite him here. His father was a great man. We did so much together to live in freedom without those Turks bossing us around.'

'Indeed, Your Highness,' Harold said without adding further comment.

'You'd better not start bossing us around too!'

They laughed then Harold took his leave and collected Violet from the ladies' court.

_ſ=ſ~

Firial made her way steadily back to port. The crew sang a special chant reserved for homecoming. Although they were weary after spending months away from home, they were happy at the thought of seeing their loved ones – and happy that they would not have to dive again for a while.

'I wonder what they'll have for dinner when I get home,' Yousef said, dreaming of lamb cooked in spices with aromatic rice.

'My mother always makes *thareed* for me even when it's not Ramadan,' Bilal chipped in.

'I just want to walk on dry land. No more rocking,' Adel said, exaggerating *Firial*'s swaying motion.

'I think I'm going to find a wife,' Yousef said. 'Slender and beautiful.'

'What girl would want you, Yousef? Away for half the year and you can't sing either!'

They laughed.

'We'll have to meet up soon. I'll miss you,' Yousef said with a hint of sarcasm.

'I don't want to see either of you for a long time,' Adel said, and they hugged each other with the camaraderie of trusted friends.

By now the small armada was making its way to Al Khor, a strong wind coming to their aid. The *joliboats*, the *booms* and *samboks* were an impressive sight. The men waved to each other, cheering at the sight of their fellow divers and all enjoying the prospect of the pleasurable days to come.

There was one final command from Captain Jamal. 'Line up on deck.'

This time they had to follow orders. It was pay time. The crew approached the task master in single file. Each man collected a different wage, depending on what the captain thought he deserved. No words were exchanged. No praise. No thanks.

The three friends looked pleased enough, for they had earned enough to get by, give their families enough to pay for daily necessities, and perhaps buy a new *thaub* or length of material for their mothers and sisters. Life was simple. They thanked the Almighty for their homecoming and found joy in simply being alive.

The singers continued their homage to the sea, praising the Creator for the bounties He had produced for them, thanking Him for their safe arrival. The drumbeats got louder and louder as they drew closer to home. This was indeed a joyous occasion. At the shout of 'Land ahoy!', all the men roared with happiness. After four months and twenty-five days of toil and graft, constant danger and confinement, they had made it back.

Gathering their few possessions, the men dressed, making efforts to look as respectable as they could, in front of the well-wishers who had gathered to greet them at the shoreline.

'Lower the mainsail,' the captain cried for the last time, and the crew pulled together to bring *Firial* into the bay of Al Khor. Among the throng Adel spotted a tiny *shui* – a craft small enough to negotiate shallow water and used mainly for fishing. In it was Salem, Lubna's brother, waving madly to his best friend.

'Salem, here I am!' Adel shouted. 'Where's all the family?'

'They're home waiting. Come on board.'

Adel hugged his two best friends and clambered down the makeshift rope ladder to the little boat below.

'OK, Salem, let's go. Yousef, I'll see you in Al Ghareyah. Bilal, we'll get together in Al Fuwairat.'

As promised, the family were all waiting. Adel and Salem had been friends, going fishing and living in each other's houses. Salem would often stay with Adel in Al Ruwais after a day out at sea. The whole village had turned out to see the divers return home.

'You know, we could have taken the gunboat provided by the government,' Harold said to his wife as they ambled along on their camels, on loan from the Kuwaiti Emir. 'But you're never one to take the easy option. The call of the desert, I suppose.'

'Well, it's the freedom, dear. There's nothing like it. I mean, look at that desert way out into the wilderness. Emptiness. Space. The vastness. It's quite spiritual. You can go by boat any time. But you wait – there will be motor cars driving through the desert before long on man-made roads. Let's relish these days of freedom where we can wander at will.'

Violet was in her element. They had been heading south from Kuwait for two days and were almost halfway to Qatar.

'I wonder how the children are.'

'They'll be fine. Muzzafar will be supplying them with biscuits and cold drinks. I expect they'll be playing with the neighbours' children too. Good for their Arabic,' Harold said, ever positive.

It was mid-afternoon when they approached the Saudi settlement of Al Hofuf. The guide the Emir had provided led the group towards a clump of palm trees – a welcome sight as this meant shade and water were at hand.

'*Sh'ryak nssawi khaym hunak ya* Um Saud?' The guide asked Violet if she thought it would be a good place to camp for the night. He liked the eccentric British lady, and called her Um Saud after her son, knowing she was fond of the desert and the ways of the Bedouin. He was not so sure about Harold, who was a little too formal for his liking.

'Jayed.' *Good.* 'Yallah. Ya seer kheer Inshallah,' she agreed, invoking the will of the Lord.

And so, the two British citizens, two Bedouin guides and two servants along with six camels made camp for the night near an oasis in Al Hofuf in the newly created Kingdom of Saudi Arabia. The guides erected woollen tents, with partitions so Violet and Harold could have privacy. The men busied themselves with making their temporary home respectable. As the sun went down over Al Hofuf, one of the servants cupped his hands to his mouth.

'Allah u Akbar, Allah u Akbar,' he chanted, summoning the rest of the party to the *azhan al maghrib* – the sunset call to prayer.

'Ashh adu anna la ila ill Allah. Ashh adu anna la ila ill Allah.'

The four Muslim men formed a line facing west towards the holy city of Mecca as Violet and Harold looked on.

'Hayya 'ala - s - Salah. Hayya 'ala - s - Salah.'

The sun had set. The soft orange and pink light glowed above the horizon for moments before darkness fell.

Violet, her head swathed in a fine silk scarf, gazed beyond the men to the darkening expanse of desert before her. The evening star appeared in the inky-blue heavens above her. She had never been so happy.

'*Ya Ob'a*, Father, come quickly. They're home! The men are back from the pearling.'

It was Salem, Nasser's son, running into the little majlis in the family home in Al Mafjar.

'I wish I could go with them. I really do.'

'You say that now,' Nasser said as he woke up from his afternoon snooze. 'But I wonder how you would feel if you had to go down to the ocean floor. You aren't a natural swimmer, I'm afraid.'

Salem had nearly drowned when he was a small boy while fishing along the coast at Um Tais. Since then his father had cautioned him against going out to deep water. Salem yearned to be like his friends, enjoying all that the sea offered, but it seemed he was destined to be confined to the land.

'I can hear them coming, Father. I can hear them!' Salem cried excitedly at the thought of seeing his friends after such a long time.

A small procession of pearl-divers came into the main square of Al Mafjar, past the tree under which Lubna and her father had sat a few days before. As the men approached their homes, families poured out of back yards and majlises to greet them, the women ululating, the children dancing. The young men thought this made the long days away worthwhile.

Lubna had been with her mother, making a large pot of mutton stew with rice, when she'd heard the commotion. Salem was already outside, but it didn't take long for Lubna to join in the excitement. She was pleased for her brother, who she knew envied the high esteem accorded to the brave divers.

There must have been twenty or so men, weary and thin, but smiling nonetheless, from boats that had started out from Al Khor and Doha. Now they had returned safely. In the minds of the people of Al Mafjar, they were real heroes – and they had come to depend on the money they brought home.

Salem was squeezed between the neighbours as the parade passed their house.

'*Ya* Lubna. Mama, come here, they're coming. Father, you too.' The family gathered to watch the celebrations, then the village suddenly burst into song praising the Almighty. A few of the older men had warmed their old goatskin drums to bang out a welcome home.

They watched the crews come along the narrow passage between the mud-brick homes of Al Mafjar. Lubna felt a sense of pride at seeing her fellow citizens come back from such harsh times. Most of them looked drained of energy. However, Lubna couldn't help but stare straight into the eyes of one young man, still walking proudly: his bearing exuded confidence and a strong character. She was mesmerised. He returned her look. She pulled her dark veil across her face as she attempted to look down, but she couldn't. The handsome young man held her gaze.

'Adel, Adel. Is it you?'

Adel hadn't expected anyone to notice him. Then he saw Lubna in the crowd. 'Hey, Lubna. This is wonderful.' Adel said warmly. 'Thank you for this great welcome. We all appreciate it.'

Salem gave Adel a big hug and patted him on the back. 'You've got more muscles! Oh, I'm sorry – this is my family. We have all come to welcome you home. But why are you here?'

'I was supposed to go home to Al Ruwais, but the captain wouldn't go any further north, so I was going to walk from here.'

'You must stay here. Please. You are welcome. Isn't he, Father, Mother?'

They agreed that he was and welcomed him into the majlis like a long-lost member of their own family.

'We shall have a big party,' Salem declared.

Lubna looked down bashfully, her cheeks reddening as she caught a glimpse of the brave handsome man.

Adel had never seen anyone so beautiful in all his life.

'Come on, Lubna,' Miriam said, suddenly realising that mutton stew alone was a rather bleak supper for such a joyous occasion and such an honourable guest. 'We have work to do.'

Salem couldn't contain his excitement. 'We'll have to go down to the sea and play games like we used to. Tell me about your days at sea, Adel. Tell me all about it.'

'Give Adel a chance to rest a little. He must be exhausted,' Nasser suggested and offered Adel pride of place in the majlis, taking his small bundle of possessions and putting them to one side.

'I don't want to be any trouble. It's very kind of you,' Adel said, making himself at home. 'We can go down to the sea later, Salem. It's going to be a beautiful evening. Now is the best time to sit and enjoy ourselves. Thank you so much for letting me come into your home.'

Um Salem was outside in the yard, looking worried. 'Oh my Lord. What are we going to do, Lubna? We can't give him mutton stew. We'll have to get other nice things from somewhere.'

'I know. I'll go down to the beach. Someone must have caught some fish today. I'll see Father's friends. You have enough rice, don't you, and maybe some *thareed* too?' Lubna suggested, appearing to be more in command of the crisis than her mother.

She sped off to the beach in search of supper. In fact, it was also an excuse. She had time to gather her thoughts. She could hardly contain her emotions. She had never before felt as she did when she looked at Adel.

She ran to her favourite part of the beach where she washed the dishes, took off her *shib shib* and splashed around in the water, trying to fathom what was happening to her. 'Dear God, why do I feel so happy? I feel like I'm in heaven already. Tell me what it is,' she pleaded.

She managed to get her long abaya wet around the ankles, but she didn't care. Still feeling as though she was on a magic carpet of delight, she saw old Abu Tamim sitting next to his fishing boat darning his nets and remembered what she was there for.

'Salam aleikum, ya Abu Tamim.'

'Ahlan, ya Lubna. Inti mastanassa el youm.' *You look even happier than usual.*

'Shukran, Abu Tamim. Andak samak akthar fil bait?' *Do you have extra fish at home?*

She told him what had happened, and he suggested she go to their house, where his wife would help. She ran along the firm sand in bare feet, swinging her shib shib in one hand and pulling up her abaya with the other. There was a gentle breeze, and the gentle waters ebbed and flowed as they had always done. She felt calm.

Um Tamim was busy gutting two large hamour when Lubna went into the back yard. Um Tamim looked up, surprised to see her. When Lubna explained what had happened, Um Tamim was happy to help out.

'Shriedge nsawi hafla ma baad?' she suggested straight away. *How about a party?*

Lubna was so pleased at the thought, she did a little dance around the tiny courtyard.

'Oh, Um Tamim, inti riyah!' *You're wonderful.* She bent down to kiss her on the forehead.

Abu Tamim had caught plenty of fish that morning, including the hamour his wife was dealing with, some sbeiti and a larger than normal catch of *saafi*, the most highly prized fish of all. As word spread of the possibility of a feast, all the neighbours knocked on each other's doors, asking for a dish of rice or a plate of dates. Hamour was used to make machbous with rice and spices; the sbeiti was stuffed with green herbs and the saafi fried whole.

The men had made their way back to their homes after saluting the divers, many of whom had been persuaded to stay for the night to break their journey to villages further north.

In the majlis Salem offered their guest coffee and dates as his father and Adel exchanged stories: Adel told tales of near-disasters at sea and Nasser recollected the battle of Al Wajbah.

'Kulla shay kheer ya umma,' Lubna announced to her anxious mother when she returned, telling her the ladies were all getting together to prepare a feast. *Everything is well.*

'*Ma shallah!*' her mother cried, unable to resist a joyful ululation, then told Lubna to go and tell the men what was happening.

Lubna peered around the doorway to the majlis. The three men were engrossed in conversation, Salem's eyes wide in awe at the stories being told.

Lubna found the confidence to announce in a loud voice, 'Fi hafla e Laila!' *There will be a party tonight.* Her father and Salem stood and gave Lubna a warm hug. Adel held out his hands in thanks, his eyes meeting hers with a longing and passion neither of them had ever known.

As the family celebrated, Um Salem burst in, in a bigger panic than ever. She demanded to know what they were going to do. How were they going to get everyone in?

'Why don't we have the party outside? It's a beautiful evening,' Lubna suggested.

'We can all gather in the square under the old palm tree,' her husband said.

Miriam looked relieved, hugging her husband and daughter for being so clever and thoughtful. It was decided: the whole village would take their dishes to the centre of Al Mafjar and celebrate. The villagers pulled together to make it an evening they would never forget.

After the *azhan al asha*, the evening call to prayer, the family made their way down to the central square, greeting their neighbours on the way. They all carried platters of home-made fare, ready to share. Salem and some of the other younger men had laid out mats made of palm leaves and brought their masanid from their majlises so the assembled families, especially the older ones, might be more comfortable.

Miriam carried a large plate of *hareess,* made by pounding wheat and flour with some old stock she had from lamb bones. Nasser and Salem carried a large tray of rice which had been infused with herbs and spices. Lubna carried a pot too.

'What's in there?' Miriam asked.

'Oh, just a little extra something for the feast, Mother, so there's more to go around.'

'Look, everyone's bringing something,' Salem said as they gathered in the square.

Adel offered to help by carrying some dates and sweetmeats a neighbour had donated to the party. He had never felt such warmth and affection, even in Al Ghareyah, which was famous for its hospitality too.

There must have been fifty or sixty people in the square, from parents and small children to older relatives staggering along arm in arm, all chatting to the pearl-divers about their days at sea. They sat down around the edge of the square, which was lit by a full moon and some tiny oil lamps. Never before had the village witnessed so much chattering and laughter. Lubna felt the proceedings needed to be called to order.

'Father, say something please,' she said.

Nasser gave a sigh and braced himself. 'Everyone, we are very happy to have our brave young divers back on dry land. This is a great occasion. Let's all rejoice and enjoy this evening together.'

A cheer went up. The women ululated, and the children jiggled around.

'Yallah, let's eat,' Nasser announced to the villagers, and they all began to tuck in.

The fish was soon devoured, along with the mounds of rice, platters of *thareed* and *harees*. The pearl-divers feasted on food they had only dreamed about for months. In fact, some of them held back in case they overdid it after eating so little for so long.

During the festivities Lubna managed to pass Adel the pot she had been carrying. She smiled at him. Once everyone had eaten their fill, Um Nasser noticed that Adel had no fish bones on his plate.

'Have you had enough, Adel?' she asked.

'Oh yes, it was lovely. Mutton stew is my favourite.'

Um Nasser was beside herself with embarrassment but managed to chuckle under her *batula*. The rest of the party guffawed.

'Do you still have those drums, Abu Talal? Abu Tamim, what about singing? You've always been the best.' Nasser was in the mood to dance. He persuaded his old friends to get their drums, and they began to perform some of their favourite folk tunes. Nasser led the dancing, beckoning Adel and the others to join in.

The divers didn't hesitate. They leaped into the centre of the square, throwing caution to the wind as they twirled and clapped, swayed and sashayed to the beat of Nasser's hastily formed band.

The women had their turn too, ululating under their batulas and rocking from side to side, alternating with the men in a flurry of dance steps that mesmerised everyone watching. The girls, including Lubna, had let down their long hair so it swayed with the music. Their jewellery glistened in the lamplight, making the spectacle even more magical. Um Nasser forgot all her troubles as she leaned on her ageing husband, knowing that this would be one of the happiest nights of their lives.

Salem had been dancing with his friends. He had noticed that Lubna and Adel were beginning a dance of their own. From their separate sections, the two met in the middle. After a while the other dancers drifted off, leaving the couple twirling around each other like two birds of paradise wooing each other. The crowd looked on in amazement at the scene in front of them – here was a moment of adoration to which nobody could object.

The couple wound around each other but made no contact, apart from with their eyes, which were constantly on each other. The band were playing a song with a slow steady rhythm; their voices were softer. After a few minutes, the gathering wound down and silence fell. Everyone wandered back to their homes, smiling contentedly.

Nasser, Miriam, Salem, Lubna and Adel stayed for a while, relishing the beauty of the evening.

'Let's walk along the beach,' Salem said, knowing they would all enjoy this way of ending the day. So, they did.

Somehow this little group felt at ease. They didn't say much as they ambled along the shoreline towards Um Tais. The waves made the only sound. Um Salem was the first to speak when they came to the spit of sand at the end of the beach.

'What a day it's been. Thank goodness it all turned out well. Look at the moon, Nasser. It reminds me of when we were first married.'

For the first time in years, she took her husband's hand as if they had just wed.

'You're still as beautiful as the day we met,' Nasser said, and the pair swung hands playfully.

The other three had begun to chat about the party and what a nice time they had had.

They were all paddling in the shallow water in their bare feet, able to see by the light of the full moon, phosphorescence glowing against the blackness of the sea beyond.

'I think we'd better go back, Nasser,' Miriam said. 'I am a little weary and need my bed.'

So they turned back. Miriam muttered, 'I can't believe Lubna brought that mutton stew to the party' as the pair headed up the beach towards home. Salem, Adel and Lubna were a little further behind, enjoying the cool evening air.

'We'll be home soon,' Salem told his parents.

The three young friends sat down outside the village, not far from where Lubna washed the dishes every day. Here on the elevated part of the beach there was shingle to sit on. They all looked out towards the invisible horizon.

'What is it like out there, diving for pearls, Adel?' Salem asked his friend.

'It's beautiful. Life underwater is even more beautiful than above the surface. It's hard work, but the pleasure I get from the nature below the sea makes it all worthwhile,' Adel said.

Lubna couldn't believe how much she identified with him. He felt the same way as she did about the sea and nature.

'If I could come back again as another creature, I would be a dolphin,' she said.

'I would be a seahorse,' Adel replied.

'And I would be a whale and gobble you all up!' Salem joked. They all laughed. 'Come on, we'd better get back. It's late and we've had a perfect day.'

'If you don't mind, I think I'll sleep here out on the beach,' Adel said. 'I find it difficult to adjust to sleeping indoors after I've been away so long. It's lovely here with the moonlight and the sound of the sea.'

'Fine, Adel. Suit yourself. You're welcome to come in any time. There's a place in the majlis for you,' Salem said.

'I hope you're not too cold,' Lubna said, as if she'd known him for years. She turned to look at him, thinking how at ease he was, how relaxed and gentle. She could see so much depth and emotion in his eyes. She found his taut bronzed body tantalisingly attractive and his face, with its growth of beard, although it was weathered from the months at sea, intelligent and strong. She longed to kiss his lips. If only she could. As they glanced at each other for the last time, Adel wanted so much to take her into his arms, to tell her he would love to stay with her like this on the beach for ever.

'Come on, Lubna. Time for bed,' Salem called to his sister.

They said good night and parted company. It had indeed been a perfect day.

Lubna lay in bed, unable to take in the events of the day. She wanted to tell someone how she felt. She was genuinely tired and tried to sleep, but sleep would not come. It was well after midnight when she left the tiny room at the far end of the house. She went to the majlis and found her father's *birnous*, which he had had since he was a young man. She tiptoed out of the house, feeling her way along the alleyway to the central square, and headed towards her favourite spot. There, where she had left him, lay Adel, asleep under the stars. Lubna put the birnous over him and crawled under it beside him.

She knew this was where she belonged.

Adel, still dreaming, took her in his arms.

3

Eastern Saudi Arabia, Qatar Border,1928

'Come on, old thing.' Harold prodded his wife awake in their Bedouin camp on their final night before entering Qatar from the desert of Saudi Arabia. 'Have some camel's milk. It's hot and frothy.'

Violet sat up, her eyes adjusting to the light outside. It was only five thirty but dawn had already broken. People were busy with prayers, camel-tending and preparations for the final stage of their journey. She drank the camel's milk, enjoying the scene outside. Here the dunes had given way to more saline land where wild desert plants grew. Since she had arrived in Kuwait she had become fond of the flowers that magically grew in the harshest of conditions. Here they could find desert roses – crystallised sand that formed into the shape of roses.

By seven o'clock they were on the trail towards Salwa, the settlement between Saudia Arabia and the Qatar peninsula.

By a twist of fate Qatar was still connected to the vast Arabian peninsula by a sliver of land like a hinge on an oyster shell. In years to come, who knows? Qatar might become an island. But the Dicksons and their party were able to cross from one country to another on dry land, skirting the sands of the inland sea and heading for the bay just above Salwa, where they had their first sight of the sea for a week.

'You know, Violet, it's not far from here, to the north I think, that our oil man from New Zealand wants to explore. He reckons there's enough oil there to last several lifetimes. Things are going to be very different in these parts in years to come. Mark my words.' Harold sounded a little pessimistic.

Violet was quick to add her thoughts. 'The simple ways of the desert will be ruined. The remarkable thing about Arabs is that they can survive in the worst conditions. The hard life they have endured over generations has created a people who are proud, strong and noble. Imagine if they had to adapt to the ways of the West. Things would never be the same again.' She looked out to sea. As they turned back to go back to their camels, one of the guides shouted out, 'Ma shallah, shouf. Shouf.' *Look. Look!*

'It must be a mirage,' Violet said as they saw what appeared to be shining mirrors glistening on the desert horizon. First one, then two, and finally several objects approached them.

'Syaraat,' the guide declared. *Cars* – several of them.

They had enjoyed days of calm and peace; the steady progress of camel hooves was all they were used to hearing. Now it was clear. This was no mirage. Some distance away, a line of motor cars headed straight towards them. In the dust they could make out a large silver Chevrolet, men standing on the running boards. Behind this were more cars, and what looked like a small lorry full of men who appeared to be in uniform. The cars screeched to a halt just before them, causing an enormous dust cloud to blow into their faces.

'Ahlan, Ahlan. So glad I found you.'

It was His Highness Sheikh Abdullah bin Jassem Al Thani, ruler of Qatar, having a day off in the desert. It was Friday, after all, and winter, so that meant hunting. No longer did the sheikh and his men have to take long journeys on horseback.

'Your Highness. It is indeed a great honour,' Harold said, still surprised the Emir had come to greet the couple personally.

'Ahmed bin Jabor telephoned me from Kuwait, telling me of your visit. And I have my spies, of course,' the wily Emir said, a twinkle in his eye. He laughed, and the rest of the party laughed too.

'Yallah. Let's go hunting. Come into the car,' the Emir ordered, leaving Harold and Violet confused. What would they do with all their things, the camels, the men and so on? Suddenly there was a flurry of activity. The sheikh's Bedouin bodyguards loaded all the Dicksons' belongings, tents and other equipment onto the lorry. The Dicksons themselves were ushered into the Emir's limousine and the camels were mounted by their guides, along with two more bodyguards, who were ordered to head for the newly built Al Koot fort in Doha. From the peace and tranquility they had experienced over the past few days, the Dicksons were in a whirlwind of cars, dust and noisy commands. They weren't sure they were grateful for the sheikh's hospitality.

'We'll go north,' the Emir barked to his driver, and the cavalcade of vehicles sped off in a cloud of dust, heading up the coast towards the settlement of Um Bab. Violet, usually unfazed, looked at her husband with more fear than excitement as they rocked from side to side, occasionally bumping their heads on the roof. They grabbed the silk rope handles and hung on for dear life.

'Welcome to Qatar,' the head of state shouted into the rear compartment, half turning his head. 'We'll be there soon. It's a good day for hunting. You'll like it. Better than Kuwait.'

The age-old rivalry between the Gulf sheikhdoms was obviously alive and well.

Sheikh Abdullah had been the leader of his country since 1913 when his beloved father Sheikh Jassim, the founder of modern Qatar, died. The fifth of nineteen sons, the Emir had come to power at a turbulent time – during the Great War, Ottoman rule and dramatic change in communications and industry. Now, sixteen years later, he had gained the experience he needed to guide his tiny country into the twentieth century – but it would be a long and hazardous journey.

'Ah, there they are. Good,' the Emir said, looking towards a group of men in the distance. As they approached, the Dicksons could see, squatting on the ground, four men and four falcons, each bird perched on a stand. The Emir's entourage again screeched to a dusty halt.

After several Salam aleikums, the men stood to attention, but His Highness bade them to take their ease. Soon they were focused on the beautiful falcons, and all formalities were forgotten.

The weather-beaten faces of the falconers, their chequered qutras wrapped around their heads as protection against the midday sun and the sea breeze, revealed a knowledge that took years to master and attain. The Emir of Qatar knew this love of nature and tradition had to be maintained throughout whatever developments might occur in his land.

'Are they ready to go?' he asked the men.

'Yes, Your Highness,' the lead falconer replied, and released the hoods and jesses to free the falcons to search for their prey.

'See the shaheen? How beautifully it flies?' the Emir asked his guests, urging them to come closer. 'The shaheen bahri comes from the sea. And that one is a gyr, the shawdak falcon. The saqer is my favourite. There she goes.'

While the men gathered the prey, Harold noticed the Emir gazing wistfully to the north, eyeing the chalk-like outcrops on the horizon. 'You see over there, Colonel Dickson? That's where our future lies, in those rocks apparently.'

'I think I know what you're talking about, Your Highness,' Harold said, realising this was a good opportunity to start his mission.

Some yards away from the hunting party a tent had been set up and the Emir's retinue had been busy preparing a lunch of freshly slaughtered goat with fragrant rice, decorated with dried lemon and cinnamon bark. The brightly coloured walls of the woven tent lent a festive air to the desert, and Violet felt more at ease as she was ushered into the enclosure, having been declared an honorary man by the Emir, which amused everyone. They sat on Persian rugs. One side of the tent had been left open to reveal a view of the rocks and the sea in the distance.

The Emir invited the British couple to sit on either side of him, Harold to his right, as guests of honour. Rolling up his right sleeve, he said 'Bismillah' as a signal to begin the feast. In keeping with tradition, choice morsels were given to the visitors. Harold and Violet were used to eating with their hands, having attended numerous lunches and dinners of a similar nature with the Kuwaiti sheikhs and sheikhas. Deftly, Violet squeezed little parcels of meat and rice together to form a ball, using the tips of her fingers and thumb to pop them elegantly them into her mouth. Harold, on the other hand, had never quite mastered the art and always ended up getting in a mess, with rice strewn all around him and his face and hands covered in food. At times like this he hankered after steak and kidney pie, eaten with a knife and fork, at a table.

As was the custom in Arabia, the meal was taken without much conversation; instead, people concentrated on the business of eating. The Emir could never understand how people could enjoy a meal, which had been painstakingly prepared, when they were thinking about matters of state and the worries of the world. No, for a while at least, here was a chance to indulge in one of life's simple pleasures: food. Harold and Violet, on the other hand, were used to jolly conversation at their numerous lunch parties, with guests exchanging news and telling stories.

Having been fed tender pieces of meat by their host, the Dicksons were full and were relieved when the Emir uttered a few words, signalling an end to lunch. They repaired to a smaller tent where the Emir reclined on cushions, inviting the travellers to join him. Their retinues were left in the dining area to finish their meal, where they could pick at the plentiful remains of the carcass and rice without having to stand on ceremony.

'So, Colonel Dickson and Mrs Dickson, I hope you enjoy your stay here. It is so much nicer in the winter. We appreciate the clement weather after the long hot summer,' the Emir began.

Already preparing a script in his head, Harold summoned up the best diplomatic language he could think of. 'It is indeed a great pleasure, Your Highness. My wife and I are extremely grateful for your generous hospitality,' he said softly, as if his words were a preamble for the more serious subject on his mind. Before he had a chance to change tack, the Emir sat upright, suddenly animated. 'Of course, you know all this area has been explored. We are sitting on vast areas of oil.'

Harold couldn't believe his ears. The crafty old devil knew exactly the purpose of Harold's visit.

'George Martin Lees was here, you know. From Anglo-Persian. He wanted to explore all around. I said OK. Go ahead. He is some sort of geologist, looking at rocks. We know all about rocks and the desert but not much about what happens underneath.' He gave a chuckle.

Harold looked worried. After a cough, he began. 'I was unaware of this visit, Your Highness. I'm sure His Majesty's government was unaware too.'

'You know, we fought against Ottoman rule and now you want to rule us.' The Emir glared at Harold. 'We are grateful to the British for their protection, but we must decide our future ourselves. We are independent people.'

'Yes, Your Highness,' Harold responded, thinking it best to keep quiet. Inside, he was furious that he hadn't been informed of this visit. What would Frank have to say?

'Come with me. May I call you Harold and Violet?' the Emir said to his guests.

'It would be an honour,' Violet replied.

Sheikh Abdullah summoned the retinues and they all got into the vehicles. 'We'll drive up the coast a little. I want to show you something.'

From Um Bab the convoy of cars and trucks passed the limestone outcrops that George Martin Lees had investigated in search of oil. It was a curious place. The desert itself was completely flat and hard so that they had a smooth drive at last, which Violet was happy about. Near one of the outcrops, which resembled the Sphinx at Giza, the Emir ordered the cars to halt. They got out and the Emir bent down to the ground and picked something up. 'Look at this. This is a desert rose. Isn't it beautiful?' He gave it to Violet. 'What do you think of that? It's taken years to form. Completely natural.'

'It's truly beautiful,' Violet said, twirling the little salt-crusted formation in her hand. 'Quite remarkable. Look, Harold.'

Harold took the desert rose and inspected it, his glasses fixed on the end of his bulbous nose. 'Wonderful. Really wonderful.'

'You see, Harold and Violet, these are troubled times. Our small country relies on pearl fishing. I have heard that there is a man in Japan who has invented a way to make pearls without diving for them. There is talk of war in foreign lands and America has money troubles. Our small peninsula could be invaded at any time by our neighbours and Persia too. So we are always wary. The people of the desert are proud and strong. Hard times have made us so. If we are fortunate enough to be blessed with oil, we will be careful not to forget our other natural resources, like this precious desert rose. Let's go home.'

With more clouds of dust, the cavalcade left the desert and the Emir guided his entourage towards Doha across the desert. Harold clutched the desert rose all the way to the capital, wondering what on earth was going on behind his back.

They followed a track of sorts, worn by camel hooves, and despite the speed the young drivers drove at, it was a relatively smooth journey. They stopped at Al Shahaneya, where large herds of camels were gathered.

'All the Bedouin are here. It's the season. They like it here. It's got water for the camels, and the families make their *azba* in the desert not far from here,' the Emir said. He clearly knew how his people liked to live. 'City life is not for them,' he said, 'and not for me either, really, but I have responsibilities. My father told me I have a duty to this country. That's why he chose me as his successor. He was raised in Al Fuwairat but I was born and grew up in Doha so I'm more used to the ways of the town.'

Violet hung onto his every word, fascinated by his revelations, but Harold couldn't stop wondering about the political situation. How could the Emir know about Anglo-Persian? Why had Frank Holmes asked him to carry out this mission when it seemed the British Colonial Office already knew and had sent George Martin Lees to explore the area to the west of Qatar? As a man of the strictest principles, Harold found the whole situation unsavoury.

The Emir's convoy drove through the oasis of Rayyan, where many of his eighteen brothers lived with their wives, sons and daughters. The date palms were a welcome sight after the monotony of the desert. At last they reached the capital. Doha was a small town with fewer than 5,000 inhabitants. At the centre was Souq Waqif. They were heading to the newly constructed fort of Al Koot.

'This is my new building,' the Emir declared as the cars came to a halt. 'We have so many thieves and vagabonds that I ordered a fort to be built so we could capture and punish them. My guards will keep our people safe.'

It was a fine example of a fort, with crenelated round towers at each corner, on top of which the Emir's men stood, each brandishing what appeared to be a large musket. Violet nudged her husband, remarking that surely no crime could be possible in such a quaint fishing town.

The fort was on a hill overlooking the souq. The azure waters of the Gulf were only yards away, and an array of craft bobbed on the water: fleets of pearling boats and fishing vessels, some at anchor and others under sail, making their way towards the little bay at Al Bidda. The capital comprised three main parts: Al Bidda to the north, Doha in the centre and Al Salata to the south. It was here that the Emir would take his guests as a final stop on their lengthy journey.

From the bustle of the central market, where a heady mixture of spices emanated, combined with the sounds of people bartering and buying produce for their evening meal, the Emir led his guests towards his palace. People gazed in awe at the Emir's motor car, taking more notice of this new mode of transport than of the man himself. He waved in acknowledgement of their greetings.

Soon they were whisked into the palace compound, which was on the shore. Large dhows were moored nearby, as well as a much larger motorised vessel at anchor some distance offshore. Harold looked at Violet, thinking it looked familiar.

'I am fortunate, am I not, to live in such a splendid place?' Sheikh Abdullah suggested to his guests.

'It's very fine, Your Highness. Very fine indeed,' Harold said. Violet was beside herself with joy at being inside such a lovely building. It was even more handsome than the Emir's palace in Kuwait, she thought.

'It was built nearly thirty years ago so I could raise my family near the sea. My father loved the sea, living in Fuwairat. Here I can be near the sea and near my people in the capital. At first it was just a collection of residences and reception halls, but ten years ago I built this central part.'

Violet looked up at the verandas where the Emir's children played. Several date palms lent some shade to the courtyards and outhouses, giving a sense of calm and coolness. They made their way across to a grand reception hall.

The Emir led Harold and Violet into a large, rather dark room. It was empty except for a man in Western clothes sitting at the far end. When the Emir and his guests entered, he stood up.

'Ah, Harold and Violet. There you are.'

It was Frank Holmes.

Harold looked as though he'd seen a ghost. Violet, the more sanguine of the pair, held her husband's arm for support, fearing he might collapse at any moment. The Emir didn't seem at all surprised to see Frank. As the Emir advanced to the end of the vast room, Holmes didn't get up, which didn't appear to bother the head of state either. Again Harold was perturbed by his lack of protocol, never mind manners.

'Had a good trip, *ya* sheikh?' Holmes asked the Emir casually.

'Yes. Not bad. Caught a few hubara. You know Harold and Violet, I think.'

'Oh yes. We're old friends,' he replied.

Harold was more baffled than ever. He wasn't sure whether he wanted to be called an old friend.

Coffee was brought in. Three servants in white thobes bearing large brass pots and tiny cups expertly poured the bitter cardamom-flavoured coffee from a great height.

'Bismillah,' the Emir began, showing that he was about to say something important. 'Ibn Saud has it, Ahmed Al Jaber has it, Hamad bin Eissa has it, they say the Trucial states and Oman have it, so I suppose so must I. But what shall we do about it, gentlemen? Oil is our future. We can't fall behind.'

'Your Highness,' Harold began nervously, not wanting to let Frank Holmes get in first. 'His Majesty's government, namely the British Colonial Office, is aware of the importance of this subject but has deemed it necessary to defer any decision until all avenues have been explored.' He felt the strain of diplomacy, knowing he couldn't commit to any deal on oil exploration with the Sheikh of Qatar sitting next to him.

Frank Holmes interjected. 'My dear Sheikh Abdullah, as you know, I first came here in 1922 representing the Eastern and General syndicate, but for various reasons these explorations have been delayed. Now I understand George Martin Lees has been here looking at the potential for discovery on the west coast of Qatar.'

The Emir nodded.

'I'm sure an agreement can be reached soon,' Frank went on.

The Emir looked relieved. Harold, on the other hand, was more nervous than ever.

'Now, if you'll excuse me, gentlemen, Violet, I must see my family. You will be taken care of and shown to your rooms. Help yourself to whatever you need during your stay,' the Emir said, rising from his cushion and going to his private quarters.

'What the hell's going on, Holmes?' Harold demanded, unable to hide his outrage.

'It's all OK, Harold. I can explain.'

'You'd better. I'm thinking that you're a cad and no mistake.'

'Perhaps you'd both like to get some fresh air,' Violet suggested, trying to calm things down. 'I need to lie down for a while. I'll see where our rooms are.'

The two men left the reception hall and headed across the courtyard towards the palace entrance in stony silence. They had just passed the bodyguards at the gate when they heard the local muezzin's call to afternoon prayer – *azhan al asr*. The local mosque was small and plain, in sharp contrast to the grand surroundings from which they had come. Worshippers scurried into the mosque, leaving their boats and chores to perform one of their five-times-daily prayers. The low winter sun cast glorious shadows from the date palms near the mosque. Children played with hoops and sticks, enjoying their freedom, too young to have responsibilities and too young to have to pray like their elder brothers and sisters.

Harold felt more at ease. The peaceful scene reminded him how much he loved Arabia.

'Let's sit down,' Frank suggested, finding a shady spot looking out to sea. There was a group of palms and some upturned boats to sit on. 'I know you're angry, and I can see why. But I couldn't get hold of you. By the time I found out what was going on, you had left. So, I took the gunboat and came here at once.'

Harold had been right. The familiar-looking boat he had seen out at sea – he had seen it before. It was the British governor's personal vessel, and usually kept in Basra. He had been on it several times on trips around the marshlands of Iraq.

'What I'm about to tell you is highly confidential, Harold, but of the utmost importance.'

Harold leaned forward, intrigued by what Frank was about to say. He'd already forgiven him. He couldn't be angry at the charming New Zealander any more.

'The governor asked to see me two days ago,' Frank said. 'I've been working hard all my life, exploring, discovering new places and new technologies to increase prosperity. I don't know how to explain.' He looked upset.

'What on earth did he say, Frank? I've never seen you like this before,' Harold said anxiously.

Frank sat up straight and loosened his stuff collar, which looked out of place on the beach. Harold would never do such a thing; a gold stud held his starched wing collar firmly in place.

'Well, the governor said he'd been told there had been some sort of secret meeting between the oil companies to carve up the oilfields between them.'

'What?' Harold looked astonished. 'How can they do this? We have a mandate to protect the Arabian countries. We can arrange the oil exploration for them, can't we?'

'Apparently not. It's all been sewn up. The governor says Sir John Cadman, representing Anglo-Persian, Henry Deterding of Royal Dutch Shell, and Standard Oil's Walter Teagle met at a shooting party at Achnacarry Castle in the Scottish Highlands last summer. They agreed it was better to share out the spoils between them there and then and save all the bickering. Like you, I was astounded.'

'Astounded? That's an understatement. It's incredible. Who knows about this?' Harold wondered what this would mean for his role as the upper Gulf's top diplomat. 'And how did the governor find out?'

'He got wind of it from the Chancellor of the Exchequer, Winston Churchill. He was aware of it, somehow, with his American connections. So now you see my predicament and why I had to rush down here.'

'What about Sheikh Abdullah? What do we do?' Harold asked his friend. 'Do we just leave him to it?'

'That's up to you,' Frank said. 'You're the diplomat. But it won't be easy. The world is changing so fast, my friend. The globe is going to need millions of tons of oil, and this is where most of it comes from. Bye-bye, pearling boats. Hello, oil rigs.'

'And goodbye to a wonderful land of tradition and culture, and hello to greedy oil magnates spoiling the desert. What a shame. What a great shame.' Harold looked desperate at the prospect of his beloved Arabia changing beyond recognition. He dreaded telling Violet.

The two men got up and made their way back to the palace, passing the menfolk coming out of the mosque. Here in Al Salata life was simple and the people happy and content.

Harold thought how unspoiled it all was. It was a hard life, he thought, but also uncomplicated, honest and pure. Neighbours and families were close, supporting each other in times of need. They cared for each other. Wasn't that what life was all about?

As they approached the large wooden gates he looked back, wondering how things would change.

4

'Ya Lubna. Ya Lubna. Where are you? Yallah. It's late.' Miriam was anxious. Today, Lubna was getting married. 'We have to go. Yallah. Ya Lubna!'

In her room, Lubna was in a deep sleep. Even the chatter and bustle from the alley couldn't wake her. She looked peaceful, lying with her hands folded under her cheek. She wore a contented smile, as if she was having a beautiful dream.

Miriam asked Salem to wake his sister. Nasser was making himself busy, managing to escape the house on various errands. Marriage was no easy business, even though the arrangements had all been made by Lubna's future husband's parents, a condition thrust upon them by the overbearing Maysoon.

'Ya Lubna,' Salem whispered, peering into his sister's room. 'Are you all right? It's late.'

He could see her lying curled up, oblivious to the commotion going on in the rest of the house. 'Lubna. It's your wedding day. Wake up,' he said nervously, not wanting to wake her, yet knowing she should be told. He gently touched her shoulder again, whispering her name, and this time she stirred.

'Lubna, you have to get up. We have to go soon.'

'Go? Where?' Lubna asked, still half asleep.

'Al Khor. It's your wedding day.'

'Oh yes. Of course. That. I'd better get ready then,' she said as if she was preparing for the worst day of her life, not the happiest. 'Don't worry, Salem. I'll be fine. Tell Mother I'll be there soon.' She gave her brother a loving smile. Salem touched her long black hair affectionately, knowing he would never be so close to her again. There was silence. They were both aware of the special bond between them.

Nasser staggered into the house, his old thobe hitched up around his waist, carrying a large collection of fresh fish. He spilled the fish, some still writhing, onto the yard floor.

'Ya Abu Salem,' Miriam bellowed. 'What on earth are you doing?'

'We can't go empty-handed, my love. It wouldn't be right.'

'I suppose they don't have fish in Al Khor,' Miriam said sarcastically. 'Did you tell the neighbours we'll be away?'

'Yes. I did. I thought you'd be pleased,' Nasser said, feigning a lugubrious look, knowing that in return he would get a warm cuddle from his wife.

'Oh come here, you silly old fool,' she said playfully, throwing her arms around him. 'We've got to get ready. The boat will be here. It's all arranged. Oh, Nasser, I hope we've done the right thing,' Miriam said, her jollity restored to its usual anxiety.

'It'll be fine. It's for the best,' Nasser said, safe in the knowledge that he was doing what was best for his daughter.

Eventually Lubna appeared, looking calm and composed. She gave her parents a warm hug.

Miriam broke away from her daughter. 'Yallah. They're here. It's time to go,' she said, feeling as if she was about to burst into tears. She continued to scurry about, busying herself, shutting away her emotions.

Nasser, Miriam, Lubna and Salem left home and walked down to the boat they had hired to take them to Al Khor. It was a small, humble vessel with old Abu Salim in charge. It had one sail and a couple of oars for calmer waters. But today there was a breeze and they would be under way within minutes, heading south past the villages of Al Ghareyah and Fuwairat. On the way, the boatman pulled into Ras Laffan, a headland where there was a beautiful beach.

'Look, Miriam,' Nasser shouted excitedly, 'remember this? Remember those dunes?'

His wife looked wistful. 'How could I forget those days, those beautiful days?' She joined him on the prow of the boat, searching for a particular place. 'That's the spot. Over there near the rocks. You asked me to marry you there and I said no.'

'And I chased you around those rocks until you said yes.'

'Not before my father agreed. Thank goodness he did.'

They laughed as they stepped off the vessel into the crystal clear water, their bare feet leaving prints as they walked up the beach, hand in hand, to relive their memories.

Lubna dangled her feet over the side of the boat and let her mind wander. The sight of her parents made her think about how her life could have been if she had been able to wait for her true love. She thought about what she had done and the decision she had been forced to make.

Salem sat beside her and put his arm around his sister.

'I know what you're thinking, Lubna. I think you're so brave.'

'Brave? Or stupid, Salem? If I had waited for him, it could have been for ever. He may never have returned. I had to think of the future. Mother and Father were worried about how my life would be.'

'I know. I know. So, you agreed to marry the rich cousin. Well, I can tell you something, Lubna, my dear. There is no future here. I will be trying to find work in Doha too. Look at them.'

They watched their parents walk back along the shore, paddling in the warm water, holding hands.

'At least we know they are happy, no matter what happens,' Salem said, 'either to you or to me.'

Two hours later, they were sailing past the green mangroves of Al Dakhira and into the busy port of Al Khor.

The journey had been quiet. Lubna knew this would be the last time they would all be together as a family.

Al Khor was full of large sailing boats, some of them out of the water to be repaired before the start of the pearling season. Lubna had only been to Al Khor a few times, for family gatherings, and enjoyed watching the busy harbour, which was a sharp contrast to the tranquillity of Al Mafjar. As the family disembarked from their small craft, they felt intimated by the frantic trading going on all around them. Although the pearling season was over, the tawashes and captains bartered on board the mighty vessels that would carry the pearls to India and beyond to be set into coronets and necklaces. It was a wonderful sight: the Indian sailors, dressed in brightly coloured lungis, and traders gave the sense that this was the entrepot of Arabia, where a man's fortune could be made with some business acumen and a bit of luck.

At the quayside waited Lubna's future mother-in-law, Maysoon. She was alone and unsmiling.

'Salam aleikum,' Miriam said politely to her elder sister, and received a perfunctory 'Aleikum e Salam' in response. Maysoon looked Lubna up and down, as if inspecting her, then turned and marched off towards her house. It was in the town centre, on a corner where much of the day-to-day business of Al Khor was carried out. It was a large townhouse, fortress-like and forbidding, with a bolted black door.

Maysoon unbolted the inner part of the giant door, the weary travellers following her. As she did so, she mumbled

'Salam aleikum' without even glancing to the right where a small man sat, bent over a tiny wooden table. He could hardly be seen below a canvas sheet that stretched from one wall of the house out into the street. This provided shade for the industrious figure to work. He was writing figures on scraps of paper.

'Salam aleikum,' Maysoon said loudly, sounding annoyed that she had been ignored.

The man muttered, 'Aleikum salam.' This was the master of the house and Lubna's future father-in-law, Faleh bin Suleiman Al Bahr, merchant, trader and owner of the largest fleet of vessels in the Gulf of Arabia.

He didn't look up as his extended family passed, his eyes fixed on calculations and percentages, adjustments and profits, losses and likely gains. He worked alone, his thoughts only on the business at hand. Lubna thought he looked rather sad.

Lubna, Salem and Miriam trailed behind Maysoon into a stark courtyard which had no charm whatsoever, with not a single green plant or any seats. Nasser was the last to enter. He was not fond of social situations, preferring to spend his time in peace on the beach further north.

'I'll be there soon,' Faleh mumbled in a conciliatory gesture to his elder brother-in-law.

The guests were shown to a reception room – not the large majlis used for dignitaries and wealthy potentates who might be passing, but a dark, gloomy room whose high ceiling boasted the obligatory dunchal, the wooden beams of tradition, brown and dull, over woven matting, which was equally colourless, in sharp contrast to the vibrant ceilings that were the norm in homes of the time.

They waited for what seemed like an eternity on long cushions that had once been white but which were now a murky grey. It was a house with no soul, and in the winter it was cold, as cold as the hospitality that was being given to the relatives from Al Mafjar.

The family whispered to each other, wondering what was going to happen. The cheerless surroundings made them even more concerned, except Lubna. She comforted her mother, who was already wiping a tear away with her black abaya, and smiled at her father and brother to reassure them. None of them realised that they should have been comforting her.

'Khaled is upstairs,' Maysoon announced. 'You can have water from the jar outside if you want; there is a cup there on a string attached to it. Make sure you leave it as you found it.' She left, and they heard her climb the stairs.

The prospect of a wedding and celebration seemed out of the question in this house of gloom, but a wedding there would be. It was left to the master of the house to announce the final arrangements. After a while, Faleh bin Suleiman shuffled into the room, frowning, looking like he was on his way to a funeral, not a wedding. Stroking his wispy greying beard with one delicate hand and clutching a sheaf of papers with the other, he sat down beside Nasser. He coughed. 'Bismillah,' he began, and with no words of welcome said, 'I have decided to give your daughter, on behalf of my son, three hundred rupees, a gold necklace and something else I will show you tomorrow. I hope that is agreeable.'

'It is very generous, Faleh bin Suleiman. We are grateful and honoured,' Nasser responded in his usual humble tone.

'In that case, we may continue with the marriage. We can go to the mosque now. The two of you can be witnesses.'

He called Khaled, and the four men went to see the imam. It paid to be on the good side of the religious, so any misdemeanours on earth could be looked on favourably in the afterlife through the intercession of the imam. Faleh bin Suleiman had supported the mosque in numerous ways when the roof needed repairing, when the carpets were worn. Therefore, he only had to beckon the imam to carry out whatever duty the wealthy merchant desired.

'I'm tired,' Maysoon said, wiping her brow as if to prove it. 'I'm going upstairs.' She made no apology or excuse as she swept out of the room.

Nasser and his son followed Faleh bin Suleiman out of the majlis, leaving Lubna and her mother alone. This was hardly the joyful occasion it should have been. Silence hung heavy between the two. Lubna sat, staring into space. Miriam, unable to say any words of comfort, knowing they would sound trite, got up and walked around, adjusting her abaya, playing with her necklace.

'Your father gave me this, you know,' she said suddenly.

'I know, Mother. As part of your dowry,' Lubna said, still gazing ahead blankly. She had heard the story of the necklace countless times.

'It's not worth much. Your father's family were poor, like ours. But I love it. I love it because I love him, and I know he loves me.'

Lubna couldn't believe her ears. Her mother had never revealed her feelings before. She got up and went to Miriam, searching her face and eyes, feeling that finally they were becoming closer, as a mother and daughter should be.

'It's been such a hard life, Lubna, for your father and me. We've had our arguments over the years, and it wasn't easy raising a family with no support from our families. But when he came back from fighting he promised he would take care of me. We were so happy in those early days, swimming and going for walks on the beach, and then you and Salem came along. We loved you, but it was so difficult trying to do what was best for you both when we had nothing. So many troubles. Maybe I was too hard on you. I wish– '

'No, no, Mother. No. Not at all.' Lubna stopped her mother, took her in her arms and hugged her warmly. There was no need for words. They cried, and at last they were close. Lubna knew that, from now on, things would be different.

'We just wanted what was best...'

'I know. I know,' Lubna said, comforting her mother.

'You know what to do Lubna, my love?' Miriam asked. She could remember her wedding night as though it was yesterday.

'Yes, Mother. I know. It will be fine,' Lubna said. She was grateful for her mother's concern but she kept the secret of her love for Adel locked inside her. She knew her wedding night would be very different to that night on the beach with Adel.

As mother and daughter chatted easily about marital matters and how to run a household – knowledge which Miriam was keen to impart, but which Lubna was not really interested in – there was a sound from the courtyard.

'Well, here is your husband,' Faleh bin Suleiman said matter-of-factly. 'We'd better mark the occasion with some food, I suppose.'

Lubna began to cover her face with her veil, but Miriam stopped her and pulled her towards Khaled. They looked at each other as if they were children who had been forced to play together. Neither looked at all interested in the other. Their eyes cast down, they stood side by side as the family joined together in silent celebration. Maysoon remained upstairs.

It was left to Faleh bin Suleiman to arrange dinner. He summoned the imam, his wife and their two eldest children to the house. Neighbours were called in to cook and act as guests for what appeared to be a wedding feast but which was merely a gathering of people.

As the evening progressed the host became more animated, largely due to the prospect of a business deal he was about to negotiate with an unexpected visitor who had heard the commotion and come in to wish the couple well. At last

Maysoon made an entrance. She went up to her husband with a look of disdain at what was happening around her. When she saw that he was engrossed in conversation, she thought better of complaining and wandered about, inspecting the crowd, trying to find someone of equal standing with whom she could share her dismay. Ladies bringing plates of food into the courtyard avoided her. They knew she didn't like them and ignored her as they carried on with their tasks. Two goats had been slaughtered and cooked in vast metal pots. The women added spices and herbs, hoping their labours would be rewarded.

The men gathered in the courtyard while the women repaired to the majlis to eat. The wedding feast was soon over and the guests, shaking hands with the groom and his father, bade farewell and went home, satisfied that they had done their duty.

There was no ululating when the newly married couple ascended the staircase to their room on the first floor of the merchant's mansion. A few words of nervous encouragement from Nasser and Miriam and a pat on the back for Khaled from his father and a cautionary glance from his mother was all the send-off they had.

Maysoon and Miriam drank tea while the two men made polite conversation until it was time for them to retire for the night. Miriam and Nasser were shown to another, equally uninviting, room to spend the night. Although they were relieved to be alone at last, they couldn't help feeling anxious about their daughter. Salem was left alone to sleep on cushions in the majlis. He wondered how his sister would endure the future with this awkward person who was now her husband.

'Are you tired?' Lubna asked her new husband.

'Not really,' Khaled answered, looking down.

Lubna felt as if she should try and make conversation, but soon realised there was no point in trying to talk to him. He didn't seem to be interested in anything at all. She felt a sense of pity for him. Somehow it didn't matter to her how she felt. Nothing could match the love she carried in her heart for Adel, yet she had tried to banish him from her thoughts. Now, though, in this unfamiliar room with a strange man, her thoughts drifted back to Adel. All it had taken was a brief shared look as Adel had walked past the house with the other divers. At that moment, she knew she loved him. If the world came tumbling down around her, she knew she would never feel the same about anyone or anything ever again.

She lay down on the nuptial bed, a high wooden carved bed with a mattress that was hard and unforgiving. It had two pillows, which were really cushions stuffed with horse hair. Lubna propped up her cushion and wondered what to do. It was so awkward. Khaled remained near the window, hardly moving, his hands on his lap.

Eventually Lubna drifted into sleep, clothed and half sitting up. She slept deeply and calmly, dreams about her lover making her smile. She was beyond caring about Khaled. He didn't matter. Whether he could detect Lubna's ambivalence was impossible to tell, but he looked relieved that she was asleep when he eventually lay down on the worn carpet near the window.

Sounds from the street outside woke Lubna. It took her a while to remember where she was. She didn't even notice that Khaled wasn't there. He had left long before, looking for leftover food from the wedding dinner then taking it up to the roof to eat.

The other occupants of the house were getting ready for the day. Nasser and Miriam, after a fitful night, were packing to go home along with Salem, who greeted them with a solemn face, still upset at the loss of his sister.

Maysoon arrived downstairs mumbling about being cold. No breakfast was provided. Just as the atmosphere was becoming tense once again, Faleh bin Suleiman came in from the street carrying milk and dates.

'If you don't have to get back to Al Mafjar, I want you to come with me,' he said to Nasser, Miriam and Salem, who looked at each other, wondering how to react.

'We don't have to go back straight away,' Nasser said, trying to be diplomatic.

'In that case, why don't you gather your things and accompany me to the harbour?'

He went to the bottom of the stairs and called for Lubna and Khaled to come downstairs at once. Lubna heard the call and looked down into the courtyard.

'We'll be down soon,' she said, peering over the balustrade. She went to look for Khaled, and finally found him on the roof, where he sat on an old bench, staring out over the rooftops.

'Your father has asked to see us. We'd better go down,' she said.

At first Khaled didn't move then, as Lubna approached, he got up. They went downstairs together to find the family assembled in front of them. Nobody said a word as the couple entered the courtyard. Lubna smiled in greeting, but her husband just looked blankly at the new relations he had acquired.

Faleh bin Suleiman had already carried out several transactions in the souq. His business had been completed satisfactorily, judging from the tune he was humming.

'If you'll come with me,' he announced, in a voice that was clear and confident in contrast to the mutters to which the household had grown accustomed. 'Um Khaled close the door behind you.'

They all wondered what was going on. Maysoon, the last to leave, caught up with her husband to ask what all this was all about, and Miriam and Nasser, arm in arm, demanded in whispers what was happening. Salem had joined his sister and Khaled trailed a few steps behind.

In a few minutes they were at the harbour. They walked past the fishing boats. Towards the end of the jetty was a large vessel, much bigger than anything else in Al Khor. It was a bakhala – larger than a boom, much bigger than a bateel. Nasser and Salem couldn't help noticing the huge boat. It had a richly carved stern, ornate and fine in every detail. It was unlike anything they had ever seen.

'What do you think of this?' Faleh bin Suleiman asked his new extended family. 'Isn't she fine?'

They all agreed she was indeed a beautiful vessel.

'Well, it's mine.'

They gasped. They knew the merchant was rich, but surely this was beyond even the riches of Faleh bin Suleiman? Then he explained. 'Remember the visitor who came to the wedding last night? He told me he had bought a large ship from a boat builder in Kuwait who had sailed it here. After much negotiation, I bought it. There you are. It's mine.' Faleh bin Suleiman put his hands on his hips and stood proudly in front of his latest purchase.

'I've hired several men to sail her for me,' he said, 'so if you care to step on board we shall sail to the capital. We'll be in Doha by the end of the day.'

The family stepped aboard via the makeshift gangplank, held steady by two young men, dark from the sun, with lungis wrapped around their waists.

Once the passengers had been settled on the luxurious seats in a cabin towards the stern of the ship, the order was given to cast off and make for Doha. The captain called for the sails to be unfurled. Within minutes, the *bakhala* had left the shallow waters of Al Khor and was heading into the dark blue depths of the Gulf. She was such a wonderful sight that a large group had gathered at the end of the jetty to watch.

'Isn't she beautiful?' Lubna said to her father. 'I never thought we would be doing this today.'

'It's truly wonderful,' Nasser agreed. 'Let's go outside.' On the deck, they breathed in the fresh sea air as if performing a ritual of renewal, reawakening their mutual love of nature and the bond between them.

Miriam and Maysoon stayed inside with Khaled, but Salem soon ventured out onto the deck, eager to feel the wind in his hair. It was an odd situation. None of them really knew what to make of it. Thrust together in such peculiar circumstances: rich and poor, the wedding that had taken place out of necessity, not desire, and this voyage. Yet somehow this unexpected journey had acted as a catalyst, a diversion, allowing them to think of nothing but the pleasure of being under sail at sea. It was a glorious feeling.

'See over there,' Nasser said to his daughter, 'that's Lusail. You can just see the coast in the distance. Our dear leader for whom I fought, Sheikh Jassim, is buried there somewhere.'

Nasser spent some time thinking of those days at war, remembering his brothers-in-arms who hadn't been as fortunate as he was, and remembering the man who had stood up to the Turks in defence of this tiny land he was proud to call home. There wasn't much response from Lubna, whose eyes were fixed on the waves rushing past beneath them.

'Lubna? Are you all right?' Perhaps you feel seasick?' Nasser asked, putting a comforting hand on her shoulder.

'Oh. Oh yes. Sorry, Father. I heard what you said about Lusail and the old Emir who died all those years ago,' she said. But her mind was elsewhere. She was wondering if she would ever see Adel again, the man she adored.

'I was just thinking how strange life is,' she said, able to talk freely to her father. 'You met Mother, you went to war, you could have died, but you didn't, and you had Salem and me. So life goes on. I love hearing about our past and the people who have made it.'

'Lubna, my love, it's your turn to carry those memories with you and build a future of your own. It certainly is a strange life. But beautiful nonetheless,' Nasser said. They looked out to sea, arms around each other.

The bakhala was going along at full speed, heading south, when the captain ordered the crew to trim the sails and change course to port to go around the coast towards the capital. As the vessel approached the shallower turquoise waters nearer land, it slowed down. The crew were out on deck, looking for hazards. Rocks and reefs could tear a fatal gash in the wooden timbers of any boat, no matter how large, and Faleh bin Suleiman was anxious that his new boat should stay safe.

Now that the boat was moving at a gentler pace, all the passengers came out onto the foredeck. Salem was the first to spot the cluster of buildings in the distance.

'There's Doha,' he said excitedly. 'I'd love to live there one day, Father.'

'Perhaps you will, Salem. Perhaps you will.'

'Look, there's another boat,' Salem said, moving up to the prow of the bakhala. 'It looks huge. It looks like there's smoke coming from it.'

As the bakhala neared the shore at Al Bida, the larger vessel came into view. It had no sails and was unlike anything they had seen before. One of the crew told the captain it was a new motor vessel. Curious, Faleh bin Suleiman told the crew to try and get near to it as it passed. The strange ship hooted, alarming the ladies. Painted entirely in grey with a black funnel, it looked menacing. Was that a cannon on its foredeck? The families huddled together, worried, watching the ship get nearer and nearer. Thick black smoke belched out into the clear blue sky, spoiling their view of Al Bida and the cluster of brown roofs and minarets.

There was another long hoot, and more billowing smoke. The vessel slowed almost to a halt as the bakhala drifted a little towards her. The captain shouted out from his position towards the stern of the bakhala, asking about their business and where they were bound.

A door opened below the funnel of the grey ship and a bearded man in uniform and cap immediately answered. 'On His Majesty's Service, bound for Kuwait. God speed.' He went back inside.

As the *bakhala* passed the ship, Nasser and Lubna noticed three figures standing on the deck, clutching the railing. They were two men in Western dress and a pale-skinned woman, elegantly dressed, holding a straw hat. They waved as they passed. The families weren't sure how to react, unused to seeing Westerners, but after a moment they waved back.

There were more difficult waters to negotiate as the *bakhala* was steered between the mainland and the island of Safliyah, a long spit shaped like a kite where migrating birds gathered to rest on their journey further south. Soon the bay of Bida was before them.

Al Bida took a while to get to. The *bakhala* was too big to moor on the shoreline. There was no harbour like in Al Khor, so she had to be anchored a little away from shore. After much shouting and commotion, a tender was summoned to ferry the passengers to land. Negotiating the gangway from the *bakhala* down to the small boat wasn't easy, especially for the two sisters, who were obliged to support each other. Khaled, equally nervous of anything nautical, had to cling to Salem so as not to lose his footing on the bobbing craft below. Nasser and Lubna were used to getting in and out of boats and took it in their stride. Faleh bin Suleiman scuttled down last, shouting orders to the crew left behind.

The entire party, except for Faleh bin Suleiman, was at a loss. Why were they here? Some had enjoyed the voyage; others less so. Some even wished they were not there at all.

'So, what are we doing to do now?' Maysoon asked her husband in a haughty voice.

'Follow me,' Faleh bin Suleiman said, beckoning. 'We shall go to the souq.'

Thankfully the sun had passed its zenith, so the walk through Al Bida was pleasant. They followed Faleh up towards Al Koot fort. They stood and admired it, and even Maysoon remarked that it was a fine building worthy of the people of Qatar. To its right, on higher ground, was a large new building.

'The Emir will be moving here soon, I hear,' Faleh bin Suleiman announced, 'from his palace in Al Salata.'

The town was much bigger than Lubna's family were used to. They missed the familiar alleys and squares of the village. So, it was with some relief that they entered the souq. Here were the ordinary people of Doha buying and selling their wares. Miriam gave Nasser a nudge when they passed a stall selling galvanised cooking pots.

'I'd love one of those,' she said, pointing to a giant platter with handles.

'What would you do with that? We won't have any more feasts, I don't suppose,' Nasser said. 'Anyway, how would I carry that all the way home?' They laughed at the idea.

There were vegetables and rice, spices shipped in from India, pungent in the afternoon air. Canvas shades draped across the souq alleyways cast shadows on the dusty ground. Donkeys were led along, carrying bundles of *bagdounis*, the bright green parsley used to enhance all Middle Eastern food. Ovens set into the souq walls were fired up, and busy bakers were making flatbreads. There was fish for sale, including huge steaks of canard or queen fish, and some fat prawns that had been caught that afternoon.

It was a wonderful feast for the eyes, ears and nose, and it slowed the members of the family down so much that Faleh bin Suleiman had to ask them to keep up. They all wondered what he was up to. When they left the souq, they walked to a quieter part of town. There was a mosque and a square with a few dusty trees trying to stay alive in the harsh desert climate. As their guide led them along, they noticed a half-built house on which several dark-skinned men were working, balancing on rickety-looking wooden scaffolding. They had completed the lower part of the house and were working on the upper floors, making arches and terraces.

Faleh bin Suleiman, who had never looked so excited about anything, gathered everyone around him and pointed at the building. 'Well, what do you think?' he asked.

After a while Nasser said, 'It's very fine. Whoever lives there is very fortunate.'

'I've built it for the newlyweds. You will live here,' he said.

There were gasps of disbelief all round.

'For me? I mean, for us?' Lubna asked, stunned at the news. 'It's very kind of you. I don't know what to say. But what about our families? How will we live?' She burst into tears and ran to her mother for consolation.

'It's very generous of you,' Nasser said. 'It's left us all speechless.'

Salem was unable to talk. Khaled reacted by walking away from the group, finding a place under a tree to be alone.

'The future lies here in Doha. This is where we must be,' Faleh bin Suleiman declared. 'I have built my business from pearling and fishing and I have done well. In Al Khor we have been lucky to become wealthy through hard work. Doha is getting bigger and even the Emir himself has come to the capital. Future trade will go through here, and we must move with the times. I have bought land here, and this house will be yours. It is up to you now.'

Nasser released his daughter and let her walk towards the house. She looked up at the high walls on which the men were working. Further along in the corner of the building a *badgeer* wind tower was under construction. She couldn't believe it. Only the very wealthy could afford to have this cooling system. Suddenly Lubna felt lost; she felt that she didn't deserve this magnificent dwelling, and with a sense of trepidation she feared that the simple life she had known and loved would be lost for ever.

Miriam turned to Nasser for comfort, crying tears of joy at Faleh's generosity, but tears of sorrow that Lubna would be so far from home. Salem gave his sister a warm hug as Khaled sat alone, unable to look at the half-built house that was to be his.

5

At sea off the coast of Qatar, 1929

'We're going further out, beyond Halul Island,' Captain Jamal boomed from his throne-like position on *Firial*. 'We need more large pearls. I want them big – the bigger the better.'

The crew were in good spirits, despite their captain's demands. They had had a good off-season, enjoying being at home with their families. Yousef, who was always smiling, had spent his time building a new room for his father and mother, who had moved in with Yousef. Bilal had occupied his time singing – he was always in demand. His neighbours wanted him to come around and entertain them. Ibrahim was happy to meet up with his friends and go on hunting trips in search of *fugga* – small truffles that appeared after the rains had come.

It hardly ever rained in Qatar, but occasionally there were heavy showers that caused severe flooding in the towns and villages which turned the desert green. Nothing was better to raise the spirits than spending a few days among the plants in the wilderness. Now, in the oppressive humidity and heat, it was only those with a vivid imagination and a good memory who could remember the winter. Somehow life at sea, harsh as it was, favoured those who could dream. The blank blue canvas of the water allowed the mind to create pictures and ideas that people on land could not. Adel was doing exactly that, sitting on *Firial*, letting his feet catch the spray as the boat sped along. He gazed into the ocean, lost in his memories of a night he knew could never be repeated. Had it been a dream? Or had it really happened? He lost himself in his imagination, enjoying the pictures in his mind. As he gazed into the sea, his memories became entwined with the ocean before him so that his love for Lubna and the beauty of the sea blended into one.

After several minutes he tried to bring himself back to reality. Why hadn't he seen her? He had returned to Al Mafjar several times throughout the winter, hoping she would be there. But he had not seen her. He had waited and waited, but all he had seen were old fishermen tending their nets. He wanted to go to Lubna's house but couldn't bring himself to knock on the door. It had preyed on his mind constantly. He knew he should accept responsibility by doing his best to find her. He wondered where she was. At the same time, he knew that their lives were somehow bound together.

'Ya Adel. Ta'al. Bisourah.' *Come here. Quickly.* It was Bilal, clambering over the coils of rope and diving paraphernalia, unsteady on his feet as the boat sped along. 'What's wrong with you? You're sitting there staring into space.'

Eventually Adel turned around and looked at his friend, not having heard a word he'd said.

'Captain has said we're going to new waters. Somewhere over between Haloul and Bahrain. We're stopping soon to get supplies. But I don't like this wind,' Bilal said, trying to get a reaction from Adel.

'I see,' was all Adel could muster. 'It's a bad season, I think. They're all worried about the Japanese. What will be will be,' he continued philosophically. 'Perhaps the good Lord doesn't want us to take any more oysters from the ocean bed. Let them sleep peacefully without us tearing them from their homes.'

'Oh yes, and who's going to put bread on the table? Answer me that.' Bilal seemed annoyed and went off to look for Yousef.

'Lower the sails,' came the order from Captain Jamal. Adel could see several large *bateels* ahead. Among them were supply vessels. By raising various flags, the captains could communicate with each other to say what supplies they needed. After two months at sea, the men were desperate for fresh water, and they were only too happy to load the barrels being sold by the Bahraini merchants. They also needed wood to make fires on which to cook their evening meal.

Meeting fellow sailors made a change for the men. Yousef and Bilal were happy to exchange tales and jokes with their counterparts. Adel too became engaged in conversation, which took his mind off the problem swirling in his head. It was all hands on deck. Camaraderie was good, and spirits restored, as the vessel took on supplies. Life wasn't so bad after all.

'You got anything for me, ya nokhdar?' It was a tawash shouting from the rocking *sambooq* that had attempted to draw alongside *Firial* just as they finished loading supplies. This agent had come from Manama and wasn't familiar to either Captain Jamal or the crew.

'Not yet. Give us a few days, maybe weeks, and we'll be back. We're going to deeper waters. Ma'asalam,' Jamal said, trying to dismiss the agent, although he was aware he had to keep on the good side of the *tawash;* he depended on him to get a good price for the pearls.

The food that was being sold looked so tempting that Yousef couldn't help pleading for more spices and *bagdounis*, brightly coloured fruits and sweetmeats.

'You'll have plenty of those if we find a *dana*,' Captain Jamal told him, refusing to take on anything he considered a luxury. Rice, water and more dates – the staples of a pearl-diver's diet – were all that was required. The captain believed that keeping his men lean and hungry meant they craved more and strove more.

The entire crew were out on deck, stowing the cargo, weighing anchor, uncoiling ropes from the bow and stern so the sails could be raised. Captain Jamal gave the order to sail to the east, into waters that none of the ship's men had navigated before. They shouted farewell to the sailors on the supply boats. Captain Jamal was agitated. He was counting the money he had left over from his purchases, and clearly resented the amount he had spent. At the same time, he was worried he had been a little too unfriendly to the *tawash*, fearing he wouldn't come back to *Firial* when they returned. He reassured himself that there were plenty more agents whose palms could be crossed with silver to do a favourable deal.

They were heading out into rougher seas, and *Firial* pitched and rolled as the crew tried to unfurl the sails and untangle the ropes. They were used to the calmer inshore waters off the coast of Qatar. This was an entirely new experience for them and Captain Jamal knew he had to be in command – not just of the money, supplies and pearls, but also of the boat.

It was a good thing that some of the older members of the crew were experienced sailors who had undergone years of unpredictable weather at sea. Living through storms had given them a deep respect for the sea and its power. Old Rashed, or Rashed al Oud as he was affectionately known, remembered being battered by a raging storm in 1914. Now his duties were limited to mending the nets and fishing for dinner, he was a valuable source of information and stories of the past. 'We thought it was the end of the world,' he said as the crew listened in amazement. 'We never went this far out, though.'

This brought a chill to some of the younger divers. Ibrahim looked nervously at his ageing comrade. 'What do we do if there's a storm, ya am Rashid?'

'Hold on tight and pray to the Almighty. It's in His hands.'

Adel, Yousef and Bilal huddled in their usual corner, trying to dismiss the tales of disaster. 'We'll be fine,' Yousef said. 'We're young and bold. No harm will come to us.'

Bilal was equally positive. He broke into song and called for the musicians to play something cheerful. Adel was cautious.

As *Firial* made her way out into the Arabian Sea she passed the occasional boom at anchor. On them were divers with nose-clips, oyster pots strapped to their bony bodies.

'Bahrainis,' declared old Rashed. 'They've been coming here for centuries. Even in the days of Dilmun they came here. Things haven't changed much. We'd better leave them alone.'

'It's our sea as much as anyone else's,' Captain Jamal grunted, even though he usually took notice of what the old man said. *Firial* was going along at full speed, her prow dipping into the white-topped waves, causing the mighty craft to heave and roll. Her crew clung to the masts, and some even lay down to avoid being tossed into the ocean. They had never known water like this and couldn't understand why they had to go so far from their usual pearling grounds. They knew something was up: that Captain Jamal would not stop at anything in order to get what he wanted, the huge pearl, the dana, and failing that two or three large pearls of the highest quality, which would outshine anything grown artificially in Japan.

Young Ibrahim crouched near the stern of the boat, cowering against the wind and spray, soaked and shivering from fear as much as from the cold. Adel noticed him first. Taking pity on him, he scrambled across the deck and held him in his arms, realising how vulnerable he must feel. Neither spoke. It was impossible to hear anything anyway. The waves crashing on the deck put paid to that. Adel knew all about being the youngest on board and immediately empathised with the young man. He wanted to prove that he was a brave man, but he was scared.

It took *Firial* the rest of that day and the best part of a night before they passed Halul Island and managed to find waters that had not already been claimed by other diving crews. Early the following day the storm had abated, leaving the Qatari men thankful they had survived. Yousef and Bilal burst into song, followed by the rest of the crew. They even managed to get young Ibrahim to join in. He was relieved that he had got through the ordeal unscathed, and his bravery and quiet demeanour had been noted by his elders. Only Adel continued to sit alone. This time he wasn't staring into space or at the ocean. He was reading.

Captain Jamal darted about the boat giving orders and making sure all was ready for a possible dive into the yet-undiscovered waters. He chided the older men for not working hard enough, he scolded the singers for making merry when, as yet, there was no cause for celebration, and he saved his harshest words for the youngest member of the crew, telling Ibrahim he was a lazy good-for-nothing. Somehow Adel escaped all his vitriol – or perhaps the captain knew he would need his star diver more than ever.

'Looks like a good place,' Yousef said, trying to think of something to say to his long-time friend. When he got no response, he continued, 'What are you reading that is so important? You're lucky you can read. No one ever taught me.'

'It's some of my poetry.'

'Can you read some for me?'

Adel gave a little cough and began to read.

'Never did I know the wonder of a silent night,

Never did I realise the beauty of a rounded moon,

Never did I understand the secret of– '

He was interrupted by an order from Captain Jamal. 'All hands on deck! Drop anchor. Prepare to dive.'

The men gathered the ropes and paraphernalia they needed. The drummers banged away, causing hearts to race and adrenalin to rush. Among the first to dive were Yousef and Bilal. They would test the waters to see if it was worth their while staying here.

'Don't go down too far,' Captain Jamal commanded. 'I want big pearls, so look for the coral and signs that oysters may be around. I don't want you to be long.'

Ibrahim was being taught to play out the rope gently and wait patiently for any sign of tugging, no matter how slight, so the diver could come back to the surface safely. He helped

Yousef and Bilal put on their nose-clips and listened carefully to the older men as they passed on their knowledge. The sea was quite calm, even though they were much further offshore than usual. How deep it was, nobody knew.

'Yallah,' Yousef called out as he and Bilal dived in. Ibrahim stood nervously by the side of the boat, hanging on to every word that was said. 'Take the rope, let it go slowly through your hands. Don't grab the rope or it will burn you.'

The rope carried on being played out longer than usual but finally it stopped, and Ibrahim could rest, waiting for his next move, which would be in two minutes at the most. Yousef and Bilal had big lungs and a wealth of experience, so Captain Jamal knew they would be able to handle the new environment. The men had gathered around Ibrahim and his mentor, curious to see how their colleagues would get on. A minute passed. One minute and a half. The sailors began to look anxious. Ibrahim looked at the others, holding the rope tightly, then gave a nervous smile when he felt a tug from below. All the men took hold of the rope and pulled, shouting and chanting, as the two explorers finally surfaced.

Still in the water, gasping for air, Yousef shouted, 'It's very deep. I've never seen anything like it.'

Bilal bobbed up and down, trying to get some words out. 'It's incredible. Nothing like the water near Qatar. It's dark. So deep. But so many corals and oysters. Here, take this.' He gave his pot to Ibrahim. Captain Jamal was quick to pounce on it and had soon collected the one from Yousef too.

The two men looked drained as they climbed back on board. The first thing they did was thank young Ibrahim for doing such a good job, particularly as he had never done it before. The ship's company patted them heartily on the back as they made their way to Captain Jamal, who had emptied the pots onto the deck in front of him. Adel looked on from a distance, having hugged his two friends warmly on their return.

'These are very good. Look at the size of these oysters. Open them up,' Captain Jamal commanded, tossing a couple of knives towards the sailors. Within seconds they had found two large, lustrous pearls. There were gasps from the men. Captain Jamal couldn't believe his luck.

'Adel,' he said turning towards his best investment, 'it's your turn.'

Adel knew this was coming. He looked skywards, asking for a blessing as he prepared for his most challenging mission.

'You'll have to lengthen the rope, men,' came the order. 'It's the deepest area we've ever been to. Adel, I want the biggest pearl you can find. These are very good. Look at their colour. It's like honey, and they're much bigger than average. Keep going like this and we'll do well. You will all be rewarded.' Never before had Captain Jamal said anything like this.

Yousef and Bilal had recovered from their dive and had been regaling the crew with tales of what they had seen – 'infinite blue depths', 'forests of coral', 'fish all the colours of the rainbow', 'such beauty I have never seen before'. Only Adel reacted calmly. He looked forward to his dive. Maybe this would be the culmination of all the wonderful dives he had undertaken since he was a novice. Bilal and Yousef noticed his serene smile. They patted him on the back, wishing him luck. He felt no trepidation as he stood waiting to dive. He put his hand on Ibrahim's shoulder as if placing his trust in the young man. Ibrahim felt honoured to be treated so well by this icon of a pearl-diver.

A new length of rope had been provided for Adel's dive. Yousef and Bilal had described how deep the water was, and Captain Jamal envisaged great rewards to be gained by going even deeper towards the ocean floor.

'Good luck,' Captain Jamal cried out uncharacteristically. He had never done such a thing before. The men followed suit. Adel placed the clip on his nose, hung the pot around his neck and held one end of the rope while Ibrahim took the other. Bilal and the crew were chanting and drumming in unison, wishing Adel the best of luck. If the best pearls to be found anywhere on earth were here, in this mysterious dot in the ocean, then their future may be secured and all worries about Japan could be banished.

Adel placed his perfectly shaped feet on the edge of the boat, his toes curling round the ledge to give him grip. He took the biggest breath he had ever taken. His chest expanded to full capacity, as though he were more animal than man, his shoulders widened, he stretched his arms upwards. His eyes dilated, taking in the last second of bright sunlight. A final smile and he dived into the water. All divers were taught to jump feet-first into the water, but Adel wanted to add grace and beauty to the art of pearl-diving. Today the crew, gathered together on the deck, witnessed Adel take flight for a millisecond: he soared skywards then pierced the surface of the sea like a sabre, his dive causing hardly a ripple. It was an unforgettable sight for the young apprentice, who held the rope loosely in both hands, letting it play out, uncoiling rapidly from the vast length that had been prepared for this special dive.

Captain Jamal would normally order the rest of the men to go about their business and not waste time standing idly by, but even he had to concede that this was out of the ordinary. He came down from his command position and joined the older divers. They were looking anxiously at the rope playing out. Never before had anyone attempted to go so far down. The next two minutes were going to be crucial.

Adel was happy to be back in his natural home again. As he leaped from the boat, he felt the freedom of flight. Under the water, he continued to fly, using his strong legs to propel himself downwards through the water. He felt comforted by the companionship of several nosey hamour who had come to see what was going on, and a shoal of sardines that darted this way and that.

Adel had never felt more alive, more alert. Occasionally he adjusted the rope and pot. Passing swaying seaweed, unfamiliar in shape and size, he began to negotiate corridors of coral that were unlike any he had seen before. They were the palest pink, reaching up like trees among the jungle of anemones, sponges and sea ferns that provided an elegant avenue on his way to the ocean bed.

At last, after days of only being able to gaze into the ocean, here he was in it. The water hugged him like an old friend. Suddenly he felt like a young boy again, darting around, spotting new sea creatures, mesmerised at being surrounded by so much beauty. Seahorses floated into view. A vast shoal of the tiniest fish in electric blue swept before him, parting to make way for this new visitor to their marine home. Adel felt that he was being given a special invitation into their world.

Through what appeared to be an arch of bright white coral Adel suddenly spotted a cave-like structure. He was on the ocean floor. Intrigued, he ventured in. The rope was at full stretch. Briefly he noted that it was taut. He was able to peer inside the entrance. There, to his amazement, was the glint of palest white. Clinging to the coral and rock, among the multi-coloured sea plants, was the largest single cluster of oysters he had ever seen.

Adel was suddenly thrown back to reality. Here was the holy grail, the most beautiful oysters on earth, and he had to get them back to the surface within the next minute. Using all the dexterity he had acquired over the years, he quickly but gently prised each giant oyster from its secret home. Ten, twenty, thirty, and that was it. His pot was overflowing. He had half a minute to get back to the surface. If he did it any faster, he knew he would risk the bends and brain damage.

Adel made his way out of the cave, but suddenly he felt the rope tighten. He tried to tug at it to let Ibrahim and the crew know it was time to come up, but there was no slack at all, making it impossible to pull. He took the rope from around his body, freeing the pot, which gave him a little more slack. He was now able to tug at the rope a little. As soon as he did so, the pot sped off upwards. It was so quick that he was unable to grab hold of the pot or the rope, leaving him without the lifeline he so desperately needed. All he could do was watch the rope and oyster pot fly away in the distance.

He had to make his way up as fast as he could, knowing the risks, but he had no choice. His lungs were at full capacity and his limbs were unable to make the climb as swiftly as he wanted to. Once he had risen above the forest of corals and anemones, he felt himself floating gently through the glinting marine world he so adored. His legs had become lifeless, with no power left. His arms hung loosely, as if he were performing a ballet. His body drifted effortlessly through the turquoise blue. He let his body and soul become possessed by the sea. His nose clip floated away. As he swayed through the shoals of plankton and starfish, expelling the last few bubbles from his worn-out lungs, his eyes were still open ... searching for the young woman he so dearly loved.

PART 2

1

Doha, 1945

Ahmed sat at the wooden table looking out across the rooftops of Doha. He began to write.

Thank goodness the war is over. It's been so difficult for those poor people in Europe. I don't know too much about it, but one day my Uncle Salem came rushing into the house, shouting, "It's over. It's over! No more war."

Ahmed had never seen his Uncle Salem so excited. He had just come from the Emir's palace, which wasn't far from Ahmed's house.

'Are you sure?' Ahmed asked him. 'We thought it was all over before.'

'Yes. Ali told me.'

Ali was the son of the Emir, Sheikh Abdullah bin Jassim. Uncle Salem was a friend of his, so he got all the news from him.

'The Americans have dropped an atomic bomb on some place in Japan. Hiroshima. It destroyed everything. The Japanese had to surrender.'

'It must have been horrible. I wonder what kind of bomb it was to destroy a whole city. I hate all this fighting and war.'

'It's for the best, Ahmed,' Ali said. 'There was another one too on Nagasaki. The Americans have been building this huge bomb ever since the Japanese bombed Pearl Harbour. That's it. No more war. Those Japanese. They took away our pearls. This is justice for all the terrible things they've done.'

It's not like Uncle Salem to be so bitter, but we have endured so much hardship it's not really surprising. I can't believe it. After five years of worry, it's finally over. I was only ten years old when it started. One day everything was calm and peaceful, and the next everyone was worried and nervous. Of course, it wasn't like being in Europe or America, where every family had a son or brother fighting, but life was difficult here too, with the pearl-diving business going and the world depression. We didn't need any more problems. I've grown up through a difficult time. I'm very lucky, though. I live in this wonderful house. I have the whole place to myself, more or less, because I'm an only child. I only have one parent, and I don't see much of him. If it weren't for Uncle Salem, I'd be completely alone. I'm used to it, though, and I like being quiet.

Ahmed put his pen down and looked out of the window towards the sea in the distance. It was lonely being an only child. He hardly knew a soul and felt left out as he tried to mix with boys his own age. Now he was on the edge of adulthood. His father was aloof and didn't speak much. Growing up in a large house in the centre of Qatar's only big town, now its capital, had been a lonely experience. There were three people in his family. Ahmed, his father Khaled and his Uncle Salem, who he secretly loved much more than his father. Salem was his mother's brother. His mother had died giving birth to him. This had caused him a great deal of heartache. He was quiet and shy and often sat, deep in thought, in his room, alone and afraid of what the future held.

Ahmed's situation was unusual. He could see other boys his age enjoying life. The streets were full of children running around, playing with their brothers, sisters and neighbours, dropping in and out of each other's houses, easy in the company of each other, with no cares in the world. Ahmed had longed for this camaraderie all his life but somehow it had eluded him. As he struggled through adolescence he become more and more introverted, dwelling on what he considered to be his great misfortune.

The one thing he took pleasure in was writing his daily journal. While the other boys played in the streets, Ahmed took out a clean piece of paper and wrote down what he had seen and done that day. If he got any information from his beloved uncle, he would write about what he had been told, and what he thought.

The house, called Bait Al Bahr after his father's family name, had been built by his grandfather, a rich merchant, as a wedding present for his son. Ahmed walked from his spacious room along the corridor on the first floor. He looked at the thermometer. Forty-five in the shade. Quite normal for three o'clock in the afternoon in August, he thought. Ahmed acted as if he was much older than he really was. He liked to sit in the corner room on the first floor under the *badgeer* – the wind tower that acted as a natural air-conditioner. He sat upright, legs crossed, almost like a buddha about to meditate. He wanted to relax and cast off his gloomy thoughts – the what-ifs and the whys, questions he constantly raised that went unanswered. He wanted to clear his mind and lie down on the cushions, but when he tried to lie down, something inside told him not to. So here he was.

In 1945, Doha was little more than a seaside town, if you could call it a town. It was more like a group of buildings haphazardly dotted about wherever anyone wealthy enough wished to construct one. The remains of the Ottoman Empire were still in evidence with Al Koot fort, once the headquarters of Turkish rule and now adapted to house the few men who had been chosen as guardians of the burgeoning capital, and the occasional thief who had been caught red-handed in the market. Nearby in Al Bida the Emir lived in his sprawling compound. Sheikh Abdullah had moved from his palace at Al Salt to establish Doha as the capital and ensure his authority was absolute.

Far away in Japan, a man called Mikimoto had invented the cultured pearl, effectively ending the natural pearl industry of the Gulf. Trade in pearls had drawn to a close: the boats and their nokhdars had retired from service, leaving their crews without work and too tired from their hard life to do much else than sit and wait for better days to come.

Faleh bin Suleiman Al Bahr sat outside his house in Al Khor, contemplating what he had achieved in his sixty-five years. He had slowed down considerably as age caught up with him. Although he had been aware of the Japanese bringing disaster on not only the pearl industry but the whole world by their actions at Pearl Harbour, he couldn't help feeling sorry for himself that all the hard work he had done over the years had ended in nothing. Thank goodness, he thought, I built that house in Doha for my son. It's up to him.

Time had mellowed him. He had had one of the finest fleets of pearling dhows and trading vessels along the shores of the Emirates from Kuwait to Oman, and during the pearling heyday of the 1920s, his name had been both respected and infamous. At one time his fine mansion on the corner of Al Khor's main square had been a hub of commercial activity. Abu Khaled now had time to reflect on those days. He let his *musbah* pass through his gnarled fingers as he wondered what he could have done better and what he would do in future. Pearling had gone, the Depression in the United States had made things even worse, and then the Second World War had put a stop to everything. There was only one thing left, but there was nothing he could do about that.

2

Kuwait, 1945

'Well, dear. All back to normal. Marvellous,' said Harold without waiting for a response from Violet. 'Back in our dear home in Kuwait. I don't think I'll ever leave it again. It would be rather rude, wouldn't it? It was rather fine of them to let us stay on here.'

'Them,' Violet said, able to get a word in at last. 'Them. Yes, dear. "Them" is the word. I wonder who "them" are. Must have been the Emir in the end. He's such a sweetie, and you were awfully good at being a political agent, even though I say so myself. As to being an oil man, we shall have to wait and see. Special advisor to the Kuwait Oil Company. I never quite saw you in trade, dear!'

They laughed and ordered more gin fizzes from the ever-loyal Muzzafar. The world was no longer at war. Here in this bastion of British civility at the top end of the Arabian Gulf there was a collective sigh of relief.

'I know, darling Violet,' Harold said, emboldened by more gin, 'let's have a party. To celebrate.'

'That's the best idea you've had for ages, dear. Oh yes, just like the old days,' Violet said dreamily, smoothing her evening dress, thinking of the ball gowns she had worn as a wide-eyed debutante just before the Great War.

During the war years, Harold and Violet had often quarrelled about decisions that had to be made, whether they concerned their future or more mundane matters such as dealing with the servants, the neighbours and the maintenance of their large beachside villa. With the war over and Harold working for the Kuwait Petroleum Company, life was much more settled. It cheered them up that they were at last seeing eye to eye on this particular project.

'So, who shall we ask? That's the question,' Violet said. 'It should be a celebration of a particular kind...'

'A gathering of the clans,' Harold said, excited at the prospect.

'Exactly. All those who've taken part in some way and made a difference...'

'Given us a reason to live.'

'British values, fighting the good fight...'

'With determination. No matter what the cost.'

'No, you're copying Churchill, my dear,' Violet said, a hint of self-satisfaction in her voice.

'Oh yes.' Harold coughed. 'So, it is. You're right. I was getting carried away.'

And they chuckled as they made their way in to dinner, summoning Muzzafar to bring pen and paper and more drinks to go with their chicken pilau.

Ahmed's world was confined to Bait Al Bahr. He didn't realise he was too young to live like this. He didn't know the consequences of living alone, of not mixing with friends and family. The path on which he had stumbled, through no fault of his own, was a bleak one. So, he thought. He dwelled on these matters for long periods of time. He sat in the wind tower, sighing with discontent. He gazed at the white stucco wall in front of him, letting his mind wander, wondering where he was going, as most adolescents do, but he was more isolated than most. His self-awareness was almost too much to bear. He couldn't imagine hoping or wishing for anything out of life; it never occurred to him that other ways of living were an option.

The silence of the hot summer's day was interrupted by the afternoon call to prayer, *Adhan Al Asr*. Ahmed stirred. He could hear worshippers making their way to the mosque on the corner, a stone's throw from the house. He thought about joining them, but his reverie had alerted in him a certain self-discovery. As he shifted on the cushion and rose to look outside, he thought that he was somehow different. He couldn't really describe how he felt, but he knew more about himself now: his time thinking in the tower had brought him some sort of spiritual comfort.

He reminded himself that he was almost nineteen.

He had dark skin compared to his father and uncle, and was tall, unlike others he had seen in the square outside. His hair was long, and he had a hint of a smile as he ran a hand through his thick shoulder-length locks. He rubbed his chin and felt the beginnings of a beard. He smoothed his thin moustache down with his right hand as if pondering a new theory by a Greek philosopher. As the muezzin chanted, calling the believers to do their duty, Ahmed was suddenly aware that he was a real person, and one he judged to be sincere despite the loneliness he had faced. In that room, he had discovered he was a man. A man of independence.

With his newly acquired confidence he rose from his position on the floor and went out onto the terrace, baked by the harsh Gulf sun. The afternoon call to prayer was done. As he looked over the parapet that surrounded the flat roof of the house he could see worshippers making their way out of the nearby mosque. The souq was coming to life too as market traders began to reopen their little stores. Those who couldn't afford any kind of shop took the sackcloth off their wooden barrows to reveal their wares. Piles of ruby-red tomatoes sat alongside sheaves of lush green *bagdoonis.* Mounds of spices were uncovered: rust-coloured ground nutmeg in pointed heaps, bright yellow turmeric, fresh from India for those who could afford it, but essential for any rice dish, cinnamon bark peeled from the tree in Ceylon only days before and, the most pungent of all, pale-green cardamom waiting for a customer to buy for his morning coffee.

It suddenly became a sensation, an assault on his youthful senses. He felt that he was in command of all he saw, heard and smelled. This was a wonderful place, he felt, a glorious place and time to be alive. He heard the door from the *badgeer* creak open. It was a while before he turned around. When he did, he saw Um Jabor bearing a tray of tea. For the first time since boyhood, Ahmed greeted her with a smile.

Um Jabor had known him all his life. She had nursed him as a baby, after his mother had died, when his father had asked a neighbour if they knew of anyone to look after his baby. From that day on Um Jabor, already a mother, hard-working and strong, had provided the care that Ahmed needed.

She looked fondly at the young man on the terrace, her lined face brightened by the smile he had given her. She wanted to hug him, to ask him questions, to advise him. But she held back.

'Ya Ahmed. Where would you like the tea?' she asked dutifully.

'Just here, Um Jabor,' he replied, pointing to a shaded corner of the rooftop.

Um Jabor laid down the tea things and left quietly. It was the first time Ahmed had had tea outside. She wondered what had happened to cause his change in routine. As she backed out through the doorway she murmured, 'Allah tik al Affyah.' *May God give you strength.*

Ahmed heard the whisper and silently replied, 'Allah ya fik'. It was meant for her. There was no need for more. It was understood.

Ahmed bent down to put a sprig of mint in the steaming tea and resumed his position looking over the parapet at the intricate pattern of passageways in the centre of Doha and Al Bida. It was almost four o'clock and the sun had begun to lose power. The market was thronged with people bustling, buying, trading, exchanging rupees and chatting. There were hagglers, raising their voices, old ladies in cloaks walking away refusing to pay even one more coin, and children racing through the crowd, chasing a worn-out wheel, stick in hand. As he sipped the sweetly scented tea it gradually occurred to Ahmed that the acedia that had befallen him was beginning to ebb away.

He couldn't help wondering why his life was so different to others. He had spent months thinking of the mother he had never seen, the father who was so distant and the grandfather who had built this house. For what? For whom?

But he had made up his mind not to dwell on it, not to feel the darkness and gloom that had pervaded his thoughts for so long. He looked down at the dusty street below and saw two young men walking arm in arm towards the market. One of them, tall, wearing a clean white thobe, was talking animatedly, smiling and gesturing. His friend cut a much more bedraggled figure. Thin, with a tattered lungi wrapped around his tiny waist, his legs and feet uncovered, the young man shuffled along, leaning on his companion for support. Ahmed realised that the poor man was blind.

He began to think about fate, destiny, fairness, justice and equality as he stood on the roof in Doha in the late afternoon sun in the summer of 1945. The introspective Ahmed was no more. From the depths of despair, unable to understand his past and present, suddenly everything became obvious. Some people were far less fortunate than him. There was hardship everywhere. Struggles. Problems. Difficulties. He watched the men until they were out of sight, then he looked out beyond the town towards the oasis of Al Rayyan – a patch of green in the vastness of the pale golden desert of the Qatar peninsula. This magnificent scene had been so familiar to Ahmed as he grew up, he thought, that he had never really noticed it. It dawned on him that it was best not only to see your surroundings, but also to keep your eyes on the horizon. He would remember this moment all his life.

Contentment was not a word that Ahmed knew. He would have to wait years to find it, but after spending more than an hour in silent meditation he had achieved a certain satisfaction with his lot in life. Turning away, he walked across the flat roof and peered down into the central courtyard of his mansion. He was level with the top of the single date palm that had been planted there when the house was built. It had grown from a small sapling taken from the north of the country to full height. It bore dates each year, which usually fell, uneaten, into a sticky mess on the courtyard floor. He was fond of the tree – and of course it provided much needed shade in the square, the hosh, that formed the heart of a family home. It was beautiful, he thought. The house felt cool and calm.

He liked that feeling. Calm and peace. All seemed well at last. And then he looked down into the courtyard again. The lone figure emerging from the small majlis was his father, Khaled. They shared the same house but hardly ever saw each other. As the muezzin called the faithful as the sun set,

Khaled made his way across the courtyard and out of the compound to the mosque. The spiritual enlightenment Ahmed had gained was at once dimmed. He had walked back and forth across this roof so many times that he knew every crack and crevice. The safe citadel to which Ahmed had become accustomed over the years was now acquiring a new place in his life. It was no longer a fortress to keep him in. No. It was now a watchtower looking out, beyond himself to the wider world. As his father left, he jumped into the air, feeling as though he could catapult himself into space, into a new world, full of new beginnings and new adventures. 'This is my time,' he said. 'I'm going to make the best of it.'

Muzzafar had never been in such a state. Up to now, life had been predictable. The colonel, since his retirement from the diplomatic service, had led a fairly quiet life and the memsahib confined her social gatherings to tea with local women. But now it was as if the world had gone mad. He had been told that the colonel was planning a special event to mark the end of the war, and that several 'persons of note' would be attending an 'At home' at their house on the seafront in Kuwait.

Muzzafar had been given three helpers to make life easier for him. 'How will I cope with all these guests coming?' Muzzafar cried, directing his plea to the ceiling – and possibly way above that – in desperation. Summoning a great force from within, abandoning all hope of heavenly intervention, he began to bark orders at the servants.

'You. Go and get those crates of tonic water from the cellar. You, stand up straight and start boiling those eggs.' Turning to a young, frail-looking teenager, he said, 'This could be the biggest night of your young life, so I need you to stay by my side and do everything I say. Understand?'

The boy, quaking with nerves, nodded at Muzzafar, who had assumed the air of a sergeant-major. With the other two servants dispatched to do their duties, Muzzafar asked him his name.

'Rami, sir,' he said quietly.

'Ah, a good Hindu boy. Right, young Rami. We have to go to work and I'm going to teach you how to make spam canapés. The master loves them.' They rolled up their sleeves and began to open tin after tin of luncheon meat.

Upstairs, things were no less tense. Violet, sitting at her dressing table, asked Harold to fasten the clasp of her pearl necklace, which she only wore on very special occasions.

'Hang on a minute, old girl,' Harold said. 'Having a spot of bother with the old dicky bow. I used to be able to do this without looking. Now it always seems to end up north–south instead of east–west. Must be getting past it.'

Heaving a sigh, Violet put the pearls down and watched her husband struggling. 'You are completely potty. Do you know that? I've known you all these years and I still can't understand it.'

Harold laughed. 'You must be mad too then. I tell you what, if I fix your pearls, will you fix my tie?'

'Come over here, then.' Violet beckoned her husband towards the dressing table. Harold took the pearls and placed them around her neck. As he attached the clasp, he bent down and kissed her gently on the cheek.

'Silly old fool,' she muttered. 'God knows what's happening downstairs. I wonder how many people will come. I hope they're all OK at the sheikh's guesthouse.'

'They'll be fine. It'll be fun. I asked Sheikh Ahmed to come, but he won't. They never do,' Harold said authoritatively. 'I expect he's laid everything on for the troops, though. Loads of space in that guest wing of his.'

'Poor Muzzafar. I must go and check everything's all right,' Violet said, getting up from the stool and smoothing her rich lace brocade gown. 'Will I do?'

'You look marvellous, dear. As always,' he replied diplomatically. 'That pale blue suits you. Lovely. Hair looks nice too.'

That took her aback, and she patted it as if to acknowledge the kindness. 'Going grey now, I'm afraid, and can't be doing with blue rinse,' she said.

'At least you've got lots of hair. Mine's almost gone,' Harold said laughingly, smoothing down the thin strands. 'We'd better go down. Some people might be on time. They never are, though.'

Muzzafar had never been so busy. He usually had all day to prepare supper for two. But today he was beyond despair. He had just about managed to get the drinks organised, but nothing was cold. It was the height of summer, and the humidity in the northern Gulf had reached 90%. Ice. Where on earth could he find ice at seven o'clock on a Saturday evening in Kuwait? Young Rami was doing rather well at chopping the slices of spam and placing them on dry crackers then spooning a blob of precious home-made chutney on the top. Muzzafar patted the young man on the back for his efforts, then showed him to make egg mayonnaise as well as Gentleman's Relish ones, which the master adored. Muzzafar thought they smelled like the backwaters in Kerala, where he came from, and would never try one.

'Oh, my goodness, look at the time!' Muzzafar yelled. 'We'll never be ready in time.' He ordered one of the men upstairs to guard the front door in case anyone arrived. 'Ask their names. Ask them what they want to drink. If you see the sahib and memsahib, call them sir.' It was all too much.

Harold and Violet came down to the drawing room, which overlooked the beach. There was a calm atmosphere on the first floor, unlike the chaos that was taking place down below.

'All seems well in here,' Harold said, making for the veranda doors. 'Let's open the doors. Looks like a nice evening out there. The moon's on the horizon. Bit warm, I suppose.'

'Just a trifle,' Violet joked as she spotted the servant standing in the hallway. 'Ah, you must be helping with the party.'

'Yes, ma'am. I am Abdul Aziz at your service, ma'am,' the young servant said, bowing. 'I am to open the door.'

'Good for you,' Violet said. 'Just direct them into the big room when they arrive.'

Abdulaziz bowed once again.

'Drink, dear?' Harold said, wondering where the drink would actually appear from.

'That would be nice, but there doesn't seem to be either drink or anyone to make that drink, dear,' Violet said sarcastically. 'I'll go downstairs.'

She was in for a shock. There were a couple of trays of half-done canapés and that was about it. Muzzafar was hopping around in panic while young Rami was doing his best to mix egg mayonnaise, a job he didn't really understand or wish to do. There was no sign of the third man.

'Where's the other one?' Violet asked.

'Not sure, ma'am. I put him in charge of drinks.'

'Sounds very strange,' she said, and proceeded to take the matter in hand.

'Right, Muzzafar, bring some gin and tonic upstairs and you, young man, finish those canapés as fast as you can. Let's go.'

As she went back upstairs she heard people talking. In the drawing room Harold was dealing with the first guests.

'Look who's here, dear. Harry St John Philby. All the way from Riyadh. It's so good of you to come, Harry. How's everything in Riyadh? You have a Saudi wife now, I understand?'

'Indeed, I do. It's good to get away, though. His Majesty's demands are such that sometimes I find it impossible to keep up. He wants everything done yesterday.'

They all laughed. Violet offered their guest a gin and tonic. He declined. St John Philby, known in Saudi Arabia as Sheikh Abdulla, had taken on the manner of a local dignitary. He stood, regal in thobe, *qutra, agal* and *bisht,* as if it was an honour for the house to receive him. There was an awkward silence until Muzzafar appeared with an *asseer limoon.* Lemon juice in hand, Philby surveyed the drawing room. Harold was about to engage him in conversation when another guest was announced.

'Major Frank Holmes,' Abdul Aziz bellowed.

'Ah, Frank, dear chap. Do come in. Glad you made it,' Harold said to his old friend. 'Look who's here, Harry. All the way from Riyadh.'

The two men glared at each other for a few seconds. They managed to say good evening, but it was clear there was no love lost between them. Although in his seventies Frank was still active, spending his time trying to do deals. He had reached Oman, the final frontier in the search for oil. Philby considered Holmes to be a rogue trader, only interested in making money. Philby, on the other hand, considered himself of higher rank and status, a senior diplomat who had the ear of the highest in the realm, wherever he happened to be. Having acknowledged Holmes, Philby managed to extricate himself by engaging Violet in small talk before whispering in her ear. 'Ghastly man. He still owes the Kingdom money. Never paid us the six thousand pounds in rent. Ibn Saud was not amused. The man seems to think he can wander around the desert, causing mayhem on the way. I hear he's down in the Trucial states now. Good luck to 'em!'

Violet nodded. 'Oh, my dear. I don't believe it! Here are the Mallomans!' she exclaimed. 'How marvellous.'

She left Philby and dashed towards the middle-aged couple. 'My dear Agatha. You look marvellous.' Violet gave the famous woman a warm hug and pecked her partner on the cheek. 'Max, you too. It's so good to see you. Harold, look who it is.'

'Good Lord. I never expected you to make it. Writing best-sellers and digging up Mesopotamia must take up an awful lot of time,' Harold joked.

'Well, my dears, Max was on a dig and I came along for the ride. All good stuff for my next novel. We'd thought we'd celebrate our silver wedding anniversary by popping down to see you.' Agatha had never looked happier, Violet thought as she caught up with her old friend. Perhaps being Mrs Malloman suited her better than being Miss Christie. Agatha had written dozens of mysteries and had met her second husband twenty-five years earlier through their shared love of archaeology.

'We didn't bring black tie,' Max declared, not in the least embarrassed. 'You know us archaeologists!'

People were relaxing and there was a lot of laughter. Drinks were passed round to those who Abdul Aziz thought would accept them. One recipient was Charles Prior, the political agent, newly arrived from Bushehr. He was His Majesty's most important representative in the Gulf – and he looked and acted the part. Ignoring the heat and humidity of the summer night, he was dressed as if he was going to the opera, in starched wing-collar shirt and immaculate black tie. He was suspicious of Philby, aware that anything he said to the Arabist in Riyadh would be passed on to Ibn Saud, the founder of the Kingdom of Al Saud and de facto father of Arabia.

'Oh Lord. It's Belgrave.' St John Philby was definitely out of his comfort zone. He hurried towards the veranda to escape yet another adversary from the past. He scurried away, his flowing ceremonial *bisht* and headgear askew.

Charles Belgrave was a tall, slender man of fifty who had worked for the past twenty years as the chief administrator to two Emirs of Bahrain: Sheikh Hamad until 1942 and since then his son, Salman bin Hamad. Belgrave knew he was in a powerful position. Highly regarded on the tiny island, he had helped create a police force and some sort of infrastructure. He was certainly in a better position than the shifty-looking Philby. Dressed in a wide-lapelled double-breasted dinner jacket and sporting shiny, swept-back short hair, he beamed as he made his entrance.

Following the dapper Charles was an elderly man dressed in Arab attire. He made his way steadily across the room to meet his hosts.

'Salam aleikum,' the man said as he approached the circle of guests around Harold Dickson, who was on his third gin and tonic. Harold stopped talking abruptly as the man reached the group.

'Bill Williamson,' he said. The guests were not expecting him to give an English name.

'Good Lord. I don't believe it.' Frank Holmes looked astonished.

'Yes, it's me, Frank. It must be twenty years. I couldn't bear the sight of you then. Time has mellowed me somewhat.'

Harold was equally surprised. 'Good of you to come, my dear chap. I never thought you'd get my letter.'

'Somebody from Basra came up with it. He managed to find me in my place at Kut-al-Hajjaj. They call me Hajji Williamson now. At least, my new wife does.'

This caused muted laughter among the guests.

'She thinks it's quite amusing. Little does she know that I became a haji when I first went to Mecca in 1894! I was twenty-two. All those travels: San Francisco, the Panama Canal, Hong Kong, Bombay and then Aden. Life was completely different afterwards.'

'I take my hat off to you, Bill – I mean, ya Hajji,' Harold said. 'There's St John Philby over there. You remember him? I'll bring him over.'

'Perhaps not,' Williamson interjected. 'Holmes and Philby might be too much to ask all at once!'

Violet was so delighted that Agatha had made it to the party and was so absorbed in the novelist's latest travels and ideas, that she forgot about her duty as hostess. Muzzafar was even more frantic than he had been earlier, with no guidance at all from his mistress.

'What am I to do? All these people coming from all over the place. And important too. Big sahibs like political agent sahib and *mustashar* to Emir and *mustashar* to the King of Arabia. What can Muzzafar do?' He cast his eyes to heaven.

Abdul Aziz had come down to see how things were during a break in announcing the guests and passing round cocktails.

'Give them some samosas. We'll never have enough food, though. Silly sandwiches. Who's going to want silly sandwiches? I ask you.'

While Abdul Aziz was downstairs, more guests had arrived. It was after nine and the party was in full swing.

'Freya!' Violet yelled. Another surprise guest had caught her unawares.

'Sorry I'm late, Violet dear. I got stuck in the Hadhramut!'

There was laughter all round as Violet, Agatha and the newly arrived Freya Stark celebrated their reunion.

'Only joking. I came down from Damascus. Finishing off editing my war letters. I would have taken the train but Lawrence blew it up so that was that! Must go back to the Hadhramut one day, though. Come with me, ladies. What a fine team we would make.'

Freya Stark had travelled through southern Arabia in the 1930s and had written beautifully crafted accounts of her adventures, most notably *A Winter in Arabia*. She was well known in the area and knew many of the guests at the party.

Just as Harold and Violet thought everyone had arrived, two young men turned up, looking somewhat out of place. After apologising for their late arrival, they straightened their crumpled tropical suits and looked around for someone they knew.

'Ah, Thesiger. Remember me?'

It was Charles Prior, the chief political agent.

'Mr Prior, sir. What a pleasure. I do indeed remember you. Those halcyon days in Addis Ababa. I remember you coming to the house when my father was the Consul-General. May I introduce my good friend, Edward Henderson? A fine Arabic speaker and servant of His Majesty's government.'

The twenty-eight-year-old Edward had spent the entire war in the Middle East and was rising through the ranks of the diplomatic service. 'It's an honour, sir,' he said, on his best behaviour. 'Wilfred is an inspiration. We share a passion for Arabia and the desert, but I'm afraid I like my home comforts. Wilfred is happier under the stars!'

Violet looked at Harold, who was looking decidedly tipsy. She mouthed, 'What about the food?' to him but all she got in return was a shrug. This could turn out to be a great entertaining disaster, she thought.

While Violet sped down to the kitchen to find out what was happening about food and more drink, the guests were beginning to shed their initial inhibitions and start to mingle and celebrate the fact that the war had finally ended.

'It was marvellous in Syria,' Agatha said to Harry St John Philby. 'We had the most wonderful time. Of course, it was all French so there was plenty of bubbly, flown in from Paris.'

Philby seemed unimpressed. 'My partying days are over, I'm afraid. I had my share of fun in Lebanon, Agatha. I leave all that to my son Kim now.'

'Look at Freya, Harry. Doesn't she look wonderful? Just like dear Gertrude.'

'Ha. Gertrude.' Philby reacted sharply. 'Miss Bell taught me everything I know. She was my controller in Cairo. She knew how to deal with the Arabs all right. I think we're losing our grip. I'm not sure how long I can go on fighting the Arab cause.'

'Now, now, dear Harry. That's not the spirit. You've been among them so long, you practically are one!'

'I'm starving.'

Freya Stark had come over to join Philby and Agatha, having taken the chance to escape from the stiffly clad and equally stiffly spoken Charles Prior.

'I knew you were talking about me. God, that man's a total bore. Diplomats are rather, though, aren't they? Where's all the derring-do? More adventure, that's what we need. I suppose the Middle East will never be the same now.'

The diplomat was wary of this self-confident and somewhat eccentric woman. He knew that, as a well-travelled expert on Arabia, she probably knew more about the people and what made them tick than he did. Prior was used to giving orders and mixing with the mandarins of Whitehall and the swan-plumed viceroys and bejewelled emirs of the Orient. He had read Freya's book, *A Winter in Arabia*, which detailed the beauties of the Hadhramut in southern Yemen and the simple life of the freedom-loving people. He was also only too aware of her more recent service in the Ministry of Information during the war. What was the *Ikhwan al Hurriya* all about? He knew from his contacts in London that she had been engaged to drum up support for the Allies from the Arabs, but could she be trusted? She had studied at the School of Oriental and African Studies and was fluent in Arabic and Persian. As far as Prior was concerned, this meant her loyalties, if not divided, were definitely dubious.

The chief political agent's sole concern was British interests in the region, safeguarding the sea routes to and from India and beyond, to maintain the image of the Empire. With unrest in Delhi and the aftermath of the war in the Malay peninsula, this was no time to be wavering over the objectives of the British government. As far as Prior was concerned, the tin pot states of the Gulf were to be ruled with a rod of iron – and if concessions were to be made on independent rule, then the United Kingdom had to use all means at her disposal to make sure those countries would remain loyal. So, when he heard Freya Stark reminiscing about her childhood reading *One Thousand and One Nights* and her nights camping under the stars in the Empty Quarter, he could barely contain his cynicism.

He should probably have been more concerned about the man she had gone over to join.

Harry and Freya had been fiercely competitive about their desert exploits over the years. In the 1930s they had vowed to be the first to conquer Shabwah in Yemen. Freya had managed to get there first and had chronicled her days there in *The Southern Gates of Arabia*, which she published in 1936. It wasn't until a year later that Philby had arrived to record all he saw in a series of maps and drawings which became *The Daughters of Sheba* in 1940. Although Freya was first and by all accounts had the edge on Philby, the Cambridge-educated Arabist had one distinct advantage: he was under the sponsorship of the founder of modern Arabia, Ibn Saud.

Ever since his days at Cambridge, Philby had been involved in matters Oriental. One of his student friends was the first Prime Minister of India, Jawharlal Nehru. He went on to join the Indian Civil Service, learning Arabic and Persian along the way. By the middle of the Great War, Philby was firmly established as a British administrator in Baghdad, responsible for the oil fields in Basra and organising the Arab revolt against the Ottoman Turks. He went on to work with a certain T.E. Lawrence. Already oil and politics were intertwined, with the Balfour Declaration and the Sykes–Picot Agreement coming into force. Although he was head of the Secret Service for the British Mandate for Palestine he was already in touch with Ibn Saud, and when it became clear that Jewish immigration to Palestine was to be allowed he resigned and went to live in Jeddah.

Wilfred Thesiger stood alone near the stone fireplace, which looked a little incongruous in the height of summer. He looked down at the tiger skin that had been used as a hearth rug ever since the Dicksons returned from the Sundarbans years before. He hated parties. Especially ones like this. All he wanted was to be among the desert people, living a simple, thoughtful and peaceful life. How could the Western nations ever understand the Arabs? he pondered, gazing around the room. It was all a big competition, he concluded. And greed. There was Philby, whose intentions had been honourable to begin with, chasing Freya around Yemen to capture their corner of Arabia. Perhaps he harboured a certain jealousy in this regard. But Philby had turned his attention to power, having gained the confidence of the most powerful man on the Arabian peninsula. That man Holmes, he thought, was typical of the kind of person who was spoiling the Bedouin traditions. He knew only too well that the people with whom he had travelled were noble and honourable, fiercely traditional in their customs and beliefs, but they were being swayed by talk of instant wealth and promises of an end to hardship and the start of a life of ease and luxury.

He looked across to the Mallomans. Max was puffing on his pipe, one hand in his pocket, and Agatha was holding forth on writing about murders in Baghdad. He felt envious that they had found each other; they seemed a happy couple. He realised that was something he would never be able to do: settle down with one person. His only love was the desert. He yearned to explore the farthest reaches of Arabia. As he gazed into the empty grate, he imagined sitting round the camp fire at night, listening to the tales of the tribal elders. He wondered why people could not be content with a simple life.

A tap on the shoulder broke his reverie.

'You look a little lost, Wilfred.'

It was Edward Henderson. The two had met before and shared a love of the Arab world.

'I confess I do feel a bit out of place. I was just planning a trip. I want to explore the Empty Quarter.'

'Haven't Freya Stark and St John Philby covered that?'

'Only the Hadhramut and Yemen. There's the entire area between the Gulf and Oman. I want to cross it.'

'You're just like Captain Lawrence, Wilfred. You'll go down in history as one of the great travellers. Mark my words.'

'Kind of you to say so. If I can get a group of young Bedouin together, I'm sure it's possible. I want to get away from all this and live a simple life. And write about it, of course.'

'Of course. You'll easily find a publisher. I wish I had your daring nature. It looks like I'm going to be stuck in the diplomatic service with all those stuffed shirts.'

'You're only twenty-eight, Edward. All your life in front of you. But with your passion for Arabia you could do a lot of good. Unlike some people, who govern from above.' Wilfred gestured in the direction of Charles Prior and Charles Belgrave, who were each holding court among their group.

The two men hadn't always seen eye to eye. Although Prior was senior and forever complaining that Belgrave was too fastidious, there was nothing he could do about it as Belgrave had been appointed personally by the Bahraini court.

'You know, I've been thinking, Belgrave. We ought to get on rather better. We've both got a vested interest in keeping everything running smoothly in these parts. There's going to be a lot of change now the war is over.'

'Absolutely. This Emir is wary of change, and with the oil companies banging on his door day and night I've got a tough job on my hands to keep things British.'

'Make sure you do. We don't want the Americans taking over. By the way, we're moving the political residency from Bushehr to Bahrain in the not too distant future. It'll be good to be nearby, won't it?'

Charles Belgrave tried to hide his astonishment that his little fiefdom could soon be encroached upon by the colonial master from Whitehall.

'We'll be more central, able to keep an eye on things in Bahrain and over the water in Qatar. Funny little place, isn't it?'

Meanwhile, Williamson was talking to Frank Holmes.

'You know, Williamson, we've got to go back to Qatar. When I went down there with the Dicksons before the war, we had a marvellous time. There are fortunes to be made. We might miss the boat.'

'My dear Holmes, I'm done with oil. I'm more or less retired. You must come and see my date palms. They yield the most wonderful fruit.'

Holmes realised there was no point in trying to engage Williamson. He had been useful to him in his day, as an interpreter with the sheikhs in Qatar and all the way down to Oman, but although they were a similar age Holmes discovered they had had little in common.

Young Edward Henderson propped himself up against the old oak dresser, which was lovingly polished and much travelled. He scratched around in the bottom of a Wedgwood bowl for the last crumbs of Bombay mix. He felt overwhelmed by the people he had been introduced to over the past two hours. Although he felt relieved to be here now that war was finally over, he couldn't quite figure out what he was doing in Kuwait, of all places. It was good of the Dicksons to allow him to tag along with Thesiger to their party, and as he had all the leave in the world he jumped at the chance of seeing another part of the Middle East. All he knew was that Thesiger loved the 'real' Arabia, as he called it, and oil had been discovered there. An intelligent and observant person, he had also witnessed the establishment of the Arab League earlier that March while stationed in Cairo. He was beginning to form a picture of how the Middle East was shaped. The German threat had been thwarted and the British presence in the Middle East had been secured. In Cairo, as the Arabs formed their league, the British were keeping an eagle eye on the Suez Canal.

He looked at Frank Holmes. He was a typical example of the expatriate exploiter par excellence, willing to smooth-talk his way to achieve his own ends, by fair means or foul, to profit both the oil companies for which he worked and the tribal sheikhs who had placed their trust in him.

Then there was Philby. Another embracer of Islam, he was the ultimate politician and could be both beguiling and duplicitous. Standing in his Arab dress, Philby wore an imperious expression, giving away nothing. Henderson understood that Philby was to be respected as a scholar, and he had vast experience in the region. He had been recruited by Percy Cox, the chief political officer, in 1915. He had journeyed throughout Arabia throughout the Great War and had worked with T.E. Lawrence on the British mandate for Palestine in the early 1920s, dealing with King George and Winston Churchill as well as the Zionist Chaim Weizmann.

By the 1930s, established as an advisor to Ibn Saud, he had negotiated with Standard Oil, Anglo-Persian and the Iraq Petroleum Company to gain lucrative rights for the Kingdom. His loyalty to the British crown came into question, however, when he suggested that the Americans run oil matters in Saudi Arabia and ARAMCO was formed. He was also involved in questionable dealings over Saudi oil being shipped to Germany via Spain at a time of high political tension.

Philby had written about his travels and had earned his reputation as an Arabist, but All Henderson felt was a sense of betrayal. Edward loved his country and believed he was in the best position to further his career as a diplomat, fostering a mutual understating between the former Empire-makers and the traditional fiefdoms of the desert. He had also come across Philby's son Kim, who was a few years older than Edward, at a social gathering in Westminster. Henderson thought there was something strange about Kim's manner. He looked as though he couldn't be trusted. Obviously, a chip off the old block, Henderson thought.

Dear old Harold and Violet. How charming they had been to invite this band of funny Arab-loving eccentrics to their house. It was a great idea to celebrate the end of this horrible war. Harold had turned from diplomat to oil company employee, further reinforcing Edward's view that oil, politics and religion were inexorably intertwined.

It was almost ten o'clock. The assembled guests were chatting happily, exchanging views on the outcome of the war, the future of the Middle East, absent mutual friends. Some were extremely tiddly, having only had crisps to eat. Muzaffar was scurrying around in a blind panic, closely followed by Violet. As the party grew louder it became all too much for Edward. Feeling rather faint, he headed for the open veranda.

Suddenly he could hear noises from along the beach. He could make out some flickering lights too. Within minutes he could hear drums and singing. At least twenty men, dressed in white thobes with maroon jackets, were heading a procession. The scene was completely at odds with the simplicity of the sandy beach before him. The noise made by the drummers finally attracted the attention of the crowd indoors, and people came out onto the veranda to see what was going on.

The drummers and singers were in front of the Dicksons' house. Behind them were more men, bearing aloft what appeared to be a stretcher.

'By Jove, it's a sheep! Look at it! It's a damn sheep, I tell you!' Charles Prior announced the arrival of a feast. Then came more servants, carrying huge platters of rice and dates, pomegranates and peaches, sweetmeats and stuffed vegetables. They were followed by more men, finely clad and armoured with rifles and shiny swords. Everyone gasped in amazement. Then the most extraordinary thing happened.

'Hello, Harry! What are you doing here?'

'Good Lord,' Harry St John Philby said in shock. 'Your Highness.'

And the crowd burst into applause. The Emir of Kuwait, His Highness Sheikh Ahmed Al Jaber Al Sabah, had decided to join in the fun. 'I didn't want to miss the celebrations. We are all grateful that war is over,' the Emir said. 'It is an honour to be among you all.'

'Three cheers for His Highness,' Harold shouted.

And the guests cheered and ran down to the foreshore where the feast was laid out before them. Cushions and carpets appeared from nowhere. Within minutes the happy throng were tucking into the lavish spread in front of them. After the hardship of wartime food, it was a wonderful sight to behold.

There was no need for a tent or awning, as it was a beautiful balmy evening. The stars shone brilliantly in the blue-black sky and the full moon was reflected on the surface of the perfectly still sea.

Violet was the only person left on the veranda. Speechless, she looked down at what she thought must be an apparition below. Harold was halfway down the stairs. He turned back towards her. 'What are you waiting for, old thing?'

'I can't believe this has happened.'

Harold came back up a couple of steps and Violet came down, whispering in her husband's ear. 'How did he know?'

'I asked him. Well, I had to, didn't I? He put up all the visitors in the guest wing at the palace, after all. Least I could do.'

'You knew all along that he was coming?'

'Yes dear. Of course.'

'And you didn't think to tell me?'

'I thought you might get in a state, old thing. Didn't want you worrying.'

'That's why you weren't too bothered about the food. Now I see.'

'Oh, that. Yes. Well, I didn't like to say. I knew he'd bring a lamb or something. You know how it is. Thought it would be a surprise.'

'A surprise? It certainly is a surprise. You crafty old devil.'

They went down arm in arm and met a weary Muzzafar, who looked dazed by the turn of events.

'Come on, Muzzafar,' Harold said, 'and you' – he turned to the two exhausted servants – 'come and join the party. You deserve it.'

Everyone feasted and made merry until the small hours.

The Emir beckoned to Harold and Violet to join him. As he did so, Harold noticed a person he didn't recognise. The stranger was squeezed between the Emir and Harry St John Philby. Although the man was in Arab dress, he didn't look like an Arab. He sat bolt upright with the poise of an Olympic athlete. Until now he had been talking in hushed tones, in between mouthfuls, to the person on his left, Philby, and, when occasion demanded, to the Emir. He seemed at ease in the ruler's presence and was clearly on familiar terms with him. Suddenly the man raised his voice, as if to make certain that everyone nearby could hear.

'Sure is good to be here, Your Highness. That was a magnificent feast. I'll be sure to tell His Majesty that all is well in the sisterly country of Kuwait.'

The Emir nodded in grateful thanks and Harold realised that the man was Colonel William Eddy, military advisor to King Abdulaziz. Earlier in the year, Eddy had been present at the talks on the Great Bitter Lake in Suez between the Saudi king and President Roosevelt. A fluent Arabic speaker, he had acted as interpreter throughout.

'Good to see so many of you British here,' he said sardonically. 'Now war is over, we can really turn the taps on.'

Philby looked sheepish, unsure of his position as a member of the Saudi court, and the diplomats, including Belgrave and Prior, shuffled and coughed, wondering what to say. The others, like Thesiger, Haji Williamson and the Mallomans, sensed that the Middle East was on the verge of great change and that things would never be quite the same again.

'Don't worry, guys. There's plenty of room for everyone,' Eddy announced, as if speaking on behalf of the President himself. 'We just have to make sure the Emir here and all his allies are in safe hands. We are securing Saudi Arabia, and here in Kuwait His Highness has been very gracious. As for you guys in Bahrain' – he looked towards Belgrave – 'we'll have to wait and see. As for Dubai' – he pointed at Prior – 'there's another story. And let's not forget the sheikhdom of Qatar. You know as well as I do,' he went on, looking at Frank Holmes, 'that Qatar's riches are undiscovered. Their time has yet to come.'

3

Doha, 1947

Ahmed decided he was no longer going to sit at home and wait for something to happen to him. After his soul-searching on the roof terrace, he couldn't stand the loneliness any longer.

'I'm almost twenty,' he said. 'I need to decide what I'm going to do. Where do I come from? Where am I going?' He gave himself a stern warning that sitting around doing nothing was not an option and if he wanted to be someone, he had to act. He rewarded himself with a rare smile. 'Ya Um Jabor. Where are you?' he called out, running along the shaded gallery. He realised it was after seven in the evening and she would be getting supper ready. He went down and opened the door to the *mutbakh* – a series of small rooms for preparing food, and where Um Jabor and her helpers could rest. Sure enough, she was there, sitting silently, her head bowed.

'I'm sorry, Um Jabor. I woke you.'

'Oh dear. I must have been sleeping. Only for a few moments, I hope,' she said, looking flustered. She was unused to any of the menfolk coming into her quarters. 'I'm getting your dinner, Ahmed. I won't be long.'

'Don't worry about that, Um Jabor. Have you seen my father or Salem?'

'Oh no. Your father hasn't been here for days. He's probably in Al Khor with your grandfather. Salem is at the palace, I should think. He's always there.'

'Oh dear. Never mind. Thanks, Um Jabor,' he said and bent down to kiss her on the head.

Um Jabor made to get up but Ahmed gestured for her to rest. Um Jabor looked shocked at this unusual display of thoughtfulness.

Ahmed didn't want to go back to his lonely place on the roof or wander around the house. He felt overcome with guilt that he lived in one of the largest homes in the capital, with everything he needed, yet he couldn't find happiness or satisfaction. He decided he had to get out of the empty building to search for something. He didn't know what. He just felt he had to do something.

Dressed in his thobe and sandals, he shut the wicket door behind him and ventured along the bustling alleyway towards the central square. The market stalls and barrows had long since been put away for the day, but as it was a warm summer evening, people were out and about, chatting, on their way to visit friends and family or cooling down in the fresh air. He walked through the busy souq, passing the famous little tea shop where men, young and old, gathered to gossip. Even though they hadn't been involved in the world war, people were happy it was over. In the tea shop Ahmed heard people talking happily.

He began to realise that the hermetic existence he had grown used to was useless. He wanted to be like the smiling men who shared jokes and tales. He stopped by a tiny barber shop, lit by a single paraffin lantern. A youngish man was having his beard shaved under the expert gaze of a much older man brandishing a cut-throat razor. Ahmed's jet-black hair was long, down to his shoulders, and he had the beginnings of a wispy beard. Looking at the man who was having his beard shaved, Ahmed thought he might feel better with less hair. Perhaps more energy would be transferred to his moustache, he thought, and smiled. He would think about it.

After a while he had reached Al Koot fort. The guards stood at ease, drinking tea outside the large wooden gates to the fort, which were open. He could have entered if he wished, emboldened as he was by his new self-confidence, but he chose instead to head towards the sea. The only lights came from the few merchants' homes near the sea front and the ruler's headquarters higher up the hill to Ahmed's left. He bade 'Salam aleikum' to the fishermen returning home from their boats. Soon he was at the water's edge. For a few minutes he stood and listened to the gentle lapping of the waves. A little further along the small bay was a new jetty.

Since the Emir had moved into town from Salata, he had asked for a place to moor his dhows. Ahmed noticed these as he walked along. A group of young boys were busy trying to catch fish from the deeper water around the small pier. Ahmed couldn't help wondering why he had never been down here before. He was enjoying himself.

At the end of the jetty, he found himself in front of a large vessel. He didn't know what kind it was. It looked old, and creaked as it bobbed on the waves. Ahmed saw piles of rope and mounds of sail cloth on the deck, and behind these a faint light. In the bow of the boat, three men were gathered around a lantern. They were talking quietly and seemed to be playing a game.

As he approached the group there was a loud thwack and the sound of laughter. Then he saw what had caused the commotion. One of them had just won the card game. The winner was pleased enough with his strategy, but the two losers were also in a good mood, slapping their companion on the back as they got up. Another had spotted Ahmed, standing alone on the dark jetty.

'Tfadal. Ahlan wa sahlan.' *Welcome. Join us.*

'Shukran. Mafee shay.' *It's fine.* Ahmed was surprised.

'Tishrab chai.' *Would you like tea?*

'Shokran.'

Ahmed was embarrassed that he had been caught looking at the men but, somehow, he felt at home. Without any further thought, he climbed on board. This was a bit of a struggle, as Ahmed was unused to boats. The man who had asked him aboard leaped to his aid, offering a hand, which Ahmed seized, thanking him. *'Tfadal. Tfadal ya akhi.'*

The group made Ahmed welcome. They asked him to sit down and join them and gave him tea. Ahmed felt overwhelmed and couldn't find any words to say except a string of shokrans.

The men carried on with their jokes and the card game. To a passer-by, it appeared that they were ignoring their new guest but, wishing to make him feel at home and not out of place, they let him adjust to the scene.

Ahmed wasn't sure what to do. His heart pounded with excitement and nerves. The men could see this, but none showed it on their face.

While the men concentrated on the card game, Ahmed began to relax a little and studied the group more closely. Were they a friendly crew taking time off from their hard life to enjoy the cool air of the evening out on deck? They looked as if they were in their mid-thirties, and they seemed to know each other very well. From his solitary days gazing down from the rooftop of his mansion, Ahmed had honed an acuity beyond his years. He felt sympathy for those he thought looked ill or sad. He chuckled to himself when he noticed a couple of weary walkers resting for a well-earned cup of tea. Sometimes he noticed a child skipping along with their mother. He also saw children who didn't skip along but tugged at their mother's abaya, demanding attention.

The older Ahmed got and the more closely he observed those around him, he more he came to realise that being happy was a rare and precious thing. His loneliness during childhood and early youth had left him in a permanent state of melancholy.

Where have I been living? What have I been doing? he thought, suddenly aware of his place in the grand scheme of things. *I am alive. I can see. I can hear, eat and breathe.*

He suddenly felt a deep contentment, as though some mystery had been solved, and found himself smiling. There would be no more sadness and self-pity. The world is beautiful, he realised, and we are lucky to be alive. *Life is precious and we mustn't waste it.*

'Chai?'

No answer.

'Ya Ahmed. Ureed Chai?'

Still no answer.

'I told you he looked ill at ease.'

'Maybe he's not well.'

'He's fine. He's young and probably confused. We are all friends, playing cards. I wouldn't have liked to be stuck with a noisy group of old farts like us if I were young like him. He seems a nice chap.'

'Give him a shake – go on.'

Ahmed came to his senses. 'Ana aasif jidaan. *I'm very sorry.*' he said, embarrassed.

'That's all right. We should have asked you to join in. Now, have some tea and relax. Let's have a song. Ya Yousef, get the tabla.'

Yousef got the tabla and the group sang the old pearl-diving songs that Ahmed had heard from time to time, sung by old men in cafés. Then he had dismissed the songs as boring and dull but now, sitting with his new friends, he realised there was a perfect harmony in how they sang and acted out the hardships of bygone days.

The largest, oldest and most jovial of the men leaped into the air and the other men clapped. Ahmed showed his appreciation with a bashful smile and more shokrans.

'You haven't lost your touch, Bilal,' Yousef told his friend, patting him on the back.

'I'm lucky to be healthy and happy. Thanks be to God. I love a good song. Singing makes you happy, doesn't it? Mind you, this one never sang much.'

Bilal's comments were directed at the tea-maker.

'Talking to me?'

'Yes, you, Ibrahim. You and Adel were always writing poetry and waiting to dive. That's all you lived for – and coming home to see the girls, of course.'

At this, the group burst out laughing. Ahmed turned a deep shade of red. 'I must go.'

'No, no. We didn't mean to embarrass you,' Bilal said.

'No, it's fine. I must get back,' Ahmed told them. 'I've had a wonderful time. Thank you for everything.'

'We haven't done anything, have we? We're always here in the evenings. Come any time. You're more than welcome.'

Ahmed got up and shook hands, reassuring the group that he would return.

'We'll cook dinner next time,' Bilal shouted out as Ahmed stepped off the boat. 'At least, Ibrahim will cook.' There was more laughter as Ahmed made his way along the little jetty. He turned to look back at the men and felt deeply moved. Then he saw the name on the bowsprit of the vessel.

FIRIAL

The old sailors weren't the only ones playing cards that night. High on the hill overlooking the capital and the bobbing dhows in the tiny harbour were Sheikh Ali bin Abdullah and his friend Salem bin Nasser Al Misfar. The two men were used to late nights, especially in the summer when they could sit out on the roof terrace and enjoy the cool breeze.

The placing of the cards had become automatic.

'Ya Salem, how long have I known you?'

'Let's see. About twenty years, I would say. We met in the pearl days. When you were at Al Salata.'

'Ah yes, Al Salata. That was the best. I loved it there. Playing on the beach, fishing for *subeiti.*'

'You can still do that, you know.'

'I'm fifty-five, and my father is in trouble. We have no money coming in. It wouldn't look very good if I was out fishing all day, enjoying myself.'

'I see what you mean. But you're not responsible for that.'

The sheikh gave his friend a long look. No words were spoken but both knew what the other meant.

For reasons best known to his father, the Emir Sheikh Abdullah bin Jassim, Ali, although the eldest son, was not his father's heir. That position was held by his younger brother Hamad. Ali had been made an outsider. This had caused an inevitable sense of resentment, especially as he had seen his country decline due to the collapse of the pearling industry and the horrors of the Second World War. He could only watch helplessly and hope for the best for his country. He enjoyed his time with Salem: he was a true friend. He was from an ordinary background, yet Ali could discuss his dreams for the future with him. Salem, raised on the north-east coast and used to a hard life, didn't wish for riches and treated Ali like a brother. He was happy to help and advise him at any time.

Around midnight, the two men heard a commotion coming from the floor below. The two friends got up immediately, thinking that some kind of intrusion had taken place. They made for the staircase to the first floor, summoning guards and bearers to the main majlis, from where the noise appeared to be coming. The group burst in, ready to face a hostile situation, but all they found was their father, beaming broadly, along with his second son Hamad and two other men, one of whom they knew.

'Is everything all right, Father?'

'Oh yes, my son, couldn't be better.'

The Emir, with his long grey beard, had been grave and concerned throughout the war. This was the first time Ali had seen him laugh in years. He sat on the floor, at the centre of this small group.

'Your father is happy because we have brought him great news.'

It was Saleh bin Suleiman Al Mana, the old merchant who lived in the second-largest house in town. His company was responsible for practically all dealings with the outside world. The third man in the group was unknown to Ali. Tall, dressed in wing collar and tie even at the height of summer, he looked distinguished.

'Gentlemen,' the stranger began, standing, 'may I introduce myself? Charles Prior, His Majesty's representative and humble guest of His Highness.'

'Ahlan wa sahlan.' *Welcome.* Ali gestured to the honourable gentleman to be seated. 'It is a great pleasure.'

Somehow the sheikh summoned the diplomatic language to deal with such a situation, even though he was unused to dealing such visitors of high rank. The ageing Emir chuckled as he explained that now, with the war over, the oil wells that had been discovered before the war would be able to start production. Through the offices of Mr Prior and Saleh Al Mana, the riches that lay beneath the sands of Qatar would be released. The future looked full of promise. Sheikh Abdullah raised his eyes towards the ceiling. 'Al hamdillallah.' *Thanks be to God.*

After years of hardship and struggle, it seemed that Qatar was about to enjoy prosperity at last. The Emir, who was in serious debt, was visibly relieved. Charles Prior began to take his leave, wishing Sheikh Abdullah every happiness for a prosperous future. He had already been given a set of rooms at the front of the building. Al Mana accompanied him out of the chamber. Outside in the corridor, they were able to talk more freely.

'I think that went rather well, don't you, Mr Al Mana?'

'Certainly, sir. We shall make ourselves available for every contingency.'

'Very good. I'll get on to IPC straight away. Whitehall will be over the moon. Of course, Churchill's not there anymore, poor old chap. He wanted to get the oil flowing again from Saudi and Iraq, and here we are in little Qatar turning on the taps again. All good for you chaps, though, and by Jove we need the black stuff more than ever. You get it sorted out this end, Saleh, dear boy, and we'll look after you.'

From that moment, the Iraq Petroleum Company, based in Basra, began to send men and equipment back to the oil fields of Dukhan through the offices of Mr Al Mana. The Emir would never have to worry about money again.

Outside, Ahmed walked home up the hill, noticing that lamps were still burning in the rooms of the Emir's palace, even though it was well after midnight. He wondered if Uncle Salem was up there. He missed him. His evening had raised his spirits to such an extent that he almost felt reborn; a renaissance had happened within his soul. He would never run for joy or leap into the air with excitement, that was out of character, but his face showed a quiet satisfaction, a deep, contented pleasure, as if at last he understood what life was all about.

Ahmed took the outer staircase two steps at a time. What had been his prison fortress was now a vantage point from which to plan, to dream, to scheme. His young mind had become fertilised with seeds of determination and ambition. He grabbed the balustrade and stood there, emboldened, strong, yet petrified at the possibilities that lay ahead. In the early hours of the summer night, ideas were coming to him. Growing inside him was a clear vision of what he would do with his life.

'I've been alone,' he whispered, 'but I won't be alone any more. I've been unhappy, unloved and unsure. Now I will be happy, I will find love, and my future will be happy and fulfilled.'

The vast inky-black sky helped him to achieve a transcendental state. The tense muscles in his face relaxed. His skin felt fresh and clean. His eyes were wide open and alert. He knew that everything made sense. He realised that his past, present and future were all connected. Somehow, while sitting on the deck of the old dhow in the harbour, life had come together. Without intending to, the men had bestowed upon Ahmed a sense of duty and pride. To enjoy life, no matter how hard the situation, to look after other people – family and friends, comrades, brothers-in-arms.

The lofty ideals which had pervaded him remained for several minutes. Once Ahmed was sure he would keep them lodged in his head, he lowered his gaze from the stars to the horizon, where the sun was rising. Although a half-moon still lingered, the silvery early morning was beginning to make its presence felt. He could make out the collection of small boats at the water's edge and the ruler's fort.

'Allah hu Akbar, Allah hu Akbar.'

The silence of the night was broken by the muezzin's call to prayer. He had seen the white-bearded old man ascend the well-worn steps to the minaret next door to Bait Al Bahr a thousand times. He had to admit, though, that this was the first time he had witnessed the dawn prayer. The muezzin's chant enhanced the images forming in Ahmed's head.

I am at ease. But there is much to be done. The words he mouthed were heard by no one. That didn't matter. All that mattered was that he heard them.

What a beautiful day, he thought. How glorious the sunrise. How wonderful the progress of the planet Earth around the sun. For the first time, Ahmed truly appreciated nature. As he turned away towards the staircase, he made yet another discovery. *I've been looking down from high all these years. Wrapped in my own self-pity, I haven't bothered about anyone else.*

He knew he needed to stop thinking of himself and to share his life with others. No more would he look down from above, remote and detached. He would create a new life at ground level and take his place in society.

'I'll get a job,' he said, setting off down the stairs.

Ahmed didn't go to sleep. He didn't even think about it. On the first floor he took a turn around the corridor that looked over the inner courtyard, passing reception rooms and bedrooms which remained empty, as they had been for many months. He let his hand slide along the wooden ledge at the top of the veranda wall. He noticed the plasterwork was peeling and the decorations fading. Rather than feeling gloomy at being alone in such a large building, he felt that he was in charge of a beautiful house, and he wanted to maintain its character as the builder had intended.

He had always regarded the house as a soulless place. His character had been moulded by introspection and sorrow here, the enclosed courtyard shielding him from the world. His physical needs had been met when he grew up: he had had enough food and clothing, a bed on which to rest and a roof over his young head. His emotional development, however, had not been given a thought, either by his distant father or by anyone else in his family. He had come to know every square metre of wall – each intricate carving, chiselled with the care and attention of only the most dedicated of craftsmen. The pillars, positioned at various intervals around the courtyard, were objects to hide behind in the darkness.

As he stood on the upper floor, halfway along the walkway, he raised his hand to the gypsum carving and touched the intricate pattern fondly, feeling the raised circles and lines that made up the complicated pattern. He closed his eyes, caressing the wood as if he were a blind man. All he could think of was the work and love that had been put into making such a thing of beauty. Opening his eyes, he looked up at the ornate ceiling. Each piece of wood was delicately arranged, bound with twine and set into the reed matting above. He wondered at the effort required to attain such uniformity, the craftsmanship needed to achieve complete harmony. The cornice was the most magical part. He hadn't realised that there were curlicues interspersed with tiny rosebuds, all painted in the finest detail; the embellishments were fading but still retained their charm.

Ahmed walked along the south side, gently touching each pillar as he passed, marvelling at every surface, noting the cracks and abrasions that had appeared over time, resolving to make them good. Finally, where the southern and eastern corridors met he leant against the massive supporting pillar and looked down at the square below. It was the hub and heart of the mansion. Looking down, he took in the various doors, the corner majlis for – rare – visitors, and the tiny staircase up to the mezzanine room where his father occasionally ate and slept. However, the space was dominated by a single date palm. He was fond of the palm. He had grown up alongside the tree, both surviving alone in their own way. Like the boy, the palm had been ignored. The only person who looked after it had been Um Jabor, who had watered it. Now Ahmed had matured along with the statuesque palm. Looking across the courtyard, he saw he was level with the tops of its grey-green spiky leaves. Ahmed promised that he would always look after the tree. He realised that the architect had added the date palm to add grace and elegance to the home, but also to provide much-needed shade. As the sun began to make its presence felt, he saw that the shadows the tree cast were long and wide. He loved the patterns they created. Staring down at the shady spot, he imagined a world full of joy. He imagined singing and dancing with cheerful conversation around the palm tree, giving them both the love and affection they craved.

In his reverie he had neither slept nor eaten. Ahmed suddenly realised he was very hungry. He poked his head into the north-west kitchen area, a part of the house about which he knew very little. The narrow wooden door creaked open and he saw a room containing trays and cooking pots. At the far end he noticed another smaller door, which he unlatched. Here was a vast walk-in larder where he discovered a half-filled sack of rice below a shelf that held jars of coffee and cardamom and a large brass pestle and mortar. On the shelves at the back of the dimly lit room were a collection of onions and dried lemons and some other dried herbs. It all looked very unappetising. Then at last his eyes fell upon a row of wooden boxes containing wrinkled dates. He was about to pick a couple when he heard the outer door creak open. Immediately he put the dates back, feeling guilty that he was trespassing. He crept to the kitchen door, which opened suddenly, revealing a small, bent figure clad in black from top to toe. Um Jabor put her hands to her mouth in shock.

'Staffar Allah al Awzeem!' she cried, asking the Lord to protect her at this moment of surprise. 'Oh, ya Ahmed, you nearly killed me. What are you doing here?'

'I'm so sorry, Um Jabor. Please forgive me. I was up early and came down here. Please sit down. I'm so sorry to have upset you,' he said. He ushered her into the courtyard and sat her down in the shade of the palm tree. 'There we are. That's better. Would you like water, Um Jabor?'

'La, la, la. Mafee mushkala.' *No problem, I'm OK now.* She looked a little better and had shed her black abaya to show her summer cotton day dress. Finally, having composed herself, she asked, 'Now, young man, what are you up to?' She gave Ahmed a knowing look. Her voice was loving; she had known Ahmed since birth. Ahmed felt nothing but affection for this kindly woman who, up to now, he had seen merely as a provider of meals. He explained as best he could the emotions and experiences of the night. All Um Jabor could do was nod in agreement or offer a smile, not understanding some of his more philosophical thoughts. He finished by saying, 'No matter what, Um Jabor, I will always look after you.'

She wiped a tear from her eye with the sleeve of the flowery dress, smiling happily.

'Um Jabor,' Ahmed said in an authoritative voice she hadn't heard before, 'I am starving.'

She stood up straight away. 'Ya Allah. I've never heard you say that before, Ahmed. There's nothing in the house. I was going to get some things. You're never usually awake until later and you're hardly ever hungry. Come.' She pulled Ahmed up from the bench, grabbed her black abaya and made for the outer entrance, holding Ahmed's hand.

'What are you doing? Where are we going?' Ahmed asked, surprised.

'We, my dear, are going home. My home. That's where we'll feed you.'

Um Jabor took charge. She almost pushed Ahmed out of the compound, stepping through the postern gate behind him and closing the old wooden door with a loud thud. Nobody bothered with keys. No visitor would dare venture inside any home without being invited to. Once outside she took him by the arm and headed away from the central souk and the sea, turning right, past the baker, past carpenters and ironmongers, tailors and suppliers of cloth, spice merchants and dealers in grain.

At the corner was her favourite shop. Um Jabor signalled to Ahmed to turn off down a narrow alley. He lingered for a moment, his eyes drawn to the tall sacks of spices on display: sticks of dark cinnamon bark, bright yellow turmeric, pale-green cardamom and cumin, hot pepper imported from Kerala, some brown but some brilliant reds and oranges. And the smell. Ahmed revelled in the assault on his senses, taking in the heady mixture with pleasure.

Um Jabor led Ahmed along a narrow sikka, one of hundreds throughout Doha. It was mid-morning and already hot. Here, away from the main road, it was cooler and darker, the harsh rays of the sun unable to enter. Underfoot was hard-packed mud. To the sides were similar mud-built walls with fissures where the dry adobe had moved and slipped over time. He followed Um Jabor, who was going at quite a pace, obviously familiar with the alley. Every now and then a person passed with a 'Salam aleikum'. More often than not, Um Jabor greeted him or her by name.

Occasionally a door would be ajar, allowing Ahmed a glance at life behind the walls. He didn't like to linger long, feeling it to be rude, but he did catch glimpses of washing on the line, mothers combing their daughters' hair and grandmothers gathered around vast trays sorting rice grains, and he heard snatches of chatter. At one point they had to dodge a pair of young boys chasing a ball. Um Jabor gave a shout of admonition.

'Ya owlad! Shbalak?' *You boys – what's wrong with you?* But she turned around to Ahmed, laughing, saying boys will be boys, when they shouted back, 'Asafeen, ya Um Jabor,' *We're sorry*, and she told Ahmed that they were actually good boys.

Now the maze that made up Fareej Al Ghanem got more complicated. Um Jabor indicated to the left between two corner houses. 'That's my mother-in-law's house,' she said. A little further along, a small crowd had gathered. Ahmed could see they all carried earthenware pots, large and small. They were mostly women, all in working clothes, laughing and joking as they set about their task. They were at the water pump. It took some effort for them to pump the water up to the surface, and they all helped each other to fill their jars and ewers. Ahmed got the feeling that this was the nerve centre of the fareej: the water pump was at the junction of four alleys.

It was Ahmed's turn to wait for Um Jabor to greet the women. After a chat, she returned to Ahmed. Some of the women giggled at the sight of a young handsome man in their midst. Avoiding direct eye contact with Ahmed, the ladies shielded themselves with their abayas, but one or two couldn't help sneaking a glance at the stranger, jokingly telling Um Jabor to take good care of him.

From the crossroads their path meandered deeper into the warren of little homes. The walls weren't so high here, and Ahmed could see more clearly what was going on inside the compounds. This part of Doha was lighter than the earlier dark alleyways: even though the land was desert, there were often shrubs and trees to break the beige monotony. It grew quieter, the sounds of commerce and voices fading, so that bird song could be heard.

Ahead there was a commotion. Several children, no more than five or six years old, had run up to Um Jabor shouting her name and tagging at her dress. She fussed over them, scolding them for being noisy but hugging them warmly too. One little girl in particular held on tightly.

'Bint binti – my grand-daughter,' she said, turning to Ahmed with a look of pride and fondness. 'My first. Isn't she beautiful?'

'She is, certainly,' Ahmed replied, unsure how to deal with the situation, and unused to small children. He hadn't even thought about Um Jabor having any family, children or grandchildren. She was just there.

In a few minutes they came to a clearing. To the left was a tiny mosque, the smallest Ahmed had ever seen. It was mud-built but had been painted pure white. The minaret was no more than twice his height, with only a few steps up to it. Ahmed loved the sight of it, and the little eucalyptus tree to the side whose leaves dangled over the low wall into the prayer area. Along the wall, next to the tree, were two wooden benches painted light blue. Sitting there contentedly, two older men were engaged in conversation, their legs haunched up and their fingers busy with prayer beads.

'Aish haalek, ya shabab?' Um Jabor asked the men how they were, addressing them as 'youth', which pleased them no end.

'Ahlein ya, Um Jabor. Allah teek al Afia,' one replied. *May God prolong your life.*

'My cousins,' she told Ahmed. 'Taking life easy, as you can see.'

Ahmed gave a chuckle. Um Jabor beckoned him across the patch of land to a low mud wall in the centre of which was a small wooden door. It stood ajar. As she showed him in, a squawking chicken made its way out of the entrance. Ahmed had never seen anything like it. The space was taken up by a yard containing more chickens, a pair of goats and, near the outer wall, a circular structure which on closer inspection turned out to be a pigeon house. Um Jabor followed, her grand-daughter in tow, demanding to be played with. Next to the goats was a makeshift kitchen: a series of pots and pans propped against the brick wall, a yard brush made from twigs, and an old carpet rolled up in the corner. The yard made up the main part of the property; the only rooms were along one side, facing Ahmed. On the right were two high beds, shaded by a well-established tree. Although it was tiny compared to where he lived, Ahmed immediately felt at ease, sensing love and warm-heartedness there. At once Um Jabor made her guest feel at ease: she asked him to unroll the carpet, placing it near the beds under the tree. She popped indoors to get a couple of cushions, which she put on the carpet.

'There you are, young man. Take your rest. Welcome to our humble home.'

'Shukran, ya Um Jabor, shukran,' was all he could say as he knelt.

It was like a secret world. He had forgotten all about his hunger, but Um Jabor began to bustle about with pots and pans.

'Breakfast in ten minutes, Ahmed. Lulua, bring me eggs, there's a good girl.'

Um Jabor's grandchild dutifully went over to the henhouse in the far corner near the goats, where she skilfully opened the cage and managed to find three eggs. She put them in a handwoven basket that her grandmother had given her and took them to show Ahmed. He gave the little girl a pat on the head, feeling honoured to be accepted by the youngest member of the family in such a way. Lulua scurried off, leaving Ahmed to lie back and contemplate his surroundings. Even though it was late morning, it was cool under the tree and there was a gentle breeze that made the branches of the old tree sway slightly. As well as the noises made by the chickens, pigeons and goats, he heard a tinkling above his head. There, dangling from the branches, were a series of metal pieces glistening in the sunlight. They had been suspended at different heights and occasionally hit each other, making the fairy-like sound as though a magic spell was being cast.

There were more elements that gave this humble home even more character. Ahmed noticed that the open-air beds next to him had intricate carvings on the legs and back. He smoothed his hand over the woodwork. Along the wall above the rooms was an exquisite frieze in a geometric design, enhanced with flowers of varying colours forming a repeated pattern in perfect harmony with the pale cream of the wall. Then something caught Ahmed's eye. Looking down, he noticed that the actual flowers painted on the frieze were there in front of him. In a neat row were the tiniest desert plants, pale purple and yellow. They had been planted in a row on either side of a short path and a pair of steps that led up to the doors to what Ahmed presumed was the only covered living area of the house. It was apparent that the family spent most their time outdoors, due to the lack of space inside and the intense heat of the summer. Over the two beds and attached to the outer wall was a simply constructed barasti made of bamboo strips. This provided a flimsy roof, and much-needed shade during the day, although at this time of day the shade didn't cover the yard. The tinkling tree shaded the rest. Ahmed enjoyed the way the pattern of fine lines fell on the beautifully carved furniture and the white cotton bedspreads. Then a place was cleared on the carpet and Um Jabor laid a platter of eggs mixed with tomatoes, chillies and onions, known as shakshuka, in front of him. Lulua carried two large round flatbreads.

'Tfadal y'azizi,' Um Jabor said, using 'my dear' affectionately: a first for Ahmed. Mother and grand-daughter withdrew, leaving their guest to tuck in.

Ahmed was used to Um Jabor's cooking, of course, but this meal tasted different, somehow. Perhaps it was the homely setting. Tearing off pieces of the freshly baked bread, he scooped up the egg mixture, savouring every mouthful gratefully. He finished the last mouthful, then Um Jabor appeared.

'You must be tired. I'm going out with Lulua to join my daughter at our neighbour's. You can sleep on the bed if you like.'

'Oh no, I couldn't,' was his immediate reaction. But Um Jabor insisted. She told him he was welcome, and it was comfortable on the bed under the barasti. So that's what he did. The house and yard were empty except for the chickens, pigeons and goats. He lay down on one of the beds. Within seconds, he had drifted off into a deep sleep. There was nobody to see the contented smile on his face as he rested.

_ᴛ−ᴛ−

Al Asr, the afternoon call to prayer, woke Ahmed. For a moment he wondered where he was, feeling briefly as though he had trespassed into a private world. He took a few moments to adjust, then decided that he loved being there. The afternoon light was less hostile, the shadows longer, less defined. He got up, stretched, deciding to look out of the entrance into the little square. Prayer-goers were emerging from the tiny mosque, lingering to chat, unlike the central Doha mosque where everyone was in a hurry. As soon as he appeared, Lulua ran up to him and tugged at his thobe. She held out her hand. In it were several little berries known as canar. The berries were delicious. Ahmed took them, showing his thanks by bending down and giving the young child a kiss on the forehead. 'Where's your grandmother?' he asked. Lulua pointed towards the bench outside the mosque. He closed the door and made his way over to the bench. There was Um Jabor along with a young woman, a young man and an older man.

'Ah, the sleepy one,' Um Jabor joked, laughter in her voice. The others laughed too. For a moment Ahmed felt himself redden with embarrassment, but Um Jabor came to his aid by introducing those around her.

'My husband, Abu Jabor.'

Ahmed shook hands with the wiry elderly man on the bench. His hands had the texture of old leather, but his grip was strong, matching the character in his lined face. He gave Ahmed a warm smile in greeting, his eyes kind and gentle.

'Our son, Jabor.'

Jabor was lean but athletic-looking, in his mid-twenties, Ahmed reckoned. His handshake was firm. His warm smile made Ahmed realise that this was a family full of love and happiness.

'And our daughter, mother of Lulua. This is Amina.'

There was no handshake this time but a mutual acknowledgement. Ahmed looked at the young woman. Her features were almost identical to her brother's: warm, dark eyes, a long aquiline nose and full lips with that now familiar smile. He found a gentle kindness in her face, thinking how she had taken on the character of her mother. This was reinforced when Amina bent down to draw her young daughter towards her like a mother hen guarding her chick.

After the introductions had been made, there was a pause. No one knew quite what to say, preferring instead to look down at little Lulua who was safely attached to her mother's side, sucking her thumb until it was gently removed by Amina. Lulua wriggled in apparent shyness as she was the focus of attention.

'Yallah,' Um Jabor declared. 'This won't do, standing around. Let's go back.' The family walked across the square, bidding their neighbours '*Fi Amin Allah*' on the way. While most of the menfolk were away working, the women and children stayed around the house, doing housework, cooking, enjoying each other's company. In this neighbourhood, doors were always open, and a problem shared was a problem halved. All were brothers and sisters living in harmony. Ahmed had never seen anything like it.

Back at the house Um Jabor made tea. The women withdrew for a while and the men sat down under the *barasti*, which had cast a shadow over the entire carpet, so they could relax in comfort against the plump cushions. They chatted about the weather, as it had been unseasonably warm of late, even by Doha's standards, then moved on to the cost of living and how difficult it was to make ends meet. Abu Jabor talked of his life as a carpenter, saying that work was now harder to find, especially as he was ageing and unable to move so well. Young Jabor chipped in from time to time, explaining that as his father was getting on it was his turn to provide the income and he had learned a lot from his father about carpentry and wood-carving. Then it suddenly dawned on Ahmed.

'Those beds. Are they your work, Abu Jabor?' he asked, turning to the old man.

'Oh yes. They certainly are. That was some time ago,' Abu Jabor reflected, looking wistful.

'My father is a master craftsman,' Jabor interjected, sitting upright, obviously proud of his father's accomplishments. 'He has taught me so many things. I just hope I can follow him as a craftsman too. I try my best.'

'That's wonderful,' Ahmed said. 'Passing a skill from father to son like you are doing is such a good thing. I wish you both well.'

They continued to talk, and shortly Um Jabor and Amina joined them, carrying a tray of tea things. The women arranged the metal pot and small glasses on the ground.

Ahmed felt a growing confidence. He knew he was among the kindest and nicest of people. Now that Um Jabor was no longer a servant but matriarch of her own family home, he felt bold enough to make a comment.

'I was admiring the work done by your husband, Um Jabor. The carvings on the beds are magnificent.'

'They certainly are, my dear, and do you know what?'

'Tell me.'

'Do you recognise the way the carving has been made? The particular pattern and style? Does it remind you of anything?'

After a few moments Ahmed suddenly proclaimed, 'Of course, of course. The carvings at home, in the Bait Al Bahr. They are the same.' His eyes lit up in wonder. Abu Jabor gave a huge smile.

'And another thing,' Um Jabor said. 'You tell him, Amina, dear.'

'My mother painted all the designs on the walls of Bait Al Bahr. Mother and Father worked as a team: Father the carpenter, Mother the painter and decorator.'

Ahmed couldn't believe his ears. He was speechless, and a wave of emotion came over him. As Um Jabor poured the tea, he couldn't help feeling shame at his attitude to her over the years.

'Now Amina is the artist,' Um Jabor said, 'and this is her work.' She pointed to the frieze along the front of the house and the intricate designs all around the yard. They were beautifully drawn and painted, the design and colours similar to those in the mansion house, but less formal. He felt that Amina had captured the spirit of the house.

Um Jabor poured the tea and they all savoured the special mix. It was a secret recipe, Um Jabor joked. After a while, Ahmed felt it was time to take his leave, but he was reluctant to go. Amina and Jabor told him he was welcome any time. He stood up and said to them, 'You look so alike.'

In unison they answered, 'Because we're twins!'

The whole family fell about laughing.

4

Cairo, 1946

Lord Killearn was in the mood to celebrate. His Britannic Majesty's Ambassador to Egypt and Sudan recalled the day, eleven years earlier, he had married his second wife, Jacqueline. He had been overjoyed at finding this vivacious woman, thirty years his junior, after the misery of losing his first wife to meningitis.

Until 1943, when he was elevated to the peerage, he had been Sir Miles Lampson, a diplomat who had arranged deals and negotiations throughout the early part of the war. The new Lady Lampson had become his co-host at the grand white stucco residence on the banks of the Nile where Britannia had once ruled the land of the pharaohs. While war raged around them, the glamorous duo had hosted Winston Churchill, even giving up their beloved bedroom to him. Cairo had become the fulcrum of battle as Hitler's lust for domination in Europe and the Middle East grew. The house by the Nile was the nerve centre of operations to counter any threat to British interests in the Middle East, notably the most important conduit between east and west, the Suez Canal.

As he strolled down the manicured lawn towards the water, he thought about those momentous days. At El Alamein, Rommel had been defeated, and in Palestine the British army had been able to maintain their presence. For now, at least, he thought, the king could be happy that he had done his duty to crown and country. This was the first chance he had had to wander alone in the vast grounds. He halted and looked out across the vast river, where the feluccas plied their trade as they had done since the Pyramids were built. At last peace reigned. And it felt very good indeed.

The couple had partied their way through the war years, using the mansion on the Nile as a gathering place for the great and good. Tonight's party had been planned for some time as a happy conclusion to hostilities and the coincidental occasion of their anniversary. Lord Lampson had reached the peak of his career having successfully steered war away from Cairo, so he thought anyway, as it was under his roof that Churchill had stayed while Rommell was doing his best to penetrate the eastern end of North Africa. Lampson could only thank God that Monty had got rid of him.

Miles Lampson treasured these private moments by the Nile. As the king's representative he had been only too aware of his crucial position in the political manoeuvres that had taken place for most of the time he had been in what most considered the capital of the Middle East. As he looked fondly at the feluccas floating gently by he couldn't help but wonder what these four years of turmoil had been all about. He homed in on the noble-faced Nubian, dressed in a sky-blue galabeya, who calmly held control at the tiller, in command of his vessel and seemingly his life. The magnificent triangle of white sail, perfectly aligned with the breeze, to create the maximum amount of power using the minimum amount of effort was a timeless sight. The newly created earl couldn't help but wonder how this simple life, unchanged since the days of the mighty Pharaohs, was the answer to all life's problems. Why do we seek to dominate? To rule and conquer? Why do we lust after power and possessions? Here on the banks of this mighty river, life suddenly stood still. Somehow the grandiose existence to which Sir Miles Lambton and now Lord Killearn had become attuned seemed pointless. The felucca captain was a silhouette against a late afternoon sun but Miles noticed that his bearing was unchanged; sturdy and strong, on course to a destination of his own making. This handsome Nubian had entered into the spirit of the noble Lord creating a symbiosis which he found both heartening yet disturbing. He almost felt like kneeling down to confess his colonial sins on behalf of the power which he represented. The silence and beauty of the scenery was to haunt him now and always. For a moment he wondered if he could have cast off his tailored pin-stripe suit there and then, to immerse himself in the waters of the Nile and the magical feeling of being free, unfettered and at one with the universe.

His reverie was interrupted by distant calls of 'Miles, Miles, what are you doing? What on earth? My dear..... you really must ....how can I?.........there really is an awful lot to do.......'

It was the co-celebrant of the occasion, Jacqueline, bounding across the lawn, awkwardly in stilettos. Sir Miles, as he then was, had been captivated by her joie de vivre and as his escort throughout his service in Cairo she had been both a dutiful wife and a supreme hostess, in charge of the numerous balls and receptions that had to be organised. All in all he couldn't have wished for a better partner. It was therefore quite easy to adjust from his mood of contemplation to one of caring husband.

'My darling, I'm so sorry. I was just having a little wander.'

'I can see that,' Jacqueline said with a critical tone. She was easily charmed though by her tall, well-respected husband and she reached up to give him a peck on the cheek which was reciprocated with a warm embrace.

'They'll all be here in an hour darling and you're not even dressed'

'My dear. I've done so many of these I can bathe, don a dinner a jacket in ten minutes and tie a bow tie blindfold!'

They laughed, easy in each other's company, the large, lanky personage of the Lord in sharp contrast to the little brittle-boned lady as they walked back up the slope towards the mansion, past the tables and paraphernalia which had been set up for the festivities by a phalanx of servants, running to and fro, bearing platters piled high with exotic-looking fruits and delicacies, sweetmeats of basboosa and khanafeya. Two tall black Nubians, clad in baggy silk pantaloons and maroon-coloured waistcoats, came down bearing an enormous domed chafing dish, under which a roasted goat was hiding. Teams of lesser vassals emerged wish similar dishes of pigeon and the rare 'farakh al Fayoumi'; the most famous chicken from the Fayoum oasis, whose flavour was considered by the Egyptians to be the best in the world.

The vast swathe of greensward that took up the expanse between the Nile and the residence had now been covered by a multitude of embassy staff and hired hands who were engaged in putting down giant multi-coloured rugs, placing brass lanterns around the grounds, various urns and plant pots, freshly cut flowers in waist-high vases, strings of light bulbs shakily hung on spindly poles along the length of the pathway that wove its way through this chaotic set-up. Now the sun had suddenly set the bulbs nervously twitched into action, their dim light not yet making their full effect felt. A chief 'mohendis' barked orders at the panicky electricians to get the power supply secured through a system of bare wires and suspicious looking flimsy cables. All down one side of the carpet covered lawn a specially constructed bar had been procured for the occasion, the trestles now being covered in starched white Egyptian linen, folded and tacked into place by the housekeeper's under maids as the major - domo commanded that champagne glasses should be in this place and whisky glasses in that, that ice should be brought from the leaded cold stores in the cellar every half an hour to make sure the bar staff were able to replenish cold drinks in an instant. Wines of Grand Cru, spirits specially shipped in from London were laid out along with silver and crystal soda syphons, quinine tonic water bottles and a vast array of sherries, vermouths and liqueurs allowing the five selected bar tenders to use their expertise to create the perfect cocktail for even the most discerning guest.

On the facing to the long bar a further team of young men and boys were arranging an octagonal wooden platform along with a score of gilt backed chairs placed in a semi-circle on the dais where music stands were being erected and adjusted. A jolly-looking group of men arrived to take up their positions on the stage. Dressed in white tie and tails they carried their instruments and music sheets carefully to their allotted positions, the maestro laughing and joking with the principal members of the band. The violins and cellos squeaked and scraped into life and the percussion rattled into action, their players seemingly all ready to strum and tap their way through the pre-planned programme of music both Oriental and Occidental.

The stage was almost set for a night that wouldn't have looked out of place in the new glitzy world of Hollywood.

As the couple made their way up to the veranda and French windows the scurrying servants briefly stopped to bow and raise their hands in salutation. This was acknowledged by the earl, briefly being reminded of the thoughts he had had at the river's edge only moments before. as he escorted his wife into the drawing room he turned around to survey the scene, Jacqueline naturally doing the same, her arm entwined in his, both unsure of who was supporting who. Beyond the hive of activity, they glimpsed for one last moment the black Nile against the crepuscular sky and Miles, drawing Jacqueline closer to him, knew this was to be the end of an era.

At precisely seven o'clock the front doors of the embassy swung open and the first carriages and cars swept up the drive to drop their passengers under the wide stuccoed portico, the white-gloved servant offering a hand to the elaborately-dressed ladies who stepped indoors, along with their husbands, spick and span in their very best. Concurrently the earl and his lady wife scurried down the grand staircase just in time to greet the first guests who had begun to form an orderly queue, all having made the effort to be frightfully British and be bang on time. Miles had transformed himself from the casually attired gentleman of the estate into the dinner-jacketed imposing doyen of the diplomatic corps in a matter of moments using his expertise having had to perform such a task on many similar important occasions, albeit with the assistance of his faithful manservant, Fakhredin, who had laid all the evening's clothes out well in advance, starched and pressed to the nth degree. Equally in her neighbouring dressing room Jacqueline's maid, Sousan, had spent all afternoon making sure Her Ladyship's sparkling evening gown was in peak condition, taken out of its tissue wrapping and hung on a mannequin so that every crease would be gone by the time she came to wear it. Now as she started shaking hands with the various wives of minor diplomats she eased into her role, smiling with the occasional pleasantry of welcome. The guests, both female and male, noticed how glamorous she looked. The ball gown was of the deepest crimson, the bodice covered in tiny marquises and rubies that looked real but were in fact paste. The off-the-shoulder design had been created by her favourite Paris couturier, the up and coming Christian Dior, whom the couple had met on a recent visit to the French couple. The figure-hugging bodice dazzled under the reception hall's magnificent crystal chandeliers and even the jewels on the full-length skirt shone like the gown of a film star. She had asked the that the dress would be as full as possible creating maximum effect when she was in full flow on the dance floor, the thing the lady loved the most. The pair of hosts, standing side by side, looked both the picture of elegance as well as authority; a manifest reminder that despite all the turmoil and talk of Arab power gaining strength that Britannia still ruled the waves. Jacqueline was happy to be swept along a tide of blind devotion to her cause, her husband was now not so sure for how long the colonial charade could continue. For now, though, for this last night at least, he was happy to celebrate the end of the war and the couple's happy marriage. Their decade together a year earlier had hardly been noted at all at the height of war but now they could rejoice with the host of dignitaries from far and wide who had come to join them for what Miles considered one last hurrah.

The punctual early arrivals were mostly third secretaries and wives from various other diplomatic missions along with all the devoted consular officials from the ambassador's bureau whose duty it was to appear well ahead of time in order to carry out their function as entertainers, at ease with small talk and handling the flow of any function, schooled in standard non-committal Whitehall jargon. As the junior officials stepped up to shake hands with their master they stiffened one by one having been minded earlier in an internal memo that all should aware that tonight's occasion should have a feeling of celebration and optimism for the future. 'Conversation should not dwell on the grim days of war but rather the exciting times ahead as Britain plays her important part role in world affairs.' Some of the staff had met together to decide what this actually meant. It was no secret that the government mandarins had serious doubts about the state of the Middle East and the consequences of any further loss of sovereignty by the United Kingdom. The Levant was being carved up largely due to the increasing influx of Jews making their homes there after the terrors of the Holocaust thus causing further upheaval in British-ruled Palestine. Although Britain was best friends with the Arab states, it had every sympathy with the aspirations of the Jews and their desire to create their own state namely Israel. The earl had been reminded of this by his dinner conversation with the outgoing Prime Minister Winston Churchill and also by the new Labour Prime Minister Clement Attlee who had asked his Foreign Minister Ernest Bevin 'to deal with it with our friends in Cairo.' What had been made patently clear throughout all the political machinations was that there was huge concern in London about the future of oil, upon which the world depended and that we couldn't live without it. The war had used up any national reserves and now that the Americans had rightly been praised for their dominant role in its outcome they felt that their presence in the Middle East was justified. None could argue with that. Nearer to home, despite the allies' victory, the ambassador now felt that he was surrounded by chaos; Jerusalem was being fought over, Palestine was under threat, and North African colonies of France and Italy were undergoing change. But it was the vast swathes of Felix Arabia that caused the greatest anguish for it was there, the Trucial states and the lands of Al Saud that held the vast untapped reserves of the future's wealth. Left in the wrong hands who knows what would happen? On top of all this the diplomats knew that whatever oil was extracted from the Orient it would have to pass through that narrow stretch of Egyptian territory made by Ferdinand de Lesseps almost a century earlier - the Suez Canal. It was to be an interesting night.

The reception was now well under way and the guests established in small groups dotted around the moonlit grounds. Most had been here before but never tired of the magnificent setting and tonight even the regulars felt that there was a special atmosphere as the band played a selection of old Cairene favourite tunes that they often performed accompanying the now famous singer Um Katlthoum interspersed with a stab at the latest Western hits by Glenn Miller and Benny Goodman. These were appreciated by the growing crowd as they were served their Martinis and Gin Fizzes.

Miles and Jacqueline were still on duty at the entrance, greeting and now often kissing and embracing as the guests became more important in status and friendship. They were both happy to welcome their old friend Freya Stark who had just arrived from Damascus. Freya had spent many happy days as a guest of the Lampsons and, with her expert knowledge of Arabia, had been occupied during the war years working for the Ministry of Information in helping to create the Ikhwan al Hurriya, the British propaganda network whose objective was to gain Arab support for the allies. just behind her was the novelist Evelyn Waugh who had served in the army during the war and now renewed his love of travel while working on his last book, Brideshead Revisited. The Lampsons had put him up on several occasions while he was involved in secret work in Libya and Crete. The ambassador immediately recalled what a poor shot Waugh had been on one of their duck-shooting parties in the desert at A Fayoum reminding him the Jacqueline had been much better than he.

Miles was pleased to see more familiar faces. Charles Belgrave who had come overland from Bahrain along with Harold and Violet Dickson from Kuwait. He wasn't so happy about the arrival of Harry St. John Philby who swept in dressed in full Arab attire, down to gold-threaded 'aqal' on his head and a lethal-looking 'khanjar' or dagger swaying from his midriff. Miles suddenly realised that the old codger had been invited some time ago, rather as a diplomatic gesture towards the Kingdom of Saudi Arabia where Philby had been special advisor to Ibn Saud. Miles had been told by the Foreign Office to keep on even terms with the Middle East veteran as he could be useful in any future diplomacy involving any potential deal involving Palestine and the possible creation of an homeland for the Jews. The earl was used to large gatherings but with pell-mell of guests from all corners of the Orient suddenly descending on his hallowed turf he felt an urgent need to escape. His head was bursting with all the negotiations involving war, the objectives of Britain's role in this fulcrum of world affairs, and the likelihood that any peace in the area looked undecidedly shaky to say the least. The sight of the duplicitous Philly had brought these emotions sharply into focus as he made his way for fresh air out on to the torch-lit lawns and the sanctuary of his beloved Jacqueline.

'Oh there you are darling. We thought you'd never get out here.' She kissed him on the cheek, comfortingly, as she began to introduce her cocktail companion. 'You don't know Mr. Sayyed Mubarak I believe dear?'

'No, I don't believe I have had the pleasure.' Miles shook hands with a tall Egyptian, in pin-stripe suit and fez.

'Mr Sayyed is with judiciary in the provinces, Miles. We have been chatting about the importance of the delta and keeping food production going.'

'Very good. We wish the best for the future of Egypt, Mr Sayyed,' Miles said in his usual diplomatic tone. 'Perhaps you will excuse me, I must move on.'

As he turned to leave a tall Egyptian youth appeared among the trio, looking rather out of place in the atmosphere of older experienced ladies of gentlemen of wealth, reputation and fame.

'Ah. Mubarak. Please excuse me Your Excellencies I took the liberty of bringing my son along. He is a good boy and studying hard. He wants to be in the military you know.'

'Of course. Good choice. Good luck dear boy.' Miles gave young Mubarak a rather sharp pat on the back. He was rewarded with a sneer not a smile, the slight rebuke in the ambassador's touch making him stand awkwardly erect, and giving him a resolve never to be touched by a human like that ever again.

Across the lawn towards the house Miles saw Jacqueline struggling to get to him through the crowd. as she arrived at her husband's side the sounds of swing from the band abruptly came to a halt. Before she had a chance to tell the ambassador none other than the portly shape of King Farouk stood centre stage on the terrace, a retinue of a dozen gathered round. Susurrations from the party-goers gave way to a squeaking sound from the little orchestra as the leader immediately adjusted to the royal situation. Luckily they were used to striking up the national anthem and they managed quite well, albeit not quite in tune causing a few tipsy titters from those who been enjoying the cocktails.

As the anthem played shakily the ambassador straightened himself wondering how on earth he could have overlooked the likelihood of the king making an appearance. He had been invited, of course, as a matter of protocol, but he never thought he would actually come. Nothing had come from Abdine Palace to say so and everyone at the embassy knew that neither Miles or his lady wife cared much for the pompous little monarch in the fez. On the last such occasion when the king danced with Jacqueline at a palace ball he blatantly showed his dislike of Jacqueline by constantly stepping on her toes and tripping her up. This didn't go unnoticed by Sir Miles who quizzed the king about why he chose to be advised by Italians he replied that he would get rid of his Italians when the ambassador got rid of his referring to Jaqueline's Italian father, Sir Aldo Castellani. The subject was never raised again.

As soon as the anthem was over Miles rushed to the foot of the stairs and the king came down escorted by his aides, both Egyptian and Italian, noses held high, as if to sanctify the air surrounding their royal ward. The ambassador bowed, greetings were politely of stiffly exchanged and the band reverted to its old familiar swing, the leader encouraging the guests to resume the party as if nothing had happened. But the mood had changed as heads all turned in the direction of the man whose word was paramount.

Jaqueline thought she better be on her best behaviour so offered the king some champagne, beckoning the waiters to bring whatever His Majesty desired. A confrontation was about to occur between her and the Italian escort when she noticed more fuss going on at the top of the staircase. She gasped in amazement as there standing with one hand on the balustrade, the other brandishing a long shiny cigarette holder was her old friend Noel Coward.

Jaqueline brushed past the king and ran up the stairs gushing with pleasure.

'My dear. How very nice.' Noel spoke but hardly moved, accepting the kiss on the cheek and the hand clutching his arm. They made their way down into the party as the assembled gathering of Cairo society gazed in amazement at the star of the day. It was all the king to do but huddle in a corner with his cronies, taking comfort in the vintage champagne. Even Miles had given up trying to amuse the surprise guest deciding to join Jacqueline, Noel and the notable travellers who had made the effort to be with him not just on this evening but throughout the horrors of the war years. As midnight approached he strolled down to this favourite place at the bank of the Nile and standing at the water's edge he turned round to see the party in full swing with men and women of all nationalities enjoying the warm evening air, dancing, drinking and chatting in their happiness. It was truly magical, he thought, and tried to imprint the scene on his mind so that he would be reminded of it in the later years of retirement when he would be Lord Killearn. Looking across the blackness of the mighty river he could barely make out the twinkly lights of a boat moored on the far side. A small group of fishermen were amusing themselves, contented to chat and sing song under the stars. He loved the simplicity of the sight before him and somehow preferred that this would be the one etched more on his ageing brain. He turned once again to see that the Egyptian guests were making their presence known to the band demanding more Oriental sounds and the king was preparing to leave. In a few minutes the character of the celebrations had changed from the devil-may-care dancing of the A list celebrities to the chanting and hypnotic melodies of Um Kalthoum. The future Lord Killearn escorted the king out of the white-stuccoed portico and wondered if things would ever be the same again.

5

Doha, 1953

'How long have we been married, Amina, my love?'

'Five years. Can't you remember? Thanks very much.'

Amina gave Ahmed a half-hearted punch on the arm. They were in bed in the first-floor corner room of Bait Al Bahr. Ahmed turned towards his wife and looked fondly at her. She had changed his life completely. Smiling, he gave her a hug as if to say thank you for the glorious months they had shared. Although Ahmed and Amina were only in their mid-twenties, they looked like a cosy elderly couple, so at ease were they in each other's company. This was their favourite time of day – when they had time to chat about things or enjoy lying together, listening to the early morning bird song. All was quiet for a while, then the peace was shattered.

'Ya 'Umma, ana burdana.' *I'm cold.* It was Lulua, who was now ten years old.

'Ya habibti, taali'i hunna.' *Come here.*

Lulua ran across the room and jumped on the bed, diving between the two adults to get as warm as possible.

'You're getting a bit big for this, my dear.'

'You love your mother and father, though, don't you?'

'Yes, Baba, of course,' she answered. Lulua and Ahmed had got on well since they met, and had not stopped talking and playing together ever since.

Then the door opened once again. A little shape, a blanket around it, stood there, half asleep, hair standing on end, thumb in mouth.

Ahmed got out of bed and went over to his daughter, Fatima, aged four.

'We are a crowd, aren't we, Tima?' he said laughingly.

Lulua rubbed her mother's stomach.

'Careful, Lulua. Can you hear anything in there?' Ahmed asked her.

'Yes, I think I can.' Fatima bent over and listened to her mother's stomach too.

'Don't tell me it's another girl,' Ahmed said, 'but he or she is due any day.'

'I know,' Amina said. 'It's all your fault.'

Ahmed couldn't help but wonder how all this had happened. How had this charmless room, where he used to be so lonely, been transformed into this happy family home?

Their courtship had been short. They had soon become inseparable. They had so much to say to each other, and wondered why they hadn't met earlier. Ahmed, apart from being instantly attracted to Amina, was interested in her views on life – that the simple life was the best, on art, about which she was passionate, about her life as a single mother following the loss of her husband at sea. Amina was able to relate to Ahmed, and they thought the same way on so many subjects. Ahmed's feelings for Amina were enhanced by the warmth he felt for Um Jabor and Abu Jabor, as well as Lulua. She enjoyed having him around, and constantly asked when he would next visit.

After his first visit, Um Jabor asked him to come round most days, either for lunch or supper or just a cup of tea and a chat. After the long, miserable months of solitude, Ahmed had realised this was the life he wanted and these were the people he wanted to share it with. He found himself excited at the prospect of going out and every day he dressed quickly, eager to start the day. He even did some exercise to shed some of the weight he had gained over the long days of lethargy.

Um Jabor still came early every morning to cook and clean, but more often than not Ahmed would interrupt her work to chat, or even make the tea himself. He asked questions about all kinds of things, but mainly about the subject that was uppermost in his mind – Amina. Um Jabar enjoyed their chats and the new character she saw in Ahmed. When he asked about her daughter, she feigned ignorance to tease him, often shrugging and saying 'Mush arifa' – I don't know – when probed too far, knowing it was driving him crazy.

Instead of slouching, Ahmed held himself erect, his shoulders back; his new confidence made him feel alert and alive. As he strode out of the wooden gates, he found himself smiling at neighbours and exchanging greetings. He realised that, since he had been so withdrawn, nobody had bothered to take much notice of him, but he told himself that to receive a smile he had to give one first.

At the fareej, Ahmed's eyes would light up at the prospect of seeing Amina and maybe Lulua playing outside in the wasteland opposite the house. He had become such a regular visitor that all the children knew him. He was never quite sure whether they liked him because he was a friendly young man or because of the little bags of boiled sweets he sometimes brought them. He thought it was probably the latter.

If Um Jabor wasn't around, Amina would be in charge of domestic affairs. The custom was that the gentlemen of the house, and especially male visitors, were not allowed anywhere near the inner sanctum of the family home, and were never seen anywhere near food and cooking. The common view was that men should sit and enjoy themselves while women rushed around catering for their every whim. Not so in this household. As soon as Ahmed arrived, he walked in, calling out 'Salam aleikum' to anyone in hearing distance. Immediately he would join in with whatever activity was taking place, be it sifting rice or washing parsley. He did draw the line at chopping onions, though, as the tears were too much to handle. Amina let him off this task, telling him with a mocking hauteur that there were some things only a woman could do. This led to a discussion on the strengths and weaknesses of each sex.

And so Ahmed was accepted into the family. It was merely a formality for Abu Jabor to agree to him marrying Amina. Everyone was overjoyed at the news, as Amina had more or less resigned herself to permanent widowhood. Lula could hardly contain her excitement at having a father again.

Their wedding was small. Simple folk called for simple ways, and all that was needed was a visit to the tiny mosque across the way. With a few short prayers, the deed was done. The only extravagance was a small goat which Abu Jabor insisted on providing, even though he couldn't really afford it. They had discussed a dowry, but as it was Amina's second marriage it didn't seem that important. Her parents hoped their daughter would at last find true happiness.

Neighbours came in to enjoy the wedding banquet. Entertainment was provided by the shabab of the fareej, who sang and danced until way past midnight. Lulua hadn't had so much fun for ages. She wore a new bright pink dress made lovingly by her mother. She had bought tiny sequins which had been painstakingly stitched on by Um Jabor every night for a month after Lulua had gone to bed. The surprise had been worth it: Lulua smothered her mother and grandmother in hugs and kisses.

After the guests had gone and Amina's parents had retired to bed, exhausted after all the festivities and the emotion of the day, the young couple stayed in the garden, enjoying each other's company and the warm evening air. Eventually they lay down on the bed on which Ahmed had slept that first summer afternoon. It was a little narrow but this enhanced the closeness they craved to seal their love. Here under the twilight canopy they wrapped each other in warmth and affection, whispering vows of eternal devotion. At last they slept.

In the following days the family gathered to discuss future living arrangements. Over cups of mint tea, they decided it would be more sensible to move to Bait Al Bahr. At least, that was the plan. Um Jabor was the first to concede that a young couple needed privacy and independence. Amina had been to the big house before, although Ahmed hadn't known that. This would be the first time they had gone there as a family. At first Amina found it hard to adjust to living in the imposing residence. Lulua was reluctant to leave her childhood home and the friends she loved, but they managed the transition well enough. Ahmed did everything he could to put Amina at ease, admitting it would be a huge task to change the vast mansion into a warm and happy home. It was a challenge that Ahmed and Amina talked about long into the night when they moved in, Lulua sleeping beside them, afraid of being lonely in a room on her own. One thing that was a comfort was Um Jabor, who considered the house almost her own, having worked there so long.

In time the family settled in, and moved the few possessions they had to the house. Amina eventually felt comfortable enough to make small changes to the house, which helped create a warmer atmosphere. She and Um Jabor found material in the souq to make cushions, and she added colour to the walls, enhancing the decorations Um Jabor had made years before. Lulua was able to make friends near the house and she began to enjoy playing in her own room, next to her parents.

With more people to cook and clean for, Um Jabor found herself getting more tired than she used to; dashing back and forth from the big house to her home became increasingly fatiguing. It was also now impossible for Ahmed to treat her like a servant, of course. Ahmed and Amina agreed they would have to pull together to run the house. It also became clear that it was better for Amina's parents to come and live with them. It was a momentous decision and a big wrench for her parents to leave the home they loved and the neighbours they cherished, but, overall, they thought it sensible.

Day by day the family grew accustomed to their new way of life. Ahmed had assumed his role as head of the household with a certain amount of trepidation. Every now and then he would go up on the roof, alone, to collect his thoughts so he could live his life responsibly and carry out the duties expected of him. The honeymoon months were blissful for the newlyweds, and they were delighted when Amina became pregnant. When little Fatima came into the world, she was immediately cosseted by her mother and grandmother, who had been on hand for Amina's labour. Lulua couldn't believe her luck at having a baby sister. She found 'Fatima' a bit of a mouthful to pronounce, only managing to say 'Tima', which stuck.

'Ya Ahmed, ta'al, Ahmed, ya ibni. Ta'al fil hosh!' Um Jabor shouted for her son-in-law, her voice urgent. Ahmed cast a look at Amina, as if to say 'What's the fuss about?' She peeled the two girls away from their father and Ahmed got out of bed, dressed, and met Um Jabor on the stairway.

'There's a man from Al Khor here to see you. He's at the front door.'

'You'd better let him in, ya Um Jabor.'

'I'm here to bring you sad news,' the man said without introducing himself. 'Your father has died.'

Ahmed sat calmly on the courtyard wall. 'I will come to Al Khor. Um Jabor, can you tell my family, please?'

With that Ahmed left immediately with the messenger, still unaware of his name or when his father died.

'You're too late. We've already buried him.'

That was his grandmother's greeting when he reached the family home in Al Khor. He had only met her once, and she had looked at him with disdain and resentment. She died some years ago, leaving Khaled alone in the house, unable to come to terms with his loss. Today the house was almost empty apart from a few neighbours who had come to do their duty. Once the mourners had drunk their coffee and sat for a while, they left. One man remained. He introduced himself to Ahmed as a representative of the company that Khaled owned.

'I have to tell you that, as your father's health declined, so did the company. There are no assets to speak of. The income you were getting monthly will no longer be available, and the company will cease to exist. Al Khor is not as it was, you know. The days of pearling and fleets of vessels have long gone, and times are changing. All the talk now is of finding oil, and the foreigners are all looking for it in Dukhan. I'm afraid our future doesn't look good. I'm sorry, Ahmed.'

Ahmed looked around the room, at the crumbling plaster on the walls, the shabby cushions and carpets. He had never known this house and he felt no emotion for the loss of his father. All he could think was that he was now on his own. He was thankful that he had been blessed with a loving family of his own, and vowed to cherish them for the rest of his days. There was no more to be done here, in this dusty corner of a forgotten town. He would head straight back home.

'Just one thing before you go,' the man said, rifling through some old papers. 'The house will go – either to a neighbour, who has expressed the desire to own it, or it could be demolished. Either way, the money raised will go towards paying off your father's considerable debts, which he accumulated since the business took a turn for the worse. He mentioned that he would like you to have the last remaining vessel in his fleet. It's an ageing pearling boat called *Firial*, moored in Doha. More than that I don't know.'

Of course, he knew *Firial*. As soon as the name was mentioned, he remembered the hot summer night he had sat with the group of old sailors on her deck and the extraordinary experience he had had afterwards on the way back to Bait Al Bahr. Had he been too harsh on his remote father? He wanted to know more. Why had he been given the old sailing boat? It had played an important part that night; it had helped him to see a path to the future.

He managed to pass the vessel on his way back home from Al Khor. It was almost sunset, and the old wooden boat was deserted. It looked a little uncared for, Ahmed thought, but still bobbed gently up and down as if claiming that there was still life left in it. He smiled and looked fondly at *Firial*, wondering if he would see the group of card players again soon. Again, he wondered why his father had left him the boat. He was determined to find out and vowed to keep the boat in good order.

Ahmed made the same journey up the hill as he had years before, but this time he had even more resolve to better himself – for his sake and that of his growing family. Although he adored his loving wife and girls, he cherished the few moments he had alone. It was a chance to restore order, to find balance and harmony. Here, on the hill, looking at the bay and the boats, he felt his sense of destiny once again. He couldn't have been happier.

'Anyone at home?' Ahmed walked into the courtyard. There was silence. He called out again but received no answer. Eventually, after climbing the stairs, he found Um Jabor and

Abu Jabor sitting quietly in the majlis. Bidding them to come with him, he went along to the bedroom where he found Amina, Lulua and Fatima where he had left them, although the three were dressed and sitting on the bed rather than in it. Amina was telling the girls an old folk tale.

'And then to their surprise the giant vanished, never to be seen again... Oh, there you are,' Amina said, looking at her husband. 'We thought you'd be away longer.'

'What happened next, Ya Ummi?' Fatima asked.

'Nothing, my dear. That's the end.'

'Well, that's a nice welcome home for your father,' Ahmed said, coming to sit with his family on the bed. Come in, ya Um Jabor, ya Abu Jabor. I have something to say. You all know my father died.'

'We are all sorry, my dear Ahmed. That's why we are quiet.'

'Thank you, my dear. You are all kind, but I didn't know my father very well and I suppose we all have to die one day.'

The girls looked at their mother, who hugged them close.

'The thing is, we have this lovely home, for which we must thank my grandfather, and now I have been given a boat. It's moored down in the harbour. It is from the pearl-diving days and we shall keep it in the family.'

Everyone looked puzzled, wondering what was coming next.

Ahmed coughed. 'The thing is, there's no more money. My father left this world with nothing, I'm afraid. So I'm going to have to get a job.'

There was a stunned silence.

'In any case, there'll soon be one more mouth to feed. We will need more money.' Gently, he patted Amina's rounded stomach.

He knew life was going to be very different from now on.

Ahmed approached the gates to the Emir's fort with trepidation. Amina had inspected him before he set off. Um Jabor had already laundered his favourite thobe and starched his best qutra. Amina thought he looked like a responsible young man, therefore most suitable for employment. 'Employment' was a word that Ahmed had never known. He had never had to think about money. He presumed his father had sent Um Jabor money each month to cover the costs of running Bait Al Bahr.

He had spent the last week wondering what he should do. He discussed it with his wife. Then Ahmed remembered his Uncle Salem and that he used to be friendly with the then Emir's son, Sheikh Ali. With all the changes in his life in recent years, he'd hardly noticed that Sheikh Abdullah had abdicated in favour of his son. Ahmed hadn't seen Salem for years; somehow they had drifted apart. As Ahmed straightened up, trying to gather inner strength, he wondered if Salem was still in the fort. He might have left. He might have got another job. There was only one way to find out.

The Bedouin guards were friendly enough. After exchanging a few words of greeting they let the young visitor through to the vast courtyard of the Emiri headquarters. Even though this was the most important building in the country, inside the atmosphere was calm. Ahmed noticed several sparrows chirping cheerily in the eucalyptus trees. Around the edges, under a colonnade, several men sat either wearing their official bishts or carrying them on their laps ready in case they were summoned into the presence of His

Highness. Old Bedouin leaders chatted together, some with one leg up on the high bench, as was the custom.

Nervously Ahmed approached a white-bearded man sitting alone, further down the line of benches towards the far corner of the cloister. His brow was furrowed in concentration, his leathery skin giving away his hard life outdoors. He played with his musbah – his prayer beads.

'Salam aleikum,' Ahmed said.

'Aleikum salam,' the man almost whispered.

'I am looking for Salem Al Bahr.'

'Salem Al Bahr?' The man looked up at Ahmed. 'Maktab Salem. His office is over there.' He pointed to a grand doorway with a huddle of people outside.

At the far end of the quadrangle were more armed bodyguards, black-skinned, tall and solid. They vetted everyone who passed, both men and women. They all carried small pieces of paper – petitions they wanted to present to the Emir. Ahmed had heard about this weekly exchange between the sheikh and his people but hadn't realised that today was the day on which the court would be open. Shuffling forward, he asked to see Salem Al Bahr. A guard with bloodshot eyes stared at him. 'Why do you want to see him?'

'He's my uncle,' Ahmed replied nervously.

Instantly the enormous African cleared a path for him. Ahmed was ushered through the throng into a vast hallway with ceiling fans, woven carpets and arched windows looking out on to the Arabian Gulf.

He continued in the direction he had been told until he reached a closed door. He gave a gentle knock and entered. There was his uncle, sitting at a large desk. Without looking up, he carried on leafing through a pile of official-looking papers.

'Ya Am Salem.'

Salem stopped what he was doing and looked up. 'Ya Ahmed! Ya Ahmed! It's really you!' He leaped up and went straight to Ahmed, giving him a huge hug and kisses on both cheeks. 'I don't believe it. It's been so long. Come in. Come in. *Tfadal. Tfadal.*'

Salem ushered Ahmed to a velvet sofa at one side of the room, overlooking the sea. He couldn't stop smiling, asking how his nephew was and asking for his news.

'I'm so sorry about your father. I should have gone to Al Khor, but I was busy here.'

'Shukran Am Salem. My father and I weren't close, as you know.'

'I know. I know.' He patted Ahmed on the leg reassuringly. For a moment there was silence.

'I came here looking for you, but thought you may have gone elsewhere,' Ahmed said.

'I'm the Emir's office manager, Ahmed.'

'Oh, my goodness. I didn't know. I'm sorry. That's why it's so difficult to get in.'

Salem gave a chuckle. 'Well, as you know, I've been a friend of His Highness for a long time. Sheikh Ali and I had similar ideas when we were younger about how our little country could develop. As he grew older, his father found the burden of office increasingly difficult, although he had done so much for the country. I had moved in here to spend more time with Ali, and it seemed natural that when Sheikh Abdullah abdicated in favour of his son that I should be on hand to help out. So here I am!'

'I'm very pleased for you, Uncle Salem. I never realised.'

'I'm always busy now. The Emir wants to do so much. We have to get ready to build a modern state. We are busy using the oil to replace pearls. It is all happening so quickly. It seems like only yesterday when your dear late mother and I played on the beach at Al Mafjar.'

Salem's eyes glazed over and he looked out of the window for a moment. Ahmed could see that his uncle hadn't changed, and wanted to renew his friendship with him.

'Ya Salem. T'al.'

It was the Emir. The connecting door to the inner office was ajar. Salem immediately got up, whispering 'sorry' to his nephew but gesturing to him to stay in his seat.

After a few minutes Salem reappeared alongside two men dressed in cream-coloured suits. Salem was talking in English to the men, which impressed Ahmed. Rather than escorting the two guests out of the Emiri Diwan straight away, Salem stopped. 'Gentlemen. May I introduce my nephew, Ahmed?'

Ahmed stood and offered a trembling hand to both.

'Sabah al Khair. My name is Geoffrey Hancock. I'm the advisor to His Highness. Good to meet you. This is Charles

Denman from Tennant and Sons. He's here to work with Mr Abdullah Darwish. There's a lot to do.'

With that, the two men bade Salem farewell and made for the courtyard.

Ahmed had got over his initial nervousness at being in such an important place, and felt bold enough to ask his uncle about his problem. 'The thing is, ya Amu Salem, my father has left me with nothing. I have a wife and two daughters and another child on the way.'

Salem gave Ahmed his full attention.

'I need a job.'

'Go! Go! Go after them. Run as fast as you can,' Salem said urgently.

Ahmed looked blank.

'Those men you just met can help you, Ahmed. Quick.' Salem chased Ahmed out of the door and waved him away. Ahmed ran across the courtyard. There was no sign of the men in suits. He ran past the guards and out into the street, fearing he had lost his chance. Then he caught sight of the men entering a white stucco building. They stopped at the entrance, giving Ahmed a chance to catch them up. Taking a deep breath, he headed towards them.

Ahmed only knew a few words of English. 'Hello. I'm sorry.'

Geoffrey Hancock asked him what was the matter. Seeing the troubled look on Ahmed's face, he told him he could talk in Arabic if he preferred.

'Yes, sir. I'm looking for a job. My uncle said you might be able to help.'

The two men looked at each other, amused by the request. Charles Denman was the first to offer a suggestion. 'Desmond Whitehouse could do with some help down at the new bank.'

'Would be useful to have a local on board too,' Geoffrey Hancock added. 'I tell you what. Pop round this evening at six. Lawrence will be here for drinks. You could meet him. Here at six. How does that suit? We'll have to teach you some English, mind.'

The men laughed and patted Ahmed on the back.

'Yes, sir. Thank you, sir,' Ahmed said, not knowing whether to bow or offer a handshake. Instead he just left, backing away from them and waving.

'Drinks?' he whispered to himself as he walked away. 'What does that mean?'

Back at Bait Al Bahr, Amina and Um Jabor were busy in the courtyard sifting rice and peeling vegetables for lunch. Abu Jabor was balanced precariously on a makeshift ladder retouching some old plasterwork.

'You be careful,' his wife said, looking up from sorting the rice. 'You're not as young as you were.' But Abu Jabor carried on, muttering something under his breath.

When Ahmed arrived, the girls ran down the stairs calling for him and telling him their news. He held his arms out to them, enjoying their chatter. Little Tima gurgled the occasional word too. While Ahmed didn't want to appear disinterested, he was itching to tell Amina about his appointment later that day.

Ahmed described the morning's events as accurately as he could to Amina and her parents, then Um Jabor brought in a sizeable baked hamour, steaming on a bed of rice and surrounded by root vegetables, parsley and coriander.

'My favourite,' Ahmed said as he sat down, cross-legged, in the shaded corner of the courtyard. 'You were up early, Abu Jabor, finding this fine fish.'

'I was lucky. My friend, Sultan, had a good catch so he gave me a good price. He's getting me some safi next week.'

They finished every scrap of the succulent hamour. Ahmed looked at his wife. She knew what he was thinking: that he never wanted the children to go hungry and that his aim was to make their future secure.

After lunch, Ahmed and Amina retired to their room. Ahmed told her how nervous he felt about his engagement at six o'clock. They wondered what it would be like. Neither of them had ever known any foreigners. They knew little of Western ways and world affairs.

'Amina, my love, I don't know English, I don't know anything about these people. What am I going to do? They said something about a bank. What will I do in a bank? God give me help.'

'Well, they must have thought you looked all right.' Amina tried to reassure her husband. 'Be strong, my dear, and think of the family. Try your best. That's all you can do.'

'Thank you, my love. I will try. Wish me luck.'

They held each other before Ahmed bathed, shaved and changed into his best thobe.

At six o'clock precisely, Ahmed peered through the old blue-painted wooden doorway opposite the Amir's fort. The pink bougainvillea that surrounded the double doors made the building less forbidding. Ahmed could hear conversation within the house. Although it was similar to his own, this house had a smaller courtyard and the walls were adorned with what appeared to be Turkish carpets and several black and white photographs. The only person he recognised was Queen Elizabeth II. He peered at the photo before being interrupted by a woman, striking in her red cocktail dress and matching lipstick and nails, who had appeared at the bottom of the stairs.

'You must be Ahmed. I'm Honor, Geoffrey's wife.'

Ahmed noticed her self-confidence and upright posture. He saw her look him up and down, checking his starched qutra and agal, his clean-shaven face, white thobe and sandals, then his nervous smile.

'Hello, madam,' Ahmed said apprehensively, accepting her hand.

'Everyone's upstairs. Run on up. They'll get you a drink.'

It was strange to be greeted by a woman in this way. It was all so fast. Ahmed had never seen anything like it. He thought she looked like a film star. He wondered what Amina would think.

'Ah, there you are, Ahmed. Come in. Come in.'

Geoffrey Hancock broke away from a circle of suited men to welcome Ahmed. 'Good to see you. What will you have to drink? We have all the wicked ways of the West here. Beer,

Scotch, you name it. Or perhaps you'd prefer something less powerful?'

Ahmed couldn't understand a word of what his host said, but realised he was being offered a drink of some sort.

'Ay shay, anything is OK, thank you, sir,' he said.

'I tell you what, have a beer. It's easier than getting juice from downstairs.'

Ahmed held a frothy liquid in his hand. He saw the other man he'd met earlier deep in conversation with the man who had come out of the Emir's office. Chatting to them was another Qatari. He was Abdullah Darwish, the leading merchant in town. Everybody knew him. There was nothing else for it. Ahmed had to pluck up his courage and head towards him. Ahmed put his hand to his mouth and coughed. 'Salam aleikum.'

Nothing happened.

'Salam aleikum,' he said again, a little louder. 'Wa Aleikum e Salam, wa Rahmat Allah wa Barakatu.'

At last. The merchant beamed. 'Well. Who do we have here? One of my young countrymen, drinking beer?'

'Uh, uh, I didn't... I mean, I haven't...'

'You British, trying to corrupt this nice young man.'

There was a second of silence, then everyone laughed.

Ahmed didn't know what to do with himself – or the beer. He looked round, trying to find a place to put it down. Abdullah Darwish, feeling that he had teased the newcomer rather too much, put his arm round Ahmed's shoulder and told him it was fine. 'I have a beer now and then too, just to keep the British happy.'

More laughter followed. Ahmed didn't understand whether he was being laughed at, or whether the group were being friendly. He soon realised it was the latter.

'You've dropped in at a good time, my friend,' Geoffrey Hancock said to him. 'We're all doing what we can to help His Highness develop your country. I hope you can play a part.'

'I hope so too, sir.'

'You met Desmond Whitehouse this morning. Des has come from the Eastern Bank in Bahrain to set up a bank here. I think he needs some help.'

'I certainly do,' Desmond Whitehouse said. 'Nobody has heard of banking here before.'

'I keep all my money under the bed. Don't tell anyone,' Abdullah Darwish said. The men laughed, unable to tell if he was joking or not.

'Well, he doesn't give me any of it, that's for sure. Whoops. Oh sorry, Abdullah. I didn't realise you were listening.'

Charles Denman, the agent from Tennant and Sons, had cracked the latest joke.

'You'll get your reward in good time, Charles,' Abdullah Darwish said, patting him on the shoulder. 'Just get all the things we need to build this country. We need roads, buildings, a hospital, concrete, nuts and bolts, engineers and technicians. You get the men and between us we'll be fine.'

Now the group became more serious.

'His Highness told me this morning that he wants the oil they've found in Dukhan to be put to good use,' Charles Denman said. 'He said we've been blessed and must not waste any time or resources. It's up to us now.'

The men nodded. Turning towards Ahmed, Abdullah Darwish said, 'Now you see why you're here at a good time, young man.'

'Come down to my house in the morning,' Desmond Whitehouse said. 'It's also the bank. I think we'll find you something to do.'

Abdullah led the little group in a round of applause. Ahmed had just found himself a job. Leaving the expatriates to their drinks, the wily merchant took Ahmed by the arm and guided him towards the veranda.

'Now's your chance, young man. Seize it. We have struggled so much over the years and now, with God's help, we can build our country and have a better life. But it's up to you. The British are here to help us, but they also want to stay here because they know how important it is. We're at the heart of the trade between West and East, and we're at the centre of the oil business now. They want to be part of the action. But we must have our say first. Good luck, my boy.'

Abdullah Darwish went back in to bid farewell to his British partners, leaving Ahmed alone to think about what he had been told. He looked at the turquoise sea and the boats, one of which was his now. They reminded him that, until now, he had been drifting. But now he had responsibilities. He vowed that he would be a good husband and parent, and he would also help to make his country a good place to live.

Neither Amina or Ahmed got much sleep that night. The family had been up late hearing all the details about the party and the all the strange ways of the foreigners. Lulua had laughed at the descriptions of the men in suits and the lady dressed in red. Her grandparents were fascinated that British people were living only a few minutes away from them. Amina listened intently to what her husband had to say, although she noticed a rather strange smell on his breath when they eventually went to bed.

The next day was Ahmed's first as an employee. He followed the directions that Abdullah Darwish had given him. It only took about ten minutes to walk to the old mud-brick house at the back of the Darwish compound. A small brass plaque indicated that he was in the right place. *EASTERN BANK*, it said. He knocked.

'Sabah el Khair. You must be Ahmed Al Bahr.'

'Sabah el Noor. Yes, I am Ahmed.'

'My name's Parker. Assistant manager. Come in.'

Ahmed thought the man looked serious as he showed Ahmed into the chaotic front room which acted as an office. Although it was a typically warm day, the young man was dressed in a charcoal three-piece suit, his blond hair flopping over his shiny pink forehead.

'Mr Whitehouse is out at the moment. He's gone to try and see the Emir. He told me about you, though. I suppose we'd better get you started. I've just transferred from Bahrain so it's all a bit new to me too, I'm afraid. Are you any good with figures?'

'Figures?'

'Numbers. Counting ... one, two, three, four.'

'Ah hissab. Math-e-matics?' Ahmed stuttered. 'I like reading and poetry.'

Edward Parker looked upwards, wondering why on earth this most unsuitable candidate to work in a bank had been sent to him.

'We had everything organised in Manama. Only the best...'

Before Edward Parker could continue, the door opened to reveal a breathless Desmond Whitehouse bearing two large velvet bags. He put these down on the stone floor.

'Phew. There we are. I had to wait ages to see H.H. What a rigmarole. Anyway, I got them. Ah, Ahmed. Good to see you. Come through. Come on in,' the manager said enthusiastically. 'Bring in one of those each, would you?'

Edward Parker and Ahmed dutifully followed their manager into the back room, each carrying a bag. The manager took his seat at the cluttered desk, which was piled with documents and files. Apart from two other small chairs, the room was bare apart from a waist-high green safe in the far corner. It bore the words *CHUBB: MADE IN BIRMINGHAM* in brass relief. From a drawer Edward Parker took out a large bunch of keys and with his back to his staff fiddled about, trying one key and then another, finally opening the safe door.

'There we are. Now, gentlemen, pass me those two, please. It's all been checked and verified. At last. I've been waiting for days to sort this lot out.'

After he placed the sacks in the safe, he asked the two men to sit in front of him. There was a knock at the door. A slim, neatly dressed woman appeared.

'Did you know the PDQL people had air-conditioning? Oh, sorry, darling I didn't realise you had company.'

'That's all right, my dear. Did you meet Ahmed at the Hancocks last night? He's our new man.'

Ahmed hadn't met the manager's wife.

'Maureen Whitehouse. How do you do?' she said in a clipped voice.

He started to get up but Maureen Whitehouse again apologised, saying she'd be upstairs if anything was needed. 'Shall I put the kettle on, darling? Anyway, I can't believe they've got air-conditioning. What about us stuck down here in this old place?'

'We'll talk about it later, dear. I'm sure Mr Darwish will spruce this place up a bit once we're organised. Now, we have a lot to do.'

Maureen Whitehouse retreated upstairs to the humble private quarters to make tea while her husband set out plans for the new branch of the Eastern Bank in Doha.

'Parker, I want you to drum up trade here in Doha. We have the Emir's account now. The two sackfuls need to be accounted for and we need more customers – the sheikhs, the merchants. I know people like to keep their hard-earned money to themselves, but as Doha gets bigger they'll need our services more and more. I know you are used to Bahrain but we can get established here in next to no time. Just you wait and see.'

Edward Parker nodded reluctantly, still wishing he was back in Manama but realising that the only way to get a promotion was to do what the boss asked.

'Ahmed, I've only just met you and you don't have any experience of financial matters, but we need a local like you to liaise and build relations. The Eastern Bank has built its reputation on excellent customer service. We will rely on you to bring customers to us. Make them confident that we can look after their money safely. Help them understand what banks are for. Parker here will help you to get familiar with our procedures and in turn, Parker, you will learn from Ahmed the ways of the local population so we can build a customer base. It won't be easy. Ahmed, I want you to go to Dukhan, where the oil fields are being drilled. That's where all the action is. We need to go there and get the workers in the field to open accounts with us. That's it. Off you both go.'

The two men got up and made their way to the front room as Maureen Whitehouse came down with a tray of tea things and some digestive biscuits she'd been saving.

'Perfect timing, Mrs W,' Desmond Whitehouse said. 'Biscuits too.'

Ahmed decided he liked his first job and these friendly people and their funny ways. As he and Edward Parker took their tea and biscuits to the front office, leaving the manager and his wife to talk about air-conditioning, he turned to his new boss with confidence. 'By the way, sir, any time you need to see the Emir, my uncle is his office manager.'

Whitehouse looked stunned. 'That's a very good start, young Ahmed. A very good start indeed. There, Mrs W, I told you we had backed a winner.'

They all laughed. Ahmed and Parker spent the morning organising the front room so it looked more like an office. Mrs Whitehouse suggested bringing an easy chair downstairs so that new customers would feel at ease. They tidied the piles of papers and arranged them in files. Edward made a mental note to order filing cabinets from Manama.

Towards the end of the morning, Mr Whitehouse put his head round the door. He congratulated them on the improvements and suggested they take a break. Ahmed wasn't sure how he would spend his time outside the office, but soon decided to take on the role of local guide.

'Shall I show you the souq? That's where everybody goes.'

'OK. By the way, you can call me Eddie. Most people do.'

<start>Ahmed led the young Englishman through the warren of alleyways that made up the souq, explaining as best he could using basic words and gestures. He described how the community was made up of fishing and pearling families who had to struggle over recent years as times got worse. As they walked Ahmed told Eddie about the Qataris who had fled to Bahrain and the east of Saudi Arabia in order to survive as there had been nothing for them here. The young bank clerk took in all the information, finding a new respect

for his Qatari counterpart. They made their way past canvas-covered stalls where traders were busy trying to sell their wares and before long arrived at the centre of the market.

'This is where I'm staying,' Eddie said, pointing to a sign which said BISMILLAH HOTEL.

'Oh I see,' Ahmed said, stifling a feeling of pity.

'But it's not for long. They're moving me to PDQL accommodation I think. I hope.'

'The owner was a friend of my father's,' Ahmed recalled, remembering the grim-faced merchant who sat with his father on the odd occasion when he visited from Al Khor. 'There he is over there.'

Next to the entrance to the hotel was a small café where the owner sat at a table, his head in his hands.

'Abu Hassan,' Ahmed stuttered nervously.

'Naam. Yes. What is it?'

'I'm Ahmed, son of Khaled Al Bahr.'

'Oh Ahmed. Yes now I know. I didn't recognise you. It's been a long time. I'm sorry about your father. We were good friends.'

Ahmed introduced him to is British colleague and they were asked to sit down and have mint tea. Although the merchant looked serious he was courteous and heard how Ahmed knew the foreigner and that he was staying in the rooms above.

'It's very difficult to survive you know,' Abu Hassan said. 'Your father died from all the worry and I may soon follow. I've suffered from losses and so I turned my building here into rooms for letting. They say oil people are coming but they are all in Dukhan. I fear I may lose everything if things don't improve.'

They drank their tea and sat stiffly feeling awkward when Eddie Parker suddenly made a suggestion.

'You know sir we can help with loans for developing business.'

The lugubrious Abu Hassan looked up from concentrating on his gnarled hands twirling prayer beads. He wondered what the young man meant exactly. Eddie explained that the new bank could offer help in the form of a loan provided the merchant opened an account and deposited his personal money there.

There was an exchange of doubtful looks between Abu Hassan and Ahmed. Leaning forward towards his father's old friend Ahmed realised that Abu Hassan was suspicious of the proposal. For decades even centuries the Bedouin and the people of the coast had guarded whatever money they acquired through fair means or foul zealously and never let it be parted from their company. Ahmed took his time to explain that things were different now and the British were to be trusted. He told Abu Hassan of the British safe he has seen with his own eyes that very morning, and furthermore he had heard from his uncle that Doha was now secure under the new police force directed by a British man.

'I like your hotel, Mr. Abu Hassan,' Eddie said, 'but if you don't mind me saying so it needs some work. I know for sure that more people will be coming to Doha soon. It is, in my view, a good investment. You are welcome to open an account at the Eastern Bank. If you do you will be the second customer after His Highness the Emir.'

At this the sad, lined face of the hotel manager brightened. He immediately stood up offering his hand to Eddie. They both shook hands heartily, all three men patting each other on the back in congratulation. They arranged to meet at the bank premises the following morning to meet Mr. Whitehouse and take it from there.

Ahmed was about to take his leave when he asked his new friend what he was doing about lunch.

'I usually eat here or in a little place along the way. Occasionally Mr and Mrs Whitehouse invite me to lunch at the bank.'

Without a moment' hesitation and not thinking at all of what meals may or may not have been prepared at home Ahmed invited his colleague for lunch.

'Come back to my house. You're most welcome.'

The two men turned up along the main street that led to Bait Al Bahr chatting as they went along, happy with their first conquest. They both felt now that as a small team they could get more accounts and that their customers were right here in front of their noses as they had proved that morning.

'I think we can call that a success Ahmed,' Eddie said patting his colleague on the back. 'I'll have to tell the boss we were working in the market for the rest of the morning, which we were. He'll be over the moon with what we've achieved I'm sure.'

It wasn't far along the dusty throughfare to Ahmed's home. Outside the faded white walls Ahmed beckoned his guest to go through the wicket gate.

'My goodness,' Eddie exclaimed. 'You live here? It's huge. I'm sorry, Ahmed, I thought you were a poor, simple man who needed a job.'

Ahmed gave a little smile as he told Eddie that the house had been his father's and that he had grown up there alone; now his father was no longer alive he had the house but no money to live on. 'But I do have a family Eddie and here they are!'

The young head of the household beamed with pride as Lulua and Tima rushed across the courtyard into his arms. Amina followed behind noticing the foreign man in his Western suit and slightly skewed tie. Unused to the presence of strangers, let alone 'ajnabis' from distant lands she positioned herself in the far corner beyond the palm tree until Ahmed said 'Taali ya habibti', come along my love. So she joined the children as did Abu Jabor and Um Jabor who came rushing out from the back kitchen in a flurry to see what all the commotion was about. Introductions were made all round. The young Englishman couldn't believe he was being made so welcome in a country that until now he thought was hostile territory.

Amina looked at Um Jabor as if to say 'what do we do now?' Um Jabor raised her shoulders and showed her open hands, indicating 'how should I know?' Ahmed realised the predicament they were in and before Amina could give him a withering look he gave her a loving smile hoping it would be a guarantee that she couldn't reprimand him in any way for inviting someone to the house for lunch without any warning.

In the end the children saved the situation. Both Luua and Tima loved the novelty of having a new person to play with. Having no inhibitions they leaped up at him like playful pets, feeling the material of the strange clothes. They all sat down together in the majlis, the girls touching Eddie's pale skin as if he were from a different planet. Although neither Eddie or the girls understood a word they managed 'yad', hand, 'rigl' leg, and 'widj' face having fun learning each other's language. Ahmed popped in to see them, observing proudly that his daughters were not only intelligent but happy to meet other people.

In the kitchen panic had struck. Um Jabor had planned to serve up the leftovers from the night before; some stock and a few vegetables with some rice. But the women of the house agreed this wouldn't do at all. Just as they were wondering what to do Lulua ran in to ask,

'Ya Ummi, wein al baydh?' She wanted one of the eggs that she had collected from her grandmother's friends' chickens earlier that day to show Eddie and find out what *baydh* was in English.

'That's it,' Amina cried out,'let's make a big omelette!'

Lulua learned from Eddie that the English word for baydh was egg and then the whole family, including Eddie, went into the kitchen to crack a dozen newly-laid eggs into a vast shallow pan, all helping to stir and add seasoning and spices. They stirred and chuckled, watching the omelette take shape until eventually it looked good enough to eat. Luckily Abu Jabor had a good friend in the baker just around the corner, so Ahmed was out and back in less than ten minutes bearing a mountain of piping hot round flat bread. A few sprinkled of parsley and some saved tomatoes added colour to the platter and they all sat in a circle around the communal dish to which they had all contributed. All agreed that it tasted wonderful as they each tore off pieces of bread to scoop up tasty morsels. Eddie loved being in the family's company and it seemed the feeling was mutual.

It wasn't until late that night, when the children had gone to bed exhausted that Ahmed and Amina were able to take in the importance of the day. It was the time they loved the best. Sitting up in bed, with peace and quiet in the house, they could discuss family problems and contemplate the future. They snuggles up together as Ahmed gave a detailed account of the morning, his first job and the man who was to be his boss. Amina wanted to hear all about Mrs. Whitehouse, and the way the bank had been set up in just an ordinary house where all the country's money was now being handled. Ahmed spoke with pride at making what he thought had been a good impression as well as securing a good customer in Abu Hassan at the Bismillah Hotel. Amina couldn't quite take it all in but showed her gratitude at her husband's efforts by taking his hand and placing it on her expanding waistline.

'It's all for this little one,' Ahmed said, looking into Amina's eyes.

'You're a good man, Ahmed,' Amina said and they fell asleep, content that at last they could build a life as a family.

6

Doha, 1953

There was already a flurry of activity at the temporary headquarters of the Eastern Bank when Ahmed arrived just before seven Eddie was almost hidden behind files and papers.

'Sabah El Khair,' he said cheerily, emerging from behind a filing cabinet. 'I've been practising my Arabic. Shams. Shouf,' he said pointing through the window at the bright day outside.

'Good. Very good, Eddie' Ahmed said. 'And I've been learning more English words. Amina is my teacher. It is nice weather today. She says the English always talk about the weather.'

'True. True. You'd better go and see the boss. He asked me to tell you to go in.'

Ahmed put his head around the door of the back room where Mr Whitehouse was at his desk, dealing with paperwork.

'Good morning, Ahmed. Come in. Come in. What a splendid morning's work yesterday. Barker told me all about it. He's going to fetch Mr Abu Hassan and bring him here later this morning. Excellent. Good start indeed. Sit down. I've got something to tell you.'

Ahmed sat down, wondering what it could be. Mrs Whitehouse came in with a tray of coffee and a few of her remaining biscuits.

'Marvellous, darling. Thank you very much. We've got to keep Ahmed here happy. He doesn't know what I'm going to tell him yet.'

'I'll be upstairs if you need anything, my dear,' Mrs Whitehouse said, leaving her husband to pour the coffee.

'Yesterday's success led me to think what an asset you are. We need locals on the ground, getting customers to deposit their money with the bank. That way we can grow and lend more money to people who need it.'

Ahmed took his coffee, still at a loss about how he could be any use when his knowledge of banking was negligible.

'You know that your country is going through a very big change. There is so much to be done. His Highness has a big ambition. He wants to build schools and a hospital and improve everything here in the capital. However, all the activity is on the other side of the country, in Dukhan. The oil company, PDQL, has been drilling oil since the end of the war and is now producing about 34,000 barrels per day, but that's going up all the time. The workers get paid direct from our headquarters in Manama. Now, we need the employees to open bank accounts here. This is where you come in, my dear chap.'

Ahmed looked puzzled. 'What can I do, sir? I am ready to help in any way.'

'I want you to go to Dukhan. Chat to the locals and make contact with the oil workers. We need to build relations with the oil company men so they'll choose this bank to keep their hard-earned money. How does that sound?'

'It sounds good. I hope I can do it. I have never been there. I only know Doha and the north. I had no idea so much work was going on there. How will I get there?'

'We'll organise everything, don't worry. I know the oil company management. But first you'd better see Cochrane. He's the head of police. We can't have you wandering around the desert without anyone knowing. He'll look after you. Go and see him now, and get ready to leave tomorrow morning. I'm going to the palace to try and see the Emir. Would you mind coming with me? I might need you.'

Ahmed couldn't have been happier that now at last he was doing something worthwhile, although it was mixed with trepidation at the thought of going across the country to unknown territory and representing the bank.

It was a short walk to the Emiri Diwan. Mr Whitehouse and Ahmed chatted easily. Up to now, Ahmed had only seen the Qatar through the prism of his immediate home and family.

Now, talking to an outsider, he could get a broader sense of what was going on in the capital and beyond. It was a new experience and he enjoyed it. All the time he listened and formulating his own ideas, gaining invaluable knowledge.

The guards at the entrance to the compound nodded at Whitehouse and Ahmed. Across the quadrangle the burly black bodyguard stood to attention, then let them pass. Salem came out of the Emir's office carrying a sheaf of papers.

'Uncle Salem. This is Mr Whitehouse, my manager.'

'Ah yes. We have more cash for you, Mr Whitehouse. I hope you're happy with your new employee,' he said, smiling at the two men.

'Very. So much so he is on a new mission. He's going over to Dukhan to get some customers for us. I'm sending him over to Cochrane to get security clearance.'

'Good. Good. There's a lot happening, Ahmed. Good luck. I think Mr Cochrane is in Al Koot fort. He was here earlier. Come, Mr. Whitehouse. The Emir can see you now. Good luck, Ahmed. If you need anything, let me know.'

Ahmed suddenly realised that it was all up to him as he crossed the patch of desert heading towards Al Koot fort, which had last been used in anger during his grandfather's youth. He wished he'd known his grandfather and what his life was like. As he approached the fort, he tried to imagine soldiers defending the capital from the upper battlements. Now there was a lone guard outside the open gate, a pale-green dusty canal tree giving him just enough shade. He didn't seem too concerned at the sight of a visitor coming through the gate and left his rifle slack at his side. In the centre of the fort a rag-tag bunch of men were attempting some form of drill, the sergeant clearly having trouble getting his squad to getting into line, as they shuffled and puffed unable to get to grips with presenting arms.

Peering into a dark room on the left under the archway entrance he saw the dim figure of a man he presumed was Ron Cochrane behind a desk. He knocked on the open door. In return for his 'Salam aleikum', Ahmed was treated to a perfectly pronounced 'Aleikum e salam wa Rahmat Allah wa Barakatu'. Clearly, Ahmed thought, this was someone who knew the Arab world well. When the man stood up, Ahmed saw that he was tall and had ginger hair and a pointed carrot-coloured beard.

'Tfadl, tfadl. Ajlis. Ismi Mohammed Mahdi.' The police officer introduced himself. 'I was Ron Cochrane, but I have become a Muslim and even a Qatari. So Ahlan wa sahlan.'

Surprised, Ahmed introduced himself and told Ron Cochrane what he had to do. It was comforting to talk in his native tongue. Cochrane listened intently. 'That all seems to be in order. Report here tomorrow morning at six sharp,' Cochrane said in English. 'I'll arrange a car and driver, probably from QGPL. We've had trouble with some of the workers. Even strikes. So, I'm not sure what their reaction will be to parting with their oil wages, but best of luck.'

He still spoke in English. Ahmed had no idea why this seemingly typically British officer had become a Muslim and a Qatari. He thought he would have to find out somehow.

Later, back at Bait Al Bahr, Ahmed and Amina discussed the next day's adventure into the unknown. Neither had travelled beyond the perimeter of the capital. For years Ahmed had gazed out into the distance from on the roof, the mystery of the desert capturing his imagination. Now he would find out what it was like. Ahmed knew when he would leave, but he was unable to tell Amina when he would return.

'I'm sure I will be back soon, ya habibti,' Ahmed said helplessly.

The girls had realised that something was up. Um Jabor paced up and down, muttering about the wilderness, the emptiness of the Sahara, and telling old stories about djinns that had bedevilled remote areas. Abu Jabor listened without commenting.

7

Neither Ahmed or Amina slept well that night. The dawn call to prayer signalled that it was time to leave. He kissed the sleeping girls goodbye, then Amina, who gave him a final hug. Just as he was leaving, Um Jabor chased after him with a large bundle.

'Ya Ahmed. Take this. A few things for the journey. God be with you,' she said.

Abu Jabor then came alongside his wife carrying a long woollen bisht, a furwah.

'Take this, Ahmed,' he said. 'This was my father's. It's a bit old but it keeps the cold out. You may need it.'

Ahmed hugged her and left, weighed down by the extra baggage. He felt he wanted to hide it somewhere – he felt sure he would be back in no time, and he didn't want to make a fuss. However, he was almost at the fort so he would just have to take what she had given him. Shortly before six, he walked up the small incline to the fort. As he did so, he saw a familiar face. It was Eddie Parker leaning against a large black car.

'Salam, Eddie. What are you doing here?'

'Good question. I've been sent to meet you.'

Ahmed put his load down and leaned against the car alongside his colleague.

'The boss told me you had met Cochrane and he would arrange everything, but when PDQL got involved it all went a bit up the spout.'

Ahmed waited for a translation, which Eddie gave, using lots of gestures and explanations of things going wrong.

'So, the boss asked me if I could drive and I said yes. Well, I drove a truck in the war when I was stationed in Tubrook. Anyway, the boss agreed, and got a car from the PDQL supply here. They said they didn't have anyone to drive and it was up to the bank. So here we are. This is it, mate, you and me. All aboard the Humber Snipe to Dukhan.'

Ahmed had only seen a few cars before. He had certainly never been in one. Only the Emir and his entourage had cars, and he felt apprehensive at his sudden rise in status from humble citizen to privileged passenger. Over the past two or three days, since he had been spending time with people who weren't from his country, he had noticed that they all behaved in a certain way. They were all very confident, as though no matter what they said or did, they would be right. They gave the impression that living in this tiny enclave in the middle of Arabia was almost like a holiday, and they didn't take anything seriously. Perhaps he was wrong. It was just an impression. Now, sitting on the tan leather bench seat next to Eddie in the front of the car, he had a sense that he was treating this venture in the same manner. It would be fun. It would be a diversion. But Ahmed knew it would be much more than that.

'The boss said they filled her up with petrol and the tyres were OK, so I reckon we'll be all right. Should be about three hours, he said. We'd better pop into Qatar Cold Stores, though, for some water.'

Qatar Cold Stores had just been opened by the Darwish family. It sold goods that expatriates might need. They drew up outside the building with a large red sign across the front. Ahmed thought it looked garish compared to the stately headquarters of the Emir opposite. When they entered the shop, it was like nothing Ahmed had ever seen. All his life he had lived simply on a diet of fish, rice and vegetables from the market. Here he saw all kinds of new produce: row upon row of coloured bottles, packets and tins. On shelves that ran the length of the shop there were tinned tomatoes and beans, jars of jam of every variety, pickles in pots, cereals in brightly coloured packages, and bottles of sauce the likes of which he couldn't make out at all.

'I come here for Marmite,' Eddie said. 'They have white bread here like in England, and I get the boy at the hotel to toast it for me then he butters it. I then spread it with Marmite. Easy-peasy.'

'What is Marmite?' Ahmed asked, bewildered by the array of unfamiliar products on display.

'Well, you either love it or you hate it. I love it. Can't explain. Sorry.'

Turning down the far aisle along the back wall was another new discovery. Ahmed saw six large containers. They were the freezers that had been the Darwish's prize investment: a collection of ice boxes that gave the store its name. He peered into the buzzing chambers, which reminded him of the igloos he'd heard about that the people in the frozen lands of the North live in. Eddie helped him to identify the various frozen objects occupying the electric sarcophagi. They were mostly meat. For Ahmed's family, meat was a very rare treat. Only for a momentous occasion would a lamb be slaughtered, cooked and eaten. Occasionally there was meat in the market, but it was soon snapped up before the flies could attack it. Here the animals had been chopped into parts: there were legs of lamb, ribs and shanks, beef steaks and finely chopped mincemeat, and finally a special separate freezer that Eddie said was his favourite. Bacon. It was all overwhelming, and Ahmed wondered how this new invention would change his family's eating habits. He loved his daily diet of fish, dates and vegetables. Would it all change?

'Ah, here's the water,' Eddie said.

Ahmed turned his attention to a corner of the shop that was taken up by crates containing bottles of water. He had never seen anything like it. Water had always been scarce but somehow they managed by buying a daily supply from a man with a donkey who brought it from a well near Um Jabor's old house. Sometimes it was a brackish, but they made do.

'They import it from Bombay, they say. Let's take a couple. I'll get some bread and cheese too, for the journey.'

It was all very strange for Ahmed. When Eddie went to pay at the counter, the man serving was an Indian, and they both spoke in English. How could he not have noticed this new way of living? Ahmed wondered. Had it all been created by the man at the party – Mr Darwish? As Eddie gathered his purchases and chatted with the swarthy man dressed in a white shirt and dhoti, Ahmed began to see that change was inevitable. It was clear that the old days were over and he wanted to be part of the new Doha.

Outside, they loaded their purchases into the vast boot Eddie placed the two water bottles and brown bag of bread and cheese between the 'furwa' and a bundle, which looked to Ahmed like a pile of washing.

'They said it'll take about three hours, but we've got to get out of town first,' Eddie said, pressing the start button on the mahogany dashboard. He cranked the gear stick into first and with a screech of tyres pulled away from the square. He headed west past the palace along the well-worn route to Rayyan. They saw a new complex being built on the right as they drove out of town. Eddie pointed out that it was a new guest palace. He'd heard about it from the expatriates he'd met. This would be where Sheikh Ali would house the various dignitaries and guests he hoped would visit his country.

Ahmed was reminded of a conversation he'd had with one of the English men at the party, a Mr Harris. He was in town to build a hospital, which would be on the road to Rayyan. It must be around here, he thought. There was already a hospital of sorts down on the seafront near the Darwish compound, but clearly there was a need for a bigger, better place to care for ill people, he thought.

They soon left the capital behind them. Eddie put the car into top gear when the dusty track became a dark brown road. 'Apparently they use some of the oil they've discovered to make the road,' he said authoritatively. 'Wind the window down and see.'

Ahmed did just that. He could smell pure oil mixed with sand – a sickly smell which forced him to close the window again.

'At least the weather's nice today. In Bahrain in the summer the roads suddenly bubble up. It's awful,' Eddie said, creating a forbidding image in Ahmed's mind. He wondered if his beautiful desert would be ruined for good.

Within minutes they were driving through Al Rayyan. They passed the walled compounds of the Bedouin sheikhs who had settled here long before, preferring the charm of the wilderness to the hustle and bustle of the capital. Al Rayyan was also a natural oasis so it had welcoming elements of green. Ahmed saw the occasional grey-green bush, tufts of grass and, behind the high protective walls, clusters of tall palm and eucalyptus trees that looked as though they had been there long before the brick encampments.

Ahmed had never been so far from the coast. He felt that he was in a foreign land. There was no doubt in his mind that he belonged to the coast. His family had lived on the north coast of Qatar for generations. Even his family name, Al Bahr, meant 'the sea'.

The two men chatted easily as they headed in a dead straight line for the horizon to the west. Occasionally they had to slow down for a camel crossing their path, the ship of the desert unconcerned by a lump of metal coming in its direction at a hundred kilometres per hour. It was beautiful, Ahmed thought, seeing the noble creature roaming in the desert. Of course there were camels nearer home, notably at Um Jabor's old house, but there they were herded and hobbled, at the beck and call of their master. This was different and altogether more pleasing.

A settlement came into view on a slight hill. As they came to what appeared to be the centre of the place, they saw a small elderly man with a stick in his hands standing by the roadside. Eddie slowed down and wound the window down. He said 'Salam aleikum' and got a mumbled response. It was left to Ahmed to communicate further. When he asked where they were, the man replied that this was Al Shahaniya and he was waiting to go to his tents in Rowdhat Rashed. It wasn't on their way but several kilometres to the south, but they decided to give the man a lift.

He sat in the back of the saloon, muttering about the weather and the state of his camels, which roamed nearby, and one of his goats, which had developed a skin condition. All this was said in a strong Bedouin accent which Ahmed struggled to understand, let alone offer any kind of translation to Eddie.

It wasn't easy for Eddie to follow the track through the desert after the relative smoothness of the oil-topped Dukhan road. But soon they were in Rowdhat Rashed, among the greenery of the tiny oasis. The man invited them to his temporary home, which consisted of a long, low black and brown tent made of rough sheep's wool supported by several wooden staves. Despite protesting that they didn't have time to stop, they had no choice but to switch off the engine and get out.

'Shismik ya akhi?' Ahmed asked the man, who was scurrying towards the tent.

'Ismi Braik. Braik Al Hajiri.'

Braik. Ahmed had never heard anyone by that name before. The reason he was scurrying was to warn his family that they had visitors. Ahmed and Eddie caught a glimpse of a black-clad woman, a purple-black batula covering her face. She went inside the tent, closely followed by three children of unidentifiable gender. Their faces were streaked with a mixture of mud and dust, their hair long and matted. They seemed happy enough, though, Ahmed thought, but they were unsure how to act in the presence of strangers, looking to their mother for protection.

The men sat in a circle some distance from the tent in the little shade that was provided by a thorny bush. They sat in silence, contemplating the peaceful pastoral scene. Apart from the children, the only sound was made by the family's two goats, who were tugging at some scrubland behind the bush. Ahmed and Eddie agreed it was a wonderful place.

After a few minutes, they heard a call from the tent. Braik went over to take delivery of a tray bearing three metal cups. He offered his guests a cup each and took one for himself.

'Labn Jamal,' he said. 'Tfadal.'

The camel's milk was warm and thick. Ahmed liked it a lot, having had plenty of it when he went to Um Jabor's old house when he first met Amina. Eddie on the other hand, wasn't so sure. He managed to finish it though, knowing it would impolite not to.

'Shokran, ya akhi Braik,' Ahmed said to their host.

'Allah teek al afya,' the man said. *May God give you strength.*

With that, they took their leave and made their way back to the car. Eddie was full of excitement. 'It was amazing,' he said. 'What a life. Living in a tent in the desert like that. I wouldn't mind it. Just for a while, though.'

'I loved being there too, I must say. The people of the desert are uncomplicated. Not like the town folk. But those children. I wonder how they will grow up without any education. We need to build schools for them.'

Ahmed suddenly felt a responsibility – not just for his own children but for the ones he had just met. This trip was taking on more significance, he thought as they arrived back at the crossroads. The journey had been delayed by more than an hour, and it was well past eleven when they turned left back onto the man road.

The long brown road before them stretched out like a thick pencil mark on a sheet of parchment. They began to talk of their families. Eddie asked about Ahmed's children and parents-in-law.

'And what about you, Eddie' Ahmed enquired, feeling he should know more about his new friend.

'I'm from a place called Swindon in England,' Eddie began. 'It's not much of a place. Famous for trains.'

Eddie painted a picture for Ahmed of a big town with many buildings and a good transport network, where trains were built. It was fascinating to hear about how people lived and worked. There were neat little houses for families, schools for every age, and a large hospital. Eddie said that up to now, he had lived with his parents, but he was saving up to buy a small house of his own. Then he had a surprise for Ahmed.

'I'm trying to save money while I'm here, because I'm getting married.'

'Oh, congratulations,' Ahmed said excitedly. 'She's a lucky lady. What's her name?'

'Thank you. That's kind. Her name Is Margaret, but she's called Maggie most of the time,' Eddie said, and described his fiancée, whom he'd known for three years. They'd met at a dance at the local church hall and had been together ever since. He said 'together' with some hesitation, as he had spent the last year and a half away from home, only seeing Maggie when he was given leave by the bank.

'We write to each other all the time and she tells me all the news. I suppose she's my sweetheart,' Eddie said, losing concentration for a second, the car wavering from its direct path. 'Wait till I tell her I drank camel's milk this morning,' he said. Both men laughed heartily.

8

Dukhan, 1953

It was well after noon. They had been on the road for more than three hours, including their diversion to the Al Hajir camp at Rawdat Rashed. They had seen how prized the Bedouin site was, being green and comparatively lush compared to the beige of the desert they were driving through. Just as the road seemed to climb a little, Eddie braked suddenly. Ahmed hurtled forward, almost hitting his head on the windscreen.

'What was that?' Eddie said frantically.

'A dhub. A lizard,' Ahmed answered in shock.

They jumped out of the car and hurried after the creature, which had scampered off the road into the desert.

'Look, there it goes. Get it, Ahmed. Go on.'

Ahmed didn't really like the idea of running off into the desert chasing a large lizard, but he did. He flung himself into action with such gusto that his qutra and aqal fell off his head into the sand. Eddie laughed at the sight of him. Then Ahmed called Eddie over.

'I think he's in there,' Ahmed said, pointing to a hole about six inches across. 'See the prints?'

'Oh, you are a Bedouin after all,' Eddie teased. 'I wonder if it'll come out.'

Sure enough, after a few seconds the lizard came out. It sat there in the sun, looking up at the invaders.

'My goodness. It's like a miniature prehistoric monster,' Eddie said.

The lizard was about half a metre long. It could almost have been a baby dragon. It was the same colour as the desert, camouflaged to perfection.

'The Bedu love these. See how fat he is. When there's no food around, a dhab makes good eating.'

Eddie grimaced at the thought. They left the dhab to bask in the sun and enjoy his freedom.

Over the brow of the hill, they were rewarded with a splendid view. Eddie wound down the window and pointed at several strangely shaped formations on both sides of the road.

'I never thought I would see this in my country,' Ahmed said, hardly able to take in the change in scenery. They drove more slowly past the formations. They weren't exactly hills, but flat-topped and white. Eddie was reminded for a second of the white cliffs of Dover. Ahmed thought he could make out some machinery between the hills. As the road flattened out, they saw the bright glistening haze of what appeared at first to be sky but in fact was the sea. They could hardly make out the horizon.

'I've always wanted to see this coast,' Ahmed said, 'and now I'm here.'

'It's beautiful,' was all Eddie could say.

'Look over there,' Ahmed said, shading his eyes against the glaring sun. He had noticed something. In the distance was a small rectangular building, alone in the desert, looking out of place.

'Blimey! It's a plane!' Eddie exclaimed. 'It's a bloomin' plane!'

'Where? I can't see it,' Ahmed said, searching the horizon as Eddie brought the car to a halt.

'Look. It's coming this way,' Eddie said, jumping out of the car and coming around to the passenger side. Ahmed got out. Eddie pointed towards a speck in the cloudless sky, gradually getting larger, just above the shimmering sea. Now Ahmed could make it out. He'd never seen a plane before, so wasn't sure what to look for.

'Here it comes. That's what the building over there is. It's a control tower, Ahmed. I wish I had my binoculars, but it looks like a biplane to me.'

Ahmed was speechless as he witnessed this new phenomenon for the first time, then heard the drone of an engine as the plane came closer.

'I don't believe it,' Eddie said excitedly. 'It's a Dragon Rapide. Well, I never. We had those in the war. The officers flew all over the place in them. Six-seater. Lovely little planes.

263

Even the old Prince of Wales had one. Well, that's enough about him.'

'I've never seen a plane before,' Ahmed said, still in awe. The plane bounced along the makeshift runway, the same colour and surface as the road.

'We've both been experiencing things for the first time, Ahmed.' Eddie suddenly put his arm round Ahmed's shoulder. 'I love it here.'

It only took a few minutes to drive to the Dukhan camp. A sign next to an open barrier announced PDQ Dukhan, and several Indians in dhotis scurried around a collection of nearby huts. Eddie leaned out of the window and asked one of the men to come over. Ahmed thought Eddie's attitude a little severe, feeling apprehensive at entering unknown territory.

'Where's the finance department? Modeer? Maloom?' Eddie asked, as if an officer addressing a private.

'Modeer over there. Seeda. Big office,' the man said, pointing at the tallest building.

'Shukria,' he said and drove on. 'It's just like when I was in the army. The camp was just like this. But I was taking the orders then.'

Ahmed sat quietly. He had never seen anything like this. It was a miniature town. There were signs everywhere with initials that meant nothing to him: DRILLING OPS. DKHN, PDQL TESTING SECT. There were shops, and a post office. Along the side of the road, small trees had been newly planted. A little further, near a long row of Nissan huts which had a sign saying JUNIOR MESS outside, was a larger building. It had an outside staircase at the bottom, and a sign saying FINANCE DEPT. Eddie parked outside.

'Here we go,' Eddie said. 'This is your job now, mate. I'm just the driver.'

Ahmed felt nauseous at the thought of meeting a whole new group of people, not knowing what he was going to say or do. He got out of the car and made sure his Qatari dress was in order – although, after spending time in Rodha Rashed and chasing a fat lizard around the desert, he wasn't sure he looked that respectable. They went up the outside staircase, then made their way to an office marked H. Jolly, Manager.

'He's not in, I'm afraid. Can I help?'

A deeply tanned man in his thirties appeared from the general office. He had short straw-coloured hair and was dressed in trousers that matched his hair and a white short-sleeved shirt. Like the other twenty or so men in the office, he wore a tie.

'Richard's the name,' he said, offering his hand. 'Not my first name. That's Arthur. Everyone calls me Rich. But I'm not. Yet.' He laughed as did the two guests. 'We got word from head office that you were coming. Come in. We can use Mr Jolly's office while he's out.'

The three men sat at a coffee table in front of the manager's desk. Ahmed felt even more out of his depth, waiting for the two Englishmen to lead the conversation.

'You know we deal directly with the Eastern Bank in Manama, don't you? Each month we go over to Bahrain by boat and collect the money, bring it back, and I go around and pay all the men, wherever they happen to be. It's quite a business.'

'Sounds like a lot of work,' Eddie said, trying to think of something more interesting to say. 'Ahmed has been put in charge of liaising with Dukhan in the hope that we may interest some of the staff in opening accounts in the Doha branch. Isn't that right, Ahmed?'

Eddie couldn't have made it more obvious. Ahmed began to talk after a couple of nervous coughs.

'Mr Richards. Rich. Mr. Whitehouse my manager, has asked me to come to Dukhan to make a connection with the people who work here. I do not know Dukhan at all, but I am very happy to be here. I hope that I can help the men to look after their money so that it is safe, and they can have a good future. Thank you.'

'Very good. very good,' Rich said, sounding surprised, perhaps at Ahmed's formal speech. 'In that case Mr. Tussler, our American friend known as Tuss, will accompany us and show us how the place operates. OK?'

'Yes. I would like that very much,' Ahmed said. Eddie was impressed by how much Ahmed seemed to care about what he was doing.

'Let's go then,' Tussler said getting up from his chair. 'I'm sorry. Rude of me. I didn't offer you any refreshment. It's a bit late for lunch, I'm afraid. Come down to the mess and see what we have. Might as well start the tour with the most important place in the camp.'

It was two o'clock, and neither Ahmed nor Eddie had had anything substantial since their early breakfast. They made their way down the staircase and along to the Senior Mess where Rich provided the two men with a pot of tea and a pile of beef and tomato sandwiches. While they were tucking in, Rich gave a brief explanation of how the operation ran.

'You'll meet engineers and other oil men who are better qualified than me to talk about the process. I'm just an accountant, but we all work as a team. When you've finished your tea, I'll take you to see some of the operations. We have a wonderful social life too. My wife is here. There are only a few couples, but we get together for darts and cards as well as the occasional birthday party. We are all happy here, I must say.'

'How often do you go to Doha?' Ahmed asked.

'Never been,' he said. 'We fly in from Bahrain, and that's it. We have everything we need here.'

Ahmed had noticed the running water and electric light everywhere in the camp – something Doha was yet to achieve.

Tuss ushered the visitors into a bright blue Chevrolet parked next to the manager's empty space.

They set off, Tuss describing the delights of Dukhan camp life. From the centre of the town they passed a medical centre, a shop marked COLD STORES and a post office. A little further along the road were a collection of pre-fab bungalows.

'That's mine,' Rich said. 'We have a nice view of the sea at the back.'

There were about ten of these. Rich explained they were for senior staff. Behind a wall that had a bright pink bougainvillea spilling over it was a much larger residence.

'That's the Operations Manager's place. We've had a couple of big parties there. Everybody comes,' Tuss explained. 'Now we'd better go and see the business end of things.

They drove back towards the gated entrance to the camp and turned left along a small desert track about halfway between the camp and the sea. Rich stopped the car in a clearing. He showed the men what looked like a large pipe with a series of bolts attached to it. The pipe stuck out of the ground. Around the pipe were four or five taps at various angles. It was painted bright red.

'I bet you're wondering what that is. Ahmed, that's your future. Come and see,' Rich said.

He led the men around the back of the odd-looking structure where a plaque had been placed. It read: *DUKHAN number 1 drilled 1939. Spudded 1949. In production 400 bpd.*

'The war stopped operations but now the well is producing, as you can see, and we go from strength to strength.'

Ahmed puffed out his chest, seeing that all this activity was taking place in his own country, but at the same time, he couldn't help feeling a little guilty at not knowing anything about it before he came.

Further north Rich drove to a drilling platform. Here was the heart of oil exploration. They approached the rig. The men were all in boiler suits, hard hats and gloves. Ahmed felt out of place in his white thobe as they made their way up the gantry to the rig platform. The noise was overwhelming. Two men operated what looked like a huge spanner, holding it as they joined the pipe attached to the drill head then lowered the sections down into the earth. All the men were busy yet looked cheerful.

Back at ground level Ahmed shook hands with some of the oil men, then realised that there were young Qatari men being taught how to be tool-pushers up on the rig. There were English and American engineers huddled together with charts and diagrams, and Indian men in the huts around the work site.

Ahmed didn't know what to say to these men. They looked exhausted, their faces blackened by dust and grime. One man introduced himself as Fahd Al Shammari. He had managed to get a job as a general worker. When Ahmed asked him about his life at the camp, Fahd talked of the hardships of shift work and the dangers involved. Sometimes there were accidents when the drill struck oil. He said it was hard work, but he was grateful to find work and the pay was good.

'My brother said I was crazy doing this,' Fahd said in Arabic, 'but I left him to his goats and said I wanted a better future.'

'What about your salary?' Ahmed asked, remembering what he had come for.

'We get paid regularly. The British man comes around and gives us money. I keep it in my cupboard at the mess.'

Ahmed told Fahd he worked for the bank in Doha and he could open an account for him. At first Fahd was reluctant but after a while said he'd think about it. He wanted his money to be safe and he wanted to save for the future and his family.

Eddie and Rich had been busy chatting to the American oil man but was time to move on. Ahmed was quiet, thinking about the amazing people he had just seen toiling away in such harsh conditions.

'We've got time to go up to Bir Zikreet,' Rich said, revving the Chevrolet. 'That's where the boat comes in. Each month our finance man goes over to Bahrain and gets the salary money and brings it over. If we hurry, we can meet the boat.'

They passed more rigs in the distance. Ahmed could picture the men drilling away, lifting and pushing, working together. He felt humbled as he looked out of the window at the rocky desert to the right and the calm beaches and bright blue sea that lay between Qatar and Bahrain.

As Rich described the oil production operation in greater detail, he drove along the clear stretch of hard-packed sand that had become a highway to the northern beaches. Ahmed was a little nervous at the speed they were doing, but Eddie loved it, urging Tuss on.

In twenty minutes, they found themselves negotiating a winding coastal path through more rocky outcrops. The hard, chalky surface was fine for driving, but now and then they had to drive around areas where the sand was like quicksand. Tuss gingerly negotiated the danger zones and breathed a sigh of relief when they made it around the final bend, to see the little jetty that had been built for the boat's arrival from Bahrain.

Ahmed stepped out of the car. In front of them lay a pure white sandy beach. To the right was a wooden jetty supported by six metal poles which looked like the pipes that Ahmed had seen being drilled into the ground at the rig. To the north-west, Ahmed could make out the group of islands that lay between Qatar and Bahrain.

'Bang on time,' Rich said, looking at his watch then indicating a small vessel heading their way. 'They could go over on the plane, but I think old Bartlett who makes the trip each month rather enjoys it.'

Ahmed studied his surroundings – another new environment. The west coast was completely different to the east; the terrain seemed to be more varied and even more tranquil, especially here in Zikrit.

The pup-pup-pup of the boat got louder. Ahmed could make out the shape of an Arabian dhow. Smaller than the ones that Ahmed was used to, and with no sail, it was a welcome sight to Ahmed. In moments the dhow drew up alongside. A man at the back of the boat threw Tuss a rope. With calm efficiency the crew drew up at the jetty. Bartlett and a heavily set dark-skinned man got out onto the jetty, then the boat turned and departed for Bahrain. The two men carried several large bags. It was just after four o'clock. Another vehicle came around the headland. This was here to pick up the 'money men', as they were known. It was a large

American station wagon. The driver opened the doors for Bartlett and his bodyguard, and carefully placed the cash in the back.

The two vehicles set off back to base. Back at the camp, they met for a drink in the mess. They ordered beers, but Ahmed decided to try something he'd never had before – Coca-Cola. Poured into an ice-filled glass, it tasted refreshing after his long day. Bartlett explained that there were more than three thousand workers in the camp and out in the field, and when they were taken on by the company they were each given a numbered brass disc inscribed with the letters PDQ. Every employee kept his disc, and a duplicate was kept in the safe in the accounts department. At the end of the month Bartlett oversaw the completion of time sheets, and when they were ready each pay packet was filled with the cash and the duplicate brass disc. At the end of each month Bartlett went around with the pay-packets and handed them over on presentation of the original disc, to ensure each man got the right pay.

Ahmed was fascinated to hear how the pay system worked – and that there were so many men on the pay roll. He couldn't help wondering if the men were doing the best they could with their hard-earned wages.

It was too late to go back to Doha. Ahmed noticed that Eddie was having a good time with his fellow Englishmen at the bar. They were invited to stay for a curry supper, then to Ahmed's surprise all the men filed out of the mess and headed for some waste ground some distance from the centre of the camp. He tagged along, wondering what was happening, thinking it might be some exercise to walk off the beers and curry and to take in the chill night air. Several rows of chairs had been set up in front of a large blank wall. Some of the wives were already there, chatting to one another. The men sat down facing the wall. Then, as if by magic, a burst of light fell onto the wall. Large black numbers counted down: 5 - 4 - 3 - 2 - 1. The audience hushed, and a crackly noise gave way to some tinny music, then the screen showed the words EALING STUDIOS presents THE TITFIELD THUNDERBOLT.

Ahmed was spellbound. The sound, the colour, the spectacle. It was amazing. He couldn't take it all in. He looked around at the excited audience, who were equally enthralled. He heard one couple say that the film was new, so they were lucky to have it. Eddie sitting next to him, passed along a bag of sweets. Ahmed took one. It was all so alien to his way of life, but somehow, he liked it. As the titles played he thought this was a good way to live: to work hard all day and enjoy yourself in the evening.

Even though he found the film exciting, he found himself dozing off. So much had happened since he left home just before six that morning. He was roused by the audience getting up and shuffling about.

'Come on, Ahmed. I guess that wasn't the easiest film to follow if you aren't a Brit,' Eddie said. 'They've asked us to sleep in the senior hut, so we'd better go.'

The guests were shown to the dormitory hut. Within minutes they were sound asleep.

9

Having explored the northern end of Dukhan to see the rigs in action as well as the landing stage at Zikreet, today Rich planned to take the men south. Just as they were about to get in the Chevrolet, Ahmed thought of his family. Would they be worried about him?

'Do you think it will take a long time?' Ahmed asked, trying not to sound unenthusiastic.

'It could be most of the morning. I tell you what, you take your car and follow me. You can take the Um Bab road back once we've finished,' Rich said.

Eddie was pleased to get back into the Humber Snipe. He followed Rich to the one-pump petrol station outside the camp compound. A lungi-wearing Keralite filled the cars, then Rich came over to pay for both cars by signing a chitty.

'The funny thing is, we have all this oil, but this petrol has come all the way from the refinery in Iraq,' Rich said. 'We haven't been able to refine it here yet, but it's on the way.'

Rich drove on and turned right, this time heading towards the rocky outcrops they had noticed on their way there. The dark brown road led to a series of hills, each one revealing more rigs. They went off-road to see one of these in action. There, Ahmed talked to more workers, trying to convince them to open an account with the bank in Doha. Word seemed to be getting around, as some of the tool-pushers already knew there was a Qatari bank man in town. They were happy to pause for a few minutes to speak to Ahmed.

'This is Fahahil,' Rich said, drawing up alongside the Humber. 'We'll spend a few minutes here and then go on to Um Bab.'

Ahmed and Eddie had learned quite a bit about the process of bringing oil to the surface. They had been introduced to geologists and technicians, labourers and office boys, all of whom were keen to know more about the new bank in Doha.

Tuss took Ahmed and Eddie a little further south, then turned off along a track heading towards the sea. They parked the cars side by side and got out to look at the view. They had a commanding position overlooking the bay.

'We are near Um Bab,' Rich said. 'It was here that they planned to build a terminal, so oil could be exported from the oil field. But it was deemed too shallow and difficult to navigate so they chose Um Said on the other side of the peninsula instead. There was even talk that this was to be the capital city of Qatar.'

Ahmed was even more amazed by this seemingly unlikely scenario. However, for a brief moment he let his imagination wander. Gazing across the stony desert that led down to the shingle beach and glittering water, he thought it would indeed make a wonderful setting for a new city. On the other hand, it was perfect the way it was.

'That's it, gentlemen,' Rich said. 'I hope you like our little town.'

'Thank you so much,' Ahmed said. 'I'll never forget these days. I've learned so much and I think we may have gained some customers too. I will probably be seeing you again quite soon.'

'You can take the road from Um Bab back to Doha,' Rich said. 'It'll take about two hours. Farewell, gentlemen. See you soon.'

The new bitumen road, which had only been laid a few months earlier, improved as the two men made their way towards the centre of the peninsula, following the pipeline which carried to the oil to Um Said on the east coast. The only sound was the gentle hum of the car's engine. They chatted about their time in Dukhan and the people they had met. Ahmed thought he had done a good job, and the bank should be happy.

After about half an hour, Ahmed asked Eddie to stop the car.

'Can we get out and take a look at the desert. It's beautiful.'

'Of course. I'll pull up alongside the pipeline.'

It was late afternoon and the sun was low in the sky. They could see the shimmering sea in the distance. It was a beautiful sight. There was total silence. Almost.

'Can you hear something?' Eddie said as Ahmed gazed at the sun.

'Yes. A sort of singing.'

Eddie walked towards the pipeline, then realised it was the flow of oil that was making the sound.

'There you are, Ahmed. That's your oil singing.'

It was the first time anyone had said that the oil belonged to him. Ahmed felt an intense sense of pride. Somehow the beauty of the desert and the flow of oil felt as one. He looked back at the pipeline and marvelled at the expertise of the engineers who had created it. This led him to wonder how much more man could do. It brought home to him how quickly everything was changing and developing – not just here, but around the world. Now man could fly from one country to the next, radio and television had been invented, so people could learn more about other cultures and ways of life. However, he thought, there had also been two world wars. It seemed to him that the world was at a crossroads. Oil could bring wealth and prosperity, but in the wrong hands it could bring death and destruction.

'Come over here, Eddie.'

'See how far the pipeline stretches. As far as the eye can see. All the way to Um Said.'

'It's amazing, Ahmed. It really is. To think that this carries the future income of Qatar is fantastic. But look what I've found.' Eddie showed Ahmed a small sandy object. 'I found it near the car. What do you think it is?'

'Oh, I've heard about these. My wife's mother told us about them. Desert roses. They're crystallised sand formed by the salt and weather conditions over here between the desert and the coast. It's beautiful. You should keep it for your fiancée.'

Ahmed took the desert rose back to the car and placed it carefully in the boot.

'Well, we'd better be off. We have a long drive ahead and it'll be dark before we know it.'

They got in and Eddie started the engine.

'They'll be wondering where we are,' Ahmed said. 'It'll be nice to get back.'

Eddie didn't respond. Instead of the car's engine springing into life, all they heard was a dull click. Eddie tried again. Nothing.

'Strange,' Eddie said at last. 'She's not responding. Petrol's OK. I've just filled her up. I'll try again.'

Click. Silence. Click. Silence. Click. Silence.

'Must be the battery. We'll have to try and jump-start her. Out you get, Ahmed. You'll have to push while I kick her into gear. So long as we can get her going down that hill, we'll be fine.'

Obediently, Ahmed began to push the old saloon. Eddie had one foot on the clutch and one on the sand to try to push the car himself, making it less heavy for Ahmed. He wasn't used to anything too energetic, and he was having trouble getting the car moving.

'Let's push together. One. Two. Three,' Ahmed called out, but the Humber stayed still, solid and stubborn. Any fondness

Eddie had had for the old saloon vanished. He wished they'd never stopped to admire the view.

'What can we do?' Ahmed asked pathetically.

'Nothing we can do, I'm afraid. We'll just have to wait until someone comes along who can give us a hand. Unless we walk all the way back to Dukhan.'

'It's too far. Now they really will be worried back home.'

'We'll just have to stay here, I'm afraid. When I was a Boy Scout, they said if you are in danger just stay put until someone finds you. So that's what we'll do.'

'You're probably right. I'm not much of a desert Bedouin, am I?' Ahmed joked, despite his anxiety.

'I expect someone will come along at some point,' Eddie said, trying to sound positive. 'We'd better make camp here.'

Although Ahmed was worried that Amina and the children would be wondering what was going on, he wasn't too concerned. After all, he had grown to love the desert and its beauty. He and Eddie began to arrange the things they had brought with them to make themselves as comfortable as possible. They had the bundle Um Jabor had given Ahmed before the journey, along with the things Eddie had bought in Qatar Cold Stores, including water. Ahmed went back to the boot to get one more item that Um Jabor had given him: the old burnoos to keep them warm. The sun had set and twilight had given way to an inky blue sky where the stars were already forming a heavenly canopy over the stranded travellers.

'We have cheese and bread,' Eddie said as they sat down cross-legged on the old ragged cloth which had been the wrapping for Um Jabor's bundle.

'And Um Jabor has given us dates, boiled eggs and a jar of fassoulia,' Ahmed said, bringing out a jar of beans cooked in spices.

'A feast!' Eddie said.

'It really is. T'fadal ya akhi,' Ahmed said, offering his friend the beans.

'T'fadal ya akhi,' Eddie bounced back, offering some bread to go with the beans.

They ate and chatted about their visit to Dukhan, laughing about some of the people they had met.

'I could murder a cup of tea.'

'Murder? No murder please. And tea? Keep wishing, Eddie. We are lucky to have water. Well, thanks to you.' Ahmed conceded.

'Aren't the stars wonderful? Look at them – millions and millions of them.'

Neither of them had seen the stars so clear and bright. Here in the desert there was no light pollution whatsoever, apart from a distant flare from an oil well to the north.

'I read that there are one hundred billion stars in our galaxy and one hundred billion galaxies in the universe,' Ahmed said.

'That's amazing. And we're sitting here on this little planet as we go around the sun, lost in space. I wonder if there's anyone else out there.'

'There must be. I wonder that too.'

Both felt in that instant that God would be the natural progression to talk about but they both remained silent. Ahmed could feel the heavens and the presence of God in the majesty of their surroundings. He knew Eddie felt the same. No discussion was needed.

They continued to gaze upwards. Eddie knew some of the constellations, like the Plough and Orion, and Ahmed pointed out the North Star, so critical to his forebears, the pearl-divers and mariners of the Gulf. They thought they saw a shooting star too.

Although it was only eight or nine in the evening, it seemed like the middle of the night. It had begun to get very cold too, so they wrapped the burnoos around them. In no time, they were fast asleep.

'Do you believe in miracles, Ahmed?' Eddie had been woken by a sound. It was still dark, but they could see approaching headlights. They raced to the middle of the road and waved frantically.

The approaching vehicle was going at top speed. For a moment Ahmed and Eddie feared for their lives but they darted out of the way as the truck sped past them then screeched to a halt, tyres burning. A hail of swear words in Arabic and English followed.

'Allah Subahna. You bloody fools. Ya Allah. What the hell are you doing? Majaneen. Crazy people.'

A bearded man in a thobe with a red checked qutra and aqal got out of the car and marched towards Eddie and Ahmed.

'I could have killed you. You crazy. What the hell are you doing here?'

'We've broken down. Our car is over there,' Eddie said when he could get a word in.

'And you? Inta Qatari?' the man asked Ahmed.

'Na'am. Ana Qatari. Any assif ala zaaj.' *Sorry to trouble you.*

By now he had calmed down a little but continued to mutter about killing the pair. Eddie took him to the Humber and explained about the flat battery.

'These old Humbers are always breaking down and getting stuck. You want one of these,' he said, pointing at his American GMC. 'I've been everywhere in this. Oil rigs, sabkha – you name it.'

His English was perfect. He had obviously been around the camp for some time. He bent down in front of the car, moving his aqal deftly to the back of his head so it wouldn't fall off. Ahmed noticed in the half-light that his face was deeply lined and weathered but his eyes were kind and generous.

'By the way, my name is Mohammed. I work for the oil company,' he said.

'Ana ismi Ahmed, and this is Eddie. We have been visiting Dukhan to meet the staff. We work for the Eastern Bank in Doha. We stayed at the camp last night. Well, the night before. We just stopped for a few minutes on the way home and this happened.'

'I'll tow her with mine. Just looking for something to hook her up to. Always the same. These town people get into a tight spot in the desert. You don't realise how dangerous it can be,' Mohammed said, as if he'd been in this situation dozens of times before. 'I saw the sheikh open the first pump in 1939 and I've been with the company ever since. Everyone knows me. I'm on the way to Al Mukainis. We heard that camels had broken the fence near the pumping station. Come on. I'll get the rope.'

They worked together to get the car on the road again. With some crafty moves on Mohammed's part, the car soon sprang into life.

'Now don't stop, whatever you do. Straight to Mukainis then Doha. Follow me and you'll be fine.'

Ahmed and Eddie were full of gratitude, but he dismissed their thanks with a flick of the hand. Dawn had broken by the time they set off. In forty minutes, they were at the junction with the Salwa Road, another new oil track between Doha and the border with the Saudi Arabia, where the peninsula of Qatar joined Arabia. Both cars turned left onto the new road, which was still merely a bitumen-topped track. After five minutes Mohammed slowed his car and turned off into the desert oasis settlement of Al Mukainis, waving the Humber onwards.

Even though they had only been away for forty-eight hours, it seemed much longer. The comparatively busy streets of the capital looked odd after the emptiness of the desert. Eddie was able to drop Ahmed right outside his front door, knowing he was anxious to get back as quickly as possible. Ahmed got his things from the boot and shook hands with Eddie. But that wasn't enough. They hugged warmly.

'Ya habibi, ya habibi Ahmed. Hamdal Allah.'

Amina rushed to the door, having seen the car draw up from her vantage point on the roof, where she had been pacing up and down all morning wondering what to do. She gave him a warm embrace, and Ahmed held his wife as the children leaped up to greet him.

'Baba, Baba,' they shouted, letting the neighbourhood know how pleased they were to see their father back safe and sound. Um Jabor came out, ululating with joy at the good news.

'We were so worried,' Amina said at last. 'What happened? Your face. It's burned. And your clothes are all dusty and dirty.'

'It's a long story, my dear. A very long story. I'm home now, though. Thank goodness. It's been quite a trip. I'll take you and the girls one day.'

This may not have been quite the right thing to say, because the girls became even more excited and demanded to go there and then. Amina gave Ahmed a look of disbelief at his tactlessness.

'Where's Abu Jabor?' Ahmed asked.

'He's not good, I'm afraid, Ahmed. Not good at all.' Um Jabor went to see how he was.

The whole day was spent washing and preparing a special dinner for his homecoming. It was as if the master of the house had been away for months, not two days. The girls

285

listened attentively to all his tales about the journey. Ahmed tried to explain the oil business to the little ones without getting too complicated and told them he had seen a movie for the first time. Everyone was mesmerised by Ahmed's description of the colourful moving pictures. Then he told them about breaking down in the desert. It was the best bedtime story the girls had ever heard.

Finally, alone together later that night, Ahmed snuggled up to Amina. Ahmed kissed his wife goodnight and fondly caressed her swollen stomach before drifting off to sleep.

10

'Ya Ummi, Ya Ummi. Taali hinna. Taali. Ya Ummi.'

Amina was about to give birth. It was the hottest month of the year, and she was in her bedroom. She summoned her mother, who was in mourning at the loss of her husband. It was late morning and Ahmed had gone to work. Lulua was at her English class, which Eddie had arranged for her with the bank manager's wife. Little Tima was in her room, playing quietly, oblivious to the commotion.

'Ma'shallah ya binti. It's come early. I thought it would. I could tell by the shape. I'll get the hakim from the souq. He'll know what to do. He thought the baby was round the wrong way when I told him about the shape.' Um Jabor was the child delivery expert and used her knowledge of herbs to cure any prenatal ailments. But Amina didn't want any such thing.

'I don't want the hakim, Ya Ummi. Get someone from the American hospital. Erjooki, please, Mother. I want this child to be delivered well and healthy. Quick.' Amina held her stomach and breathed through a contraction.

These days, Um Jabor had trouble with the stairs. It took her what seemed like an eternity to get downstairs, but she knew what to do. She had to find her son, Jabor. He had been busy in recent years, getting married and raising a small family of his own, but since his father had died, he had spent more time coming to the big house to see his mother and Amina.

She went as fast as she could along the alleyway behind the house and found Jabor in his small workshop. As soon as she had told him about Amina, he ran through the souq towards the sea, passing the Eastern Bank house. He popped his head in the door and asked for Ahmed, but he was out on bank business.

From the bank it was only a quick dash across the road to the large two-storey house that was the American Mission hospital in Doha. Jabor went in. In the inner courtyard, twenty or so patients were queueing up, waiting to be seen to. Jabor didn't have time to queue. He saw a foreign woman crossing the courtyard and went up to her.

'Sorry, madam,' he said not knowing how to address her. 'My sister is going to have a baby. I need help.'

'Where is she?'

'At home. At Bait Al Bahr. Not far from here.'

'OK, honey. Just wait there.'

Jabor had never heard an American accent before. Within a minute or two she was back with a bag, a hat and a parasol.

'Let's go, honey. Lead the way. By the way, I'm Mary Allison. Doctor Mary Allison.'

At the house, Amina was gasping in agony.

'OK, honey. Deep breaths. That's right. There we go. Hot water and towels, please. And fast.'

Luckily, Um Jabor had boiled water while her son was away, knowing the routine. She found some towels in an upstairs linen cupboard.

An hour and a half later Ahmed arrived back for lunch, having picked up Lulua from her English lesson. As they crossed the courtyard, they heard screaming. Ahmed looked at his daughter in horror and leaped up the stairs, two by two. He burst into the bedroom to find Jabor, Um Jabor, Tima, Dr Allison – and Amina, cradling a tiny baby.

'There you go, sir. Congratulations. You have a fine healthy boy.'

Ahmed was stunned. He ran to his wife and his newborn son, gathering Lulua and Tima around him too.

'Nice of you to come,' Amina said. She couldn't be angry, though.

'How was I supposed to know? I don't believe it. I mean, he isn't supposed to be here for another month.'

'I told you he'd be early,' Um Jabor said with the voice of wisdom.

'You should always listen to your mother-in-law,' Amina said, panting.

'Thank you, doctor, for coming. We haven't met. I'm Ahmed bin Khaled Al Bahr, and this is my family.'

'Well, it's good to meet you at last, Ahmed. If it wasn't for Um Jabor's quick thinking, things may have turned out differently. Thank goodness everything's OK. We have too many patients at the little hospital. Good thing they're building a new one. It's up at Rumaillah. It should be open in a couple of years. No more babies until then.'

'Don't worry, doctor,' Amina said. 'There's no chance of that, I can assure you.'

They all laughed again.

Ahmed had been gazing at his new baby. He turned to his wife and said, 'My dear wife. I know we should discuss this in private, but since we are all gathered here, can I say how proud I am of you? And my sincere thanks to you, Dr Allison.'

'Call me Mary.'

'Mary. We'll have a party at the weekend, and we all want you to be there.'

'It's a deal!'

Salem was working late in the Emir's office. During the hot summer months Sheikh Ali insisted on working from early in the morning until eleven thirty then breaking for lunch and a rest, returning to the office at four and staying until eight or nine, even later, depending what had to be done.

One evening around nine o'clock, the Emir asked his office manager to come and see him. Usually there was a line of visitors waiting to see the sheikh, but tonight it was particularly hot and humid so most families were at the coast, trying to keep cool. Here in the corner office the Emir, cooled by a solitary ceiling fan, toiled away, listening to the BBC on the radio.

'Ya Salem. Ajlis. Sit down. Let's have a coffee and think about what we've done. You know more than anyone about my intentions and ideas for our beloved country.'

'Thank you, sahib ismu. It is an honour to serve you.'

'Since we have found oil, we have attained great wealth. That wealth has largely gone to the oil companies, namely the Iraq Petroleum Company. Now we have established the Qatar Petroleum Company, the state is taking fifty per cent of the profits. This will allow us to make more plans. The people should benefit from our oil. Our citizens do not like foreigners taking jobs and money from them.'

Salem nodded politely in agreement, sipping his coffee. He was tempted to give an opinion but thought it better to remain impartial.

'We need to build schools and hospitals for our families and future generations. We need roads and drinking water, the telephone and radio, as well as a good police force. Rumaillah is almost ready. You know Harris came to see me today? It should be ready by the end of 1956. We must make sure the British help us. We need them for protection, but Cochrane needs to improve the police force. We need to help the Palestinians too, and play a part in foreign matters. There is so much to do. You have been my right hand, Salem, but now I think it is time for you to leave me.'

Salem looked down, unable to take in what he had heard. He had worked all hours in the service of the state. He was about to say something when the Emir continued.

'It is for this reason, Salem, and I have given this considerable thought. I only trust a handful of people. One of them is you. I want you to be my Minister of Finance. You will be responsible for all the economic matters I find so burdensome. Will you accept?'

Salem looked up in shock, this time with a broad grin.

'Of course, Your Highness. Thank you. It is such an honour. I hope I can do it. It is such a big job. I am at your service.'

'That's good. We have to form a proper government administration. Your part will be essential. You will head a government department and be responsible only to me. Your final job here is to find a replacement for you. That will be your most difficult task. Good luck.'

Salem thanked the Emir once again and backed out of the room into his outer office, where he sank into his chair in disbelief.

11

Bait Al Bahr had never looked so splendid. Although it was hot, the night air was not as humid as it had been. It was late August. Ahmed had waited a few more weeks to hold his party. Amina understandably didn't feel up to a big social occasion so soon after the birth of their son. Husband and wife agreed it would be a big occasion. For the first time, they were able to live quite well with the income from Ahmed's work at the bank, where he was doing well. He and Eddie had secured more and more accounts every day. He had invited his manager, Mr Whitehouse and his wife. Mrs Whitehouse gave Lulua English lessons and had become friends with Amina. Through the expatriate community, the couple had begun to meet people from all walks of life.

Eddie was already at the house. He and Ahmed had a lot of time discussing the party while on their visits to potential clients in Doha and in Dukhan, where they travelled once a month. The pair had become locally famous. At first, they were treated with suspicion by the local tradesmen, with their traditional ways, and by the oil workers, who were only interested in getting their pay packet and saving it until they went home.

They made an odd sight – one in pure white Arab dress, the other in a crumpled cream linen suit, talking in a mixture of Arabic and English to match the occasion. While Ahmed dealt with most of the potential accounts in Dukhan and Eddie the merchants in town, Ahmed had charmed the engineers and management with his easy manner and Eddiehad delighted the business community with his animated conversation. He was never short of a tale to tell or a joke to share. Both were always welcome to the offices of the influential as well as the simple dwellings and workplaces of the humble.

They knew they needed good food, a wide selection of drinks and some kind of entertainment to have a successful part. They enlisted the help of the Qatar Petroleum Company. To cater for the growing number of British and American engineers and administrators in Doha and in the field, a special outlet had been set up where employees could buy drinks and produce not found in the local market.

During the days leading up to the party, Ahmed and Eddie had chatted up the outlet manager, a Mr Jackson, commonly known as Jack, and had persuaded him to open an account at the bank. Jack had only been in the country for three months and was expecting his wife and two children to arrive in the coming week. He needed a bit of cash to 'tide him over', as he put it, so Ahmed arranged a short-term loan at very favourable rates. In exchange, Jack was more than willing to let Ahmed have a few cases of this and few cases of that at cost price. Now the two men arranged borrowed trestle tables in the corner of the courtyard. They would store half the drinks there. The rest had been taken up to the roof, where another trestle table had been placed so guests could choose to be on the roof in the fresh air.

Amina and Mrs Whitehouse, meanwhile, were busy in the kitchen, along with Um Jabor. Over the years Amina had picked up more and more cooking tips from her mother. Now that she was quite frail, Um Jabor was more of a supervisor. They had been getting things ready for almost a week, and all they had to do was to bake and heat up food. Mrs Whitehouse had raided Qatar Cold Store and the oil company outlet to bring a taste of Europe to the proceedings. As well as samosas and other little meat pastries, spicy fishcakes made from freshly caught hamour, and beans, salads and flatbreads, there were dishes of tiger prawns brought in from Bandar Abbas with an accompanying pink mayonnaise, a vast tray of shepherd's pie Mrs Whitehouse had made, with the addition of some garam masala she'd got from the souq and mixed in with the mince and onions to 'make it more interesting'. The pièce de resistance from the expat kitchen was two large dishes of coronation chicken. Mrs Whitehouse had tasted this shortly after the Queen's coronation, for which it had been invented, and vowed to make it herself. She had told the manager at Qatar Cold Stores to save all the chicken breasts he could find, and she had baked these before mixing with curry powder, sultanas and Heinz salad cream, the latter being the most difficult ingredient to find. Even Lulua came in to lend a hand. She had learned to make crème caramel and falouda, which weren't quite special enough for this occasion. Amina had asked Um Jabor and Nasser the baker to make some delicious cakes using rosewater and over-ripe dates. These, together with an enormous trifle that Mrs Whitehouse's expat lady friends had made, looked very impressive. Never before had any of them seen such a spread. All the food was going up on the roof. Abdullah Darwish had asked six of his office staff to help out for the night. The clerks were only too happy to do something completely different to their normal routine of typing and filing. At seven o'clock they trooped in, smart in white shirts and black trousers. Eddie told them what to do. Some would serve drinks, while others would pass drinks around or serve food.

Amina went upstairs to see to the children. Her newborn son wanted to be fed and her daughters demanded attention as they put on their new dresses. Lulua's dress was a floor-length purple satin and lace whereas Tima had chosen pink, her favourite colour. It was made of the softest chiffon, creating the effect of a little ball of candy floss.

Then there was a loud rat-a-tat-tat at the front gate along with several hoots from a car horn. Ahmed left Eddie and the waiters and went to the gate. There was a tremendous fuss going on outside. Then he remembered. Surely it can't be, he thought. They didn't take me seriously, surely?

But there they were. Taking up the whole of the pathway was the GMC pickup truck that had towed Ahmed and Eddie's car out of trouble the month before.

'I told you we'd be here. Here are the boys. Where do you want us?'

It was Mohammed. In the back were Tuss, a large man wearing a stetson, another Qatari, much younger than Mohammed, and a thin dark-skinned man with a moustache and slicked-back black hair.

'This is my son, Badr,' Mohammed said, pointing at the young Qatari. 'Come on, guys. You'll meet them properly later. You go in. I'll leave the Jimmy around the back.'

Ahmed was speechless. During his last couple of visits, he'd met Mohammed again by chance at the club in Dukhan. He mentioned he had just had a baby boy and invited Mohammed, along with anyone else he cared to invite. He hadn't thought for a minute that Mohammed would come, let alone with others from Dukhan.

Ahmed led the four men inside. They carried bags of varying shapes and sizes. Strange, Ahmed thought.

'Wow! Is this all yours, Ahmed?' Mohammed asked.

'Yes. It is. I inherited the house from my father. It's nice to put it to good use.'

Eddie appeared and greeted the three men who introduced themselves; Mohammed's son who was under training on the oil rigs, the tall thin man said 'I am Fuad. I'm Palestinian but lived in Beirut until I came here. I work in the school, teaching music.' The American was called Terry, a large jolly man whose job in Dukhan was dealing with disasters.

'If there's a fire, I put it out. If there's a leak, I seal it up. And if there's a blow out, I blow it up!'

Everyone laughed.

'My dear Mohammed, it's so good to see you, and you are all most welcome here. But what on earth are you up to? What are you all carrying?'

'Oh, didn't I say?' Mohammed said teasingly. 'This is my drum kit. We're the jazz. Did you say you had a roof? Come on, boys. We'll set up there.'

And before Ahmed had a chance to say anything, the band were off upstairs, ready for the night ahead. Ahmed looked at Eddie then his wife.

The waiters were all at their stations. Amina went around the house lighting little lanterns around the arches and pillars on the first floor. Mohammed came hurtling down the stairs, followed by his band.

'I almost forgot. Quick, guys. Come on. It won't take a minute. Can I borrow some of your waiters?'

Moments later they were back, carrying an upright piano.

'Brought her all the way from Beirut.' It was Fuad, the musician with shiny black hair. 'Well, not from Beirut tonight, but you know what I mean.'

It took eight men to get the piano up onto the roof. Terry decided he was too large to help and headed straight to the bar.

'Any chance of a cold one?' he asked.

'Of course,' Ahmed said. And so, the party began. The door opened, and Mr Whitehouse walked in, to be met by his wife. He was followed by Abdullah Darwish with his son. They brought along two other men who were in Doha to build a desalination plant. Ahmed and Amina stood near the entrance, shaking hands with guests as they arrived. They hoped they wouldn't have to stay there for long, as it seemed too formal, but thought it best for now. The political advisor came in next, with his wife and two boys, on holiday from boarding school, and Charles Denman, who was passing through Doha for discussions with the Emir and the Darwishes about supplying materials to build roads and new government buildings. John Harris, the architect, who was in Doha putting finishing touches to Rumaillah Hospital, was next with his wife. Uncle Salem came in a new gold-trimmed bisht, befitting his new status as a minister. Amina's brother Jabor arrived with his wife and two children. Just as Ahmed was thinking about going to mix with those who had already arrived, there was a flurry of activity in the street outside.

'Here we are, gentlemen. The Bait Al Bahr.'

It was Dr Mary Allison from the American Mission. Looking glamourous in a green satin frock with a shawl to match, she wore her long blonde hair down over her shoulders. She had brought two doctors with her.

'Hi Ahmed. Hi Amina. You look well. These are Doctor George and Doctor Farouk. I hope you don't mind.'

'Not at all,' Amina said. 'You are all most welcome. Come in. I may be needing you again. You never know.'

'Not tonight, I hope. We're here to have some fun.'

The courtyard was buzzing with guests, chatting over drinks. Lulua loved the spectacle and Tima chased around the palm tree, attracting attention. Um Jabor remained upstairs looking after the baby, who stayed fast asleep in his cot in his parents' bedroom.

The polite introductions over with, Eddie went upstairs to see how the band was getting on. They had assembled and set up their equipment in a corner.

'Let's begin, boys,' Mohammed commanded from behind his drum kit. 'How about Glenn Miller to kick off? Let's break 'em in nice and gentle. A one two, a one two three four...'

And in perfect harmony the quintet played 'Moonlight Serenade'.

The guests looked upward as the gentle notes floated from the roof. Ahmed was talking to Salem and Eddie when Mary Allison approached them and offered her hand to Salem.

'Mary Allison. Doctor at the Mission.'

'Salem bin Nasser Al Bahr. Minister of Finance.'

'Oh, I'm sorry. I never realised.'

'That's OK. It's nice to meet you. Another drink?'

'Yes, that would be nice. Thanks.'

'You?'

'I'll stick to orange juice. I tried champagne in Beirut. Didn't do much for me, I'm afraid. Have you met John Harris?'

They wandered off and found Harris, Denman and the political advisor in a circle with Abdullah Darwish, who was chatting near the palm tree.

The courtyard was quite full, and even more people had appeared.

'I think people must be getting hungry,' Amina said, nudging her husband. 'It's all ready up on the roof. Mrs P and I and some of the other ladies have been running up and down the stairs, in case you hadn't noticed.' She shot a pointed look at Ahmed.

Eddie shouted, 'Supper's ready, upstairs on the roof!' Everyone proceeded up the stairs. The band had played all Glenn Miller's hits, and were having a break.

An orderly queue formed, and the guests helped themselves to food. There weren't enough tables and chairs, so everyone spread themselves around the house: some in the majlis, happy to sit on cushions on the floor, others in the courtyard on the high benches that had been there since the house was built, and others on the roof.

'Wonderful spread, dear boy. Absolutely first class. What an evening, eh?' It was Mr Whitehouse, bearing a plate of prawns and coronation chicken. 'I'll have this then I have to take my leave. Off to the airport to meet the management from Bahrain.'

'Oh, sir. I didn't realise. Perhaps you can come back afterwards. Bring the management. They sound important. You're the only management I know!'

'Chaps from Manama, checking up to see how we're getting on. Don't worry. With you and Eddie on board doing all the hard work you're doing, things are looking very good.'

Waiters continued to buzz around, topping up drinks and replenishing plates. The ice had been broken: people mingled with friends and strangers alike. Salem hung up his gold-edged bisht in a reception room and escorted Mary Allison to the roof. The oil company men from Doha and Dukhan, most of whom were in the band, chatted with guests.

Ahmed took a moment to survey the scene. He had just come out of his bedroom, where Amina was with all three children, giving Um Jabor the chance to have a break and some food. He leaned on the balustrade overlooking the courtyard and couldn't believe how the house had been transformed. As the band started up again with some lively swing, his foot began to tap. The house has become a melting pot, he thought. My people, the Qatari people, from all walks of life, together with the British, Indian, Palestinian, Lebanese, American – all here to help build this country, all represented in this house. This is where I want to be. This is my destiny. He felt truly happy.

The sound of a female voice singing brought him back from his reverie. Up on the roof, Mary Allison was with the band. All eyes were on the young American. She was belting out Ella Fitzgerald's 'Anything Goes'. The audience lapped it up.

'Yallah, habibti ¬– let's dance,' Ahmed said, knowing Amina would say no.

'OK,' she said, catching her husband off-guard. 'I know this one. I heard it on Mrs Whitehouse's gramophone.'

There was more applause as the hosts danced in front of the band. They managed a sort of jive crossed with a waltz. It wasn't that great, they had to admit, but it was fun. Then the band swung into 'Too Darn Hot' and the whole rooftop became a dance floor. Even the single men jigged around, freestyle, their hands in the air. The only exception was Eddie, who was looking away across the rooftops.

'Come on, Eddie. Come and join us,' Ahmed shouted, and brought him to the centre of the rooftop. It seemed that Mary Allison was an Ella Fitzgerald fan. She continued with more Cole Porter songs: 'Anything Goes' segued into 'Just One of Those Things'.

Lulua and Tima had never been up so late. It was so exciting that they couldn't think of going to bed yet and spent all the time running around, Lulua showing off her English skills by saying 'Hello' to everyone, even her uncle and great-uncle. Tima followed her big sister and danced in her pink chiffon dress.

After dessert, the band were about to start up again. It was almost midnight, and people were still arriving. Ahmed looked down to see who it was.

Mr Whitehouse came through the door followed by two men in suits. The management, Ahmed thought, looking at Eddie who nodded. Following them were three women, smart, young and pretty in summer dresses.

'Well, we've come back, Ahmed and Amina, as you suggested. What a splendid evening! I've brought Jack and Lucy Dunbar and Mike and Jean Jamieson – they've come over from Bahrain for a two-day visit. I had to show them Qatari hospitality in action. This has been an amazing night – thanks to you both and to all those who have made it so special. Ahmed and Eddie have worked endlessly to get the Eastern Bank started here, and for that we are all most grateful. They have managed to open accounts for so many young people here in Doha and Dukhan. By the way, if you don't have an account yet, see me afterwards.' This drew hoots of laughter.

'There's one more thing. There's someone else out here. Eddie, I think you may have met her before.'

Eddie couldn't believe his eyes. It was Maggie.

'Oh, my goodness. What are you doing here?' he shouted as everyone applauded and cheered. He ran down the stairs and, taking her in his arms, twirled her around the courtyard.

'This is the happiest day of my life,' he said. 'What? How?'

Before anyone had a chance to speak, Maggie glanced over at Mr Whitehouse, who put his forefinger to his lips.

Eddie didn't care how she happened to be there; he was just pleased to see her.

Back on the roof, the band struck up 'All Through the Night'. The happy couple, Maggie looking dazed, danced close to Eddie. Ahmed and Amina danced together along with the rest, all squeezed onto the roof like penguins huddling together. They danced and partied into the night without a care in the world.

12

Ahmed couldn't quite believe all that had happened over the past two days. He needed time to take it all in and reassess his life. When he'd finished work at the bank he'd wandered down to the jetty, to the boats bobbing up and down. He didn't often go to see *Firial*, preferring instead to let the old group of friends use the vessel as a meeting-place to enjoy their retirement. When he had met them again, he didn't let on that the boat belonged to him, but now he thought she needed some repairs.

'I thought I'd find you here.'

It was Salem. He looked concerned. 'I saw you from up there,' he said, pointing to the Emiri office.

'Oh, of course. Your new job. Minister Salem. You are a very important person now.'

'I know, Ahmed, I know. But the responsibility is huge, and I doubt my ability to do it. Sheikh Ali expects a lot from me. Ach, I'll be OK. I'm just nervous.'

'And who is the office manager for His Highness? Did you manage to find someone?'

'Well, you won't believe it, but I asked Jabor, your brother-in-law. He said he would think about it. This morning he came to the office – he's agreed to do it. I have every confidence in him.'

'That's good. Jabor needed a good job and he's very reliable and trustworthy. It's a great honour for him. I must tell Amina and his mother, if they don't know already. They'll be so happy. Come, let us walk along the jetty.'

Ahmed was pleased to have met Salem. They strolled, talking about the wonderful party on Thursday.

'Your English friend looked so shocked at the end when his fiancée arrived from London,' Salem said.

'I know. I won't ask what time you left the party, Uncle Salem, or about your new American friend.'

They laughed. Guests had stayed up until dawn, then had slept wherever they could find a place. Ahmed told Salem he had found musicians asleep in the wind tower room, and Eddie and Maggie had been asleep on the roof in the corner as the sun rose. It had taken all day to clear up the debris and get Bait Al Bahr back to normal. Ahmed wondered whether it had been too much: the noise, the celebrations. 'I wonder what His Highness would think.'

'He would probably have loved it,' Salem said. 'He knows we have to keep up with the times. If we want new buildings and roads, hospitals and schools, then we need people from outside. We can't do it on our own. In any case, it makes life more interesting.'

'Ya Salem, tfadal, tfadal. Shlonak ya Salem?'

As they walked along the jetty to *Firial*, old Bilal shouted Salem's name.

'You know those men?' Ahmed asked Salem.

'Oh yes. I've known them for years. They were all in Al Mafja when I lived there. We grew up together in the pearl-diving days. They still come down here on their old boat to relive the old days.'

'I know. I met them several years ago. I was walking down here, before I got married, and they asked me on board. I come and see them from time to time.'

Ahmed wanted to tell his uncle the boat was now his, but something told him to hold back. For a moment there was a silence between them and Ahmed sensed that Salem was also reluctant to talk about *Firial*.

The two men went on board and stayed to drink tea, play cards and chat with the old sailors. Ahmed and his uncle loved listening to their stories and hearing their opinions on everyday matters.

Neither Ahmed or Salem said anything about their lives, or how they had been entertaining Westerners only two days before. They kept quiet. Their time on *Firial* was a reminder that they lived in a traditional country with traditional ways and they were responsible for keeping the Qatari way of life going.

When the time came for them to leave, they walked back along the little jetty towards Doha's. They climbed up the hill to the Emir's headquarters, where their paths would split.

'Ahmed,' Salem said turning to his nephew, 'I've been thinking. You've done so well at the bank and judging from the party on Thursday you have gained a lot of respect within the community. May I offer some advice?'

'Of course, Uncle Salem. I would value it greatly.'

'We are fortunate to be in a position of great influence. I am shortly to be responsible for the economic growth of the country. Of course, any major decisions will be made by the Emir himself, but now we have Jabor at his side. If any of you Qatari want to succeed in business and commerce, no one is better placed to do so. Think about your future – for you and your family. You have the chance. Seize it. Seize it with both hands.'

'Shukran ya Ami Salem. Alf shukr.' I shall remember your words.

The two men embraced warmly and looked out across the harbour they loved.

13

Events had taken over. Since the party, Ahmed and Amina had hardly spent any time together. When he eventually got back to Bait Al Bahr, he found the girls playing in the courtyard, enjoying the warm summer evening air. Amina was upstairs lying down with the baby.

'You look happy.'

'It's strange having a boy after the girls. He seems to want to move about already!'

'We haven't given him a name yet, Amina.'

'Oh no. There's been no time.'

'How about Fahd? A fahd is the fastest creature on the planet. He'll win all the races!'

'OK. Fahd it is,' Amina said. 'Welcome to the family.'

Ahmed told his wife that her brother had been chosen by Uncle Salem to be the Emir's new office manager. She gasped in surprise, then shouted 'Ya Ummi, Ya Ummi' to summon Um Jabor, who was overcome with pride and emotion. It was just sad, they thought, that Abu Jabor couldn't be here to share their happiness.

Ahmed told her about Salem being the new Minister of Finance. It looked like there were good times ahead. He said he would stay at the bank with Eddie and do his best to find more customers, so he had a steady income.

When Ahmed arrived at the bank the following morning just before seven, he found a flurry of activity. Mrs Whitehouse was running down the stairs, carrying her husband's hat and a clothes brush.

'Whatever would His Highness think if you didn't look like a proper English gentleman?'

'I'm sure he'd be more than happy.'

Mr Whitehouse sifted through a sheaf of papers while his wife brushed his shoulders and his hair, straightened his tie. Eddie walked in, looking weary. He glanced at Ahmed and mouthed 'good morning' at him.

'I'm in a bit of a hurry, chaps. The Emir has summoned me to the palace. Had a call at six o'clock from some new man there. Chap by the name of Jabor. Yes, Jabor, I think it was. Told me to get there ASAP. The Minister of Finance is coming too. Seems like things are moving. Better be on parade and let them know the bank is ready to help in any way it can. What do you say, chaps? Eddie you'd better man the fort while I'm away.'

Ahmed coughed, as if to say, *what about me?*

'Ah, yes. Ahmed, we'll be getting busier so be prepared to get out and get more customers. Those oil men all need bank accounts.'

'Yes, sir. By the way, sir, Jabor is my brother-in-law and the new Minister of Finance is Salem, the previous office manager and my uncle.'

'My dear Ahmed' – Mr Whitehouse put a hand on the young man's shoulder – 'That is very good news. We are going to be well placed.'

He made his way out into the already blazing heat of the August day. Ahmed and Eddie had soon divided their work between them: the Englishman would go after any potential expatriate clients and the young Qatari would attract as many Qataris as he could to open a bank account. After that there were possibilities of loans and investments with the country on the brink of rapid change. The two men decided to discuss things over breakfast.

'How are things at Bismillah?' Ahmed asked as they walked along.

'OK. But we'll have to find a place of our own soon.'

'Follow me. I know a place you will either love or hate.'

Ahmed led Eddie into the depths of the souq, passing the merchants and stallholders, all of whom could be potential customers. Ahmed noticed that one of the little shops was closed, the empty frontage looking out of place against the frenetic activity of the neighbouring businesses. Ahmed wondered what had happened. He was about to say something to Eddie when he decided to keep the thought to himself. The café was two doors along.

'Here we are. Abu Firas. Best breakfast in town.'

They took their places at a table and Ahmed greeted Abu Firas warmly.

Within minutes, two portions of fried chopped liver and onions arrived with a pile of flatbread. With a little guidance from Ahmed, Eddie dived in, tearing the flatbread, making a little spoon with it and scooping up the liver and sauce.

'Wonderful,' Eddie exclaimed at the end of the meal.

The friends began to plan their strategy at the bank. Eddie was willing to meet the newly arrived engineers and planners who had been engaged to build the infrastructure that Sheikh Ali and his advisors had envisaged. Ahmed agreed those accounts would please Mr Whitehouse.

He looked around at the busy café. The customers were all wearing different clothes: some in thobes, wearing not the Qatari aqal but a white turban. He thought they were from Iran, Iraq or Yemen. Others were wearing the shalwar khamees of newly created Pakistan. Their Indian counterparts dressed in chequered lungis with a vest on top. Ahmed wondered how many of the men had made the long journey to Doha to make money for their families, just like he was trying to do.

'Eddie, I'm going to talk to some of these men. Do you want to get on with trying to meet some of your British managers?'

'Very well, Ahmed. I'm going to find out about a house for Maggie and me too, because we can't stay at the hotel much longer. It's not fair on Maggie.'

The two men parted, leaving Ahmed to chat with the café customers. He learned that most of the men worked as porters, or coolies, as they were known in India. Their main task was to carry the heavy equipment needed for the oil wells, to run errands for their new masters, and work long, hard hours doing the most menial tasks. It was tough out in the desert, which Ahmed had already discovered, but he hadn't realised until now how important a role these men played in the discovery of oil.

By the time he had finished his tea, there was a circle of ten men around his table all telling him how they had arrived in Qatar, and how they had left their families. They all wanted to work hard to better themselves and have a brighter future. He felt as if he was on a mission to help them in any way he could.

'Shukran ya Abu Firas,' Ahmed said, paying for his meal. He shook hands with his fellow diners, vowing to meet again and enjoy more conversation.

As he emerged into the dusty market he realised he hadn't done anything about his task: to drum up trade for the bank. But, how could he? How could he ask these poor people to talk about their finances when he'd only just met them, and in any case all they probably wanted to do was get whatever meagre salary they had and send it home? Then it dawned on him. He stopped dead in his tracks when he reached the boarded-up shop. That was it. These men needed something other than a bank – something less formal and forbidding. He turned back into the café, calling Abu Firas.

'Ya, Abu Firas. That shop next door but one. What happened to it? Do you know?'

'Oh, it was very sad. Poor old Abu Omar – the trader, remember? He died. His family don't seem interested in the shop.'

'Where can I find the family? I might be interested.'

Abu Firas told Ahmed the family lived in Al Salata, but Abu Omar's son had the small grocery in the street opposite the fort. Ahmed was off, a spring in his step, his head buzzing with ideas. He wanted to go to the grocery straight away but thought he should head back to the office, having been out all morning supposedly finding clients. He had certainly found those, but he wasn't sure whose clients they were going to be – his or the bank's.

That afternoon, Mr Whitehouse and the two men discussed plans. He told Eddie and Ahmed what had happened at the palace that morning. He knew there were going to be some big contracts coming up. They would have to work hard, he said, because British companies as well as many from the Middle East were coming in to take advantage of the construction boom. The bank would be called upon to provide loans – and, as the Emir's chosen bank, the future looked promising.

Later that afternoon, as the children played in the courtyard Ahmed managed to have a quiet moment with Amina. He asked her to come upstairs, and they walked arm in arm along the balustraded veranda looking down at their little family. Um Jabor sat under the palm tree, rocking baby Fahd, as Lulua and Tima ran around trying to catch each other. The couple laughed when Um Jabor asked the girls to calm down – as if they would.

Ahmed took Amina into the wind tower room, where he had spent so many lonely days and nights in his youth. They sat down on one of the long mattresses by the wall.

'You know I've always wanted what's best for us for both, don't you, my love?' Ahmed said. putting his arm round Amina.

'Of course, I do. Ahmed,' she answered.

'And I want to discuss everything with you.'

'I know. That's the best way.'

He explained what had happened that day and how he had listened to the men in the café. 'I'm doing well at the bank, but I want to help these people. They're just ordinary folk who need somewhere to keep their money, where they can send any money they have to their families.'

'You're a good man, but what can you do about it?'

'I want to open an exchange house. Just a small place where the men would feel comfortable and they could go every month to send their salary home. I've found a place, I think.'

'But what about the bank? You have a good job there!'

'I think I can do both. I'll work at the bank in the morning and run the exchange house in the afternoon.'

Amina thought for a moment, unsure what to make of the plan. Would it be too risky? Could they afford it? They talked and talked until in the end Amina gave her consent. They kissed each other lovingly.

'I'll make some tea. I need a cup after all that,' Amina said. She was about to ask Ahmed whether he would like one, but it was too late. He was up and at the door.

'I'm just popping down to the souq. To that grocer's opposite the fort. I won't be long.'

'You're very naughty. As bad as the kids. Go on, off you go.'

The children could hear their father running down the stairs, something they were always told never to do.

'Daddy, you shouldn't run down the stairs,' the girls told him teasingly, thinking he was joining in their game. He felt like a child himself, he was so happy at Amina's approval.

'Let me go girls, please,' he pleaded. 'I've got to go. I won't be long. I'll be back soon, I promise.'

And the girls let him go.

In the souq Ahmed found the shop Abu Firas had told him about. It was next to a new baker's called Habib. The shop was small but was filled with all kinds of goods that Ahmed hadn't seen before. Lots of tinned food, neatly displayed on shelves, and in the centre were huge tins of olives and cheese, sacks of grain and spices that gave off a wonderful aroma. At the back of the shop a stout man, dressed in a thobe but with no headwear, was talking to a man who looked Indian – he was in a plain light blue shirt with a multi-coloured checked sarong wrapped around his lower body.

Ahmed was grateful for the ceiling fan that whirred in the centre of the shop. He gave a cough. 'Excuse me. I'm Ahmed Al Bahr. I hear that you have a shop next to the old café behind Al Darwish,' he ventured.

'Ahlan wa sahlan,' the stout man answered. 'Yes, that's true. Our family no longer has use of it.'

'Would it be possible to rent it?'

'I don't see why not. What do you need it for?'

Ahmed thought about telling him his plan but decided to be vague, saying it was to be used for clerical work. No food would be involved. He didn't want to give away his secret scheme, yet he wanted to assure his prospective landlord that he wouldn't be competition for his own grocery business.

'Very well. Sanjay, could you get the keys to the other shop?'

They discussed terms and over tea reached a compromise, then shook hands. Sanjay handed over the keys.

'Mukherjee here is from Bombay. He's very bright. He does all the accounts for me and is in the shop all day. We have many contacts now over in Bombay, so we can order goods quite easily. He's a great help.'

Ahmed's mind raced ahead, thinking of men like young Mukherjee who could be potential customers. He thanked the two men for their help and promised to be in touch again, telling them he was sure his wife and Um Jabor would visit their shop.

There were smiles all round as Ahmed left the grocery shop and stepped out into the warm night air. On his way home, he went to his new premises, where he stood outside, wondering what the future would hold. Nervously, he opened the door. There wasn't much light, but he could see the shop was in good order. It was small, and a few tables and chairs were piled up in the middle of the room. He imagined a counter towards the back of the premises and possibly a desk in the corner. Yes, he thought, I think we are in business.

14

Jabor was getting to grips with his new job. Although Salem had spent many hours with him showing him the ropes and giving advice, he still found it difficult to deal with all the new things he had to learn, as well as be on hand for anything the Emir demanded.

'Ya Jabor. Ta'al.' It was the Emir bellowing from his neighbouring office. Jabor dropped everything and sped to the desk as fast as he could.

'Shoof. Shoof ya Jabor.' Sheikh Ali was looking out of the window at the sea. He pointed to a flotilla of boats heading towards the harbour below.

'British flags. What's happening, I wonder?'

'Jabor, where is Cochrane? I need him here now. Find him for me.'

'I'll get him, Your Highness. I'll find him right away,' Jabor replied. He summoned two of the palace guards to go to Al Koot fort to find Cochrane, who was responsible for policing the country. As he did so, two more visitors arrived in the outer office. One of them Jabor knew. Abdullah Darwish was back again, constantly with the Emir, ready to take part in any future business deals. The other was Charles Denman, British businessman Darwish's associate.

'Sit down, gentlemen, please. His Highness is very busy this morning,' Jabor said politely.

Not used to waiting, Darwish reluctantly sat down alongside his business partner. They could hear discussions going on in the Emir's office, and he wondered what they were about. Within minutes Cochrane arrived, out of breath, having run from the Al Koot fort. He knew why he had been summoned and went straight into the inner office.

'Cochrane!' the Emir shouted. 'What's going on? Mohammed Al Attiyah here is saying there aren't enough Qatari policemen. All are foreigners. What do you have to say?'

The British policeman twitched nervously, trying to think of the most diplomatic words.

'There are strikes, Your Highness. The oil men aren't happy. We are trying to keep calm. I can't find enough men from Qatar who are willing to do the job and keep the peace.'

'Mohammed Al Attiyah will work alongside you and establish a joint force. You understand? We must stop the strikes immediately. You may go.'

Jabor escorted Cochrane out of the office. There was a commotion at the palace entrance, and he rushed down to see what it was about. He could see three tall men in uniform, one with white plumes in his helmet. Of course – it was the men from the British flotilla.

'Let them in. It's OK. His Highness will see them. Mafee mushkilla,' Jabor said to the heavy-handed guards, who put their rifles down and let them through.

'Salam aleikum ya Sahab ismo.'

'Aleikum salam ya Sayyed Hay. This is an unexpected surprise.'

The Emir, while remaining polite, couldn't help showing his disapproval at the sudden visit. 'I hope all is well.'

'I apologise for the unannounced visit, but my people in Bahrain were unable to get through on the phone. I am here to introduce my successor and a new advisor for Your Highness. Bernard Burrows will be the new political agent for the Gulf representing Her Majesty's government, and Geoffrey Hancock will take up his post here with immediate effect.'

'I see. So Plant has gone already. I can't say I'm surprised.'

The group stifled a chuckle. They all knew that Captain Philip Plant had made rather a mess of things during his short tenure.

'Ahland wa sahlan ya sayyed Hancock, Welcome' the Emir said shaking the new man's hand.

'Shukran ya Sahib Ismo. Ana ureed alaqat jaid bain al baladain shaqeeqain,' Hancock replied, expressing his wish that relations would be good between the two countries.

'You speak Arabic well, ya sayyed Hancock.'

'It's improving, I hope.'

Bernard Burrows stood to attention. 'I am happy to be here as Her Majesty's representative. My first duty is to hand over an invitation from Her Majesty for you to attend her coronation in London in June. Her Majesty has asked me to convey her greetings and would be most honoured if you would attend.'

Sheikh Ali opened the large stiff cream envelope bearing the royal coat of arms. Finally, he resorted to using a small ceremonial dagger on his desk.

'I am happy to receive this, Mr Hancock, but I am very busy these days. There is a lot of work to be done here, as you can see. I will send my son Ahmed on my behalf. I am sure he will be a good representative. Please pass on my thanks and congratulations to Her Majesty.'

The delegation left the office, and in walked Abdullah Darwish with Charles Denman.

'Welcome, gentlemen. It's a busy morning, as you can see. What can I do for you? Good to see you again, Mr Denman. Abdullah, you seem to be in my office every day!'

The Emir and Darwish knew they needed each other at this critical time. The wily merchant was keen to maintain his position as the merchant to whom the Emir turned for any major requirements. Denman was the principal conduit for any major purchases and supplies from the former colonial power.

'You may have seen the new advisor as you came in,' Sheikh Ali said. 'He seems to be an Arabist. That helps. We need someone who understands what's going on. From what I hear from Cochrane, we need more Qatari men in the police force. Denman, find me British officers who can teach my police. We need more engineers and doctors too.'

Before Charles Denman could reply, Abdullah Darkish stepped in, saying, 'Of course, Your Highness, we'll do that.' He knew that any future contracts would go through him and he would take his cut.

The Emir asked the men to look out of the window. 'You see how our country is small and not yet ready to meet the challenges of the current times. Trouble is spreading throughout the Arab world. Look at the tragedy of Palestine, and how Egypt is looking for a better future without Britain. We love the British, but my people want to have their own struggle too. Many of the oil workers are not happy. They see the British, the way they live here, and they want the same. You can't blame them.'

The two guests looked at each other, gauging how to respond. They knew the Emir was right. Abdullah Darwish had been aware of a few men demonstrating outside his office near the seafront only a few days ago, and Charles Denman, having served his country as a soldier in Egypt during the war, was only too aware of the situation.

'Your Highness speaks with reason,' Denman said, the voice of diplomacy. 'I am sure with a little help from professionals Qatar will find her own people willing to run the country in years to come.'

'We should send some of our best people to study abroad so they can come back with the skills they will need,' Abdullah

Darwish suggested, knowing he could make the arrangements with Denman for that all-important fee.

'By the way, you'd better look after my son when he goes to the coronation,' the Emir said, turning to Denman. 'I'll try to visit Britain later in the year, if the situation here allows.'

'Very well,' Denman said, 'it will be an honour. Now we must go. Mr Darwish and I will be meeting the new advisor and working on contracts for the new schools and hospitals. I am currently bringing engineers to build a new road to Saudi Arabia too, Your Highness.'

'Good. Good. Just make sure we can get supplies from across the border. But don't make it too easy for the Saudis to get in. We don't want to give the impression this is an open invitation.'

All three laughed, knowing that Qatar was dwarfed by its neighbour.

'Ya Jabor,' the Emir barked. 'You see, gentlemen? You have met young Jabor. He has to do everything here. It was difficult at first, but now he is doing well. In fact, I couldn't do without him.'

Jabor bowed his head with embarrassment but felt proud as the Emir stood up to say goodbye to his guests. 'Yallah, gentlemen. Jabor, there's work to be done.'

The Emir and Jabor spent the day ploughing through paperwork and receiving petitions from elders who had come into the capital from their desert dwellings to ask for financial assistance. As the Emir dealt with Bedouin tribal sheikhs and former pearl-divers who were finding it difficult to manage, he felt a huge burden weighing on his shoulders. How should he handle the new oil wealth, so it could bring a better life for all his fellow citizens? Whenever there was a gap in the procession of penitents, he confided in Jabor how hard it was for him to see these fine old men suffering hardship.

It was almost dusk when Sheikh Ali headed back to his private quarters and the sunset call to prayer. He loved the sight of the calm sea at the end of the working day, calming his troubled mind. In the corner of his eye he noticed the grey gunboat and support vessel still moored at the jetty. 'So they are still here,' he thought. 'I wonder what they are up to. The British have been here since 1916. Why do they love the place so much? Is it just oil? Power? The attraction of the Orient? I'll never know.'

As His Highness looked forward to a peaceful evening with his family, things were getting under way opposite the Diwan Emiri. The advisor's house had been decked out with lanterns along the balcony and in the dusty palms that swayed in the evening breeze as guests assembled for drinks.

It was an all-British affair. After the lacklustre performance of the previous political advisor, the new political resident, Bernard Burrows, based in Bahrain, was keen to 'rally the troops and put on a good show', as he termed it.

Few wives had accompanied their husbands. Those who had gathered to share their stories of settling in to this desert land.

'Well, we had the war to contend with, so this can't be any worse,' exclaimed one bright expat in a floral print and with upswept hair, freshly rollered.

The half dozen women all knew each other, having been invited to each other's homes for coffee mornings – part of an unwritten code that made sure any newcomer was shown the ropes of living in a new, unfamiliar country. Some had been posted overseas before and were used to hardships like disease and heat, some having lived in the Far East and India during the pre-Independence years.

One of the newer arrivals was Maggie, Eddie's wife. She looked a little nervous.

'Still in a hotel, dear?' It was the woman in the floral dress. 'That won't do. They should find you somewhere decent. I'll speak to Tommy. You know my husband, don't you? Head of Ops.'

'That's very kind, Mrs ... er...'

'Hughes, dear. Hughes. Call me Dorothy.' Dorothy offered her hand with a generous smile. She sounded as though she was used to getting her own way.

Then there was a tinkling noise. It was the political resident. 'Gentlemen, ladies. Your attention, if I may.'

The chat around the room died away.

'We are gathered here to welcome George to his new posting. Please support him as best you can. He knows the challenges ahead. We need to maintain our position in Qatar as Her Majesty's government strengthens her role in the development of the country. We are playing our part in

Qatar's oil development, with British interests both onshore in Dukhan and offshore in the Arabian Gulf. We must be careful to keep the Emir as a friend, and so we have been generous in rewarding him personally for the contracts we have won.'

The British engineers looked at each other with wry smiles. Only a few months ago a new treaty had been signed whereby the Qatar government received 50% of the profits from oil. Petroleum Development Qatar had been formed, but Shell was in the forefront of any future development.

'Among us this evening, are those responsible for establishing various government departments. Geoffrey will oversee this. His Arabic is good, and he has already made a good impression on His Highness.'

Geoffrey Hancock acknowledged the compliment by giving a slight bow. The other guests were not quite sure what to make of the new man. Arabic-speaking expatriates were often regarded with a certain amount of suspicion.

'My dear Ron.' Burrows addressed the police superintendent, who was dressed not in a suit but a flowing robe. The short, rather overweight man looked out of place in the formal British gathering.

'It's been a difficult time, I know. To maintain law and order when the locals aren't used to rules and regulations is a challenge. These demonstrations must be stopped. We can't have discontent on the streets. The people must have confidence in their leader and our system of government will ensure this.'

Cochrane dabbed his forehead with a white handkerchief. He had become a local in matters of religion and dress, but he had never adapted to the heat. His weight added to his discomfort. Knowing that the political agent was referring to him alone when it came to the strength of the police force made him even more uneasy. He sensed the well-to-do expatriates around him shying away from him.

Burrows ploughed on, talking about new roads, schools and hospitals. The senior management teams of the engineering companies were all present, as well as Whitehouse and Eddie from the bank which, Burrows reminded the audience, was ready to supply funds for any major project.

'Finally, ladies and gentlemen, let us remember Her Majesty the Queen, who will be crowned in June as head of state of the United Kingdom and the Commonwealth. There may no longer be an empire, but here in the Gulf we fly the Union flag as a symbol of our strong links across the globe with India and the colonies of Hong Kong and the dominions of Australasia. May I propose a toast to the Queen?'

'The Queen,' all said loudly, thrusting their gin and tonics towards the stucco ceiling.

15

Ahmed could think of nothing else. He kept Amina awake at night talking about his plans, excited at the prospect of starting his own business, imagining the office and how it would help the workers he'd seen in the café. At the same time, he tossed and turned, anxious about the huge task ahead. Could he manage such a project? What would the bank say? Could he cope with the responsibility? What if it all went wrong?

'I want to build a future for our children, my love.'

'I know. I know, Ahmed. You're doing a great thing. We'll help you as much as we can. Don't rush too quickly. All will be fine. Just you wait.'

Amina's calm reassuring voice gave her husband more confidence. Unable to lie in bed any longer, he got up and made his way to the roof. It was barely dawn, and the muezzin was summoning the faithful to prayer. He felt energised, and thanked God for all the blessings in his life.

He ran down from the roof, washed his face and changed into the nearest clean thobe he could find, kissing Amina on the cheek before she could ask where he was going. He had barely got to the wooden postern gate when he heard her call out.

'I think you've forgotten something.'

'Keys.'

Another grateful kiss and he rushed through the early dawn worshippers towards his new office. Nothing else mattered. He could manage a couple of hours work on the new premises before started work at the bank. The old blue door opened after a bit of gentle persuasion. Although the sun was up, the dark souq allowed no light into Ahmed's new world. He could just about make out the leftover furniture propped against the back wall. His office was small, shabby and uninviting. After his initial excitement, he now felt a sudden melancholy, thinking that the enterprise was beyond him. He shut the door in a temper, taking out his annoyance on the old bolts and key, then decided to go next door to the café to cheer himself up with a big breakfast.

The café was busy as usual. Ahmed looked for a table in the corner where he could be quiet in order to rethink his plans.

'Ya Ahmed? Ya ibn ami waynak?' Where have you been, my nephew?

It was his Uncle Salem. Ahmed should have realised that Doha was so small, and the café had such a good reputation, that he was bound to meet someone he knew.

'Tfadal. Tfadal ya achi. Please after you.'

Salem rose from the table near the window along with Jabor, Ahmed's brother-in-law.

'This is a nice surprise. Sit down, ya achi. I see you've discovered the best breakfast. I come here nearly every day,' Salem said. 'Jabor wanted a few tips about running the Emir's office, so here we are.'

'Your uncle has been very helpful, Ahmed,' Jabor said. 'I'm finding it difficult to cope with all the comings and goings and arranging the day. So many people want to see His Highness. In fact, I'll have to go soon.'

'How is everything with you?' Jabor asked.

Ahmed told them how he had rented the office next door and that it was probably going to be a disaster.

'It sounds like a great idea, Ahmed,' Jabor said in between bites of his kidney and onion sandwich. 'The people need something like that, for sure.'

They looked around at their fellow diners.

'There's something that unites us all. We all like good food to start the day. It doesn't matter where we come from.'

Ahmed ordered a sandwich and sweet milky tea. He told them that the old office was in such bad state of repair it wouldn't be possible to start an exchange house there after all.

'Nonsense,' Salem exclaimed. 'You can do it. I may be a minister now, but I can help you get set up. I'm still good with a bit of hard manual work.'

'I can help too,' Jabor said. 'After all you've done for me, it's the least I can do.'

Ahmed felt buoyed by this support from his family. At that point a woman came into the restaurant. There was a hush, as it was unusual for this to happen, and so early in the morning. It was Maggie. Holding the door open for her was Eddie. All three men got up to welcome the couple, slightly unsure how to arrange the seating.

'I thought I'd bring Maggie along,' Eddie said. 'After we had such a good breakfast the other day, she wanted to try it instead of the dreary fare at the Bismillah. So here we are.'

'Welcome. Welcome,' Jabor and Salem said, making them comfortable.

There was more talk of Ahmed's project. Eddie and Maggie were happy to offer their services. 'Give me a mop and bucket and I'll clean all day if you like,' Maggie said.

Eddie looked a little concerned. Ahmed hadn't mentioned the project to him. After a while, he said he would support Ahmed. Ahmed breathed a grateful sigh of relief.

'Mr Ahmed.' Another call from across the café. It was Sanjay Mukherjee, the grocer whose landlord owned the building next door. 'If you need any help, let me know.'

'I may need you soon, Sanjay,' Ahmed said. 'I need an accountant. I don't think I can manage on my own.'

'I'm busy all day but will try and make some time for you. My brother, Vijay, is a qualified accountant. He studied at Bombay University. I can ask him to come over if you like.'

'Yes please,' Ahmed said.

'It sounds like you're in business, dear Ahmed. Mabrook,' Salem said. 'Let's all meet later after work. Say four o'clock?

See you later. I've got to see the Emir. Jabor, you'd better come with me too.'

Ahmed was dazed. All his friends were behind him. The despair he had felt less than an hour ago had turned to elation. He walked with Eddie to the bank, thanking him for his support. Maggie went to Amina to ask her to bring Um Jabor's brushes and cleaning cloths in the afternoon.

At the bank Mr Whitehouse was waiting for his two staff members in the hallway. He looked anxious as Ahmed and Eddie came in, apologising for being late. Ahmed felt a twinge of guilt when Eddie explained they had been engaged in drumming up trade. A white lie, Ahmed thought. Yes, they had been engaged in financial affairs, but the business wasn't for the benefit of the bank at all.

'I've seen Hancock,' Mr Whitehouse announced. 'You'd better sit down. There's a lot happening. Through Darwish and Charles Denman in London we've been asked to finance the loans for the new hospital and two schools. We'll also be involved in the new road to Saudi Arabia. We're going to be extremely busy. I may have to go to Bahrain to arrange things. I may need you to work more than usual.'

Eddie asked for more details. Ahmed wondered if he could handle the extra work along with his new business. He was suddenly panic-stricken at the thought deceiving Mr Whitehouse. To make himself feel better, he promised to work hard for the success of the bank. Ahmed noticed Eddie looking at him and felt an uncomfortable awkwardness between them.

Back home, Ahmed barely touched the lunch Amina and Um Jabor had made.

'Aish feek, ya habibi? What's the matter my dear' Amina knew there was something wrong.

Ahmed waited for the children and Um Jabor to finish and go upstairs before answering.

'Amina, you know all I want is the best for us all, but I've always said that the simple way of life is the best.'

'Yes. I know that. That's why I love you.'

'Well, things have just got complicated. I don't know how I'm going to manage working at the bank and running the new business. Mr Whitehouse has asked me to do extra work. It doesn't seem right.'

'You'll have to tell him, habibi. Best to be honest, isn't it?'

'I suppose. But what if he's angry? Eddie gave me a funny look today. I don't know what he thinks about it all. Perhaps I should just forget the new idea. We can carry on living on my salary from the bank if we are careful.'

'But it's a great idea and I'm sure it will be successful. You have to take risks sometimes, Ahmed. Everyone is behind you.'

Ahmed thought for a moment. 'All right. I can't do it without you, though. I need your support.'

'You have my support, dear Ahmed. Now look at the time. We'd better go.'

Leaving baby Fahd at home with Um Jabor, Ahmed, Amina, Lulua and Tima made their way from Bait Al Bahr down to the souq, all carrying cleaning items. When they arrived,

Salem and Jabor were already there with two other men bearing tools and equipment.

'Once we've cleaned the place up, Hussein here can start to do some woodwork. Mohsen is from the Darwish stores. He can get the paint – whichever colour you like as long as it's light blue.'

Everyone laughed. Ahmed opened up the shop doors, letting in the afternoon light. Maggie and Eddie came along a little later too. Amina popped next door to get tea for everyone as they got started on scrubbing floors, washing down walls and dusting the ceiling. A small crowd had gathered outside, curious. Ahmed, bewildered by all the interest, didn't have time to worry any more. The die was cast.

16

Desmond Whitehouse called Eddie and Ahmed into his office. It was Thursday morning and business was coming to an end for the week.

'Gentlemen, I have something to announce. I'm being transferred back to Bahrain. I am to be manager there. A promotion, I suppose.'

Eddie and Ahmed offered their congratulations, happy for their boss.

'Bahrain have said it's up to me to choose a successor. I'm happy to say that Eddie will be taking over as manager here in Doha. Ahmed, you may be disappointed but since you have your own business I thought it best that the bank be run by someone who can devote all their time to the task. My wife and I have enjoyed our time here immensely, and I'm sure we'll keep in touch. We'll be leaving at the end of the month.'

Ahmed turned to Eddie to congratulate him. A distance had grown between the two friends recently. Since the exchange house had been established, Ahmed had been very busy. Eddie and Maggie had moved into a new house in Rumailah. Maggie hosted coffee mornings and had formed a small amateur theatre group. It had been a long time since they had been to Bait Al Bahr for family lunches now that Ahmed was so busy, and Amina had started work at the Women's Hospital.

Then there was a commotion outside the office. They got up and peered out of the front office window, and saw a procession of men marching and shouting, banners held high. The men looked like a mixture of Qataris, Egyptians, Indians, Yemenis and Palestinians.

'Down with Britain! Down with the colonial power! Freedom for Egypt! Freedom for the Arab world! Justice for the workers! Fair pay for all!'

'What on earth's going on?' Mr Whitehouse said in disbelief. 'I've never seen anything like this in all my days in the Gulf.'

'Must be about Suez. The British aren't too popular at the moment,' Eddie answered.

Ahmed kept quiet. He had sensed something like this might happen. He had bought a new radio when Nasser had come to power in Egypt and was following events closely. Britain's part in the Suez crisis, he realised, would not go unnoticed.

'There must be more than a thousand people out there,' Whitehouse exclaimed. 'I'm going up to see Hancock and

Cochrane to find out what the situation is. Eddie, you'd better come too.'

Ahmed felt left out. He followed the men out of the bank and walked along beside the protesters. He recognised some of the workers as customers at the exchange. They came in every Thursday or Friday afternoon to send whatever they could back to their families in the Middle East or India. They all looked determined and angry. It was also a demonstration against the conditions under which the men were working, and their right to work for a fair wage. Ahmed knew that since the oil had been discovered, and later exported, only a small percentage of the profits went to the people.

He made his way past Darwish's office, where the demonstrators had stopped to shout, obviously aware that Darwish was a friend of the British. Ahmed decided to walk up to the Emir's office and see Jabor. The men continued to shout as they marched on and gathered at the new clock tower outside the palace.

The guards knew Ahmed well and gave him a friendly nod, despite the trouble brewing not far away. As Ahmed glanced back at the crowd, he noticed Mr Whitehouse and Eddie walking into the political advisor's residence opposite. He made his way across the vast courtyard, admiring the Emir's new Chrysler gleaming in the noon sun.

Upstairs, Jabor was dashing backwards and forwards to Sheikh Ali's office as usual and asked Ahmed to wait. He looked out of the window at the jetty, spotting *Firial* moored at the far end. The Emir's vessel was nearer the shore. He thought how sad it was that they were hardly ever used and vowed to go and chat to the old crew more often and maybe take *Firial* out one day.

His daydream was interrupted by Jabor, who came bustling in. 'You see what's out there, Ahmed, apart from your beloved *Firial?*'

Ahmed then spotted a grey ship moored some way offshore.

'HMS *Flamingo*. The British navy are here. Can you imagine?'

'Oh dear. That is serious. I've just seen the demonstration.'

'Darwish is in with the Emir now, deciding what to do. The sheikh is worried. No doubt Hancock and Cochrane will be over soon to offer their advice.'

Jabor said the word 'advice' with a smirk. Ahmed nodded ruefully. Then Salem came in.

'What's all this? I saw them from my window. I came here as fast as I could. Can I go in?'

'You'd better wait a minute. He's with Abdullah Darwish.'

'He's part of the problem. Too many merchants in league with British companies. The people want to have their say. Looks like we can't escape it here. You can't blame them. As long as they just march and shout, that's OK, but any more trouble... Where's Cochrane? You know about Suez? The British have landed troops there. First the Israelis in Sinai, now this. We'll never get our oil through the canal. The British had a plan all along. It was on the radio. If Hancock comes over here, I'll give him a piece of my mind.'

'You can go in now. Good luck.'

When they were alone, Jabor asked Ahmed to sit down.

'I'd better go. You're busy.'

'OK, but between you and me, the Emir isn't happy. This will make it worse. He says he's had enough. The long days and all the problems of running the country – so much has happened in such a short time. He doesn't think he can handle it. He wants to step down.'

'Ya Jabor taal. Come here.'

It was the Emir. It was time to go. Ahmed wished his brother-in-law well and left. At the clock tower he saw the British entourage walking briskly across to the palace. Eddie waved, and Ahmed waved back, but Eddie didn't smile.

The crowd gathered on the newly asphalted seafront road, one or two men the obvious leaders, encouraging the crowd to repeat their anti-colonial slogans. Ahmed went home. He opened the postern door, thinking how complicated life was getting. All he had wanted was to live a simple life. Little Fahd toddled up to him with a broad grin.

'Baba, Baba.'

It was more than enough compensation. The girls ran into his arms too, Lulua rushing to tell him about her morning at school and Tima showing him a drawing of a house with a bright red sun in the corner.

'Is that our house, Tima? Our happy house?'

'Naam Baba. Naam. Yes, it is, little one. Is it beautiful?'

'It certainly is.'

341

'Wain Mama?' he asked, then realised she must still be at the hospital.

Um Jabor came out from the kitchen to tell Ahmed Amina would be late back today. They were short-staffed at the hospital.

'Lunch is ready.'

It felt strange to eat with the children and not have Amina to chat to about his day. He missed her saying 'Don't talk with your mouth full' and 'Tima, finish your salad. You want to be a big, strong girl, don't you?' The children were quiet. He felt he had little time to spend with his family, to read a favourite story to Tima or make one up, which was her favourite thing. Ahmed told the children to be good while he was at work. As he was leaving Amina came in, looking tired.

'I thought I might catch you. A lot of babies are being born at the moment. I had to stay on.'

'Lunch should still be warm. I'd better go. Have you heard about the demonstrations?'

'Some of the mothers said something about it. Can't blame them, I suppose. When will I see you?'

'Not sure. I'll see how things go at the office.'

Ahmed gave his wife a kiss on the cheek and made his way out into the busy souq. Thursday afternoons were always busy, but today there was a feeling of uncertainty in the air. Doha had always been peaceful. Now it felt as if it was changing.

It was three o'clock. When Ahmed arrived at Al Bahr Finance and Exchange, proudly looking up at the red sign, as he always did, there was a small crowd waiting to go in. He had seen many of the men down near the seafront earlier, taking part in the march. They hushed when Ahmed opened the door. Vijay, the accountant, was already there. He had been a godsend. Over the past three years, the exchange house had become the place for workers to come and send their earnings back home. It had been a source of pride and joy and Ahmed had reaped the rewards of his idea, supplementing his income from the bank. In recent months Amina too was bringing home a small salary from the Women's Hospital. She loved her family dearly but found she wanted to make a difference and do something useful as her country started to improve.

The expatriate workers formed an orderly queue. Vijay stood behind the counter to deal with the first customers. Ahmed stood alongside him, making sure everything was going properly. After half a dozen men had been dealt with Ahmed, looking over Vijay's shoulder, noticed the remittances weren't as much as usual. They were only tens of rupees. They wondered what had happened. He asked an Indian oil worker why he was not sending as much as usual.

'We've been on strike, sir. All of us. We want more money. We are working from six in the morning until six at night. We can't continue like this.'

'So the company has docked your pay?'

'That's right. We don't know what to do. This is all I have to spare to send home to my wife and daughter.'

Ahmed made a mental note to see Uncle Salem. If anyone could help, it would be the Minister of Finance.

Men continued to come in, but not as many as usual. Each of them told stories of their ill-treatment in the camps. Now they had less money, they would have to return to the long hours and stop striking.

Ahmed tried to calm the situation by telling them he would do what he could to help, but he knew it was all up to the oil company and the managers in Dukhan. When the last customer left, Ahmed and Vijay closed the business, hoping for a better day tomorrow.

Now the sun had gone down, there was a chill in the air. It was time to start putting on warmer clothes. Ahmed would change to a thicker wool thobe and his red-patterned qutra instead of the white one. He didn't mind the summer, but in November you could be outside more, enjoying the days without having to constantly find shade. On his way home, he chatted to the neighbouring businessmen, with whom he had become friendly. All the talk was of the demonstration in the morning. Some of the older traders, sitting outside their establishments, playing with prayer beads, looked concerned and predicted difficult days ahead.

As Ahmed walked home, he was happy that he was improving his life and the lives of his family, but a nagging feeling gnawed away deep inside. A Chevrolet truck passed him, and Ahmed stepped aside to make way for the large vehicle. There were more cars and trucks on the streets, thanks to the oil money, and proper roads had been made. He couldn't help wondering how things would change. He thought about Jabor's revelation that the Emir wasn't happy. At the gate he thought of *Firial* and the pearl-divers. He promised himself that next morning he would go down to the jetty to buy fish and chat to the old men.

Later that evening, when the children had gone to bed, Ahmed and Amina went to their favourite corner room upstairs. The wind tower wasn't really needed at this time of year, but that was where they had decided to put the new radio. Abdullah Darwish had imported several large Bush radios from London and offered one to Ahmed at a discount price.

Ahmed twiddled with the tuning knob until the crackles stopped and a deep male voice with an Egyptian accent announced, 'Hunna Misr. Izza' Sawt Al Arab.' This is Cairo. The voice of Arab radio.

The couple listened intently as the announcer spoke. 'Foreign invaders have arrived on our dear nation's shores. The British have landed at Port Said. The French have landed too and are attacking Port Fuad. The Israelis continue to invade our country and there is fighting in the streets of Sinai and Suez. We ask you citizens to pick up arms and fight the aggressors. His Excellency President Gamal Abdul Nasser has declared this "the people's war".'

Amina and Ahmed held each other tightly, unable to say anything.

'It's not surprising the Egyptians were demonstrating today then,' Amina said eventually.

'No. But this crisis is affecting us here too. It's all to do with oil. The British hate Nasser since he nationalised the Suez Canal. Nasser wants to control the Arab world and get rid of Britain and France, and he even hates Iraq, which is worrying. And Israel, of course.'

'And what about the United States and the Soviet Union? This could lead to another world war.'

Late that night, there was a banging on the outside door.

'Who can that be at this time of night?' Amina wondered.

Ahmed rushed downstairs and found Jabor at the door.

'I'm sorry to disturb you, but I've come from the palace. I need to talk to you.'

Amina was pleased to see her brother but concerned at the late-night call. Jabor told them about his terrible day. He needed to talk about things to calm down. They discussed what they'd heard on the radio, and how events might unfold.

Um Jabor heard them talking and came out to greet her son. The warm embrace she gave him gave him the comfort he needed after working with the Emir all day. She made tea for everyone and brought out some biscuits.

'I'm sorry, Jabor, but you look terrible. You must be exhausted,' Amina said, looking lovingly at her brother.

'I am. All day there are visitors coming and going, trying to get an audience with the Emir. Then after they've gone the Emir pours out all his sorrows. He's thinking of handing over power to Sheikh Ahmed.'

'I suppose a younger man would be able to handle the responsibility better. After all, Sheikh Ali is sixty,' Ahmed said.

'But Sheikh Khalifa has his eyes on power too. They were all in there today. When Sheikh Abdullah abdicated in favour of Sheikh Ali, Ali promised that his successor would be the son of Hamad. Sheikh Khalifa supports the workers' right to strike and he's trying to get money to send to Egypt to support the Arab cause. And as all this was happening, Hancock came in with Burrows from Bahrain.'

'What is happening to our country, Jabor?' Amina said.

'We have become mixed up in this power struggle. It all comes from oil. It's a blessing which we have turned into a curse,' Ahmed said.

'The British have made a big mistake with Suez,' Jabor said. 'Of course the sheikh couldn't say that to Burrows and Hancock. If the nationalist fervour gets stronger, the traditional way of government here and in the rest of the Gulf will – well, you can imagine.'

With a better life came additional worries brought on by being busier and knowing more about world affairs. Was life better in their fathers' and grandfathers' day? They finally said goodnight to each other. Jabor was too tired to go home and slept under a blanket in the majlis.

17

Friday started as usual with the children getting into bed with their parents. They had already found their Uncle Jabor snoring peacefully downstairs.

'Ya Ummi, ya Ubbi. Ami Jabor ragid fil majlis.' *Mama, Uncle Jabor is asleep in the majlis.* Tima brought them the news.

'OK, Tima. We know. It's OK. He's tired. Leave him alone, please,' Amina said. 'Why don't you ask your sister to make some tea?'

Ahmed was slow to wake. He had had a strange dream. 'We were all in it. You, me, the children, even Jabor. We were all flying somewhere. We had wings.'

'That's why you were making funny noises in your sleep.'

'I've got an idea, Amina. Can we all go down to the harbour and see *Firial*? I want to check she's OK and see if the pearl-divers are still there. It would be fun for the children too.'

'Sounds like a good idea. I'll get them ready.'

After breakfast the family walked down to the jetty. Jabor went along too. He had slept well and was happy to have a break from the strain of the palace. The November air was fresh and just the right temperature. The girls skipped along, hand in hand. Fahd took a few steps but then had to be carried by the grown-ups.

Ahmed led the way along the jetty to the far end where *Firial* was moored. He saw a small boat coming alongside. It was Uncle Salem.

'Ya Ammi Salem. Forsa saida.' A happy chance.

Salem thanked the sailor who had rowed him ashore and climbed up onto the jetty from the boat. 'I've come from the British gunship, HMS Flamingo,' he said. 'She's over there, see? Burrows has just gone back. He stayed last night at the British residence. I was there last night and this morning having discussions. Do I look tired?'

'You certainly do,' Jabor said. 'You must have seen them just as I was leaving last night. What's the latest news?'

'Everyone's worried about Nasser. Burrows knows his government has made a mess. He thinks Eden will have to go. Despite that, he thinks he can manage the situation from Bahrain so has gone back onto Flamingo.'

'Exactly what we were saying last night,' Ahmed said. 'Jabor stayed with us. We've come down to see *Firial*. Here she is. Remember, Uncle Salem?'

'Of course, ya Ahmed. Oh, those days. Hard times but so lovely.' Salem's mind seemed to wander.

'Baba, where's your boat?' It was inquisitive Tima.

'It's our boat, Tima habibti. There, look. Your great-uncle Salem remembers this boat from when he was a boy. Let's go and see.'

Lulua and Amina held Fahd by the hand. Jabor and Salem decided not to talk about the events of the past day and to enjoy this family time together. Ahmed led the way. He thought that, now he could afford it, he would try to get *Firial* painted and restored.

Three men sat at the stern of the vessel. They were sitting exactly where they had been when they had invited him on board to play cards.

'Bilal, is that you? Yousef? And Ibrahim?' Uncle Salem looked in awe at the three men.

'Ya Salem. Praise be to God. It's been such a long time,' Bilal said, and they hugged.

Ahmed realised the men must be childhood friends of Salem. They were all from Al Mafjar. Salem hadn't been a pearl-diver, but here they were all reunited.

Ahmed introduced the men to his family and they all got on board. The children loved having a new place to explore. Yousef sat on the old nokhdar's throne-like seat, cracking jokes about the joys of being retired, and seemed blissfully unaware of the political turmoil. He was tall and thin, unlike the large, dark-skinned Bilal, who sat on his right enjoying a bubbly bubbly.

They all had lots to say. Salem was unable to stop talking about the old days. Jabor and Amina were enthralled by the sailors' pearl-diving stories. Ibrahim showed the children around. Tima was very interested in a wooden box they found at the back of the boat.

Suddenly Lulua spoke up. 'Where do you sail to?' she asked.

The men looked at each other. 'We don't sail anywhere. We just come here every week or so to chat and think about the past.'

'Doesn't *Firial* want to move? She's a boat, after all.'

There was laughter. Then Ahmed said, 'Good question, Lulua, my love.'

'It's been a long time,' Yousef said. 'I'm not sure she could move now.'

'Please,' Lulua said. 'Can we sail *Firial* somewhere?'

'Well, I don't know,' Yousef said, looking a little anxious.

'I think it's a great idea,' Ahmed said.

'So, do I,' said Salem.

'Yallah, let's go then.' Yousef got up and, as if he was thirty years younger, ordered his crew to prepare for sailing.

Each of the old sailors took a newcomer and showed them the ropes. Jabor was in charge of the rope at the front and Salem the one at the stern. The sailors took the oars and hoisted the tattered old sail.

'Here we go!' Yousef shouted. 'Cast off.'

Jabor and Salem let go of the ropes. The sea was so calm that *Firial* hardly moved. The sailors took up the oars and pushed the boat off from the jetty. Slowly but surely, *Firial* broke away from the jetty, creaking and groaning. Everyone lent a hand rowing, Yousef continuing to issue commands. They rowed for about twenty minutes, out into open water.

'Look at Doha. Look how beautiful it is,' Lulua shouted, hugging her mother. Everyone looked around. The turquoise sea was flat, with hardly a ripple. They could see the British gunship on the horizon, making its way back to Bahrain.

Fahd sat on his father's lap as Amina pointed out to him the buildings on the shore: the new mosque near the palace, and the clock tower. It was so peaceful at sea. There was no sound apart from the lapping of the waves against the ship.

'She seems happy enough,' Yousef said. 'I think, Lulua, you had the best idea ever.'

Lulua was very pleased to hear this.

'What a joy it has been to come here today,' Jabor said, patting Lulua on the back.

Salem was lying down at the front of the boat, unable to speak. He raised his hand in gratitude. He hadn't been so happy for years.

The family rowed back to the jetty. They decided to leave putting up the sail for another day. It needed repairing, and there wasn't any wind anyway. It was time to go home.

It had been a memorable day. They moored *Firial* in her usual place, and the old sailors stroked her fondly as they disembarked.

18

Doha, 1961

Maggie sat in her favourite wicker chair on the veranda of their villa in Rumaillah. It was two o'clock. Eddie should be back from the bank any minute, she thought. They were lucky to have one of the new houses that had been built for government and oil staff. After months of living at the Bismillah Hotel, she was delighted to have somewhere they could call home, and they settled in quickly.

It was hot, so fans were whirring indoors. Today, though, there was a breeze. She wore a sleeveless cotton floral dress. Maggie was nine months pregnant and the baby was due any day.

'Abdou,' she called out to the houseboy, 'Nimbu pani, please.'

Maggie had spent her childhood in India, so she could speak Hindi, which came in handy. 'Nimbu pani' was lemonade, and 'mali' was the word for gardener, whom she watched watering the crimson bougainvillea.

She heaved herself up from the chaise longue to take the cold lemonade from Abdou. 'Something smells nice, Abdou. Thank you for helping. It's difficult for me at the moment.'

'You're welcome, madam.'

Maggie didn't ask what was cooking. It was curry, she could tell. Probably mutton. She thought that she would stick to boiled rice and salad. She loved the green salad that Abdou got from the souq early in the morning, along with lemons and spices. These days, she had to be careful. She walked into the living room. On one side was the dining table, a present from her parents-in-law. It was teak and had a matching sideboard, over which was a colourful landscape of the Kerala backwaters painted by Maggie's father. It was mainly of palm trees against a powder blue sky. The trees were reflected in the still waters, along which a man rowed a narrow boat. It was a gentle, peaceful picture of life in the watery wilderness. Every time Abdou dusted the gilded frame he gazed at the scene: it was his home state and made him think of the family he had left behind.

On the left was the sitting area, with two large pink squashy sofas supplied by the bank. On the walnut coffee table were copies of The Lady and The Illustrated London News. There was a white painted wall unit on the far side facing the front window, and on this sat a gramophone. Eddie and Maggie had brought some new LPs back with them from their last leave. She put on Ella Fitzgerald's new song, 'Mack the Knife'. She hummed along.

Maggie had never been drawn to a career. Her parents had placed no demands on her to follow any particular path. All they had wanted was her to be happy and to marry the right kind of man. Now she was a bank manager's wife, and she was about to start a family. Maggie had taken this in her stride as if it was her destiny to be a home-maker. Eddie was getting very excited about the birth, constantly asking how his wife was, and making sure she didn't overdo it or eat the wrong things.

Abdou was in control in the kitchen so Maggie resumed her semi-supine position on the chaise longue, looking out for Eddie. She cast her mind back to when she had arrived in Doha, and the party at Bait Al Bahr. The Bismillah Hotel wasn't her favourite hotel, but somehow, she had got used to the noise and living in the centre of the souq. Any other expat woman might have insisted on leaving at once, but she had spent her childhood among the dhobi-washers and stallholders of Delhi, and she loved the colour and excitement of life in the souq.

Maggie's reverie was interrupted by the sound of Eddie's Humber swinging into the drive. He looked marvellous, she thought, at the wheel of the white saloon: like a movie star, she imagined. Even the tyres had white walls specially ordered from the UK.

'Hello, darling! Good day?'

Maggie was getting up to greet her husband when she suddenly gasped and fell back down. She clutched her stomach.

Eddie ran to her, dropping his hat and briefcase.

'It's all right, my love. I'm here.'

'I don't know what...'

'Don't talk, my dear. Don't tire yourself. We'd better get you to hospital.'

'But it's not– '

Eddie didn't let Maggie finish. Abdou had heard the commotion and ran out from the kitchen to help.

'Abdou, can you take madam's arm please? I'll take the other. We're going to the hospital.'

They managed to walk Maggie to the car. She felt like screaming but stifled any sound, although her contorted face showed that she was in agony. Eddie helped Maggie in the back and asked Abdou to sit beside her. The new Rumaillah Hospital, the first of its kind in the country, was only just around the corner. The Humber screeched to a halt under the entrance's portico. Eddie left the engine running while he flung open the rear door to help Maggie inside.

'Hello? I need help. My wife's expecting a baby. Anyone?'

There were a few people waiting in the reception area. They looked aghast at the scene confronting them. A nurse in a starched white uniform sat behind a desk, doing paperwork. 'No midwifery here. You'll have to go to the Women's Hospital, sir.'

'What? But this is the new hospital, isn't it?'

'Yes, sir, but all deliveries and maternity care are at Hamdy Hospital. It was for TB; now it's for maternity. You'll have to go there.'

'Can't you...'

'No, sir. Sorry.'

Maggie, bathed in sweat, was making the most awful noises. They made their way back to the car.

'Where's Hamdy Hospital, Abdou?'

'I know, sir. I'll direct you.'

Abdou got in the front this time and directed Eddie while Maggie writhed in agony on the back seat.

'It's OK, darling. It won't take long. We'll be there soon,' Eddie said, not sure if it was true.

'Turn left here, sir,' Abdou said, confidence in his voice.

They headed back into the centre of Doha, Eddie driving far too fast, swerving past cars and bicycles.

'I think the baby's coming!' Maggie shouted just as they arrived at the hospital. Eddie screeched to a halt outside the doors, and the men rushed Maggie indoors.

'Another one? What's going on today?' asked a tall woman in her fifties. 'Well done for getting her here.' She pointed at two nurses. 'Let's get her along the corridor. We'll get her seen to straight away. Deep breaths, dear, come on. First one? Yes, looks like it.'

Maggie was wheeled on a trolley along to the far end of the corridor. Eddie was told to wait in reception. Abode waited outside in the car.

'Let's examine her,' the woman said to the nurses. 'Looks like she's in labour.'

Maggie didn't have to wait long. She was fully dilated. The woman and her assistants told Maggie to push. Maggie concentrated hard. There was no more yelling. After what seemed like forever, in a daze she found herself looking at a tiny red-faced baby, who was screaming.

'Congratulations, dear. You have a fine baby boy. By the way, my name is Doctora Hamda Iqbal, and this is my hospital. I'll get your husband.'

Before she could offer her thanks, she heard another voice. 'Maggie? Is that you?'

It was a patient in the bed not far from her own. Maggie looked over, still in shock, cuddling her baby.

'Maggie. It's me.'

'Amina! It can't be.'

'It is! I've just had a baby boy. My second. We have three girls and two boys. Ahmed will be here soon, I think.'

They looked at the entrance to the ward – and there were Ahmed and Eddie, beaming with pride.

19

Lulua, Tima and Fahd had just got home from school, their uniforms dishevelled after the hot walk home. Lula loved all subjects, devouring facts and figures from the Egyptian teachers. Her parents had told her she was so lucky because they hadn't had any proper education. Her Uncle Salem had helped to establish the Ministry of Education, convincing the then Emir, Sheikh Ali, that all citizens should have a good education. Sheikh Khalifa had been nominated as Minister of Education and in recent years more and more schools had been built. Lulua was fifteen now. She knew she was fortunate – one of the few girls in the country to enjoy this new right of every citizen. Ten-year-old Tima and eight-year-old Fahd had the big school to look forward to. They were at junior school, which was nearer home. Lulua always collected them on the way home.

Lulua put her school bag down in the hall then popped in to see Um Jabor, who was old and frail. Tima and Fahd were already halfway up the stairs. They wanted to know what had happened to their mother. Had she had the baby yet? They gathered around Amina and Ahmed's bed to meet their new little brother.

'You'll have a brother to play with, Fahd, dear,' Amina said, holding the baby boy up for everyone to see.

Fahd was quiet, unable to figure out what to say. Amina could see he was happy, though. The girls were so excited: they wanted to pick him up, as though he was a doll.

'So, it's decision time,' Ahmed said. 'Names, please!'

'Michel,' Fahd shouted straight away.

'Michel?' his parents said in unison, puzzled.

'He's my teacher. Ustez Michel.'

Everyone laughed.

'Michel is a nice name, Fahd, but it's not a Qatari name,' Ahmed said, trying to be diplomatic. 'Ustez Michel is from Syria. Let's think of something else.'

After a lot of debate, they decided on Jassim for the new member of the Bahr family. It had been Um Jabor's father's name, so she was especially happy.

'We never see Jabor these days,' Um Jabor said, suddenly reminded of her son.

'He's very busy with Sheikh Ahmed,' Ahmed said. 'Since Sheikh Ali stepped down at the end of last year he hasn't stopped. He's even busier than before.'

'I miss him.'

'I know, Um Jabor. I'll go up there later and see him.'

While the children fussed over their new brother and Um Jabor made sure her daughter was well, Ahmed excused himself and went up on the roof to gather his thoughts. He had to take stock. Everything in his life had changed so rapidly. He was thirty-one, married to a beautiful, kind, caring woman and the proud father of four children; he had a good job at the bank and was running his own business – all this in just over a decade.

Here on the roof he tried to come to terms with the events that were unfolding in his life. Amina knew her husband needed time on his own, and she let him go sometimes so that he could think. He loved her more for that.

Gazing out across the rooftops, he realised that Doha was getting bigger. He compared the view from his childhood days – when he could see the desert quite easily towards the south and west – with the view today. He could see the new hospital, schools, and more shops and homes. He could hardly see the horizon.

He wondered what the future would hold for baby Jassim. What view will he have from the roof when he's my age? Will he be a doctor or an engineer? He already had hopes for Fahd, and was certain that Lulua was going to do well. Tima would always be sweet little Tima, no matter what path she chose. He would never admit it, but she was his favourite.

His thoughts then turned to meeting Maggie at the Women's Hospital. Eddie had never mentioned that Maggie was pregnant. Although they still worked together, their relationship had been strained since Eddie had been promoted to manager. Initially he had encouraged Ahmed to start up his own business, but then had started to discourage him from spending too much time concentrating on matters that weren't related to the bank.

Socially, the couples had drifted apart. In the early days Eddie and Maggie were always coming around to Bait Al Bahr for lunch or tea. Now that never happened. Ahmed and Amina had even been invited to their new villa in Rumaillah.

Perhaps this will change everything, he thought, with the two babies being the same age. He hoped they could all be friends again. He wondered too about Jabor. He worried about him working too hard. He decided he would do as he had promised and go up to the palace to see him.

By the time Ahmed arrived, it was almost five o'clock. He had popped into the exchange house to make sure Vijay was all right. The June heat was less harsh at this time of day and Ahmed enjoyed the exercise. There were lots of changes happening to Doha. A new post office had been built next to the central market. In some ways Ahmed missed the old days, but he felt a sense of pride as he walked past the new offices and shops that heralded a new way of life in the country.

The coast road had been newly asphalted. It looked like a road from a movie, with the Cadillacs and Pontiacs driving along it. He strode past the clock tower to the shining new Diwan Al Emiri. The onion-shaped arches added a sense of grandeur to the former palace. The entrance gate was huge, and guards stood on either side of the double gates, which were wide enough for the largest limousine to pass through.

On his way up the gentle slope he glanced to the left at the British political residency. Its cream plaster was crumbling, to reveal dark grey patches. It looked out of place beside the new shiny polished concrete walls of the Diwan. Ahmed had heard from Uncle Salem, who was now Minister of Planning, that the colonial days were coming to an end.

Only a few months ago, Ahmed could walk straight to the Emir's office manager without being challenged. Today the guards picked up their rifles. A messenger was summoned to inform Salem he had a visitor.

Eventually Ahmed was escorted across the polished marble-floored courtyard and into a vast lobby with chandeliers and velvet curtains. Ahmed was led up a curved staircase. At the top of the stairs his young escort gestured for Ahmed to walk to the end of the corridor. Ahmed almost tiptoed along the deep-pile Persian carpet. There were offices to each side, with what Ahmed presumed were servants sitting outside. The corridor ran the whole length of the Diwan.

A man about Ahmed's age, with a small goatee, cloaked in a black and gold bisht, was heading towards him, followed by half a dozen men in bright white thobes. The group walked so quickly that Ahmed stepped to one side to get out of the way. To his surprise, the man stopped when he saw Ahmed. Ahmed felt he ought to know him but couldn't bring himself to say anything.

'Ahlan Kaif ha lak ya aikhi? Aish ismik?' the man said, asking Ahmed's name and asking after his health.

'Ahmed bin Nasser Al Bahr.'

'Ahlan wa sahlan. Shoufak. Alakheir Inshallah.' The retinue moved on at top speed along the corridor and down the stairs. Ahmed felt embarrassed that he didn't know to whom he had been talking.

In the far corner was Jabor's new office. Ahmed heard people talking behind the doors so sat down to wait on one of the comfortable velvet couches.

Jabor appeared through the double doors, his back to Ahmed, nodding in agreement with Sheikh Ahmed bin Ali. He finally turned round, and dropped a bunch of files and papers he was carrying.

'Ya Ahmed. Ya salam. It's been a long time.'

Ahmed got up to rescue the papers and to embrace his brother-in-law. As he held Jabor, he felt his ribs and realised he had lost weight. Hie eyes looked sad.

'I'm very busy, Ahmed. I'm sorry.'

'I understand. I just wanted to see you. Your mother was asking for you.'

Jabor collapsed into his chair. Piles of paper covered his desk. 'It was bad enough when Sheikh Ali was in charge, but now it's even worse. Every minute of every day there are appointments and contracts, calls to be made and diplomats to see. He relies on me for everything.'

'I can see that,' Ahmed said. 'You don't look very well. Who was that last man? He nearly ran me over with all his staff.'

'Who was that? His Highness Sheikh Khalifa bin Hamad, the heir apparent and Prime Minister. He wanted to be the Emir, but the role was passed from father to son, as you know. But there's a lot going on behind the scenes.'

'You look exhausted, Jabor,' Ahmed said. 'Why don't you come to the house when you finish here and see your mother? We have another surprise for you too.'

It wasn't until ten o'clock that Jabor finally arrived at Bait Al Bahr. Um Jabor heard her son coming in, sitting as she always did in the corner of the courtyard by the kitchen.

'Ya Jabor? Mashallah.' She gave him a loving hug.

'Wain ik ya ibni?' Where have you been, my son? 'You don't care about me any more.' Then she stopped, realising it would upset him more. Instead she told him he had lost weight and was working too hard. 'I've made fassoulia beans with oil and khubuz. You must eat, my son.'

Slowly, Um Jabor got up and shuffled to the kitchen to get a tray of beans and bread. Ahmed and Amina made their way down the stairs. It was Amina's first time out of bed, but she felt the need to walk a little. As it was such a warm evening, it would be good to sit by the palm tree in the courtyard.

Amina and Jabor hugged warmly. Instead Amina told her brother that he had become an uncle again and baby Jassim was asleep upstairs. Jabor congratulated them, secretly wondering if he would ever get married and have children.

'Sit down, Jabor. Sit. I'll get tea,' Ahmed said. 'Talk to your sister.'

'It's so nice to be here again, Amina, my dear sister. I should come more often, I know. I can't get away, though.'

'I know, Jabor. But you can't go on like this. There are other people they can ask.'

'I suppose they've got used to me doing everything. I know all the ways and people to find the answers to their problems.'

'But you're just an ordinary man, Jabor. You aren't wealthy with servants and cars. You must try and find happiness.'

'Inshallah. Inshallah, I will.'

Ahmed and Um Jabor brought out the tea, and supper for Jabor, and they sat in the moonlit square chatting and enjoying their time together. After talking about all the latest news from the palace and catching up on Ahmed's business and the progress of the children, Jabor said he should be going.

'But there's one more thing before I go,' Jabor said. 'His Highness is going to visit London. He had such a good time there when he went for Queen Elizabeth's coronation, he keeps going back. This time, he wants me to go with him.'

'Well, that sounds good but not if he will make you work all the time,' Amina said.

'Ahmed, I was wondering whether you could come with me. You are right. I do work too hard. I get fed up with it all sometimes. I would love it if you could come with me to take my mind off work and make sure I rest.'

Jabor was stunned at the invitation. Without hesitation he said, 'No, I couldn't possibly. I've got the family, a new baby, the business, the bank– '

But Amina immediately said, 'Go, Ahmed. It'll be good for you. We can manage.'

'Are you sure? How long for?'

'Maybe two weeks, maybe a month. He likes to go when it's hot here. Everything would be arranged for you. I don't want to pressure you, but you would be welcome.'

'What about the bank? Ahmed said, looking at Amina.

'I'll talk to Maggie. When we were in hospital, I asked her to come here. I think we'll be friends again.'

Ahmed smiled. 'I suppose I could ask Uncle Salem to keep an eye on the exchange house. Vijay knows what he's doing, anyway. I don't know what I'd do without him.'

Jabor patted Ahmed on the back. 'The sheikh wants to go in July. Please, Ahmed. I need a friend now more than ever.'

'That's only next month. But there's so much to do first,' Ahmed said, excited and worried at the same time.

Jabor stood to leave, saying he was tired, but he swayed with exhaustion. 'I think I'd better stay here again tonight.'

'Of course, Jabor. Of course.'

Ahmed led him into the majlis where he lay down and slept straight away.

PART 3

1

London, 1961

It was six o'clock in the evening. Ahmed had been awake for an hour. He had flung open the heavy curtains in his room at the Dorchester to marvel at the vivid green plane trees on Park Lane and the expanse of Hyde Park beyond. His room wasn't at the front of the hotel. That was reserved for the Emir and his family. The side view was good enough, though. It was such a new experience that Ahmed found it hard to adjust. He's only ever been as far as Dukhan and only seen sea and desert. He wiped his eyes, wondering still if the crystal-clear colours of a London summer were real and not just in his imagination. Then he remembered Jabor telling him why they were all coming to the ruler's favourite city.

Sheikh Ahmed had stayed at the Dorchester every year since he had seen the young Elizabeth crowned. Representing his father, he had been accorded all the pomp and circumstance of a head of state, a limousine taking him from his guest suite at the Dorchester in procession to Westminster Abbey. He couldn't get over the crowds in their thousands lining the street even in the incessant rain. His car had followed the open landau carrying Queen Salote of Tonga who beamed and waved all the way, umbrella in her hand. Coming from a barren desert land where life had been relatively simple although hard the young sheikh was impressed by the courteous people he had met and the warmth of those well-wishers. After the harsh climate of Qatar, he loved the rain, walking among the trees and chatting to ordinary passers-by; total strangers would raise their hats and say, 'Good Morning' and when he met the Queen for a private audience she had said 'I hope you'll come again soon.' And so he did again and again. They had set off two days earlier from Doha's new airport on a British Airways VC-10, stopping off in Beirut. Ahmed and Jabor sat together in the front seats of the economy section, the curtain dividing them from the VIPs in first class. Ahmed was apprehensive about flying, but he kept talking to Jabor to take his mind off it. Looking out of the little cabin window, he was amazed by the sight of the mountains of Lebanon as they landed for the first time. When they took off again, Ahmed began to relax and started to enjoy the food and drinks that were being served. It was all so new and exciting. The pilot announced that they were crossing the Alps, so Ahmed and Jabor leaned over to see the snow-topped mountains through the clouds under the silver wings of the plane. It was all like a dream,

Ahmed thought, and vowed to bring his family on a similar trip one day if he could.

As the plane made its descent into Heathrow, all Ahmed could see were patchwork fields of greens and yellows. He couldn't believe his eyes. The captain pointed out the round tower of Windsor Castle and River Thames, which Ahmed had heard about in stories about London.

A gang of porters lined up to take all the trunks the family had brought. The airport manager and Charles Denman were on hand to greet Sheikh Ahmed, who was whisked to his limousine with his immediate family. Jabor and Ahmed, along with the bodyguards and other assistants, were driven into central London in a fleet of taxis.

'All right, lads?' the cabbie asked them.

'Shinoo?' *What?* They looked at each other.

'London. We go London,' Jabor said, making an effort to speak English.

'I know that,' the cabbie said, laughing. 'You're all going to the bleedin' Dorchester. You lucky sods. Welcome to London.'

They all understood the last part. Along the Great West Road, the traffic got heavier, but it was a beautiful evening and Ahmed couldn't believe how light it was for eight o'clock.

The cabbie pointed out places of interest along the way. 'That's Harrods, boys. You'll have to take your girlfriends shopping there. Oh, I'd better get out of the way.' He moved into the nearside lane as a bright red open-top sports car sped past.

'Shuf, shuf ya shabab,' one of the bodyguards shouted as the car zoomed off into the distance.

'He's doing the ton. Must be. First one I've seen. New E-type Jag. More money than sense, I reckon. Macmillan says we've never had it so good. Looks like he's right.'

Ahmed looked at Jabor, wondering what on earth the cabbie had said.

The cab drew up next to a gleaming Rolls-Royce parked in front of the hotel. They had arrived at the Dorchester. It was hard for Ahmed to think about Amina and his family in Bait Al Bahr in these opulent surroundings. There was a lot of cream and gold and paintings on the walls with a little brass lamp over each one. It was like being in another world, Ahmed thought, gazing out of the French windows. Through the plane trees he saw families strolling in Hyde Park, the afternoon sun casting sharp shadows on the dappled pathways. He couldn't quite believe the beauty of the light and colour. It was such a contrast to the hazy pastel shades of home. Within minutes he had collapsed onto the luxurious double bed, wishing Amina was beside him.

Before he had a chance to take a nap after the long journey, Jabor was by his side calling him to get ready.

'Good thing you left the door open. The sheikh has asked us all to go out for the evening. Put on your best suit and tie. We're leaving in ten minutes.'

Half-awake, Ahmed stumbled around, looking for his suit. His clothes had been packed into a well-worn suitcase Amina had borrowed from Maggie. Thank goodness she had had the presence of mind to pack Eddie's old suit, which he had passed on to Ahmed for the occasional British party. With a little help from Jabor, he managed to make himself look reasonably presentable, though he had to ask a chambermaid to do his tie for him.

Within minutes Sheikh Ahmed met the party in the grand foyer. Ahmed hardly recognised him without his Arab dress and official gold-edged bisht. He too was dressed in a dark charcoal suit and held a set of worry beads. Jabor was busy arranging cars for the family. When everyone was ready, a tall figure, clad in a black *abaya* led a group of women down the stairs and out to another set of cars. The Emir's wife Sheikha Maryam was not to be left out of the party. Ahmed wondered what was about to happen. Outside, the sheikh headed for the first Daimler and turned back to address the rest of the group.

'I hope you all like Frank Sinatra. See you all at The Talk of the Town.'

'Wait until I tell Amina about this. She's always talking about him with Maggie and they play his records all the time.'

The cars made their way along Piccadilly, the driver pointing out Fortnum and Mason and slowing down at Piccadilly Circus to admire the statue of Eros surrounded by all the flashing lights and glamour of the electric advertising boards. On Shaftesbury Avenue they gazed at the theatre signs and the well-dressed people walking along.

'Look at that,' Ahmed shouted, his eyes wide. It was a young couple, their arms around each other. The young man wore tight satin trousers and a bright red vest. His girlfriend had long blonde hair amd wore a strappy dress that reached the top of her thighs. The men in the car looked back in awe.

'We love mini-skirts,' the driver laughed as he turned into Charing Cross Road and pulled up outside the Hippodrome, now renamed The Talk of the Town.

Ahmed and Jabor took their places at one of the round tables set out for Sheikh Ahmed and his guests. They wondered what to do with all the sparkling crystal glasses and gleaming silver cutlery. A team of waiters poured champagne into saucer-shaped glasses; caviar came around served on ice, followed by lobster and strawberries. No fruit had ever tasted so sweet or so delicious. Then with a drum roll the orchestra played a medley of Frank Sinatra's songs before the compere came out to announce the star of the evening.

'Ladies and gentlemen, the one and only Mr Frank Sinatra.'

The curtains parted, and Sinatra made his entrance from the back of the stage, lit by a single spotlight.

As Ole Blue Eyes crooned his way through 'Fly Me to the Moon', 'I Get a Kick out of You,' 'My Funny Valentine' and half a dozen more songs, all Ahmed could think of Amina and his family back home in Doha. London was such a contrast to Qatar. As he listened to Sinatra, his mind drifted back to his earlier years and his struggle to make ends meet to raise his young family. He couldn't help but wonder if the sheikh's extravagant lifestyle and constant travel to foreign lands was the right one. Ahmed was overcome with a sense of moral righteousness he hadn't known before. Yes, Ahmed desired wealth to improve his life and that of his family – but, more than that, he wanted to better the lives of his neighbours and friends too. He wanted to help those who were in need. However, he vowed there and then to shun any form of overt wealth. He certainly didn't want his children, or grandchildren, to be spoiled.

Ahmed was woken by a tap at the door.

'Hello, sir. Room service. I've brought your breakfast.'

Ahmed wasn't sure what to do but said 'Come in'. A young woman came in carrying a large silver tray.

'It's a lovely day, sir. Sun's shining, birds are singing. What more do you want?'

'Thank you,' Ahmed said, not quite understanding her colloqualisms. 'My name is Ahmed.'

'Oh, you're welcome, sir... Mr Ahmed,' the waitress said.

'Your name?' Ahmed asked.

'Me, sir? Oh, my name's Jean. I do room service. I was a chambermaid then got promoted. Lovely hotel innit, sir?' She looked down, cheeks reddening. 'They said I couldn't do room service. It's a man's job, they said. I said, give me a chance. I'm strong and can do the work. Oh, I'm going on, aren't I?'

'Yes. Yes. My friend Jabor is in the next room.'

'I tried next door, but I think he's still sleeping. I'll try again soon. Enjoy your breakfast, Mr Ahmed.' Jean backed out of the room, leaving Ahmed standing in the centre looking at the tray.

Ahmed decided to explore London. Having eaten as much of the full English breakfast as he could, he bathed and dressed in a fresh cotton shirt and a pair of Eddie's trousers. Taking a deep breath, he ventured outside. He crossed busy Park Lane and went to the park. There, Ahmed felt at ease, alone with nature: the trees were in full leaf and the vast swathe of grassland was a brilliant lime green. He wandered down to the Serpentine via the rose garden at Hyde Park Corner, passing courting couples and nannies pushing prams. It was a glorious morning. He noticed men raising their hats to fellow walkers, saying a cheery 'good morning'. At the lake he couldn't help thinking of Lulua, Tima and Fahd when he saw children feeding the ducks. It was an idyllic scene, he thought: one that would stay in his memory.

Back at the Dorchester, Ahmed was greeted by Jabor, who had been worried about where Ahmed had gone.

'Ya Ahmed. Wainak ya akhi? Yallah.' It's time to go.

'Go where?'

'Sheikh Ahmed is going shopping with his family. We're going to Carnaby Street.'

'Where's that?'

'You'll see. The driver is taking us. And tonight, we're going dancing.'

'Dancing?'

'I have a new friend, ya Ahmed habibi. Her name is Jean. She's taking us dancing tonight. This is the life.'

_ᴦᴧ_

2

Abu Omar surveyed the scene. He could easily build a new row of shops here. He wasn't content with the grocery shop Mukherjee ran, and the small shop he rented out as an exchange house; he felt he should own more property. Luckily one of his customers worked at the Diwan Emiri so he was able to get clearance to build wherever he wanted. His contact had also put him in touch with an architect specialising in retail development who had just arrived from Beirut. The two men stood outside the exchange house, discussing how they should go about the project.

Abu Omar found it hard to follow the architect's Lebanese accent as the young man described what he could do with the land in front of them.

'You could build six shops with apartments above, maybe two floors high.'

His name was Pierre. He was an engineer who had been advised by his father to seek work in the Gulf, where he was told he could make his fortune. First, he had gone to Saudi Arabia, but he found the people of Riyadh difficult to deal with. While he was there, he met some oil drilling engineers at ARAMCO, who put him in touch with the operation in Dhahran. Eventually he ended up in Doha.

Abu Omar stroked his beard, wondering if he should trust this unknown person. He thought he had just about enough money to afford the project – and, in any case, he would quickly get the money back through rent, as he had done in the past.

'I can build you six small shops with accommodation above. This will be the first building of its kind in Doha. My design will be the best. My father has a building like this in Beirut. You will love it, sir.' Pierre quoted a price to which Abu Omar reacted with a sharp intake of breath. They bartered briefly. Then a pause.

The figure he had been quoted was double the amount he had expected. He had to think quickly. He had no choice but to go to the bank and ask for a loan. He totted up the potential rent he could bring in each month and was satisfied that he would be making a profit within a year or two.

Before he agreed to proceed, he took one more look at the site. A sense of pleasure coursed through his veins as he saw that the fine merchant house, which had once been the focal point of the centre of Doha, would be dwarfed by his new building.

The men shook hands and the deal was done.

–⊢⊤–

Jabor and Ahmed waited nervously outside Lyon's Corner House in Coventry Street, along from Piccadilly Circus. Jean had told Jabor to be there at four o'clock. She had managed to get time off work.

'Are you sure this is all right, Jabor? It's better if you meet her alone,' Ahmed said, wishing he could escape and go for a long walk alone.

'It's fine. Take it easy. It's a chance to meet new people, make new friends.'

Ahmed wanted to say that he didn't want to do any such thing but kept quiet. Then Jean arrived with another young woman.

'Hello, Mr Jabor, Mr Ahmed. You're here! I didn't think you'd come. This is my friend Shirley.'

Ahmed gave Jabor a look. Had he arranged this behind his back? They all went into the tea shop and were seated at the window table, with a prime view of the bustling street outside.

Jean chatted non-stop while they ordered a pot of tea, bread and butter, and jam and a selection of French fancies. 'I waited for Frank Sinatra to leave after his show. Got his autograph. I couldn't believe it. And you lucky things saw him sing. Oh, I'd love that, I really would.'

Jabor sat opposite her, gazing into her eyes, apparently mesmerised by her. All thoughts of the Emir and the daily worries of his life in the Diwan had been banished.

Shirley had hardly said a word. Dressed more soberly than Jean in a floral print with a beige cardigan, she had a pale complexion and short wavy hair. Her horn-rimmed spectacles gave her the air of a librarian or teacher.

Finally, when the tea arrived Jean included her friend in the conversation.

'Shirley's my best friend. Aren't you, Shirls?'

A dutiful nod.

'We were at school together, weren't we, Shirls?'

Another dutiful nod.

'Now I'm at the Dorchester slaving away, but Shirley here is in the Home Office, would you believe? In the Civil bleedin' Service. I ask you!'

'What do you do there, Shirley?' Ahmed asked.

Shirley blushed. 'It's all very hush-hush. I can't say anything about it.'

Jean placed her forefinger on her lips.

Ahmed offered to pour Shirley's tea.

'Ooh, Mr Ahmed's being mother. That's nice,' Jean said. 'Now, afterwards we're all going off shopping. Let's go to Carnaby Street. It's the latest place. All mini-skirts and Mary Quant.'

'I'm not sure the gentlemen would be interested in those,' Shirley interjected.

'I need a new suit,' Ahmed said. 'I can't keep wearing the same clothes.'

'Simpson's is just down the road,' Shirley said. 'We can go there.'

'I think Mr Jabor might be more Carnaby Street,' Jean said. 'We can go there after. Then how about the pictures? Cliff

Richard's in The Young Ones at the Empire. They say it's fantastic.'

While Jean and Jabor popped into each little boutique, Ahmed tried to explain to Shirley how different London was to his life in Qatar. The beat music booming from every store and scantily clad women made him both excited and overwhelmed. Shirley understood this and guided him to a quiet corner near Liberty.

'There's Cranks,' Shirley said. 'It's a new place where they only serve vegetarian food. Would you like to go there?'

Ahmed agreed, but when they asked the others to join them they said they would find somewhere that served meat, like a Berni Inn.

After much discussion, they split up, While Jabor and Jean went off for prawn cocktail, rump steak and chips followed by a banana split, Shirley introduced Ahmed to nut cutlets, bean salads and avocados. He loved it: the way people helped themselves from big bowls of healthy food, and the way the customers behaved. It was all much quieter than the madness outside. As they sat at their scrubbed wooden table, the pair began to learn more about each other's lives.

It was still early, and they wondered if they would continue their night out together. Shirley confessed that she didn't much like the idea of The Young Ones, then asked Ahmed what music he liked. He tried to describe some of the famous Middle Eastern artists, like Um Kalthoum and Farid Al Atrash, both of whom he admired. The only Western singer he could think of was Frank Sinatra.

'How about Ella Fitzgerald?'

Ahmed gave her a quizzical look.

'Worth a try?'

'Of course.'

'In that case, we'd better be quick.'

They hopped on a 159 bus in Regent Street and sat upstairs to get a good view. Shirley proudly pointed out the landmarks they passed: Nelson's Column in Trafalgar Square, Admiralty Arch, through which they caught a glimpse of the Mall and Buckingham Palace at the far end.

The bus made its way down Whitehall. As it came alongside Horseguards Parade, it came to a stop. A policeman on a motorcycle came towards them on the wrong side of the road and signalled for the bus to wait. The conductor came to take the fares.

'Oh dear. Now what? Must be somebody important come to see Mr Macmillan,' she said, taking their money.

In front of them was a Cadillac with an American flag on its bonnet.

'Blimey,' the conductor gasped, 'it's President Kennedy!'

'Of course,' Shirley said, standing to get an even better view, 'Mr Kennedy is here at the moment. How marvellous. Look, Ahmed.'

Ahmed was amazed. He remained speechless as the bus started up again to approach Westminster, Big Ben and the Houses of Parliament. He realised he had fallen in love with London. And he was beginning to grow fond of Shirley.

From the bus stop they raced along the South Bank to the Royal Festival Hall. Shirley, a regular visitor, headed for a little booth with a sign saying Returns over it.

'Any chance of anything, Mr Thompson?' she said to an elderly man.

'You're in luck tonight, darlin',' he said. 'Two up in the gods if you're interested.'

'Oh, yes please,' she said, smiling at Ahmed.

They watched the first lady of jazz hold the audience in her hand for two hours. Ahmed loved it all. The evening had been tremendous. To finish it off, they walked to Waterloo Bridge where they watched the lights of Westminster. Ahmed was aware of a frisson between them. He knew he liked her, and he wondered how she felt. He knew he had to tell her about Amina. The embankment lights twinkled in the background as he explained that his wife and children were waiting for him back home, and he loved them dearly. It was only fair, he thought. Shirley was quiet.

Then, 'Do you like tennis?' she asked, out of the blue.

'I'm not sure,' Ahmed replied, surprised at the change of subject. 'I've never seen it being played. The only sport in Qatar is fishing, if you can call that a sport.'

'I've got a couple of tickets for Wimbledon. I would love to take you there.'

'That's very kind of you. Yes please.'

'I'll meet you at the Dorchester the day after tomorrow at midday.'

It was time to go home. Shirley said she would take the Tube to Ealing where she lived. Ahmed hailed a taxi to get back to the Dorchester.

It was 45 degrees on the roof of Bait Al Bahr. Amina had come up to hang washing out to dry. Um Jabor was getting frailer by the day, and the summer heat had confined her to the relative cool of the ground floor.

Amina had managed to get the children up in the morning, and the girls off to school. She was buying food in the market and looking after Jassim. Without Ahmed, it was becoming a strain. The responsibility was taking its toll. She was short-tempered and fractious with her mother and the girls. She didn't like who she had become. The truth was, she missed her husband very much. With a huge sigh she took the damp clothes from the basket and pegged them out along the rope. As she did so, she was reminded of her children: the cotton dresses the girls had worn, the tiny baby clothes Um Jabor had made for Jassim. They brought her joy but when she had finished, she burst into tears, wishing Ahmed was with her. He was so far away. What was he doing? Who was he meeting? How was he spending his time?

She rested her head in her arms on the parapet and looked around at the hazy sun-baked scene, at the rooftops and dusty palms. Not a soul was out in the scorching heat of the day. Then her eyes wandered down to street level. She had to look again because she couldn't quite believe her eyes.

Below her were half a dozen men digging what appeared to be a large trench. There was a man in Western dress watching over the group. He was wearing sunglasses, had a sheaf of papers in his hand, and was carrying a tape measure.

Then Amina noticed that the land next to the house had been marked out. There was a long piece of string attached to four wooden poles that stretched from the nearest neighbour, fifty metres away, across another twenty metres and back down to the wall of her home. What on earth could be going on?

Amina ran downstairs and grabbed her abaya. She went outside, over to the man in sunglasses.

'What do you think you are doing?' she barked without any form of salutation.

Taking his time with his tape measure and looking down at his papers, he eventually responded. 'Madam, this is building land. You will have to excuse me. As you can see, I'm busy.'

'You can't build anything here. This is our house. My house. My husband – my family. It's been ours– '

'That is not my problem, madam. I am here to build on the site that I have laid out as agreed by my client. It will be a very nice building with six new shops, and you will have neighbours on the upper floors too.'

Amina saw that he was smiling, which enraged her. 'How tall do you suppose this building will be?'

'Quite a bit taller than your house, I would think, madam. Don't worry – there will be many more like this now we are here to turn this little village into a proper city.'

'You will be sorry for this,' Amina shouted. 'Wait until I tell my husband.'

'Ah yes, the man who rents a shop from my client. Ha!'

He carried on measuring. Amina withdrew to her home to weep.

Shirley was outside the Dorchester waiting for Ahmed. It was another glorious summer day. Ahmed came out, looking at ease, in a lightweight blue jacket, and grey trousers. Shirley had cast off her beige cardigan and wore a pink rose-patterned cotton dress with cream sandals and bag. They walked along to Hyde Park Corner. Ahmed was looking forward to taking a ride on a Tube train. Shirley laughed as he stepped gingerly on to the escalator, uneasy at first but then enjoying the sensation. They emerged some time later in Wimbledon.

There was half an hour before the match they were due to see, so Shirley said, 'How about strawberries and cream?' They had to queue for a while, something Ahmed found fascinating. That people would simply form an orderly line without being asked to, was a revelation. They took their strawberries and sat on the grassy bank watching the tennis fans coming in. Shirley had to explain the rules of the game, but Ahmed couldn't take them all in. He was fascinated by the calm beauty of the surroundings: the overall sense of lush green grass and trees, with the buildings painted green to match. The men all wore straw hats and cream linen jackets, and he thought the women looked glamorous and full of self-confidence.

On Centre Court, they were escorted to their seats by a young naval officer. They sat down, and Ahmed thanked Shirley for organising the tickets. The grass had been mowed and rolled to perfection. Soon, the two players in the women's singles match were announced.

'Ladies and gentlemen. Christine Truman and Margaret Smith.'

3

Amina desperately needed her husband. She sat in the wind tower room, her head in her hands, away from the children and Um Jabor, not wanting to show how distraught she was. She could hardly bear to think that men were behind the wall she was resting against, digging and scraping to build something that would dominate their home. To Amina, it felt as though a monster had come knocking at their door, and she had to try to keep it at bay.

More than anything, she thought of Ahmed and how he would feel. It had been his home since birth, and she knew how proud he was of the family he had raised there and his house's special place in the neighbourhood. She couldn't turn to him or to her brother, who would know what to do. He could easily tell the Emir, who would put a stop to it. But they were all in London, oblivious to the goings-on in Doha. She decided there was only one person she could talk to – Maggie.

Amina told the girls to be good and look after Jassim. She looked in on Um Jabor, who looked more tired and thin than ever. The children would keep her company for the rest of the evening, and there was some food left over from lunch that they could have.

It was quite a walk from Bait Al Bahr to Maggie and Eddie's house in Rumaillah. It was still hot at four o'clock when she strode out along the Rayyan road past the Emir's palace. She had never walked this far from home before, and soon saw that the builder was right. Shops were being built on both sides of the road. Taking care to avoid the trucks and vans that sped past, forcing her onto the dusty verge, she passed mud-built houses that were being knocked down in between the occasional street stall selling drinks and nuts. As she neared Rumaillah, a group of a dozen or so men appeared, holding a banner that said Jobs for Qataris. They chanted that they needed work and they were born here not like the foreigners who had come to take their jobs away.

She turned off the main road towards the sea. Rumaillah was a haven of calm after the noise and commotion she had just witnessed. The low bungalows set back from the road looked inviting, and in some ways, Amina envied the quieter life here. Expatriates had their own school and clubhouse where they could relax and enjoy each other's company.

Maggie was dozing on the veranda when Amina walked up the gravel drive. A mali was standing in the middle of the lawn spraying a bank of crimson calla lilies with a garden hose. Amina didn't want to disturb the peaceful scene. Maggie looked so comfortable, lying there in her steamer chair, a two-month-old copy of The Tatler face-down on her lap. Amina coughed to signal her arrival, wondering if she had done the right thing by coming here. She sat down on the wicker two-seater, glad of a little rest after her walk.

'Oh dear. I must have dozed off. Dear Amina. What a surprise,' Maggie said when she woke, unused to seeing her friend without any prior arrangement.

'I'm sorry, Maggie. I had to come. There's a problem and I don't know who else to turn to.'

'There there,' Maggie said, getting up and moving to sit next to her visitor. 'You can talk to me, you know that. Any time. I'm pleased you came. Babu,' she called to her houseboy, 'bring nimbu pain please. Is the baby all right?'

The servant nodded and backed away to get the lemonade.

'How's Jassim?' Maggie asked.

'He's doing well, thanks. And yours?'

'He's great. So, what's the matter, Maggie dear?'

Maggie took Amina's hand and Amina poured out all the details of what she had seen earlier in the day: the workmen digging next door to her house, the pompous builder, the fact that Ahmed was away, and she was lonely.

Maggie put her arm round Maggie's shoulder, trying to comfort her.

'Try not to worry. I'm sure something can be done. Eddie will be home soon and maybe he can help. When is Ahmed due back from London?'

'I don't know, Maggie. That's the problem. It's up to the Emir, I suppose. It's so difficult waiting – and now this.'

'I wonder if we could get the British advisor involved. He might be able to track Ahmed down. He would know the Emir's movements in London.'

'I don't want to make too much fuss. What would they think of me?'

As the two women tried to find a solution, Eddie arrived back home in his new cream Humber Super Snipe, the white-walled wheels crunching on the gravel.

'Hello, darling,' Maggie greeted her husband. 'Look who's here. A surprise visitor.'

'Hello, my love, and hello, Amina. Long time no see. Ahmed still away? Phew, it's been a busy, hot day. I'll just get a beer and be right back,' Eddie said, loosening his tie and tossing his briefcase onto a chair.

Maggie asked for tea and some fruit cake, then she went to get the baby and brought him out to show to Amina. Seeing mother, father and son together as a family made Amina even more upset, but she managed to keep her emotions under control as she explained to Eddie what had happened.

'It's bad. Very bad. But I can't say I'm surprised. It's crazy at the bank. So many people coming for business loans. I suppose, with the price of oil going up and more oil fields coming on-stream, there's more money about and people want to make the most of it.'

Amina forgot about her own problems for a moment,

reminded of the demonstrators she had encountered on her way there.

'So, if there is so much money coming in, why are the workers marching in the streets? I saw them on the way here.'

'I saw them too,' Eddie said. 'I'm afraid the oil men, the riggers and tool-pushers, the lower-paid workers, are seeing none of the profits, that's why. A lot of the men are Yemeni too, and their country supports the United Arab Republic.'

Maggie, wanting to get back to the family problem, interjected, asking whether they could get through to London.

'I could ask the advisor to speak to London, I suppose. In fact, the way things are, it might be unwise for the Emir to stay away much longer. I'll see what I can do. I have to tell you, Amina, that without Ahmed at the bank it has been difficult to cope. His absence has been noticed by HQ in Bahrain.'

Amina, even more concerned, thanked Eddie and said she had better be going. Eddie offered her a lift home, and she accepted, relieved that help might soon be at hand. When they arrived at Bait Al Bahr, Eddie saw for himself the work being carried out in front of them.

'It's disgraceful, Amina. Some unscrupulous businessman has decided to build and develop without any consideration for the neighbourhood. If this is the way Doha is going, it will be a total mess. Who could possibly have done this? Whoever he was knew exactly what he was up to.'

The Emir spent the summer days strolling in Hyde Park with his wife and children, enjoying the simple pleasures of feeding the ducks and taking tea at Fortnum and Mason. This meant Jabor was rarely required to be on hand for any matters of state. He and Jean, Ahmed and Shirley spent more and more time together, going to the Oxford Street shops and taking bus rides out to Putney and Greenwich for impromptu picnics. When the women were working, Ahmed and Jabor went to Speakers' Corner. They loved listening to political views being aired in the open, whether about banning the bomb or the plight of the Palestinians.

Ahmed was beginning to feel as though London was his second home. He enjoyed the long summer days and the cool evenings, catching a bus or buying a newspaper and taking it to the park. The people were pleasant and courteous, and made him feel welcome. Every night before he slept he would pray that his wife and children were safe at home and that one day they too would come to this beautiful city.

He usually met Shirley near Parliament Square after she had finished work. They never talked about her work, but when they met for a cup of tea in Victoria Street on day, Shirley looked like she had something on her mind.

'Are you all right, Shirley?' Ahmed enquired.

'Yes, I'm fine, thanks, Ahmed. Been busy, that's all. I hope you like ballet.'

'Ballet? You mean dancing?'

'Yes. I mean Rudolf Nureyev and Margot Fonteyn at Covent Garden. He has defected from Russia and is here tonight performing in a charity gala. I've got two tickets. Would you care to join me?'

Ahmed held Shirley's hand and thanked her again and again for being so kind. 'You've introduced me to so many things, Shirley, so many things I would never have done without you. Of course, I would love to come. Let's have dinner together first.'

They headed towards Covent Garden via Simpson's in the Strand where they dined on prawn cocktail and roast beef. Over dinner they talked about their lives. Shirley was fascinated by Ahmed's description of the tiny desert sheikhdom from where he came and his life at Bait Al Bahr. She warmed to him more and more. Ahmed, in turn, enjoyed Shirley's knowledge of history and the arts. He longed to learn more about the theatre, about writers, poets, artists and playwrights. He longed to travel, to broaden his mind. As Shirley talked to him about ballet, all he could think of was that he wanted his children and grandchildren to be as knowledgeable, if not more so.

The performance was sold out. Nureyev, the new sensation who had left Russia to enjoy the freedom of the West, had curtain call after curtain call. When the applause eventually died down, Ahmed and Shirley went to the Crush Bar for a final glass of champagne.

'I'm going to leave you now, Ahmed,' Shirley said. 'Thank you for your company.'

Surprised by her tone of voice, Ahmed asked when they'd meet again.

'I don't think there will be a next time, Ahmed. You will be going home soon. Goodbye.' She kissed him on the cheek and left him standing there, wondering what she meant and how she could possibly know.

Amina sat by her mother's side holding her hand. Um Jabor hadn't eaten for days, and Amina had to encourage her to take regular sips of water. The girls had been told that their grandmother was ill, and she would be resting more and more. Lulua had taken more responsibility for looking after Jassim and helping to prepare simple meals. Tima was more difficult. She couldn't understand why Um Jabor wasn't around to cook and tell them stories any more.

It was clear that Um Jabor did not have long to live. She had never been the same since the loss of her husband, and she had been telling Amina how much she missed him and that she wanted to be with Abu Jabor again. Just when Amina needed her mother more than ever she was dwindling away, unable to offer the comfort and kindness she had always shown.

All evening Amina sat by her mother's side keeping vigil, dwelling on what Eddie said about Ahmed's job. What would they do if he was told to leave? she wondered. She thought of the house being destroyed by the work going on outside and she thought of her children and what kind of future they would have. She thought of Maggie and her comfortable way of life: her husband, secure in his job, and a son whose future would be planned and paid for. But most of all she thought of her husband and what he might be doing. It pained her to think of him elsewhere, out of her world, the only world she knew.

Amina was jolted back to the present by Um Jabor's heavy breathing. She lay as still as a stone in the low glimmer of a single lightbulb. Amina didn't want to leave her, but it was time to make sure the children were getting into bed, so they would be rested for school in the morning. Just then, the door creaked open. Her children stood there – with Jabor!

Jabor ran straight to his mother, unable to contain his shock and sadness at seeing her so close to death. Amina let him take her place and left the room – and there was Ahmed, waiting in the courtyard. He had come home. They exchanged no words, just the warmest hugs.

Um Jabor died peacefully in her sleep with Jabor and Amina to witness the end. With all the arrangements they had to make, there wasn't much time to discuss matters with Ahmed. However, the next day Ahmed could see for himself the work taking place next to his home. Amina tried to explain as well as she could during the little time they had earlier that morning, but the funeral took priority over everything.

They held a wake in the courtyard and majlis, in which Jabor became the focus of attention. Mourners arrived throughout the day, telling Jabor how good it was that he got there in time. The children passed round tea and dates while Ahmed looked on proudly, but with a sense of shame that he hadn't been able to give Amina the support she needed.

It wasn't until the following day that Ahmed went to find out what was going on. He was furious that someone had gone behind his back while he was away. It was a matter of principle. As the workers dug and chiselled away, Ahmed saw the man in sunglasses who Amina had described. Taking a deep breath, Ahmed went up to him.

'Salam aleikum. My name is Ahmed. I am the owner of this house, Bait Al Bahr. It has been here since I was born forty years ago.'

'Ahlan wa sahlan. I am Michel, architect from Beirut,' the man said, smiling. 'This work is none of your business. I am here to supervise the work.'

'Who asked you to do this?'

'I couldn't possibly say.'

'My uncle is a government minister. If you don't tell me, I'll have you thrown out of this country within minutes.'

Now the architect took off his glasses and looked more serious. 'He calls himself Abu Omar. He has a grocery shop– '

Before he could finish, Ahmed had left.

When he arrived at Mukherjee's shop, he was sitting outside, his worry beads in hand as always.

'Ahlan ya Ahmed. Wainak ya akhi, where have you been?' Abu Omar said, greeting Ahmed like a long-lost friend.

'What's going on next to my house? Who gave you permission to build six shops and accommodation over them, so they will overlook my courtyard? Have you no shame?'

'Azizi, Ahmed. This is business, my boy. You see an opportunity and you take it. That's all.'

'Who gave you permission?'

'I have my contacts at the palace.'

'You haven't heard the last of this.'

'Are you threatening me, Ahmed? By the way, you are due a rent increase, I believe. If you can't afford it, I have plenty of people who would like that shop.'

Ahmed stormed off, leaving his landlord chuckling to himself. Frustrated, he went down to the seashore to think. He couldn't go home yet. Amina and Jabor would still be mourning their mother and it wouldn't be fair to trouble them. With London still fresh in his thoughts, he became suddenly confused. Only hours ago, he had been at the ballet. Back home, he felt at a loss. He felt like a stranger. He had no idea how to cope with people who had no culture or respect. He headed to the jetty and to *Firial*.

The old sailors were there, as ever, even older and greyer. He was pleased to see Uncle Salem among them. Gradually his negative thoughts faded away as he chatted to the sailors. The pearl-divers' genuine fondness for him and the way Salem greeted him made him realise that, no matter how sophisticated London was, this was his home.

4

Time seemed to have stood still. The men played cards and poured tea as they had done since Ahmed had met them all those years before. When Ahmed said he had been in London with the Emir the men teased him, saying, 'Doha not good enough for you now, eh?'

'You'll be eating with a knife and fork soon, Ahmed,' Bilal said, laughing his head off, 'and drinking tea from a cup and saucer.'

They all joined in the laughter, Ahmed included. It was fun to be home. Then Ahmed thought of the troubles he was facing and asked to speak to his uncle privately.

'I don't know what to do, Uncle Salem,' he said, having explained the situation about the building about to go up next to Bait Al Bahr.

'Ya Ahmed,' Salem said, holding his nephew by the arm, 'Qatar is changing. More people are coming here every day. We need them to develop our country. We may have a new oil field out at sea at Halul. There will be even more money for the country. We have to find houses for more families and shops for people who need more goods. It's happening in Kuwait and Bahrain. We don't want to be left behind.'

While Ahmed agreed with what his uncle was saying, he was surprised at his lack of concern for Ahmed's situation. 'But can people build anywhere they like?'

'It depends who they know and how much money they have. If you can find out how he got permission and the funding, maybe we can help. He must know someone at the palace – and for a project like that, he must have got a bank involved. Good luck, Ahmed. Life isn't as simple as it used to be. Those men on *Firial* had a hard life but look how content they are now – happy with each other's company and a pack of cards.'

For the first time since he got back, Ahmed spent time with his family. He gathered Lulua, Tima and Fahd together in the wind tower room to catch up on everything that had happened while he was away. Lulua was doing well at school, top of the class in mathematics and science. She loved history too and wanted to study more when she left school next year. Tima would play all day if she could; she found school difficult. At ten, Fahd was already an artist. When school was over he would come home and draw with bright crayons until it was time to do his homework.

The children wanted to hear all about London and what it was like. Their father told them all about the red buses and the soldiers guarding Buckingham Palace. He told them about the theatres and museums and all the beautiful parks. The children's eyes sparkled with delight at the thought of such a magical place.

'If you're good, my darlings, and I do well,' he said, 'I will take you there one day and you will see for yourself. Would that be nice?'

They all gave Ahmed a huge hug and went off to their rooms. Ahmed now had to tell Amina everything that had happened in London. She had to tell him that Eddie had implied that his future at the bank may be in doubt.

Eddie sat at the manager's desk, first to arrive at the bank as usual. He had several pressing matters to deal with. Now they had installed a phone, he could talk to the main branch in Manama quite easily. Several merchants had been setting up businesses as agents for oil-related equipment and the bank had been required to finance them. The palace also relied on the bank to handle the ever-increasing income that was coming from oil.

There was a knock at the door. Ahmed came in, wondering how he would be received.

'Good morning, Ahmed. Good to see you.' Eddie shook his hand. This was hardly the greeting of an old friend. 'I thought you were never coming back. We're very busy, as you can see.'

This made Ahmed feel out of place and unwanted. 'We were at the mercy of the Emir, Eddie. You know what it's like.'

'Well, you'd still be there now but the British advisor intervened. There's been a lot of trouble in town. The people aren't happy with the Emir being away so much. They can't understand why there's more money coming into the country and they aren't seeing any of it. It's an awkward situation for us all.'

'I'll try and help as best I can,' Ahmed said apologetically. 'But I have an urgent problem. Eddie.'

'I've heard from Amina. You're lucky I'm a friend of yours, and we need you to keep the Qatari oil workers' accounts, because otherwise you'd be looking for a job. With your private interests, I can't guarantee anything here. Bahrain is asking questions.'

'Has my landlord been here asking for money?'

'I've been looking through my files. He came in a couple of weeks ago asking for a business loan.'

'And you agreed?'

'Yes.'

'Knowing he planned to build six shops and flats next to Bait Al Bahr?'

'No. I didn't know that. He told me it was to expand his business, that's all. The policy from the palace is support the local business community as best we can, so that's what we did.'

'There's an enormous hole outside my front door, thanks to him.'

'I'm sorry, Ahmed, there's nothing I can do. He must have got permission to build from the palace. You better see them. Now, I'm busy – and you should be busy on bank matters too.'

Reluctantly Ahmed left the room, wondering where their friendship had gone. He went into the front office to start dealing with the business of the day, but as he worked on the ledgers and bank drafts his mind wandered to his personal problems. The morning dragged.

On the way home, he had to do two things. First, he went to the palace. After being stopped several times by the Bedouin guards, he managed to gain entry into the Emir's official quarters, where he had been welcomed so many times. In the outer office there was no sign of Jabor. Instead there was a smartly dressed Qatari with a trim beard.

'Yes?' was all he said.

'I'm Ahmed Al Bahr. Jabor, my brother-in-law, is usually here. We've just come back from London with His Highness.'

'Jabor is no longer here. I have been managing the office since the Emir went to London. I have been asked to take over permanently. Anything else?'

'No. No, thank you.'

Ahmed turned to leave.

'Oh, there may be something. Do you know Abu Omar? He has two shops. One a grocer, the other an exchange house.'

'Ah yes. A very good friend. Such a good businessman. We need men like him to build our country.'

'Yes. Yes. Thank you.'

Now he knew. Ahmed went out into the midday heat, past the fort and into the souq. At the exchange house he found Vijay busy with a queue of customers.

'Hello, sir. Nice to see you, sir,' Vijay said while sorting out transfers for the workers.

'It looks busy, Vijay. How is business?'

'More people every day. We are doing very well, Mr Ahmed. It's difficult on my own, though.'

'I'll give you a hand.'

And they helped men from India, Pakistan, Iran, Yemen, Oman and other Gulf countries send money back to their loved ones. At last Ahmed felt a sense of achievement.

Afterwards, Ahmed went back at the jetty to tell Salem about his encounter at the palace.

'I know that miserable new office manager,' Salem said. 'Leave it with me. He needs to be taught a lesson.'

A week had passed since the funeral, and Amina was coming to terms with life at Bait Al Bahr without her mother. Now she would have to assume the role of housekeeper. She sat with the children as they did their schoolwork, and told them they would have to help more in the house. Jabor had been staying with them since he came back from London. Now seemed a good time to confront him about the situation at the palace.

'Do you mind if I ask you about the palace and why you're not there?' Ahmed enquired carefully.

'It was going to happen sooner or later. He was put there while I was in London. To tell you the truth, Ahmed, I'm relieved. You saw how much I was working, and I couldn't take it any longer. That nasty toad they have there now will run the office just how they want it. It's no place for someone like me. In fact, now my dear mother has died I think my place is with Jean. I miss her already. I've decided I'm going back to London. Jean says I could find work quite easily there. In a few days I'll be gone.'

'I don't know whether to be happy or sad, Jabor, but I can't say I'm surprised. Jean is a great girl and she has changed you from a nervous wreck to a happy person. We'll be sad to see you go, especially Amina, but she'll get over it. You never know, you might bring Jean here one day. That would be fun.'

They laughed, remembering the good times they had shared over the summer. Hugging him, Ahmed left Jabor to break the news to his sister.

Just as Ahmed was about to leave for the exchange house, Uncle Salem arrived at the front door.

'Ahlan ya Ami Salem. T'fadl, t'fadl,' Ahmed said warmly. Come in, come in.

'Before I do, let's go and see what's happening next door. That's why I've come.'

The workers had moved away from the house and the hole was partially filled. The two men saw the Lebanese architect turn away from them.

'I'm afraid we can't stop the work altogether,' Salem said, his hand on his nephew's shoulder. 'As I mentioned, we have to encourage development if Doha is to thrive. However, I found out that permission was given without the proper authority and I've managed to reduce the size of the plot. I've ordered the plot to be ten metres away from your house, and there should be no more than one more floor. So, he will build four shops with one floor above. This is the best compromise, Ahmed. I hope you agree.'

Ahmed thought for a moment and then nodded, smiling gratefully.

'Shukran ya Ami Salem. Shukran. Now we will still be independent. Bait Al Bahr will continue to stand alone. I will just have to put up with that wretched landlord of mine and do as he says.'

'Sometimes you just have to work things out the hard way. Business is difficult, as you know, and not everyone is as kind and charming as you, dear boy. From time to time you have to be as cunning as your opponent. Otherwise they'll walk right over you.'

'Let's go and tell Amina. She'll be so pleased, and I have a feeling she could do with some good news.'

5

Sir William Henry Tucker Luce, newly appointed as Her Majesty's political agent in Bahrain, wasted no time in making his presence felt when the Emir arrived back from London. This was one man Sheikh Ahmed's new office manager would have to usher through without having to wait. Arriving directly from the airport he was greeted cordially by the Emir, who agreed that only they would be present in the private office overlooking the Gulf.

He came straight to the point. 'Your Highness. My government is most concerned that, as a British protectorate, your country should be secure. Much as we appreciate your family's desire to enjoy the benefits of our capital city, I must urge you to exercise the greatest caution in these turbulent times.'

The Emir gave a wry smile. 'I shall give the matter my most careful consideration, Your Excellency.'

'You know that Iraq has attempted to annexe Kuwait and that we have given Kuwait urgent assistance in this matter.

Also, with the continued hostilities between you and Bahrain over the islands of Hawar, we propose that a joint task force operates in the region. The people are rebelling, Your Highness. The United Arab Republic is getting stronger by the day, trying to destroy the status quo in the Gulf. The situation is dangerous. Can I count on your support?'

The Emir paused, aware that whatever he said would be reported back to London immediately.

'Our position is quite clear. The people of Qatar appreciate all the efforts of Her Majesty's government, but we can resolve these disputes between ourselves. You know the people of the desert are tribal. We have fought battles for centuries and we make peace in our own way. We have made further discoveries of oil and will soon be exploring at sea, thanks to the British oil companies who have come here to make vast amounts of money. May I respectfully remind you that my nation is a peninsula at the heart of the Arabian Gulf. We have been blessed with this natural energy resource for which you and the West have a great need. It would be wise, therefore, for you to inform Her Majesty's government that it is in its interests to protect us at all costs.'

The Emir rose, signalling the audience was over. The surly office manager was already at the door to escort Sir William out.

Ahmed arrived home with a new sense of confidence. The family were upstairs, so he sat for a while in the shade of the central palm, closing his eyes to meditate. He had learned to do this while in London: to be in the moment and enjoy the silence. He realised that problems could be overcome, and that sorrow and pain can lead eventually to joy. All you needed was patience and the will to see things through. He breathed deeply, a smile of contentment on his face. A few minutes later, he called for the children to come down. It had been a while since he had had a good talk with them, and since he had been away he thought they had become a little distant. It was time to resume his role as loving father.

They appeared one by one. Lulua was eighteen, tall and beautiful. Tima, at thirteen, fun-loving and playful, and Fahd was ten. He spent his time quietly drawing with his coloured pencils.

Sitting under the tree with the girls either side and Fahd on his knee, Ahmed told them how sorry he was that Um Jabor was no longer with them and he knew how much they missed her. He told them how much he loved them and promised to take care of them, no matter what. He told them they had the best mother in the world. Taking their hands and drawing them close to him, he promised that Bait Al Bahr would always be there for them to come home to. Lulua asked him what London was like and he described it all in great detail. Fahd interrupted him, asking how and why about every aspect of life in the city. Tim begged to go there for a holiday, insisting it was now the best place in the world.

Ahmed asked the children to look up into the palm tree. 'What do you see up there, my dears?'

'Dates,' said Fahd, first to answer.

'Shall we pick some?'

'How can we do that, Baba? They are too high,' Tima said.

'But if we help each other, we might be able to do it,' Ahmed said.

He stood up on the seat and asked the girls to put Fahd up on his shoulders.

'Now reach up as high as you can, Fahd. Can you reach?'

'Nearly. I'm trying. I can't do it, Baba.'

Ahmed put Fahd done and asked for Tima to be put on his shoulders. She struggled for a moment then got her fingertips to the lowest bunch of dates.

'Go on, Tima, you can do it,' Fahd shouted.

Lulua lifted Tima up a little more off her father's shoulders. She could finally reach the dates. She passed them down one by one until they had more than a dozen.

'We did it,' the children said. 'We did it.' They danced around the tree, happy with their achievement. Then they heard clapping. They all looked up. There was Amina, looking down from the balcony, proud of her husband and the children they had raised.

Jabor arrived to see the family gathered in the courtyard. He had been given two large hamour by one of his fisherman friends, so they all set to work making a fish dinner in honour of Um Jabor. As dusk came they took the platter of fish and rice, salads and the dates the children had picked onto the roof and ate in the cool evening air. Everyone agreed that Jabor should follow his heart and wished him happiness. The children, especially Tima and Fahd, continued to demand stories from him about London. Amina and Lulua were more interested in knowing more about Jean.

'To the future,' Ahmed declared, his hands outstretched either side. His family joined hands, shouting out across the rooftops, 'The future!'

At last Amina had her husband to herself. It was almost midnight by the time he had told her about Jean and Shirley, the concerts he had gone to, and the ballet. He told her that the British studied hard and worked hard, and that men and women were equal, with equal rights. There were so many aspects to life there that he admired.

Amina had to admit that she was lonely while he was away, and she had worried he might be enjoying himself too much. Ahmed confessed that he enjoyed Shirley's company, but had only realised at the end of his stay that Shirley wanted more than friendship.

'I felt sorry for her in a way,' Ahmed said. 'I don't think she'll ever find happiness. She's married to her work, I think.'

'What does she do?' Amina asked.

'I'm not sure. Works for some secret government department. But she knew we were all going home before we did.'

'And Jabor?'

'Jean came along at the right time. He was exhausted working at the palace. He had had enough.'

'I told you I went to see Maggie. I was worried about you.'

'I know,' Ahmed said, pulling her closer, cradling her head in his arm. 'One thing I know, my dear. The business seems to be going well. If we can afford it, I think we should try to send our children to London for higher education, if they agree. What do you think?'

'I think it's a wonderful idea, habibi. I really do.' Amina drew Ahmed closer to her and whispered in his ear. 'You know I love you more than ever? After tonight you might have another child to send to London.'

6

Doha, 1968

'I'll take you for lunch at the Oasis, Ahmed, if you're not busy.'

Ahmed was surprised by the invitation.

'Yes, OK. Thanks. I'll phone Amina and tell her not to expect me home.'

'I'll just finish some paperwork then I'll bring the car round.'

Eddie had always insisted the bank provide him with the latest car. Now he drove a light blue Chrysler Imperial. It was large and luxurious. Ahmed had never had the desire to drive. He thought he was lucky to live in the centre of town and liked walking to work each morning.

'It's got air-conditioning,' Eddie said proudly as Ahmed sat beside him on the red leather bench seat. 'So much better when it's hot outside.'

Ahmed wanted to say that it wasn't that hot, but he kept quiet, feigning interest in all the chrome switches and dials. They drove along the newly created seafront carriageway past the Ministries of Education and Finance. Shoppers were making last-minute purchases at the new vegetable market that had been built alongside the post office and central police station.

'There have been quite a few changes since I've been here, that's for sure,' Eddie said. 'Remember when it was just the bank, the palace and Qatar Cold Stores?'

'Yes. The first time we went to Dukhan? Salem has never been busier with all this construction going on.'

They passed fishing dhows and the old Emiri palace before turning into Al Hitmi and the Oasis Hotel.

'Maggie's with the children at the Beach Club. They love it there and they can play with the other kids while Maggie gossips with her friends.'

'How many have you got now?'

'The eldest James is at the English-Speaking School, of course, but we also have Sally, who's coming up to his sixth birthday. Yours are all grown up now, aren't they?'

'Almost. Lulua is in Kuwait, as you know. We wanted her to go to London, but she wanted to be nearer home. She'll be here for the holidays soon. Tima is nineteen and hoping to marry soon. Fahd is seventeen, the same as your eldest. Remember when they were born?' The men laughed. 'Then there's Jassim, who's seven now. He's a clever one. He loves school already, thank goodness.'

The Chrysler pulled up at the Oasis, which was built ten years earlier by Abdullah Darwish, who had seen a gap in the market for visiting businessmen.

'You can tell Abdullah enjoys Beirut, can't you?' Eddie said as he and Ahmed crossed the shiny marble floor to the glass-doored dining room. 'It's all glass and mirrors, just like the Commodore.'

'Oh yes, now you mention it,' Ahmed said. 'These brass chairs with black velvet seats are a bit much for Doha.'

Several other tables were occupied, only by men, who looked like businessmen.

'So many travellers coming through. You see that man over there?' Eddie said, trying not to attract his attention. 'He was in the office this morning. Palestinian. He and his family moved to Kuwait after the Israelis kicked them out. He came down here to start a trading company. He told me his family had an orange farm in Palestine – hundreds of hectares. It's tragic.'

'I know. And now with Sinai occupied, who knows what the Israelis will do next. We have a Palestinian in the shops next to the house, and one of Fahd's teachers is Palestinian. They're good for the country but it's not the solution.'

'Nasser closing the straits of Tiran started it all off. The shipping lanes should be open to all countries,' Eddie said, 'otherwise the whole world suffers.'

'True. It's tragic to see Egypt, Jordan and the Palestinians being bullied by the Israelis. We have to support the Palestinians as much as we can.'

When the Egyptian waiter came over, Eddie ordered skewers of lamb with flatbread and a salad of tabouleh and fattoush to go with it. 'Now, Ahmed, I have something to tell you. I won't be at the bank much longer. The Emir's office has asked me to set up a new currency. We can't go on using the rupee now that Qatar is gaining such a high profile as an oil producer. It will take quite a while and I'll have to be in London to coordinate the production of the new notes and coins. I'm sorry to break this to you, but that's why I asked you here today. I'm afraid HQ have found a replacement, and it's not you.'

Ahmed looked a little taken aback. Eddie was not expecting his reply at all.

'Well, that's perfect, Eddie., because I'm leaving the bank too. I've decided I can no longer work for you in the morning and myself in the afternoon. I intend to put all my energy into my own business. We're doing well, and I have every intention of doing even better.'

'I hope you know what you're doing, Ahmed,' Eddie said as the food arrived. 'It's a hard world out there, and with all this turmoil in the Middle East you'll be at the mercy of the politicians. But I wish you luck. I really do. You're certainly going to need it.'

After lunch, Ahmed asked Eddie to drop him at the harbour. There wasn't much chat on the way; they realised that they were going their separate ways and may not meet again for a long time.

As usual, Ahmed took refuge at the water's edge to gather his thoughts. Had he actually given in his notice? Had he done the right thing? Could it be the worst decision he'd ever made? All these things swam around in his head as he walked along the jetty. Salem was visiting the old pearl-divers, Bilal, Yousef and Ibrahim. As ever, it was a comforting sight. Politics and business meant so little when he saw *Firial* swaying gently to and fro, the awning over the deck giving the four friends shade.

'Salam aleikum,' Ahmed said as he boarded *Firial*.

'Aleikum salam wa Rahmat Allah,' the men replied.

'My dear friends,' Ahmed said, coming to the point, 'I may be needing your support. I have left the bank and am going to concentrate on my own business. From now on, I'm on my own.'

The men patted him on the back and wished him luck. Only Salem looked perplexed at his decision. Ahmed sat with them and tried to reassure himself that he had done the right thing.

'You know something, Uncle Salem, Bilal, Jousef, Ibrahim? Today is my fortieth birthday. Would you do the honour of coming to Bait Al Bahr this evening? Bring your wives and children. I would like to fill the house with my dearest friends and family.'

Amina had no time to quarrel with her husband. The shock of him telling her he didn't have a job any more was banished by panic at having to welcome an unknown number of people into the house in a few hours.

'We never celebrate my birthday – and now this. What's got into you, Ahmed? How are we supposed to get food for such a gathering? And to celebrate the loss of a regular income?' Amina gave a laugh. 'I could strangle you. You're crazy.' Then she hugged him and kissed him, whispering in his ear, 'Happy birthday, old man.'

Somehow, they managed to get cold meats and salads from the shops that had opened up in the new block along the street. The Palestinians had brought in new products in the last few months, and it was a chance to try them. As well as succulent black olives, there were cured and smoked meats, jars of feta cheese in brine, halloumi and *jibna baida*. Tim was dispatched to get more bread. She brought home a pile of khobz Irani wrapped in newspaper to stop her hands from burning.

Fahd was called down from the roof where he was drawing the view over Doha on a large piece of cartridge paper he had procured from school. Nothing much fazed the seventeen-year-old, so being asked to find two dozen lemons to make juice was easy.

Amina sat Jassim down in the kitchen to watch her make something out of the leftovers of lunch.

'You're only seven, Jassim, but you can help me too. These potatoes I want you to mix up with this cooked fish. I'm going to make fish cakes.'

Ahmed put his head round the door.

'Such a good team we have, my dear. Any help?'

'Jassim is making fish cakes. I'm helping him. You could fry them for me as we make them.'

In no time, the food was ready. As darkness fell, Ahmed switched on the newly installed electric bulbs that dangled around the courtyard, creating a warm glow. They put the food and drinks on a long trestle table. Ahmed, Amina, Tima, Fahd and Jassim were all at the front gate as the guests arrived.

Bilal, Yousef and Ibrahim all brought their wives and ten children altogether. They all brought dishes with them, so Amina needn't have worried. There were stuffed vine leaves, tiny pastry parcels filled with spiced mincemeat, and lots of sticky sweetmeats. Uncle Salem, still unmarried after all these years, arrived bearing a large basket of Lebanese chocolates, causing great whoops of joy from everyone.

As usual all the men congregated together, their sons forming a sub-group. The women enjoyed meeting each other and talking about the house, the neighbourhood and the latest goings-on. Daughters helped to hand out the food and gradually the men mingled with the women and the boys began to befriend the girls. Then there was a great shout of joy.

'Ya Lulua! Ya Lulua!'

Tears streamed down Amina's face as her eldest daughter stepped through the doorway. Ahmed and her brothers and sister ran towards her.

'We weren't expecting you so soon,' Amina said, struggling to hold back the tears. 'Come along. Meet everyone.'

'Happy birthday, ya Baba,' Lulua said, giving him a kiss and a large envelope.

Ahmed and Amina proudly introduced their daughter to each of the families, telling them she had decided to go to Kuwait to study law. She told them how hard it was to leave home and to be in a different country, how she missed her family, but she felt she had done the right thing.

Ahmed decided to make a speech. 'Thank you all for coming,' he began. 'You are the dearest people in my life. Today I decided to give up my regular job at the bank and to try and expand my business. It was a hard decision, but one that I feel is best for the family. Lulua being here has made it such a special night. Thank you.'

'Open the envelope, Father,' Lulua called out.

Ahmed took out a large stiff piece of paper from the envelope.

'Lulua Ahmed Al Bahr. Graduated from Kuwait University as Bachelor of Law. First class honours.'

Great cheers erupted in the courtyard. Ahmed waved Lulua's degree in the warm evening air. Amina couldn't stop crying. Tim, Fahd and Jassim danced a jig around the palm tree as Uncle Salem and Bilal brought in an enormous cake, on top of which forty candles flickered for the master of Bait Al Bahr.

7

Geneva, 1971

'Forgive me, Your Highness, but you really ought to go back to Doha. If you're out of the country when such an important event is taking place, who knows what may happen.'

Edward Henderson had travelled to Sheikh Ahmed's Swiss hideaway on the orders of the Foreign Office.

'Khalifa seems to be getting on without me,' the Emir said of his cousin. 'The other states are all arguing about the proposed union. Let them get on with it.'

'With respect, Your Highness, Sheikh Khalifa has been working tirelessly to form a union with the Emirates. He has even been to see King Faisal in Jeddah to ask for mediation, to no avail. We have it on good authority that President Nixon is concerned.'

'Of course, they are concerned. Oil – that's all they want.'

'That may be so, but your country is in an extremely vulnerable position, sir. If you sign the article of independence from Britain and become a sovereign nation represented at the United Nations, you will get all the support you need.'

'Very well. I'll sign it right here and you can do with it what you will.'

Edward Henderson, having witnessed the Emir's signature, left the ruler to live undisturbed by matters of state in his luxurious mountain villa.

By the time the Arabist arrived in Doha, the state of Qatar had been an independent nation for two whole days. Instead of being an advisor, Henderson had become the first British ambassador to the country. He had to set up a new mission. No longer would the former colonial power be able to command and control, but it would join a long list of other countries offering their assistance.

Qatar was an OPEC member and had a seat at the United Nations in New York. Since the Emir insisted on staying put in Switzerland, the country was being run by the heir apparent, Sheikh Khalifa. Now that independence had begun the people, although pleased, wondered what it would mean for them.

Edward and Jocelyn Henderson soon established themselves at the new mission in Rumaillah. It was built next to Rumaillah Hospital and opposite the compound where Eddie. and Maggie had lived.

_ᛁ⸗ᛁ⸗

8

Doha, 1971

Ahmed was at the exchange house every morning at eight o'clock sharp. Since he had left the bank he was able to see for himself how business was doing. He and Vijay rearranged the office so Ahmed had a corner to himself where he could deal with prospective customers. He decided from the outset that he would try to be friendly to all who walked in, and made sure Vijay had the same attitude. It paid off. From the time Ahmed was there all day, the number of customers almost doubled, and profits rose accordingly.

At home Amina busied herself in the kitchen. She had gone shopping that morning at the newly refurbished Qatar Cold Stores and filled her Hotpoint refrigerator with fresh and frozen foods as well as the vegetables from the market. The new cooker took a little getting used to: you had to adjust the heat in advance so that pans didn't boil over. She made herself a cup of mint tea and took it along to the downstairs family room where ten-year-old Jassim was watching television. Ahmed hadn't wanted to get one, but Amina thought it might be good to keep in touch with the news now that so much was going on in the world, seeing pictures rather than just listening to the radio made such a difference. The family had gathered round the black and white set to see the funeral of President Nasser in Cairo. Vast crowds had turned out to line the streets and mourn the man they all idolised. Ahmed agreed then that television had been an asset to the family, and reluctantly watched the news every evening.

'How was school, Jassim habibi?' Amina asked her son. 'You'd better do your homework before your father gets home.'

She felt sorry for the boy now that his brother and sisters had left home. They had all smothered him with love and affection and he looked forward to seeing them. Thank goodness Tima lived nearby and could pop in to see him. She had married Tareq, Bilal's grandson. They had met at Ahmed's fortieth birthday party. They lived happily in Farij al Najma. Ahmed was over the moon that the two families were intertwined.

Lulua had also married. Following Ahmed's birthday, when she had appeared so unexpectedly, she told her parents she had met someone at university. A fellow law student, he was from a wealthy family, and the couple convinced their parents that they were right for each other. Once again Bait Al Bahr was the scene of a celebration. Her parents had spoken to Lulua and were satisfied that their daughter, an extremely intelligent girl, knew what she was doing, so they gave her their blessing.

And then there was Fahd. Jassim didn't speak for three days after his elder brother left home. He had heard his parents discussing the matter for days beforehand. Fahd had always loved to draw, and after he finished secondary school at seventeen his father suggested he go to study in London. Ahmed had seen for himself the rich culture in England's capital when he had visited. Amina naturally felt uneasy at the prospect of her son living so far from home. In order to ease her concern, he assured her that he would ask Jabor, who lived in England with Jean, to look after Fahd. When Fahd received an offer to study fine art at the Royal College of Art, Amina had to agree it was the opportunity of a lifetime.

Once Jassim had finished his homework, he asked Amina if he could go out for half an hour. One thing he looked forward to was his regular knock-about with a football on the remaining land between Bait Al Bahr and the row of shops. When he walked home from school with his friends, he would fix a time when they could gather. There wasn't enough room for a proper game, so they made do with a couple of old tin cans for goalposts. They kicked the ball, on permanent loan from one of the teachers, around until dinner time. Jassim was always the last to go home; he liked to carry on playing keepy-uppy on his own, trying to improve his personal record.

9

London, September 1971

Jabor had been living with Jean in her one-bedroom rented flat over a Chinese takeaway in West Hampstead ever since he had returned to London a decade earlier. Jabor, who had had a string of part-time jobs, had a job as a night porter at the Cumberland Hotel, Marble Arch. Working at night paid well, so they weren't badly off. The only problem was, while one went to work the other was coming home. They cherished the period between four o'clock and eight o'clock in the evening when they had supper: this was the only time they could be together except weekends, which they spent in bed.

Their routine was disrupted one summer's afternoon when Jabor received a letter from Ahmed and Amina asking him to look after Fahd, who was about to start studying in London.

'How on earth are we going to look after him, Jabor?' Jean asked. 'Where will he sleep? How will we cope with our shifts and everything? Doesn't your sister realise?'

'He's family, Jean. He's my nephew,' Jabor said, knowing Jean was right but giving her a look of desperation. 'It's what we do. We look after each other. He's only nineteen. He'll be fine, I'm sure.'

So Jean agreed he could stay. Fahd arrived, fresh from Doha Secondary School, in the rain a few days later. He began his course the next day, and Jabor took him all the way on the bus to Kensington.

'Your father loved it here,' Jabor said as they sat on the top deck, passing Lord's cricket ground. 'That's why you're here, you know.'

'The reason I'm here, Ami Jabor, is because I'm good at art.'

Jabor was taken aback at his response.

'My father may have loved it here because he enjoyed seeing beautiful things. My intention is to create beautiful things.'

'I see,' Jabor said. 'In that case, I wish you well.'

The pair sat in silence for the rest of the journey, getting off at the Royal Albert Hall. Fahd thanked his uncle for accompanying him and said he would see him later.

'But I'm not sure how long I'll be staying with you. It's a bit far from college,' Fahd said, turning and running up the stairs to the Royal College of Art.

Fahd never returned to the flat over the Chinese takeaway. As soon as he walked into the college, he felt at home. It was a glorious space filled with creativity. Sculptures suspended from the atrium ceiling, 'ban the bomb' symbols painted on the walls, and a noticeboard plastered with announcements of meetings, seminars and splinter groups. The Students' Union had set up a counter for subscriptions alongside the Marxist society and the Gay Liberation Front.

Fahd immersed himself in this new environment. He was confident – even arrogant. He strutted around, aware of his good looks. He'd have to grow his hair, he thought, seeing the shoulder-length hair of his fellow students and lecturers. The conventional shirt and trousers he had worn for the flight would have to be replaced by velvet flares and a tank top. As he sized up the students assembling for the first lectures of term he decided he would be exotic, enigmatic and desirable. If he was to do well and make the best use of his time here, he would have to get to know all the right people. Holding his head high, he knocked on his tutor's door.

'Those rooftops were good, I must admit. Sit down, Fahd. My name's Andy Rice. I'll be guiding you through your Fine Arts degree course.'

Andy Rice, middle-aged with a mass of grey curly hair and beard to match, wore a purple suede jacket over a black T-shirt. He didn't get up, so Fahd couldn't see what he was wearing below his waist, but he guessed jeans that were probably a little tight.

'You've got a sense of space and form which I like, but colour is lacking. I suggest you forget everything you know and start again.'

Fahd gave a broad grin. 'Exactly what I'd hoped you'd say, sir,' Fahd said politely.

'Call me Andy. I'll see you once or twice a month, but if you're interested there are a few of us getting together this evening in the bar. You're welcome to join us.'

It was music to Fahd's ears.

Ahmed went over the figures, sitting at his desk in the exchange house. Vijay was dealing with a queue of customers. He had been concerned that the formation of the new Qatar riyal would upset things but, if anything, it had made it easier for transactions to be processed. A new confidence was emerging in the market as oil continued to flow from the west coast in Dukhan to the new offshore fields near Halul Island.

He watched Vijay handling each customer like an old friend, feeling a sense of pride at what he had achieved. His thriving business meant that his family were well cared for. Amina was able to spend her time enjoying the latest goods available. Apart from new labour-saving gadgets in the kitchen, there was the television and modern furniture, home decorations that she bought from the latest shop, Modern Home, and he had promised her they would install an air-conditioner in the TV room for the following summer.

Ahmed knew these material comforts were a replacement for her mother and Lulua, who had settled in Kuwait with her husband. Amina missed them both. He wished that Amina could see more of Lulua and hoped he would be able to take Amina soon to visit. Thank goodness Tima was happy with Tareq, Bilal's son, and they visited quite often. He wondered how Fahd was doing in London. He imagined Jabor and Jean showing his son all the sights. For a moment he reminisced about his time in London and how much he had learned about art and culture. He though how lucky their children were. *They have opportunities we never had.* He allowed himself

445

the pleasure of imagining his eldest son becoming a famous artist and how gratifying it would be. He smiled to himself. Poor Jassim missed his brother but was working hard at school. Should he encourage Jasim to play football, since he enjoyed it so much? He made a mental note to discuss this with Amina.

The daydreaming came to an end when Uncle Salem appeared in front of his desk looking agitated.

'Ya Ami Salem. Ajlis. Sit down. You look upset.'

'I've just come from the hospital. It's Bilal. They think he's had a heart attack. Tareq is with him. Yousef and Ibrahim too.'

'I'm very sorry to hear this, Uncle Salem. Thank you for letting me know. I hope he will be OK.'

'I should go back to the office, but I need to sit here for a minute. I don't think Bilal will be with us long. I keep remembering the old days, when your mother and I used to see Bilal and the others come back from pearl-diving. They were all so happy and full of fun, even though their lives were hard. Such brave men. Things are so complicated now.'

'It must be hard for you. I was just thinking how life for us is improving. Perhaps I'm being selfish, thinking just of my family and my business.'

'No, Ahmed. I'm sorry. It's just such a mess at the moment. I am trying to run my ministry to plan the future – build new roads, hospitals, schools – but we have no leader. The Emir has gone away yet again. This time he's gone to Iran on a hunting trip. How can we get anything done? People aren't

446

being paid on time, decisions aren't being made, and there's a lot of ill-feeling. Jabor is lucky to be out of it. Sometimes I wish I was in London with him.'

'I didn't realise it was so bad. The oil is flowing, isn't it?'

'Yes, but now the British are no longer in control and we're supposed to be independent, everything takes much longer. At least the oil companies are still coming in looking for oil. It would have been so much easier if we had joined the Emirates. God knows what's going to happen.'

Ahmed had never seen Salem look so despondent.

Fahd finally woke up just before midday. He looked around the bright white bedroom.

'Good morning, Mr. Sleepy. Breakfast?' The voice came from a hair-haired young man in a baggy tie-dyed T-shirt, and pantaloons.

'Er, just coffee, please,' Fahd replied, trying to remember the name of the man.

'Was fun last night, wasn't it?' the stranger asked, going into the galley kitchen to pour coffee from a glass percolator.

'I'm sorry, I don't remember much about it. Where am I? Who are you?' Fahd asked without any hint of embarrassment.

'That's nice. I provide a bed for the homeless and offer breakfast in bed and you don't even remember my name. Well, it was quite a night... I'll forgive you. I'm Alexander.'

'Oh yes, now I remember. You were dancing near the bar.'

'That's right. Friday nights at the RA are famous for their music, and I love dancing. You came over when the Doors were on. 'Love Me Two Times' drives me crazy and I have to dance. You happened to be there.'

Fahd got up to get the coffee, yawning and stretching.

'I'd better take a shower,' he said, leaning on the doorpost in his underpants, running his hand through his tousled hair. 'I'll need some clothes.'

'There are a few clean things in the spare room. I don't suppose you remember what I said about that either.'

'What?'

'After the RA disco we went to Sombrero's,' Alexander said, raising his voice when Fahd turned on the shower. 'It was packed. Maybe you couldn't hear above the noise. I said you could stay at mine. So we came back here. You never made it to the spare room, though.'

'What time is it? I've got a lecture at two, I think,' Fahd said, popping his head out of the shower.

'Same as me. We're both doing fine art.'

_⌐⌐_

Fahd fell into a routine of work and play. Alexander was happy to introduce him to his friends, and his favourite bars and clubs. Ahmed sent him money, and Fahd bought a second-hand bike, so he could explore alone, leaving Alexander to run the household. He made sure that each day was full of interesting things to see and do because he wanted to be the best fine art student of his year. To do this, he had to focus on art. He couldn't think about anything else.

Andy Rice introduced Fahd to new artists who were trying to make a name for themselves. Fahd absorbed all the latest thoughts on the contemporary scene. Conceptual art was taking prominence, and Fahd went to go to new galleries, such as the Hayward, where experimental spaces were transformed into vast weird installations. Andy suggested Fahd move away from painting simple landscapes to more figurative work, which would be more challenging. Fahd had never done well with painting people and, at first, he was reluctant. One thing that changed his mind was a chance meeting with Francis Bacon.

Once a week Fahd cycled from the flat to Oxford Street along the Bayswater Road. Along with seeing the latest art, he wanted to read the latest literature and hear the newest music. He continued along Oxford Street until he was almost at Tottenham Court, and found the place he'd been looking for. Alexander had suggested Virgin Records was the best place to get LPs. He left his bike propped against the shop front and headed to the first floor.

'Hi. Can I help you? My name's Richard. Would you like a coffee?'

'Thanks. I'm looking for Leon Russell.'

'Ah yes, and the Shelter people. Right over there. Brand-new album. Buy three and I'll throw in a fourth for free.'

Coffee in hand, Fahd browsed through the shiny covers, finally choosing Leon Russell, Chick Korea, the Doors and J.J. Cale, who he'd heard in the background at the Nuthouse vegetarian restaurant a week earlier.

Richard handed over the records. 'Pop in any time. Here's my card.'

Fahd looked at the card before putting it in his pocket.

RICHARD BRANSON,

VIRGIN RECORDS,

FIRST FLOOR

24 OXFORD STREET, LONDON

Back on his bike, Fahd headed for Soho. He recalled Andy recommending the French House as a good place to meet fellow artists. He cycled along Dean Street, relishing the bohemian feel of freedom in the air. His father had told him about the jazz clubs and thought he should go there sometime. He spotted the pub and ventured in, clutching his bag of music. It was warm at the bar, so he took off the blue greatcoat he'd bought at the weekend from Kensington Market and laid it on the bar stool next to him.

'Shandy, please.'

The barman poured his drink.

Fahd noticed a half-full glass next to his and wondered to whom it belonged. He didn't have to wait long.

'Would you mind removing your coat, my dear?'

A rather short, tubby man propped himself up on the stool and proceeded to light a cigarette.

'Another, please, Jack,' he said to the barman.

The barman filled the glass with vodka, leaving little space for tonic.

'Haven't seen you in here before,' the man said to Fahd.

'No. First time,' Fahd said, wondering how to handle the situation. 'It was recommended by a fellow student.'

'Where are you studying?'

'Royal College of Art.'

'My old stomping ground. Well, I never. Fine art, I hope?'

'Yes. First year.'

The man held out his hand.

'Francis Bacon. Would you sit for me? I'd love to paint you.'

Within a month Fahd had established himself as a member of the trendy arts scene as well as a regular on the party circuit. He loved working hard – and playing hard. At the Royal College his tutors were happy that he had settled in so quickly and was willing to learn. Having sat for Francis Bacon, he now had a good idea of how to work on a portrait himself. For a week his class did life drawing – a male model posed in the winter light coming through the glass ceiling in Kensington Gore. Unlike the other students, Fahd chose to concentrate on the creases and folds in the sitter's skin and the sadness in his eyes. Electing to paint in watercolour, his usual medium, he gave the cartridge paper a wash over the subject, keeping the background white. The finished piece was stunning in its simplicity.

Francis Bacon was pleased with his portrait of Fahd. It had only taken three sittings to complete. Francis was mesmerised by Fahd's description of his home country, so by the time he'd finished Fahd was portrayed as a character from the Arabian Nights. Dark purple and crimson added to the rich mysticism in the picture. Fahd was overcome at seeing himself in such a way and gave Francis a warm hug. At last he had found people who were on his wavelength, he thought as he sped home on his bike. He ached to find out what would happen next in his life.

He didn't have to wait long.

'You know Powis Terrace?' Alexander said as Fahd came through the door. He was making pasta.

'No. And don't make any for me. I'm going to the Hard Rock. Andy asked me.'

'In that case, you won't want to come to the party.'

At the word 'party' Fahd stopped in his tracks. He went to his room and changed into a bright red satin shirt and pink velvet cords he'd found at Mr Freedom in Kensington Church Street. He felt it might be a night for Cuban heels too.

'Where is it?' Fahd said, one Cuban heel on the landing already.

'Powis Terrace. South Ken. I'll be there about nine.'

He took the Tube to Hyde Park Corner where Andy was waiting for him. The newly opened Hard Rock Café was the place to go for burgers and music. They had to wait for twenty minutes for a table, so had a tequila sunrise at the bar while they waited.

Andy admired his party clothes, asking where he was going.

'Oh, just some party in South Ken. The usual, I expect.'

'You know, you're very talented, Fahd. Once the figurative work is done we want you to explore other forms. Maybe abstract? Have you considered that?'

'Not really.'

'You're very privileged to have sat for Bacon. I'm not in his league, I'm afraid.'

Andy paid the bill and Fahd headed for the Tube and South Ken. It was almost eleven o'clock by the time he got there. He heard the thumping beat of dance music coming from the first-floor flat in Powis Terrace.

The door was open, revealing a dark smoke-filled space with psychedelic lights flashing. It was hard to make anybody out, but soon Alexander had found Fahd. 'Let me introduce you to a few people,' he said. 'This is Jason. Jason, this is Fahd. He's on the course with me.'

Fahd could just about make out a shortish, slim man of about forty with a shaved head and one earring.

'Hi, Fahd,' Jason said in an American accent. 'Alexander has told me all about you. Are you enjoying London?'

'I'm enjoying working. Art is my life,' Fahd said, choosing his words carefully.

'That's good to hear. Refreshing, I must say. My life is art too. I'm a dealer. I represent David in London and the United States.'

'David?'

'David Hockney, dear. This is his apartment.'

The party went on until three in the morning, by which time Fahd had met every person there. Like some desert prince who could command attention with a glance, he gained the attention and admiration of the hippest gathering in town.

Freddie Mercury wanted to know all about him, Serge Gainsbourg asked him to dinner, and Gilbert and George invited him to their latest show. He was about to leave when Jason tapped him on the shoulder.

'By the way, Fahd, David likes you. He would love it if you come to California for Christmas.'

10

Amina knocked on Jassim's bedroom door. Friday morning was always different. No school and no exchange. Bilal had died, and Ahmed had gone to be with Salem, Ibrahim and Yousef.

'I'm going to Beirut to get foul and falafel, Jassim. Do you want to come?'

She knew it was early but sometimes Jassim enjoyed going out on Friday mornings with her. She poked her head through his door to find Jassim in bed, just waking up. His walls were covered in posters of his favourite footballers, including Johan Cruyff and Gordon Banks. There was also a giant picture of Abdul Haleem Hafiz, his favourite singer.

Amina went downstairs to wait for him. She had something else on her mind. She hadn't heard from Fahd since he'd left a month earlier. Even her brother hadn't been in touch. It was difficult to get through, and she thought she might go to Cable and Wireless to place a call to London.

Eventually Jassim appeared in a crumpled thobe, a gaffeya perched askew on his luxuriant wiry hair.

'Yallah habibi,' Amina said, opening the wicket gate.

The tiny Lebanese restaurant, Beirut, was on Electricity Street, close to their house. It served the best breakfasts in town. Salem had told Ahmed about it, so most Fridays the family ordered several foul and falafel sandwiches to take home and share. They used to have to order a huge pile of little round flatbread sandwiches oozing with tahini paste and garlicky beans, but now half a dozen would do.

'I think I'll be a goalkeeper,' Jassim said, having been silent since they left home.

'That's nice. Good. I'm sure you'll be a very good one, just like Gordon Banks,' his mother said, making Jassim smile. 'Now, Jassim, my love, can you take these home for me? I want to go to Cable and Wireless to call your Uncle Jabor. I won't be long,' Amina said.

The family had a telephone at Bait Al Bahr, but it was only for local and incoming calls. To make an international call you had to go to the central office, which was a five-minute walk.

Jabor would be finishing his night shift, Amina thought, as London was three hours behind Doha time. She had the number of the Cumberland Hotel written down in a letter that Jabor had sent when he first got the job there. She loved getting his letters, with news of his life in London.

As it was early, there was no queue and she was able to make her call straight away. After a few distant rings she heard the operator say, 'Cumberland Hotel. Can I help you?'

'Is Jabor there, please?'

'Sorry, madam. Who?'

'Jabor. He works there as the night porter.'

'Ah, Jabor. I'll see if he's here. Who's calling, please?'

'Amina. His sister.'

There was a pause, then she heard her brother's voice. 'Hello?'

'Jabor?'

'Ya Amina. Are you OK?' Jabor asked.

'Yes. Thank goodness I found you. It's Fahd. How is he? I'm worried about him.'

'I don't know, Amina. I'm sorry. He didn't stay with us. He left straight away – he said our house was too far from college. I suppose he's living somewhere else.'

'Oh dear. I don't know what to do. I asked you to look after him, Jabor. Just this one thing. I thought you would be responsible for him. He's only nineteen.'

'I'll talk to Jean. I'll try the college and see if they know, then I'll ring you at home. I've got your number. Maybe this evening. Okay? But try not to worry. I'm sure everything is fine.'

Amina couldn't concentrate on anything else for the rest of the day. Ahmed came home for lunch, but soon went back out to deal with customers who came in on their day off to send money home. She didn't feel like unburdening her secret to her husband just yet. She paced around the house. Jassim had gone to play football with his friends and she had the place to herself. What if he's ill? Where can he be? I knew it was a bad idea to let him go to London, she thought. The hours went by so slowly until Ahmed came back in the evening.

'I have something to tell you,' she said as he came through the door. 'I called Jabor in London. Fahd isn't there. He's gone.'

'Gone? What do you mean, gone?'

'I knew he shouldn't have gone to London. It's all your fault, filling your head with grand ideas. He should be here with us, Ahmed. With his family.'

Ahmed went to give Amina a hug. As she tried to shrug him off she burst into tears, unable to contain her angst any longer.

'I'll try to find out in the morning. Don't worry, Amina. I'm sure he's OK. He's very independent.'

'Well, Jabor said he would call me this evening. I'm waiting.'

Finally, two hours later, the phone rang in the majlis.

'Jabor? What have your heard?'

'The college is closed for the Christmas holidays. The operator doesn't have any information on students. I'm sorry. We'll have to wait until the new year when the new term starts.'

Amina put the phone down and turned to Ahmed, burying her face in his comforting embrace.

Fahd decided he wasn't a great fan of Hockney. Having been plunged headlong into the ferocious world of Francis Bacon, he thought Hockney's paintings were too tame. As he began to grapple with figurative work, he felt drawn to Lucien Freud, where the subjects were exposed in all their raw nature. He would work late into the evening, even using Alexander as a model.

As Andy had asked him to explore other forms of art he worked on larger canvases, sometimes splashing paint on them randomly. He'd seen works by Jackson Pollock at the Tate and identified with the sense of freedom in the work, but somehow when it came to colour he couldn't manage any kind of distinct style. Each time he finished a painting he stood back and saw a dark blanket of dirty browns and grey.

His ticket to Los Angeles arrived at the perfect moment. Term had finished, and even though he would miss the Christmas party season in London, he was looking forward to leaving the rain behind and heading for Hollywood. Alexander was openly jealous, but Fahd was dismissive of his feelings. He left the flat to take the Tube to Heathrow, clutching an overnight bag, a quickly procured visa and the ticket that would be his entrée into the Californian world of make-believe and glamour for the next three weeks.

The Pan-Am 747 took Fahd to LA in time for poolside drinks at Jason's villa in the Hollywood Hills. A driver bearing a sign saying *FAHD* was waiting in the arrivals lounge. Looking out of the back window of the Ford Pontiac he saw multi-lane freeways, high-rise blocks of offices and apartments, and smiles on the face of every person he saw. This was the obvious difference between California and dreary, wintry London. However, as the car moved away from the airport and out of town, he began to realise that the landscape reminded him of home. This came as something of a shock. For a moment he felt homesick and a longing for his family. But he forgot this as the car swept up into hillier terrain into a residential area with lush green lawns and swaying palms. All the properties were long and low, surrounded by stone walls. The driver dropped him off outside a house on Woodrow Wilson Drive. Fahd was admitted to the house by a smartly dressed servant.

'Fahd! Come in. Come in. Let me introduce you. Everyone, this is Fahd from London. Well, not from London but at the Royal College. He's going to be a big name in painting one day. Let me tell you.'

Fahd made his way around the pool, where the lights had just been turned on. The man who had opened the door for him offered him a turquoise cocktail containing a cherry and an umbrella. All the guests were suntanned, slim and attractive, he noticed. Many of the older men wore gold jewellery and silk shirts and loafers. The younger ones had shoulder-length hair and wore a vest and shorts. The music was Latin American. Tito Puente segued into Santana as the drinks flowed and the conversation grew more raucous.

'Is there somewhere I can change?' Fahd asked Jason, making the point that he hadn't yet been shown where he would stay.

'Oh, I'm so rude. Of course. Carlos, Carlos. Show Fahd his room in the guest wing.'

Fahd decided to establish himself as the star turn by appearing in the skimpiest bathing suit he could find at Harrods. Already tanned – something the other boys worked to achieve – he posed for a second then dived into the deep end. There was a wild round of applause.

In moments Fahd was surrounded in the pool. Everyone tossed aside their clothes and jumped in. He was splashed and teased for his charming good looks.

David Hockney wasn't there that evening. He was working on a major new piece and he stayed at the studio until late. He did stop by in the morning to meet Fahd and asked him to lunch around the corner at his own villa in Montcalm Avenue.

Soon Fahd was accompanying David to his studio on Santa Monica Boulevard, driving there each morning in a red Mercedes open-top sports car. Gradually Fahd began to relax into the LA lifestyle, enjoying plenty of painting and parties. He listened to Hockney explain that London was great as a cultural centre but that the weather and lifestyle in California were so much better for work. He'd had huge success with *A Bigger Splash* – a painting of his own pool. Now he was putting the last touches to Portrait of an Artist (Pool with Two Figures), which featured his former lover Peter Schlesinger, uncharacteristically in jacket and trousers, leaning over the pool. As they drove, David explained how hard it was for him to paint it.

'If you want to get out in the car and explore, feel free,' David said one morning, seeing that Fahd was stuck for subjects.

'I can't drive.'

'Sam will take you wherever you want to go.'

Sam, one of the assistants, took Fahd out in the car and asked where he'd like to go.

'The desert?'

'OK. If we drive due East, we'll hit the desert.'

During the two-and-a-half-hour drive, Fahd saw the scenery around him change. He listened to Sam tell him about the Mojave and Colorado deserts, which came together at Joshua. It had become a haven for artists and nature-lovers wanting to escape Los Angeles.

Sam stopped the car, so Fahd could sketch the giant boulders and cactuses. Further east, where the desert was flatter, he took the time to wander, drawing and absorbing the eerie atmosphere. Once again, he was reminded of home. He promised himself that, whatever he learned here, he would remember to use in Qatar, although he couldn't imagine living back there again.

Each day brought a new experience, with new techniques and ideas. He watched Hockney's use of colour and began to experiment with acrylics as an alternative to watercolours and oils. Once the Schlesinger portrait was done, David took Fahd out on drives himself. He took his Polaroid camera and took photos along Mulholland Drive – the road, the road signs, the hills, the highway itself, even the yellow road markings. Once back in the studio he created a montage then started a giant painting using the references. Fahd had never seen anything like it. He picked up the ideas, saving them for the future.

Christmas and New Year were lively affairs, with pool parties for both. Jason did most of the hosting: he enjoyed inviting people from different walks of life, mixing them up and seeing what happened. This was not entirely social. As an agent his role was to introduce the wealthy to the artists, so by the end of the evening cards would have been exchanged and potential sales made.

Fahd had the freedom of the guest wing at Jason's, the use of the Hockney studio and his car, and the occasional lunch at the Hockney residence. It was at one such lunch between Christmas and New Year that he met another artist, Richard Diebenkorn. The other guests were the writer Christopher Isherwood and his partner Don Bachardy. They were fascinated to hear about Fahd's life in Qatar, which had the same population as Beverley Hills. They'd heard about Saudi Arabia and its oil wealth, but Fahd had to explain how life in Qatar had been so different before oil. He surprised himself by how well he could describe his country to others.

He loved listening to the quietly spoken Christopher Isherwood and his memories of Berlin. He should have felt privileged to be in such esteemed company, lunching al fresco on salmon and strawberries in the middle of winter, but he felt it was his time and he wanted to make the most of it.

After working in the studio all morning one day, Fahd decided to go to the coast. He loved the sea and thought he might look in on Richard Diebenkorn, who had a studio in Santa Monica. Sam dropped him at 2448 Main Street. At dinner, Fahd heard how the artist had moved here to paint Ocean Park, once a theme park to rival Disneyland but now derelict. Inside the bright factory-like space, Diebenkorn was busy scraping layers of paint across a vast canvas. In the background Bach played as he went over and over his work, correcting and correcting. Fahd saw that he had captured the bright California colours: that special blue and a thin line of ochre at the very top. An even thinner line of red and green drew his attention upwards, and he felt torn between carrying on the complicated figurative work he'd been doing and working like Diebenkorn.

They hardly spoke, but they didn't need to, the mentor and the mentee. His colours were similar to Hockney's but here there were no figures, buildings or trees you could recognise. They were there in different forms – uncluttered, cut back, restrained. He had to go and look at the remains of Ocean Park to see for himself what had sparked these gorgeous works.

Fahd explored Ocean Park, with its rusty helter-skelters and rides. At first, he wondered how anyone could find inspiration in this apocalyptic place, but then he took out his sketchpad and began to draw the twisted shapes before him. Rather than the objects themselves, he concentrated on the forms in between them. Feverishly he made strong, bold lines, vertical, horizontal and diagonal, a dynamic painting appearing in front of him in his mind's eye. He did three such drawings in different areas of the park until, exhausted, he headed for the coast to think about his work and where he was going with it. He strolled along the near-deserted pier before making his way along the equally deserted beach, where he sat down to listen to the waves crash on the shore.

It was the first time he'd been on his own since he'd been in California. After all the experiences he'd had, he started to reflect on his recent past. He finally admitted to himself that he was struggling to find his identity as a painter. He had been introduced to so many ways of working. The walk around Ocean Park had convinced him that he had to find a style. How could Diebenkorn find such beauty there? He found this fact depressing. He thought about his lifestyle and all the parties he'd been to since he arrived. He hadn't met anyone he could call a friend. He realised he hadn't even wanted a friend – he had merely sought out contacts for his own gain. Looking back to his life in London, he began to see that he had been using people ever since he'd arrived. Poor Alexander doted on him, but with no return. All his fellow students thought him unusual and interesting, yet he couldn't be bothered to search for anyone special to share his thoughts. The worst thing was how rude he'd been to Jabor. It dawned on him that he really wasn't a very nice person at all. Tears rolled down his cheeks as he thought of his mother, father, brother and two sisters at home.

'Hi! How're ya doing? Kinda nice out here, ain't it?'

Fahd was shaken out of his reverie by a tall youth in jeans and bomber jacket with a mass of brown curls and a canvas shoulder bag dangling from his shoulder.

'Er. I'm OK thanks. just enjoying the air.'

'Where you from?'

'The Middle East. A place called Qatar.'

'Woah, dude. That's cool. Never heard of it. Can I sit down?'

'Sure,' Fahd said.

'I'm Dexter.'

'Fahd.'

'Nice to meet you, Fahd,' the young man said as they shook hands. 'You on vacation or something?'

'Sort of. Staying with some people. I'm a student in London.'

'I see. How's London? My dad had been there, but not me.'

'It's a big capital. Not as big as LA, though. The weather's not so nice, that's for sure.'

'I'm staying just over there if you'd like to come back for a coffee and meet my friends.'

'Sounds nice. Thanks.'

They got up and walked towards the ocean boulevard. Fahd was surprised when only after two minutes Dexter stopped in his tracks. 'Here we are, Fahd. This is home.'

In front of them was what looked like a luxury hotel. Pillars and palms graced the front entrance.

'You live here?' Fahd said in disbelief. 'Your dad must be rich.'

'My dad don't live here, Fahd. My friends do, though. Come inside and you'll see.'

Curiosity took over as Fahd walked up the marble staircase to the foyer. It would be nice to make real friends, he thought.

Inside, Dexter took his new friend's coat and bag containing his art materials and gave them to a young woman, who seemed to be some kind of receptionist.

'This is Sarah. Could we have some coffee, please?'

The two sat in an anteroom and drank the coffee, Fahd looking around at the ornate white and gold decor. On the walls were Italianate murals in gaudy colours. When they had finished, Dexter guided Fahd to a set of double doors off the anteroom. He opened them to reveal another larger room, again in the Italianate style. In the centre were a group of twelve or so men and women of about Fahd and Dexter's age. They sat in a circle, their hands placed neatly on their laps. At the head of the circle was an older man who directed Dexter and Fahd to empty chairs directly opposite him.

'Welcome to our family, Fahd. My name is Chuck.'

Fahd felt a little uncomfortable, for some reason. He remained quiet.

'So, you've met Dexter. Such a nice young man, isn't he?'

The rest nodded in agreement.

'You're probably lonely, Fahd. You may find happiness here I can assure you. Welcome to Synanon. The 'syn' means 'togetherness' and 'anon' means 'unknown'. So, you can be here with us all and nobody need know. Isn't that great?'

Nobody reacted.

'Today is the first day of the rest of your life,' Chuck said. 'Now let's play the Synanon game. Dexter, perhaps you'd like to begin.'

Dexter stood up and began to tell the others what he'd done that day. 'I woke up late and didn't help with the breakfast things.'

'Shame on you,' one of the group said. 'You're wicked. Never do that again. You should be punished.'

Others followed, saying all the bad things they had done over the past twenty-four hours. In the end Fahd was asked to stand up.

'And what about you, Fahd?' Chuck asked.

'I've been cruel to my family and abused my freedom.'

'That's good, Fahd. You will like it here. We're your family now. What do you think, everyone?'

'Give him chores and let him sleep on the floor,' one said.

'No dinner tonight. We must purify him,' said another.

'Remember, children,' Chuck said, 'we must renounce the sins of the world and keep our planet pure and clean. It's the only way. Your old ways of selfishness and desire will be banished if you do what we command. Go in the peace of Synanon and live in harmony.'

Strangely, Fahd felt rejuvenated by the orders. He thought his punishment was justified. The others got up and walked to the far door. Dexter took Fahd by the arm. As if in a trance Fahd walked with them, away into seclusion.

11

It had been three days since Fahd had gone out. He had never returned. Jason asked David if he'd seen Fahd. David asked Sam the driver, who said he'd taken Fahd to Diebenkorn's studio. Jason called Diebenkorn, but Diebenkorn said he had left days ago. 'I know young people in LA. They get invited to parties and weekends away and never tell anyone. That's probably what he's done,' David said.

'But he's supposed to be going back to London in two days for the new term. It's odd, you must admit.'

'I'll have to call someone in London if he doesn't show up soon,' Jason said, sounding anxious.

Two days later, in Doha, Ahmed made a call from his office to Jabor asking for the number of the college. He and Amina were increasingly concerned. Amina hadn't been eating and kept blaming her husband for letting Fahd leave home at such a young age.

Eventually Ahmed got through to Andy Rice.

'It's the first day back, Mr Ahmed,' he said. 'Very often students are late back. Perhaps he'll be back tomorrow. I was away over the holidays. If he doesn't show up, I'll ask his flatmate.'

The following day, Ahmed tried again. Andy Rice said he had some surprising news. Ahmed sat down, composing himself.

'I've spoken to Alexander, another first-year student who shares a flat with your son. He tells me that Fahd went off to Los Angeles for Christmas. I'm sorry, sir. I wasn't aware of this. However, it's not our responsibility, of course.'

'Los Angeles?' Ahmed repeated, incredulous at the thought. 'How did he get there? Why?'

'Alexander tells me he met a group of artists and they invited him there. I would imagine he's still there. If I hear anything, I'll let you know.'

Ahmed had to face Amina and tell her the news. After he had told her that Fahd hadn't turned up at college and was on the other side of the world in Los Angeles, she screamed out in rage.

'You shouldn't have let him go!' she cried, beating her fists against Ahmed's chest. 'That brother of mine too. Good-for-nothing. Where is Fahd? Something terrible has happened to him, I know it has.'

'It's OK, Amina, my love. I'm sure it's nothing. Let me phone a few more people,' Ahmed said as Amina stormed off to bed, her wailing echoing through the house.

Fortunately, Salem was at the jetty, about to board *Firial*.

'Ya Ami Salem. Something terrible has happened. I need your help. Fahd has gone missing. He went to Los Angeles and hasn't gone back to college.'

Salem thought for a moment. Who did he know? How could he help?

'I'll see Edward Henderson, the British ambassador. They have contacts with all the special services and Interpol. I'm sure he must have some ideas. What about your friend in London?'

'You mean Shirley?'

'Yes. She works for MI6, I think. They know everything.'

'But Los Angeles is a huge city. He could be anywhere.'

'You'd better call the college again. His fellow students might know more.'

Ahmed went back to the office to make more calls. He managed to find out that Alexander knew the art dealer who'd sent Fahd the air ticket. Someone called Jason. Ahmed found Shirley's number on an old scrap of paper in his desk and tracked her down at her desk. She'd already had a call from the embassy about Fahd.

'Lovely to hear you, Ahmed, although not under such circumstances. I'll do the best I can, but I can't promise anything.'

The waiting was tortuous for Amina and Ahmed. It affected Jassim too, who had heard his parents arguing at night about whose fault it was that Fahd was missing. The only consolation was Tima, who came around every day to comfort her mother. Ahmed had already been in touch with Lulua, who promised to come home as soon as she could.

A week passed. There was no news. Then one afternoon the phone in the office rang. It was Shirley.

'I'm afraid it's bad news, Ahmed. I've just received a fax of today's Los Angeles Times. Can I read you the headline?'

'Go ahead. I'm listening.'

"YOUNG MAN FROM MIDDLE EAST HELD TO RANSOM IN LA." There's a picture of Fahd on the front page.

Ahmed couldn't believe it. 'Go on.'

'It's a statement from the group that is holding him. They're called Synanon. They say, "Synanon wishes to announce that we are keeping Fahd Al Bahr here at our headquarters. He has joined us as one of our family, who have renounced all worldly pleasures, seeking peace and harmony in nature. He joins us in demanding an end to the exploration of Mother Earth's natural resources".'

Ahmed couldn't tell Amina. He didn't think she would be able to take the news. He went home and pretended he hadn't heard anything for three more days, while Shirley gave him updates each afternoon. The press had made it a huge story, and it was finally picked up by the international media. He would have to act fast or he knew the news would reach Doha. Each day after he finished work, he met Salem to confer. Salem told Ahmed he'd had to tell the palace, as one of Qatar's citizens were in danger in another country. The United States had yet to establish diplomatic relations with

Qatar, so Salem relied on Edward Henderson to do all he could in diplomatic circles.

Shirley described front-page pictures showing demonstrations outside the seafront mansion where they thought Fahd was being held. Placards read 'Free Fahd,' 'Allow People to be Free,' 'Close Down this Hell-Hole,' and 'Synanon is Corrupt.' The press ran articles about the cult and its strange rituals.

Ahmed kept reassuring Amina that every effort was being made to find their son. When she tried to prise more information out of him, he refused.

They didn't have to wait long. It was nearly February when the good news came.

Ahmed hovered over the office phone, waiting for Shirley's call.

'It's over, Ahmed. Your son is free.'

'Hamdilallah.' Thank God.

'Our boys got on to the Navy Seals, who raided the place last night. According to my sources, it was a swift operation. They managed to gain entry and snatch Fahd at four in the morning. Shortly after dawn, the LA police swooped in and arrested the cult leader. He's in custody and the people he recruited are being united with their parents. Fahd has been taken to the airport and should be in London tomorrow morning.'

'That's fantastic, Shirley. Thanks so much. You're amazing. I can't thank you enough. I must go and tell Amina.'

Ahmed ran all the way to Bait Al Bahr and up to the bedroom.

'He's all right, my love. He's allright. I just heard. He's free, and on his way back to London.'

'Really? Really? Are you sure, Ahmed?' Amina was in shock, hardly able to believe her son was safe after weeks of worry and fearing the worst. 'Hamdillah. Hamdillah.'

Then she hugged her husband as if she would never let him go.

With Fahd safely back in London, there was much debate as to his welfare. Amina was the first to speak to her son and then questions raised about his behaviour. However, the conversations were cordial, with Fahd promising to see his uncle more often. He had already told Alexander how happy he was to have him as a friend. He apologised to Andy for his behaviour.

Jabor came around to see Fahd more often. For weeks they wondered what had happened and why Chuck had done what he did. Ahmed had kept in touch with Shirley, who told him she thought it was purely for publicity. Salem told Ahmed that the government was prepared to send ransom money, but, in the end, it wasn't needed. The most pressing question was how Fahd had got kidnapped. That would have to wait.

By the middle of February everything had calmed down and life was more or less back to normal. One day, Ahmed had a visitor.

'Good morning, Ahmed. Hope I'm not disturbing you.'

'My goodness. Eddie. What are you doing here? I thought you were in London. Sit down. Sit down. Tell me all the news.'

'There's not much to tell, really. As you know, the new currency has been made and is in circulation. The job's done. Maggie and I missed our old home, so we're back.'

'That's great. I must tell Amina. She'll be so pleased. In fact, we're going down to *Firial* tomorrow for a picnic and a trip around the bay. Would you like to join us?'

'Yes, please,' Eddie said enthusiastically, his old friendliness restored.

Amina had been baking, and the aroma of home-made bread wafted through the courtyard.

'Oh, it's only you,' she said as Ahmed opened the kitchen door.

'That's nice. Thank you,' he said sarcastically. 'Everyone will be here in a minute.'

'I know. I know. Why do you think I'm running around like crazy? Look at my hair, my face, my dress.'

'You look lovely as always, my love,' he said, putting his arm around her waist.

'Stop it. Stop it,' she said, giving a little giggle.

It was too late. Their guests were arriving.

First Tima came in, Tareq holding their new baby boy.

'Look at me, Tima. What will Tareq say?'

'You look lovely, Mama.'

Amina heard a taxi draw up outside. It was Lulua. She was carrying a baby daughter, but no husband was with her.

'Ya Umi, ya Abi. This is Buthaina,' Lulua said.

Jassim came running down the stairs to kiss his sisters and greet his brother-in-law.

They all sat down to lunch outside, as the weather was just right. Then there was a knock at the door.

'Can you go, Amina, love?' Ahmed said with a grin.

'Why always me me me?'

Then she opened the door.

Fahd stood in front of her. She couldn't hold back the tears, putting her hands up to her face.

'No kiss for me, then?' Fahd said, starting to cry as well.

Amina was speechless. She hugged him as if she would never let him go.

Finally, she ushered Fahd in to see the rest of the family. 'Remember when you put me on your shoulders, Lulua, and I got the dates? Baba said we'd always be welcome back home. Well, here I am, and it feels fantastic. They gave me special leave to come back for ten days.'

It was a glorious family occasion, and they celebrated being back together.

12

The family, Eddie, Maggie and the children got on *Firial* laden with picnic things. Ibrahim and Yousef were there. The old captain's seat was left vacant as a mark of respect to Bilal, who had always sat there.

The sea was calm, and everyone was excited at the prospect of a trip to Safliyah island. They had to wait for Salem who arrived at a run, out of breath. Stepping on board, he said he had important news. 'I've come from the palace. Sheikh Khalifa is now the Emir. He has taken over. All the government support him.'

'It's been coming for some time, hasn't it?' Ahmed said to his uncle.

'Yes. All those foreign trips he took. He was never here. We had no captain. You have to have a captain.'

They all rejoiced at the prospect of better days to come. Then they cast off the ropes and cheered as the boat set off, Ibrahim and Yousef showing Fahd and Jassim what to do.

Several other boats were out, including some smaller sailing boats from the expat sailing club.

Firial ploughed through the calm sea. After lunch on the island they reboarded, and Ahmed said he had something to say. 'You see that my good friend Eddie and Maggie have come back to their second home. On this special day too. We are happy we have a new leader and of course grateful that we are all safe and well – especially my eldest son.' He gave a little cough. 'Therefore, I am happy to announce that the exchange house will be closing.'

There was a gasp around the deck.

'I am launching the new Al Bahr Bank, and Eddie will be the general manager.'

Everybody cheered and slapped Ahmed on the back.

Filial set sail, heading for home. Eddie felt on top of the world as he sat on the noqada's wooden seat. Just as they moored at the jetty, he felt the old wood of the seat. It made him wonder about the old days, and he asked Yousef and Ibrahim about the pearl-diving. He stood up to inspect the seat a little more. Feeling along its edges and back, he discovered that the seat lifted up to reveal a large empty space.

'That's where the captain kept the pearls,' Ibrahim said. 'We were never allowed to go in there. That's why he sat there all the time.'

Just as he was being told all about the rarity of the pearls and how hard it was to find one, Eddie saw another that the space at the bottom had an extra compartment. He could feel gaps set into the base. 'What's this?' he asked the divers as the rest of the party gathered around.

'Not sure,' Ibrahim said, looking at Yousef.

Eddie used his penknife to prise open the internal lid at the base of the trunk. Inside was a small chest, the size of a tea caddy.

Salem was the first to speak. 'Could I have that, please?' he asked. 'I never thought I would see this. I'd heard about it but I presumed it was lost during a voyage.' He took out a folded piece of parchment and read aloud:

'Never did I know the wonder of a silent night,
Never did I realise the beauty of a rounded moon,
Never did I understand the secret of one true love,
Until that night with you.
Ya Lubna. You are my only love.
I dream of you day and night as we sail the seas,
Waiting for your sweet caress.
I'll always be yours,
Forever.
Adel'

Salem folded the note and replaced it in the box, taking out a small velvet bag.

'This has remained untouched for forty years,' he said, cradling the bag in his hand. He opened the bag. Inside was the largest, most magnificent pearl they had ever seen.

'*Al Dana*,' Salem said. 'The most beautiful pearl in the world.'

Ahmed and the family sat in silence until Ahmed asked, 'Who is Adel?'

'He was your father.'

The family walked back to the house in silence, Ahmed some distance from the rest, taking time to absorb what he had just discovered. Amina tried to comfort him, but she asked her to leave him alone. She hurried the younger children along, away from Ahmed.

At home, Ahmed headed straight upstairs and onto the roof, where he had found solace all those years before. Could this man Adel really be my father? Not Khaled, the man I thought was my father all along? The man who built this house, which was handed down to me? Am I not from his loins, from his blood? Incredulity built up inside him, turning to anger as he paced the rooftop.

He had never known his mother, except for the little that Salem had told him. he had mourned her loss over the years, but now felt a surge of animosity. I am not the man I thought I was, he said to himself. I am the product of lust – of a pearl-diver and his woman. Who am I? Nothing at all. I shouldn't be here.

He heard the family whispering downstairs. Tears began to pour down his cheeks. He could no longer keep his emotions in check. He felt that all the long years and hard work he had put in to raise his family had all been for nothing.

Salem had waited long enough. He had spoken to Amina and the family and now braced himself to face his nephew. Climbing to the top of the staircase he approached the roof, trying to find the right words to ease Ahmed's shock. He coughed to signal that he had arrived. Ahmed seemed not to hear, still gazing across the rooftops towards the distant desert.

'I'm so sorry, Ahmed. I couldn't tell you.'

Ahmed continued to look into the distance, apparently unwilling to look at Salem, whom he had always adored and trusted.

'Your mother swore me to secrecy.'

More silence.

'All I can say is that you were born of love. A perfect love.'

Ahmed finally turned towards his uncle. 'So who am I, Uncle Salem?'

'You're the same person you've always been. The nephew I have always loved and cared for, as I promised your mother I would.'

'Who was this Adel? I want to know. It's my right.'

'If you're ready, come downstairs. Please, Ahmed habibi. Your wife and family are waiting. They have as much right to know as you.'

At first Ahmed was reluctant to hear his story in front of his family, but slowly he saw sense in Salem's proposal. The men embraced and made their way down the stairs to the courtyard, where Ahmed's family were gathered. Holding back the tears, Ahmed looked lovingly at Amina, trying to apologise with his eyes and tell her how much he needed her.

Salem felt he had to take charge of the situation, so he asked Fahad and Jassim to get one of the large carpets from the majlis as well as the cushions. Lulua and Tima hurriedly made mint tea which Tareq, Tima's husband, passed around.

Although Ahmed was head of the house, he felt so weak that he had remained quiet and still, sitting beside Amina. Maggie suggested that they should leave but Amina told them to stay; they were considered part of the family.

Once everyone was settled Salem, his legs crossed, prayer beads in hand, began to address everyone. 'I don't have to tell you that we belong to a very happy family. I am proud of Ahmed, my dear nephew, for all he has done for you. I need to go back many years, to when I was a young man – not unlike you, young Fahd. Well, maybe not quite like you.'

This caused a little laughter, which defused the tension. Ahmed let Amina hold his hand as they sat waiting.

'My parents were the happiest people alive, and my sister Lubna and I had the best childhood you could ask for – carefree, playing on the white sandy beach of Al Mafjar. We were poor, but we were able to survive on the simple things – all the villagers helped each other. We all relied on the pearl-divers. Without their income we would have had nothing at all.'

Ahmed felt a twinge of nervousness. He crossed his legs once again, drawing his wife and children closer for reassurance.

'I remember that hot summer day,' Salem went on, 'when we all ran down to the beach to welcome the divers home. They had been away for weeks and weeks, and we were all concerned about them. Mother, Father, Lubna and I were so pleased to see them. Ibrahim, Yousef and Bilal were all there, as well as Adel. His parents were so happy to see him home safely. But I noticed that my sister was quiet around him. She confided in me that she liked Adel, and told me they had met several times before, whenever he was back home. His parents knew our parents and it was like one big family in those days anyway.

'All the villagers decided to celebrate their safe return. Everyone rushed around cooking, and we had a feast in the centre of Al Mafjar. It was a wonderful night. The drums were heated around the fire to make their skins taut, the drummers made wonderful music and we all danced. We all felt relief and joy at seeing the divers return home. I had always been envious of my friends going out to sea, but early on the nokhdar said I wasn't cut out for such a harsh life – something to do with my lungs. I couldn't stay under the surface for more than half a minute, unlike Ibrahim and the rest, who were on the sea bed for up to three minutes at a time.

'Everyone felt compelled to dance that night. Even my parents, Nasser and Miriam, danced. I remember Adel taking Lubna's hand and twirling her around in the middle of the square. We all stood around, clapping to the drumbeat, as the flames lit the happy faces of the divers and their families. Children played all around, even though it was getting late. The full moon cast such a bright light that nobody seemed to care what hour of the day it was.

'I remember Adel looking as though he could burst with joy as he danced with Lubna, leading her through a series of steps. Lubna's hair swayed back and forth as she swung her head downwards then up to the sky, holding up her bright red dress, her bare feet almost touching her partner's. Adel had his eyes closed as he held his hands aloft, his thobe tied up around his waist. We all stood in amazement, watching them fall in love.'

There was silence.

'We were all overjoyed, yet tired from the events of the day, so the party broke up and we all went home. We knew there was something special between Adel and my sister, but we let them say goodnight alone and we went to bed.

'It was only later that I wondered where Lubna was. What I haven't told you so far is that Lubna was due to marry her cousin the following day in Al Khor. You have to understand, we were very poor. All my mother and father wanted was for their daughter to have a secure future. Lubna had reluctantly agreed to marry Khaled to please them – she loved her parents more than anyone. But that night changed everything. It was as if Lubna was having her last moment of freedom. I'm sorry, Ahmed, but I know she was dreading marrying a man she didn't care for – and it seemed that Khaled didn't want to marry Lubna either.

'She had to be up early the next morning as we were all going to Al Khor. It was almost dawn and I couldn't find her in her room, so I went to the beach. There they were, asleep on the beach, in each other's arms. They looked so happy and at peace that I couldn't disturb them. It was obvious they were deeply in love.'

Ahmed had to wipe away a tear. Amina patted his arm comfortingly. Lulua, Tima and Fahd were enthralled. Jassim had gone out to play football, to his parents' relief.

'We all went down to Al Khor. Lubna married Khaled and, as you know, his father built this house for the newlyweds, so they could start their life together. The early days were very difficult. I had decided to leave Al Mafjar as well and try and find work here. There was nothing for me up north and I could no longer be a burden to my parents. For a while I stayed with them here in this house, looking for a job. I can't remember them talking much to each other. Khaled started going back to Al Khor more and more, leaving Lubna alone. In desperation I went to the sheikh's palace in Al Hitmi and asked if they needed anyone to work there. I started in the court pouring coffee for guests, fetching and carrying for the family. In return I was given a bed there, food and a tiny salary. Of course, I saw my sister whenever I could. After a few months she confided in me that she was pregnant, and Khaled couldn't possibly be the father.

'Khaled didn't react when he found out Lubna was pregnant. He just found a servant who could help in the house. That was Um Jabor. I don't know what we would have done without her.

'From what Um Jabor told me, the birth was difficult. I was at the palace when it happened. Um Jabor said that labour lasted all night. The baby was stuck. Lubna had struggled and fought so much, she couldn't carry on. Finally, she screamed,

"Take the baby, not me, take the baby!" She died that morning giving birth to a baby boy – you, Ahmed.

'I was devastated. I didn't eat for days. My beautiful sister had been taken away from me. The worst thing was having to tell my parents. I hadn't seen them since we had come to Doha. Sheikh Ali gave me permission to go and see them. By the time I got to Al Mafjar, they were already frail, and they had summer flu – it was particularly bad that year. They were so ill they hardly recognised me, and I didn't have the heart to tell them their daughter had died. I stayed with them for a month as they faded away, first my father and then within a week my mother. Her last words were, "Look after Lubna, won't you?" I said, "Yes, of course."'

'You grew up in this big house all alone,' Salem said to Ahmed, 'except for Um Jabor, who came in every morning to cook and clean. It must have been so lonely for you. Lucky for me the sheikh seemed to like me, and I got on well with his son. I came to see you as often as I could, but it was hard in those days.

'The only pleasure I had was going to meet my old friends on *Firial*, which your grandfather kept in Doha. The retired divers gathered there most days, and we used to chat. Then I learned that Adel had gone on a particularly dangerous dive, trying to get Al Dana, the prized pearl of the ocean. They told me he had dived down with the rope as usual, but minutes went by and there was no sign of him. They all dived in, searching for Adel, but he had vanished. Eventually they pulled the rope in, only to find a basket with one huge pearl. Adel had found Al Dana – but, in doing so, he perished.'

'Was he Adel Al Nuaimi?' Amina asked.

'Yes. He was from the Al Nuami family.'

'Lulua's father used to talk about him. I remember now. He used to talk of this diver who had extraordinary powers, diving to unimaginable depths. He said he loved the sea so much that he wished he could live there beneath the waves. Mubarak died at sea too, and I thought my life was over – until I met Ahmed.'

'Here you are,' Salem said looking at Ahmed, holding a small wooden chest. 'Here is Al Dana, the finest pearl there is.'

Ahmed stood up to take the chest. Shaking with emotion, he tried to convey his thoughts as best he could. 'Shukran ya Ami Salem. Thank you for everything. Without you and Amina's mother I don't know what I would have done all those years growing up. Now I know the true story of how I came to be here, I feel strangely content. It all seems to fit into place. I'm also so lucky to have Amina and our beautiful family. I suppose I have two fathers – one who provided this house and *Firial*, of course, and the other, whom I never met. But I know Adel will be in my heart forever. As for my mother, she sounds like an amazing woman – brave and beautiful.'

He looked at his children, and to lighten the mood said, 'And our first grand-daughter will be called Dana.'

'Well, it won't be my child,' Fahd said, to laughter. 'I see you've got a record player. Can I play one of the records I brought back with me?'

'Of course,' Ahmed said, puzzled.

'It's John Lennon.'

After a crackle or two, gentle piano notes echoed throughout the courtyard and Lennon sang: 'Imagine there's no heaven, It's easy if you try, No hell below us, Above us only sky...'

Ahmed's family gathered around him to support him.

Then the front door burst open. It was Jassim, in shorts and T-shirt, caked in dust from playing football in the street.

'Have I missed anything?' he said innocently.

'You could say that.' Ahmed lifted his younger son high in the air.

Glossary

Ahlan wa sahlan – welcome – literally 'the family with you'

Abaya – a woman's cloak, usually fine black thin material, worn over her head and dress

Abu – the father of

Adhan Al Fajr – dawn call to prayer

Adhan Al Dhur – noon call to prayer

Adhan Al Asr – afternoon call to prayer

Adhan Al Mughreb – sunset call to prayer

Adhan Al Isha – evening call to prayer

Akhi – my friend

Alhamdulillah – Thanks be to God

Aqal, agal – rope-like cord, usually black, that holds the man's headscarf in place

Azba – desert camp

Badgeer - windtower

Baghla – largest type of boat

Bait – house

Al Bahr – the sea, family name

Barasti – traditional roof/ceiling made from palm fronds

Bateel – long streamlined sail boat

Bagdounis - parsley

Batula – type of ladies' eye mask worn in public

Boom – large to medium-sized type of boat

Birnous – a blanket

Bisht – cloak worn by sheikhs often with gold embroidered edging

Bismillah – In the name of God

Dana – largest and most beautiful pearl

Dhow – traditional sailing craft of the Gulf

Dhub – spiny-tailed lizard

Fagga – desert truffle

Farwa – kind of thick winter coat worn by the Bedouin

Fassoulia - beans

Fi aman Allah – goodbye – literally 'with God's protection'

Ghutra – cloth worn on men's head either in white or red check

Habibi, habibti – my love, my darling, my dear – first to a male, second to female

Hamour – brown-spotted reef cod

Harees – porridge-like dish usually served in Ramadhan, made from wheat, butter and meat

Imam – person who leads prayers in a mosque

Jaliboot – straight-keeled boat with an upright prow

Jibna Bayda – white cheese

Lanj – another name for a boast possibly derived from 'launch'

Labn – fermented milk

Lungi – a type of sarong

Machboos – traditional Gulf dish of rice usually made with lamb or chicken

Mafi Mushkila – no problem

Mafi Shay – nothing, it's nothing

Majlis – room in the house, sometimes separate, where guests are entertained

Maloom – from the Hindi word for understood, often used with Indian servants

Ma Salama – Goodbye – literally 'with safety'

Mashallah – God has willed it

Matbakh - kitchen

Mudeer – manager

Mustashar - advisor

Nokhdar – the captain of a pearling boat

Naam – yes

Qutra, ghutra – headscarf made of cloth

Saafi – the most highly prized fish in Qatar waters

Sabah Al Khair – Good morning

Sabkha - mudflat

Sahab Ismu – Highness: the form of address for an Emir

Sambooq – pearling boat

Sbeiti – highly sought-after fish

Shari – highly prized fish

Shlonak? - How are you? (in Gulf Arabic– literally - what colour are you?)

Shuw'I – most common boat in Qatar used for both pearling and fishing

Shibshib – sandals

Shaheen – species of peregrine falcon

Shukran, shokran – thank you

Syara – car

Tabla – a drum covered in goatskin

Tawash – pearl merchant

Thobe – men's dress – white cotton for summer – black or brown thick material for winter

Tfadal – After you – polite word of invitation

Thareed – traditional dish made from pieces of bread and meat broth, popular in Ramadan

Rulers of Qatar 1851 - 1995

1851 – 1878

Sheikh Mohammed bin Thani

First ruler, uniting the tribes of Qatar

1878 – 1913

Sheikh Jassim bin Mohammed bin Thani

Founded the state, fighting many battles as a military leader

1913 – 1949

Sheikh Abdullah bin Jassim Al Thani

First oil well drilled under his rule

1949 – 1960

Sheikh Ali bin Abdullah Al Thani

First oil exported and a new period of development

1960 – 1972

Sheikh Ahmed bin Ali Al Thani

Advisory council formed

1972 – 1995

Sheikh Khalifa bin Hamad Al Thani

Government reorganised, hospitals and university built